Critical Acclaim for LEST DARKNESS PREVAIL

Beautiful cover! [Sandra Valencia] ...has a clean and poetic writing style. Descriptions bring to mind strong visual images. [The author] ...has an excellent ear for dialogue and has done a good job of creating worlds.

—WRITER'S DIGEST

Lest Darkness Prevail is a work of metaphysical science fiction with political and cultural themes. [This book] ...forms the third and final installment of The Chikondra Trilogy, penned by author Sandra Valencia. Things haven't been easy living the diplomatic nightmare that Sirinoya and Sandra have been through, but the couple has weathered the storm so far thanks to their differing but complementary perspectives. Now with a newborn son in the mix, the quest for peace for the next generation is more important than ever, but the threat of galactic war still lurks in the shadows. Once again, old mysticism and fairy tales may hold the answers.

...[T]hese metaphysical, romantic, and intense novels [in The Chikondra Trilogy] have always sustained their central tension and pace, thanks to the solid relationship of the Senior Field Minister and his innovative, intelligent lifemate. Sandra feels the most developed in this last installment, in which spirituality and reality collide very powerfully as the ultimate test rears its head—just when our couple thinks the peace they have cultivated might be sustainable at last. Author Sandra Valencia always works a lot of description, atmosphere, and heart into each of her scenes, and this final novel seems to perfectly balance the cultural and political arts of war, the mystifying ideas of spirituality, and the real, grounded love of a strong bond. Overall, *Lest Darkness Prevail* brings The Chikondra Trilogy to a superb close. Highly recommended.

—5-Star Review
KC Finn, Readers' Favorite

Lest Darkness Prevail

THE CHIKONDRA TRILOGY: DARE TO LIVE THE LIGHT

SANDRA VALENCIA

Dare to strive for the best. You deserve it! Sandra Valencia

LCCN: 2020911903

Hardback ISBN 978-1-63337-394-5
Paperback ISBN 978-1-63337-395-2
E-book ISBN 978-1-63337-396-9

Printed in the United States of America

1 3 5 7 9 10 8 6 4 2

Dedication

Writing the ending of this book has been an experience far more emotional than I ever could have imagined. The Chikondra Trilogy has been an integral part of my daily life for several years now. To bid farewell to the beloved friends in this saga is to say goodbye to an incredibly rich phase of my life. Still, with their story chronicled within the pages of books where they will always live, I know I can someday return for a visit.

In the meantime, I am blessed with a devoted family and extraordinary people who are always with me. They reach out from near and far to grace my life with their presence.

As always, I cannot fail to mention the continued friendship and support so generously given to me by Jan Thompson and Philippa "Rosie" Ede. They made every step of this long journey to Chikondra with me, and I am forever grateful.

I would also like to thank two extraordinary Viking friends from Sweden, Jan Gunnerdal and Rolf Parlhem, for helping a simple girl from the Midwest discover more of the world and to see it through bold, new eyes. Their influence, their humor, and their wisdom enriched both my life and my creativity.

At this moment, I also think of friends who lost struggles against terrible illness but always found time and energy to encourage me to carry on with my writing. Robert Delamora, Debbie Walters, and Bernice Hause: each forever holds a special place in my heart.

This final book in The Chikondra Trilogy, ***Lest Darkness Prevail,*** **is dedicated to these treasured friends.**

Prologue
From: Whispers from Prophecy

Returning from their honeymoon, the newly unified Warnach Sirinoya and Sandra Warner begin their life together with unswerving support from his family. While she tackles the final phases of her education at the Chikondran Academy of Diplomatic Sciences, Warnach immerses himself in the less-than-satisfying routine of home duty. Although longing for the challenging rigors of his field service career, he reminds himself that solidifying the foundation of his unification is well worth the sacrifice of a single year of Ku'saá on Chikondra.

Before the Sirinoyas reach the end of their first year of unification, civil war erupts on a densely populated world and threatens many nearby planets. Pressured by Chancellor Edsaka, Warnach reluctantly decides to set aside his commitment to Ku'saá to undertake the emergency mission. Terrifying consequences result as separate events nearly claim his life and those of his brother and his new lifemate. Upon his return to Chikondra, Warnach must contend with guilt that Sandra almost died because of his actions while wrestling with resentment and anger toward his once-beloved godfather.

Upon Sandra Sirinoya's graduation from CADS, she visits Earth before embarking on her new career as her lifemate's primary diplomatic aide. Her reunion with her family quickly turns into a bitter confrontation with her father. Soon, however, she departs with Warnach to launch the diplomatic career of her dreams and quickly proves the value of her work ethic, exceptional observation skills, and powerful intuition.

Incidents across the Alliance continue to erupt and threaten violence that cannot be contained within the single worlds where they originate. The planetary union's diplomatic corps travels incessantly with individual field ministers often joining efforts to stem the increasingly turbulent tide of political instability. Their missions are endangered by deception and outright attacks, which prompt painful soul-searching and troubling decisions.

In the midst of the hectic pace of field missions, Sandra Sirinoya becomes ill. Her doctors discover the cause of her illness is both life-threatening and miraculous. When she tells Warnach that they have conceived a child, each of them must look at their future in totally different terms

Upon learning of the pregnancy, Warnach's family is overjoyed. In some, however, that joy is tempered by secret questions. The pregnancy is something that should not have happened. Is there a more powerful explanation than simple miracle to explain the conception of this child between Chikondran and Terran?

As ***Lest Darkness Prevail*** begins, Senior Field Minister Warnach Sirinoya cherishes the joys of unification and new fatherhood while he yet again turns his energies toward his career as peacemaker. Uneasy with the future, he gratefully relies on the wisdom and strength of his Terran lifemate.

PART ONE

The ancient legend in Sandra Sirinoya's book...

The Coming of Mi'yafá Si'imlayaná

The Great Spirit, in all His wisdom, looked down upon the beautiful face of Chikondra. Watching as vile spirits approached the peaceful world He had created, Yahvanta sighed. What should He do? Should He intercede and drive away those dark forces? Or should He entrust His favored people to defend and protect the beautiful Chikondra He had given them?

After much contemplation, the Great Spirit reached a decision that troubled His eternal spirit. Still, knowing so many souls would begin to doubt, Yahvanta knew clearly that His people would need to recall ancient lessons delivered to them with the revelations of Meichasa. They would also need to prove themselves worthy of the great gifts they had received.

Speaking to His legions of ageless spirits, the Great Spirit began to weave His story of prophecy. He told of the coming of the Mi'yafá Si'imlayaná.

Cradled by spirits of ground and sky, a solitary voyager sought comfort from Mamehr Chikondra. Cheerless and lonely, discouraged and weary, this guardian spirit struggled to fulfill his share of the mission mandated to his people through Meichasa. Too far from home, too long in darkness, the protector pursued elusive peace. Disenchanted, the saddened child of Chikondra slipped further and further from light as his strength waned. Dwelling in shadows, his soul found no solace, no peace, until a solitary voice cried from within his heart. Only in light could he discover comfort and harmony to revive the essence of his innermost self. Craving redemption, the defender rallied and clung to faith as if to life. Hope reawakened and, undefeated, the guardian retreated from gloom's abyss and sent sacred prayers to touch the Great Spirit's heart.

Unto those prayerful entreaties, Yahvanta did listen. Into the soul of Chikondra's child He did probe. Discovering honor and courage, devotion and purpose, the Great Spirit smiled. In renewed faith, this child had stepped forth. This child had weakened beneath his burden but had at last returned home. With darkness looming in greater threat, Yahvanta sighed upon the breast of His precious Chikondra. His champion had she borne. His steadfast warrior had He found.

Arduous would be the paths to peace. Yahvanta's champion must no longer face life alone. To the blessed wisdom of angel spirits, the Great Spirit did hearken. Upon His vast universe did Yahvanta look, seeking kindred spirit to ease the difficult path traveled by the woe-filled child of Mamehr Chikondra. Finally, holy eyes fell upon a helping spirit. Alike yet different, a perfect match was this other child. Again did the Great Spirit smile.

Satisfied, Yahvanta issued His sacred decree. From the warm embrace of a faraway star to Chikondra would journey a new light. Borne by that light to the Great Spirit's precious world would be soft rains of sadness and shining rays of hope. Still, with strength ever-present, that strange mystic glow would kiss the heart of the world to which it had come. Infused with essence of blessed love, the new light would shine upon Yahvanta's chosen - upon Chikondra's own great guardian warrior.

Fresh. Clean and bright. Arriving light would step upon precious ground and into the hallowed waters of Mamehr Chikondra. In joy would the holy guardians of Meichasa acknowledge this new child from the distant star as into joy would this helping soul come to deliver from sorrow Chikondra's steadfast warrior.

Upon their love, Yahvanta would smile. Upon their hearts He would bestow His blessings. Bound they would be to one another in holy vows and sacred intent. Seizing anew the sacred mission, they would journey far from Chikondra's loving embrace. From endless quests for peace to Mamehr Chikondra they would always come home, yearning for respite from relentless trials.

Seeking renewal and revival, to Meichasa's spirits they would return. Always waiting, always listening, the guardians of Meichasa would welcome home their new light and her valiant warrior. Strengthened and healed, their spirits restored, the two again would venture anew. Traversing the expanse of the Great Spirit's universe, touching the hearts of His many peoples, the chosen defender would journey with the light of his soul. In purpose united, they would continue their duty. Together, they would seek to fulfill tasks revealed at the coming of Meichasa.

Despite dwelling in faith and filled with their love, the two great lights silenced empty chill. Longing did they know, yet they continued their quest. Neither cried for secret sadness nor complained of empty wishes. So great were the gifts granted to them that each light sought reminder within and chose thankfulness instead.

Always watching, always listening, Meichasa's spirits bore fervent pleas unto the Great Spirit. These faithful lights never deserved such gloom when into shadows they must surely yet go. Wise in heart, the Great Spirit again hearkened unto Chikondra's sacred guardians. Indeed, those angelic guardians truly understood. Much aid would Mamehr Chikondra's defender spirit and his helping light need.

New warmth to chase the empty chill. New light to fill longing hearts. Wise and thoughtful, Yahvanta banished their sadness. With tears of joy did Mamehr Chikondra welcome Yahvanta's newest creation, faithful guide granted to her courageous warrior.

But look again did the Great Spirit. Shadows of darkness continued to encroach, their plague aloft, their poison spewing as the dark cloud poured out its anger. Toward Chikondra, the shadow its foul breath blew. Shuddering in anger yet true to His course, Yahvanta cast his gaze again upon His chosen warrior.

True in heart and firm in faith, the guardian spirit stood fast at the side of the helping light dispatched from the faraway star. Despite their spirits blessed, even more help would they require to defeat powers of darkness. What gift should I send? What help will they need? These questions Yahvanta did ask of Himself. His ear again He turned to the ageless legions filling His Heavens. To the guardians of Meichasa those legions did send Him.

Wisdom of ages granted eons ago. Hearts open wide with purpose unbroken. To Yahvanta's inquiry, Chikondra's guardian spirits did reply.

"Here, Great Spirit, You sent us to love Your people. To this world You did send us, their spirits to guard. Beneath the breast of Mamehr Chikondra, we do reside. Beneath her starry eyes, we do dance. For her, our songs we do sing.

"Now, Mamehr Chikondra's guardian child does come to us, led by the heart of another light to which he gratefully clings. With their whole selves, they shield the guide You already sent to still their longing. With hearts overflowing, they pray their gratitude for Your compassion that has banished their sadness.

"To us, they listen and extend their hands. With us, their love they always share. His eyes to the universe turn; Your mission, Your bidding, he takes up again. He shakes off the dread. He clutches her hand. Together, they will forge ahead.

"Sacred One, O Great Spirit wise, we presume not to advise. Only our hearts speak out as the guardians You commanded us to be. No doubt exists. Great threat approaches, blacker than any night. To dispel the threats, hesitate You must not. To Mamehr Chikondra, You must send brighter light."

Their wise counsel did the Great Spirit heed, so upon His helping child He again did smile. Although the portal would be closed by brilliance unrivaled, His most sacred of lights would He send to bring hope to Yahvanta's own Chikondra. Radiant in beauty, cradled in love, Mi'yafá Si'imlayaná, Yahvanta's own Guardian of Light, would shed grace and courage upon the people to whom the Great Spirit had entrusted His beloved Chikondra.

Child called Light. Guardian of Light. Mamehr Chikondra could sigh her relief. Salvation would swell as the Light would brighten. For Mi'yafá Si'imlayaná to Chikondra had come.

And the years would pass. Protective the great warrior would remain with his helping spirit ever by his side. In love and courage, custodians they would be, ever watchful, ever faithful, to the guide of faith and the sacred Light to become known as Mi'yafá Si'imlayaná.

Malevolent shadows continued their spread through the heavens, threatening the sacred mission of Meichasa with darkness foul. Defeat would become the word no true Chikondran heart would utter. Gathering their strength and bonding their lives in sacred intent, Yahvanta's bidding they would honor.

Mamehr Chikondra, so sweet and lovely, would bear the ultimate anguish. Her beloved children would face the fight; their blood unto her core would flow. Rivers of tears would she be forced to cry With heart rent open, upon her own body would Chikondra wear the scourge of war.

Ever the mother, she would shield brave children with breath and tears, seeking to protect the faithful whose hearts held fast. Still, too many souls of beloved children would she be forced to cradle in chaotic repose. Her maternal heart, swelling in grief, must wait yet longer for the promise to be fulfilled.

Her warrior child, in valor and pain, had dispatched afar his beloved helper. Sent away to the safe embrace of her faraway star, he had bidden her protect the lights entrusted to them. Remaining in sorrow with the embattled Mamehr Chikondra, his defender spirit would never surrender.

Waiting and hoping, recalling the prophecy, Mamehr Chikondra embraced her warrior within the depths of her heart. In secret, she clung to the ancient promise. Mi'yafá Si'imlayaná would surely return; such had been Yahvanta's sacred vow.

Unable to withstand exile from her own beloved warrior, to Meichasa's guardians did the helping light return and did seek their aid. Driven by love and unwavering devotion, to the weary warrior she finally returned. Together, two lovers stood in black of night, resisting the shadows with all of their might.

Then, when all seemed lost, dark skies shuddered. Following in the wake left by love inspired, the faithful guide did approach. To the weeping Chikondra, he also returned and with him, did he bring the sacred Mi'yafá Si'imlayaná.

Fortified by the breath of Mamehr Chikondra, Mi'yafá Si'imlayaná arose from churning seas and stepped out upon hallowed ground. Behind her, ever watchful, shone the gaze of Meichasa's sacred angels. Their breath they blew across her shoulders; their blessings they sent to fill her breast. With no fear of night, she celebrated her homecoming - the fulfillment of promise from ages ago.

Ever-sensitive, the warrior's helper had sensed the flight. Through forests deep, o'er rocky heights, beneath the watch of a thousand eyes, the helping light reached out for the brilliance of Mi'yafá Si'imlayaná. When hand took hand, they changed their course. Light so intense could not be stopped.

Unto the great warrior, whose heart pounded with fear, returned his most precious lights. Reminded of courage, guided by faith, Chikondra's defenders took new heart. Listen they would to words borne by the Light. Cast aside the pain. Follow the path. Cling to hope. Embark into night. Embrace the Light.

Mi'yafá Si'imlayaná had come home. Yahvanta's holy promise to Mamehr Chikondra was coming to pass. Time would press onward. Tears would still fall with lives yet to yield. Despite tribulation, steadfast hearts would continue true.

Truth was the legend; prophecy it held. The Guardian of Light, Chikondra's own daughter, had bravely marched forth. Her sacred sight would pierce the veil of blackest night. Spirits evil could not prevail for the Great Spirit's Light had appeared to cast them into void.

Mamehr Chikondra's tears began to subside. Her lost children's souls she guarded inside. With aid from the light of a faraway star, she had been defended by the great warrior whose own light never dimmed. Then, guided by faith strong and bright, Mi'yafá Si'imlayaná returned in beauty to bathe the beautiful Chikondra with the Great Spirit's most sacred gift of peace.

PART TWO

In love, there is new life...

Chapter One

Time. Perspective on time. For Senior Field Minister Warnach Sirinoya and his Terran lifemate, both time and perspective assumed dynamically new dimensions following the birth of their son. Morcai's miraculous arrival completely transformed their awareness of minutes, hours, and days.

By the time he took his family home from the hospital, Warnach Sirinoya had already gained confidence in performing the fine art of changing diapers while simultaneously dodging unexpected showers. Finding it necessary to supplement Morcai's diet of breast milk with special formula, the new father also quickly learned about feeding and burping his baby. From the very start, he undertook his new role in life with humor, patience, and devotion.

The first months of Morcai's life passed in an absolute blur. In the beginning, there were nights of interrupted sleep to nurse and change a demanding newborn. Daytime brought calls, visitors, and deliveries of gifts for the newest member of the celebrated Sirinoya family. Medical appointments. Diapers.

Family photos. First teeth. Hours spent playing on the floor. Baby toys scattered in the most unlikely places. Life adjustments.

While weeks whizzed happily by, Sandra Warner Sirinoya watched with affectionate amusement and utter amazement arising from memories of Warnach as he had been when they first met. Recalling their initial meeting in John Edwards' office on Earth those many years ago, she certainly would have considered Chikondra's famous Minister Sirinoya as the galaxy's most unlikely candidate for parenthood.

Turning over, she slowly opened her eyes. Soft blue light glowed from the monitor linked to the baby's room. Happy cooing sounds had awakened her to a new day. Contented and drowsy, she mumbled a quick prayer of thanks that Morcai's transition to a room of his own had gone so smoothly. After ten months of sharing his parents' suite, Morcai had taken less than a week to adjust to sleeping alone in the nursery. Grinning to herself, she thought Warnach had suffered more separation anxiety than the baby.

A few minutes later, she stood in the hallway by the nursery's open door and peeked into the cheerfully decorated room. Gladness filled her heart. Chubby baby hands gripped the soft rail of the crib while active legs flexed. Black curls bounced. Dark eyes sparkled. Suddenly, Morcai emitted a shrieking baby laugh.

"Shsh! You don't want to wake Momma!"

Although her hand covered her mouth, Sandra unsuccessfully stifled giggles. Striding inside, she greeted her lifemate with a stirring morning kiss. "Too late, my dear Minister Sirinoya."

"Mmm," he murmured in a deliberately sexy voice just as Morcai laughed out loud and reached for his mother. Twisting to glare at his son in mock dismay, he winked. "Perhaps we should send her back to bed so you can wake her up again. I could use another greeting like that."

Sandra also winked at the baby. "Close your ears, Morcai." Shifting her gaze back to her lifemate's face, she smiled seductively. "This, my good minister, would have been the perfect morning for you to stay in your own bed for an even better wake-up greeting."

Following morning prayers and breakfast, Warnach prepared to leave for an important meeting in Kadranas with Farsuk, Rodan, plus Masters Barishta and Devorius. Discussions would focus on plans for an upcoming summit on Mijadka. The top-level conference would draw leaders from around the Alliance for consultations regarding heightened levels of violence attributed to Zeteron influence. Rapidly increasing concern and otherwise inexplicable hostile incidents were finally forcing member planets to seriously assess threats either too long underestimated or ignored altogether.

Thoughtfully, Sandra adjusted the straight collar of Warnach's black, elegantly cut coat. "You know you have my support should you change your mind about attending the conference on Mijadka."

Tipping his head forward, he lightly kissed her Kitak and then her forehead. "The summit takes place in two weeks. My exceptionally efficient deputy doesn't reenter service for another six. Traveling off-world isn't so attractive without her."

Nodding, she smiled. "Even without her, you're methodical, intuitive, sensible, and wise. That's a rare combination. Your presence would be important because people trust you. They also respect both your judgment and experience."

"Despite whatever validity your observations contain, me'u Shi'níyah, I now view life from a totally different perspective."

Directly staring into his eyes, she answered, "Yes, and just as our son is the source of that different perspective, he's also the strongest reason for you to attend this summit. His could be a questionable future if Zeteron efforts at destabilization aren't derailed. The only possible defense is to strengthen the Alliance and expand its commitment to broaden resistance."

Warnach's full lips tautened into a narrow line. "Leaving the two of you isn't something I wish to do."

"Nor do I want you leaving without us. However, this may be the best chance to start building a consensus on the problem. We both know that inaction poses far too much danger. No one can argue that point more effectively than you, my dear Minister Sirinoya."

His jaw twitched from side to side as he thoughtfully weighed her words. "I promise to consider your opinion carefully." Forcing a smile, he kissed her lightly and left.

Later, inside Farsuk's office, objectives were clear. Effective strategy, however, proved elusive. While Master Barishta listened quietly, the others debated possible tactics. With the variety of proposals expected, the first and most crucial obstacle was defining the key issue and how to present it for maximum impact. Secondly, they would be challenged to glean the most valuable suggestions from hours of expected political rhetoric. Developing a stratagem capable of garnering widespread endorsement would require masterful diplomatic finesse and arm-twisting.

"Warnach, I still believe your unique understanding of Terran mentality makes your attendance essential," Master Devorius argued again.

Warnach's eyes met the wide, nearly transparent irises of the venerable Kurulian diplomat. "A year on Earth hardly qualifies me as an expert on the psychology of a people who populate half the known galaxy."

Farsuk smiled wryly. "True, especially considering they're one of the most culturally diversified races in the known galaxy. However, there are consistent factors in their character. You comprehend that on a different plane."

"Fundamentally, I agree with you, Farsuk," Rodan interjected, sensing his best friend's rising personal conflict. "However, you rely too heavily on experience derived from his unification with a Terran. Sandra is far from typical when it comes to Terrans."

Master Devorius conceded the point but pressed ahead. "Atypical she may be, but you must admit there are ingrained characteristics that could lend valuable insight when dealing with Terrans in positions of leadership."

Devorius turned from Rodan and faced Warnach. "For years, you've excelled at delving into the psyches of different races and cultures across the Alliance. In doing so, you've achieved unparalleled success in negotiating solutions to all sorts of disputes. You can apply that same inborn talent with the intuitive comprehension of Terrans that you now possess. Your combined skill and knowledge should provide us a unique advantage. We can dare to have hope of leaving this summit with more than a glimmer of optimism."

Pensively, Warnach rose and stared outside a window. Never had home held such importance as it had since the birth of his son. Not once had he regretted the six-month sabbatical he had taken from work to concentrate his attention exclusively on Sandra and their baby. Neither did he regret the additional six months of home duty taken to spend extra time with his family. Still, as he listened to opinions from some of the most renowned diplomats of the era, her words echoed inside his head. Morcai's future could well be affected by whatever outcome emerged from the impending summit. Dreading separation from his family, he comprehended how much he would willingly sacrifice for the benefit of his lifemate and their son.

As he turned around, his bearded jaw set in a firm line. Black eyes no longer shone with indecision. "There is little time to define our strategy before we depart for Mijadka."

While Warnach sat on the floor playing with Morcai, Sandra smoothed clothing neatly packed inside luggage. Glancing upward, she noted her lifemate's smile but also detected his distress. Even Morcai sensed something amiss. For days, he had clung to Warnach and had cried more easily, constantly reaching out and calling, "Badah! Badah!"

Closing the travel cases, she crossed the room and stretched out on the carpet with her family. "Having fun?"

Affectionately, Warnach reached out to stroke her cheek. "Enjoying our son while you did all the work."

Her expression softened as she tilted her cheek against his palm. "I didn't mind. I still have a few weeks of playtime." Her voice broke. "You have to leave tomorrow. Enjoy what time's left."

Later that night, humming a lullaby, Warnach stood over Morcai's bed. He silently watched huge eyes grow drowsy before heavily lashed eyelids opened and closed until they could no longer resist sleep. An odd thought struck. He had worked his entire adult life pursuing peace. How many times had the endeavors seemed pointless? Suddenly, he realized that every long night, every frustrated hour, and every avoided tragedy had been not just for himself or even for the peoples he had sought to help. Each effort had been for the sake of the family he now possessed, the same family he never before realized he had wanted so much.

Returning to the master suite, he discarded his robe. Lowering onto the edge of the bed, he tasted playfully sweet kisses awaiting him. With exploring hands and lips, he paid rich tribute to the woman whose soul gave him satisfaction soaring far above the physical desires she fulfilled with such energy and passion. Taking her as part of him made his body feel vibrantly alive. Loving her always encompassed every aspect of his being, sating his body's needs while continuously regenerating his spirit.

"Hey! Deputy Minister! Can a lowly advocate join you for lunch?"

"Druska! Good grief! Where've you been hiding?" Quickly, Sandra got up and threw her arms around her friend in a boisterous hug.

Sitting down across the table from Sandra, Druska laughed while signaling an attendant for a menu. "Hiding? Wish I could, but Minister Thapord insists that I traipse across the galaxy at his heels."

"Oh, yes, I forgot. He has one of the worst territories. Not a single planet is closer than a three-week journey."

"It's good I don't suffer space sickness. Now, what are you having for lunch?"

"Soup and salad," Sandra replied wryly. "Morcai's almost a year old, and I still can't get rid of these last two kilos."

"You must be the only one who notices," Druska chuckled in response.

When lunch was served, their conversation veered. "How are things going with Peter?"

Druska's eyes darkened. "He's still mad that I accepted the position with Minister Thapord."

"If I know Peter, he's complaining about never seeing you, especially since he's traveling so much with Rodan."

Druska nodded and swallowed a leafy bite. "Exactly. It makes it really hard to plan time together, but Peter seems to completely disregard the fact that I wanted to enter field ministry as much as he did." She paused. "Do you think I was selfish in taking the job with Minister Thapord?"

"Absolutely not!" Sandra exclaimed. "You deserve the chance, Druska. You worked hard and graduated in the top five of the class." She paused. "Did he really accuse you of being selfish?"

Druska's face dropped, and her lips pressed tightly together. "Yes."

"Then, as far as I'm concerned, he's the one who's being selfish. I know he loves you. He's also a worrier. I'm sure he'll come around, but you need to be true to yourself. You have every right to pursue your career dreams."

Druska smiled heartfelt appreciation. "Thanks. Mom and Dad told me the same. It just helps hearing it from you since you and Peter have been close for so long."

Sandra reached out and touched her friend's hand. "Listen to your Mom and Dad and keep those spirits up. This will work out if it's meant to be."

Laughing lightly, Druska added, "Mom and Dad told me that, too."

"My advice? Listen to your folks."

Tension hung like winter storm clouds inside the lounge area of Premier Carlsson's luxurious suite. His taut expression revealed burgeoning apprehension. "Excellency, Premier Mazzini and I are convinced that the Zeteron threat is growing faster than ever. Our elections in three months are still much too close to call. With our fellow premiers vacating their posts, Earth desperately needs to elect replacements who understand the potential for galactic crisis. If de Castillo or Yu wins, we carry the majority. If both win, we face little difficulty in continuing our support. However, if neither wins, I sincerely fear what the future will bring."

"Crister, there's little that Alliance leadership can do other than offer endorsements. I need fresh ideas because, in truth, we have no direct experience with candidates sympathetic to our cause." Frowning, Farsuk shook his head.

Warnach leaned forward. "That statement isn't entirely true."

Farsuk's brow lifted. "Explain."

"I worked extensively with Eduardo when I was on Earth. So did Sandra. Although we can offer Yu only limited help, we can certainly throw our full public support behind Eduardo. Right now, Sandra is Earth's only citizen with minister's status in the Alliance's diplomatic corps. We plan to visit her family just before general elections. The timing could be perfect."

Master Devorius cocked his head in question. "Are you certain she'll endorse Yu and de Castillo?"

"We've discussed upcoming elections. She has little respect for Dorn and doesn't trust Schneider. Yu is a relative unknown. On the other hand, based on past experience, she admires de Castillo very much. Yes, I believe she'll willingly support him."

Farsuk sat back in a comfortable chair and loudly exhaled a relieved sigh. "With all that's happened lately, I had nearly forgotten. If Rodan succeeds in his private meetings with the representatives from Mendara and the Qamazir Coalition, perhaps we can begin to broaden our circle of consensus. Gentlemen, we mustn't fail. Evidence can't be ignored. Zeteron infiltration continues to expand. We must find means to deter them before they further undermine our strength from the inside."

Warnach gazed grimly at Carlsson. "You do understand how key Earth's role is in this equation, do you not?"

Carlsson's once blond hair fell in a straight shaft as his face dipped. "You refer to the many worlds settled by Terrans."

"I do," Warnach replied. "Petty disagreements or competitive posturing will have little significance. Earth will always be the grand source to which Terrans turn. Ties existing between your worlds are deeply embedded, no matter what. We must do everything possible to maintain that emotional advantage."

Master Devorius stood and paced. "Let us pray, gentlemen, that the notoriety Deputy Minister Sirinoya has earned during her short career will prove an effective weapon once released from our reserves."

Farsuk glanced at Warnach but was unable to discern any of his godson's thoughts. "Perhaps she won't appreciate being perceived in such light."

"She will not," Master Devorius said. "However, her value in this matter must not be underestimated, most especially not by her. We must maintain Earth's open support, and I firmly believe she can energize the necessary momentum."

Finally, Warnach stood and strode across the room. Pouring a glass of brandy, he took a drink and swirled the liquid around his mouth. "Gentlemen, my ki'mirsah fully comprehends the significance of Earth's elections. She's also staunchly dedicated to the peace we all hope to preserve. I will speak with her when I return home."

Two days later, Rodan stared into a glass of red wine. "I honestly believe Zeteron influence has already weakened planetary governments throughout the Mejazar Sector. We're fortunate that the Mendarans remain steadfast supporters."

"And you, my friend," Warnach commented, "proved your great value in securing commitment from the Qamazirans. I admit that I was quite concerned on that count."

A terse smile crossed Rodan's face. "As was I. However, now that their coalition's ruling council is predominantly female, there seems to be less egotistical posturing and more calculated analysis. Intuitively, they sense the danger and understand that fear must be contained within calm. I've no doubt that they'll be among our most vital allies."

"Allies we shall need. Rodan..." Warnach's voice trailed off. Recollections of his recent pilgrimage raced through his mind. How had the voices in meditation phrased it? Something about never surrendering to dreadful darkness approaching.

Seconds crawled. Rodan straightened in his chair. "What, my friend? I read in your expression worries far exceeding the tone of our discussions with Farsuk and Master Devorius."

Warnach shook his head and set aside the stemmed glass of wine he hadn't even tasted. "I'm frightened, Rodan. When Badrik and I made our pilgrimage to Efi'yimasé Meichasa, we received dire warnings. Vague though they were, I do not doubt them. I question the effects of our political and diplomatic positioning because I believe with all my heart that our future holds war."

Biting into his lip, Rodan stared at Warnach's grim face. "Are you so certain?"

Warnach's chest rose and fell several times. Resting his elbow on the arm of his chair and lifting his hand, he let his fingertips track circles above his Kitak. "My belief is that we both need to look beyond Council's current cycle. In five years, Farsuk completes his final term as chancellor. We both recognize the vision and strength he's brought to Alliance leadership. It's far too early to predict his successor. Whoever becomes chancellor afterward may not possess his fortitude. I expect the Zeterons to avail themselves of the transition and grow increasingly active."

"Your suggestion?"

Deriving deep comfort from touching his Kitak, Warnach sighed and replied, "We have precious children to protect. I believe we must plan for their safety - away from our homes on Chikondra."

Smooth turquoise colored the bright skies of late summer. While Araman watched over her napping grandson, Warnach walked with Sandra along familiar paths toward the old tower. Glancing around, he noted concentration on her face and a faraway look in her eyes. His grip on her hand tightened as he led her toward the ancient Brisajai that was the last vestige of his ancestors' first home on the estate.

Inside, cool stone shaded them from warm afternoon sun. Both had discovered sanctuary in a place that had sheltered the meditations of generations of Sirinoya. Each had felt strong need to escape for private prayers in advance of their departure for Earth the following week.

Neither spoke as Warnach produced candles and two cones of precious Efobé. Nestled into smoke-scarred niches, the incense began to produce its richly fragranced plumes of smoke. Short, stout votives supported yellow flames waving back and forth as gentle breezes sneaked through open windows. Captivated by the hypnotic effect, Warnach and Sandra drifted into deep meditation.

By the time he fully emerged from his trance, dim light filled the Brisajai. Outside, elongated shadows revealed that his meditative state had lasted more than two hours. His left brow crinkled slightly as his attention turned to Sandra. She had quite obviously waited some time for him.

"Do you remember?"

Her question confused him. "Remember? What am I to remember?"

Her head shook back and forth. Shrugging her shoulders, she answered, "I really don't know. You were deep in conversation, but I didn't quite understand. It sounded like the old form of Chikondran."

Several deep breaths finally cleared his mind. Still, he had no clear recollections from the trance. Instead, feelings swept through him. Gazing at her, he felt profound peace. "I seem to be at a loss. What about you?"

Again, she shrugged. "Are we still going to the beach tomorrow?"

Spontaneously, he grinned. "Of course."

"Good. Rodan. You must call him. He is to go with us. I'll contact Nadana."

Dark eyes locked onto her face. "Will they come?"

Reaching for his hand, she stood and pulled him up with her. When she looked upward into his face, her smile reflected the perplexity in her thoughts. "Remember. I'm only the messenger."

"The messenger, me'u Shi'níyah, or the beacon?"

Something in his question prompted soft laughter. "Whichever, I grow more and more curious. However, curiosity will have to wait. We need to get back. Morcai is likely making his maméi-mamehr frantic."

Rodan's cinnamon-colored features enhanced the brilliant white of his smile. "I feel like a schoolboy sneaking off for an afternoon swim when I should be studying."

"Ah, my good friend," Warnach replied, "a bit of play is sometimes necessary."

Speculatively, Rodan eyed both Warnach and Sandra. "Play? When you called last night, your invitation sounded more like business than recreation."

Sandra's eyebrows lifted sharply. Remaining quiet, she left conversation to Warnach, who cocked his head sharply to one side and said, "I'm thinking what a shame that Mirah is in Dihmi'ishna with Kaliyah. Visits to the beach often provide unexpected entertainment."

Amusement shone in Rodan's black eyes as he stared at his old friend. "You seem to have learned very well your ki'mirsah's convoluted technique for communicating nothing and everything via open circles that leave people like me dizzy and thoroughly confused."

Sandra's spontaneous burst of laughter startled Morcai awake. Although he didn't cry, his lower lip, as full and richly curved as his badehr's, protruded in a quivery pout. Stroking her baby gently and cooing softly, she coaxed him back to sleep while making faces at Rodan.

Suitably contrite, Rodan continued, "My comment was merely an observation, not an insult. You must admit. Both of you seem to be hiding something."

Nodding sympathetically, Warnach agreed. "Even you must agree that certain situations require patience to allow proper time to develop. Resulting surprises can be exceedingly satisfying."

Seeing that he was making no progress at uncovering hidden intentions, Rodan tossed his hands in the air while his eyes glittered with good humor. "Patience is not the word I would choose in this instance; however, I do recognize defeat."

Warm breezes rustled lush green fronds ringing the tops of tall, slender tree trunks. Conversation blended happily with the soft background rush of ocean tides curling onto sandy shores. Summery scents filled sea-freshened air and stimulated spirits as well as appetites.

Through the window above the kitchen sink, Araman thoughtfully gazed outside. Leaving home early that morning in a transport piloted by one of the estate employees, she had arrived in Tichtika. After joining her sister for tea and toasted sweet bread, the two had departed for Tlalpilistlah. Not during their breakfast, the trip, or meal preparation had the sisters discussed reasons behind the unusual midweek trip to the beach.

"The table is set. Are we ready to serve?"

Araman turned and smiled. "Everything is ready. Did you call everyone in?"

Nadana nodded. "Rodan and Warnach just finished hanging the hammocks. I saw Sandra bringing Morcai back from the beach."

Midway through lunch, Warnach's head shook quickly to and fro as he tried not to laugh. Morcai seemed to be wearing more food than he was eating. Red gadrichar was smeared from the corners of the baby's mouth to his earlobes. With efforts to keep him moderately clean proving useless as little fingers crammed fat, sweet berries into bulging cheeks, Sandra surrendered and let him eat his own way.

Chuckling, Rodan looked at Warnach. "Such changes do children bring."

"Meaning?" Warnach asked as he deftly snatched from mid-air the empty bowl Morcai tipped over the edge of his tray.

Rodan laughed aloud. "My friend, I never imagined you as a doting badehr, but it is one role that suits you exceedingly well."

Reaching for the warm washcloth Araman offered, Warnach grinned as he wiped Morcai's sticky cheeks so Sandra could eat in peace. "I thank you, Rodan. More than ever, I understand why you and Mirah have been so happy since Kaliyah was born."

Undaunted by damp, berry-stained clothes, Rodan stood and lifted Morcai from his seat. Holding the baby high, Rodan affectionately gazed at the happy, cherubic face framed with long, curly locks. "My dear godson, what a sight you are!"

Swallowing a bite, Sandra laughed and then warned, "Just be careful..."

Suddenly, Rodan jumped. His strong arms shot out and held Morcai at arm's length while the baby squealed in laughter. "You little chu'tibíl!"

Sandra grabbed Morcai while Warnach got a clean napkin from the table for Rodan. "Morcai! Bad boy, Morcai! How many times must Momma tell you? You aren't supposed to keep food in your mouth to shoot at people!"

Sternly scolded, Morcai immediately began to wail. While Sandra disappeared inside the house to change her son and console his wounded feelings, Araman entertained everyone with a similar story from Warnach's baby years. Half an hour later, happily forgiven, Morcai snuggled into a hammock with his baadihm as everyone prepared to enjoy a summertime nap.

Within lazy afternoon dreams, memories unveiled images from the past. During the Chikondran month of Ferzhama, she had first visited the seashore with Warnach and his family. Smiling, she had lain asleep in his arms. How beautiful that day had been. Her first glimpse of ci'ittá-shivayah. Her nervousness over her introduction to Araman Sirinoya. The hilarity of meeting Badrik Sirinoya a second time. The amazing sense of calm as Warnach had held her while breezes gently swayed the wide hammock.

Gliding upon a glistening ribbon of dreams, she saw another day in Ferzhama. Standing barefooted in the sand, she wiggled her toes as ocean waters danced a frothy ballet of rainbows and bubbles around her ankles. Glancing over her shoulder, she had seen Warnach's pensive smile as she spoke of the sea's secret murmurings.

Time transformed into a river of multi-colored images flowing through her mind, carrying her to yet another Ferzhama. Tears, borne from his soul, had glazed Warnach's eyes as he saw his newborn son for the very first time. Her heart had overflowed that night when she first touched a true miracle, her baby whose very life had been considered an impossibility.

Easing awake from precious dreams, Sandra cocked her head slightly backward. Very quietly, she whispered, "Warnach, wake up."

Heavy lids reluctantly lifted. A lethargic smile curved the sensual lines of his mouth. His free hand slid slowly beneath her rumpled blouse and moved upward to cup the fullness of her breast. "Me'u Shi'níyah, I don't want to wake up."

Smiling lips received his kiss. "You have to. It's time."

"Time for what?" he mumbled thickly as his eyes closed again.

Sighing regretfully, she pushed his hand away and, shifting her weight, swung her leg over the side of the hammock. Escaping his firm grasp and climbing out, she leaned over and dropped a lingering kiss against his cerea-nervos. "Warnach, wake the others. Then, get Morcai and put on his swim vest. Meet me by the water. Hurry!"

Wakefulness penetrated his brain. Climbing out of the hammock, he stripped away gauzy white shirt and trousers, leaving him clad in only his swim trunks. After waking Araman and Nadana, he very gently lifted Morcai and touched Rodan's shoulder. Already roused by the women's voices, Rodan's brow creased in question. For as many years as they had been friends, never had he known Warnach to behave so mysteriously.

Once straps on the baby's swim vest were secured, Warnach led the way to the beach. Stopping, he watched Sandra's still figure as she stood ankle-deep in silvery waters rolling onto shore. Beneath the calm glance that Araman turned to Nadana lay excitement for yet another chance to commune with sacred spirits. Meanwhile, Nadana's eyes glistened with joy at the prospect of seeing Quazon again. The mere thought of touching one excited her as nothing else ever had.

Puzzled by such strange, obvious anticipation, Rodan stared as Sandra finally began to move further from shore. His left brow dipped. "What is she doing? Why are we just standing here?"

Warnach smiled. "Patience, my friend. You shall soon discover the real reason we came today."

Frowning slightly, Rodan looked back toward the water just as a sleek, silver shape broke the ocean's surface and launched into the air. Startled, he watched the long body curve an arched trajectory that carried it above Sandra's head and back into the water. In rapid succession, three more forms hurtled upward and then re-entered the sea with mighty splashes. Incredulous eyes stared at fabled creatures whose contemporary existence some had begun to doubt. "W... War...Warnach?"

Baby Morcai squealed in laughter as he watched Quazon leaping and dancing around his mother. Briefly, Warnach touched cerea-nervos to those of his son. "Quiet, my little one."

Rodan's arm extended from his side. Tightly gripping Warnach's arm, he tore his gaze from Sandra and the Quazon for a matter of seconds. "Tell me I haven't lost my sanity."

Before there was a chance to answer, Sandra's voice called out. "Warnach! They're inviting everyone in!"

How well did he comprehend the shock on Rodan's face. "Prepare to meet the sacred spirits of Meichasa, my friend."

Gentle swells of water rose around them as they slowly advanced farther from shore. Unafraid, Araman stretched out her right hand and stroked one of the smaller Quazon as it swam close to her. Initially feeling reticent in the presence of the magnificent creatures, Nadana's face suddenly shone with delight as the large male gently slapped his tail, deliberately splashing her with seawater. Rodan's eyes swiftly darted around as enchantment replaced disbelief.

Cautiously playful, all four Quazon lavished attention on Morcai. Buoyed by his flotation vest and tethered to straps held by his protective badehr, the toddler thoroughly delighted the aquatic visitors. The baby boy squealed with excited laughter as plump hands patted sleek bodies gliding past him. At one point, one of the smaller Quazon gently nudged Warnach away, creating sufficient space to move underneath until Morcai straddled the creature's smooth back. Alternately, the adult female circled the women while the other adult divided attention between a mesmerized Rodan and the two youths playing with Morcai.

Gradually, all antics abated. Tranquility marked graceful sweeps around legged friends. Rodan repeatedly directed questioning gazes toward Warnach. Simply nodding, both men focused full attention on Sandra, whose lips steadily moved in conversation unheard above rushing tides. Transfixed by something that defied every ancient text she had ever studied, Nadana also watched.

Evening descended in tranquility upon the Sirinoya household. Bathed and wearing cheerfully patterned pajamas,

Morcai relaxed against his badehr's chest. Adoring fingers gently twirled black curls until the tired little boy fell fast asleep. With a tender smile, Sandra lifted her son from Warnach's arms and excused herself to carry the baby upstairs.

Peaceful quiet saturated the family lounge. Nadana appeared with a tray of cool, lightly spiced beverages. Araman, comfortable in Rodan's presence, dispensed with formalities and tucked her feet beneath her on a plush chair. Neither sister spoke, although Nadana's mind continuously reached far back into memory, seeking some explanation for the rare and wonderful honor granted by the angel spirits of Meichasa.

Rodan's black hair swished with the almost constant twisting of his head as he somberly addressed Warnach. "Yesterday, when I agreed to go with you to the beach, I wondered what could have prompted such a midweek invitation." He paused, awe still clearly written on serious features. "Not in a million years would I have suspected you were taking me to see Quazon."

Warnach's head dipped forward. Pensively, he lifted a tall glass to his lips. "I fully comprehend. Even though this wasn't my first time with them, I find it so difficult to…"

Nadana smiled at her nephew's abrupt loss for words. "I believe it's impossible for any of us to simply accept Quazon visits as mere happenstance. After extensive research of this phenomenon, I have found not a single mention of any comparable appearances."

Rodan noted Nadana's contemplative expression. "Their repeated presence must bear meaning. Is their intent a warning? Do they herald impending change? I cannot help believing that they come with some great purpose."

Threads of a remembered tale flitted in and out of her mind. Nadana's slim shoulders lifted. "You're right on one point. They would only come with purpose, but what that might be..."

Interrupting them with a serene expression, Sandra lowered herself onto Warnach's lap. Affectionately, she kissed his cerea-nervos and then shifted her eyes around the room before finally meeting Rodan's perplexed gaze. "A piece of advice. If what you say is true, then you must be patient until they reveal their purpose. I'm convinced they'll let us know when the time is right. I also believe they will never abandon us."

A widening smile brightened Nadana's face. "Child, your ability to accept their comings and goings only heightens the magnitude of the mystery. You are, however, right. We must be grateful for their confidence and show patience until the time of their choosing."

Rodan heaved an enormous sigh. "How does one commune with angels and not question why they choose to reveal themselves to him?"

Warnach's eyebrows arched high. "How would any faithful Chikondran explain their telepathic communications with a Terran? In itself, the very idea boggles the mind. I suggest that you consider my approach."

"And that would be?"

Spanning Sandra's waist with long hands, Warnach lifted smiling eyes to his ki'mirsah before answering the question. "Cherish unparalleled honor. Savor the experience. Relegate all questions to the corner of your soul that guards the mysteries and promises of our faith. Believe that all will be revealed when the Great Spirit chooses."

Hours later, Rodan lay awake. Sleeping without Mirah was rarely easy. Still, solitude seemed appropriate since his mind could not escape the day's astounding events. Memories, fresh and vivid, intrigued him. Quazon. Foundation for legends. Inspiration for art. A wish entertained at least once in every Chikondran's life.

Nadana's words echoed inside his mind. Quazon allowed themselves to be seen only by those whose lives held good for Chikondra. Rodan wondered. Rare occasions existed when one would hear of a faith leader glimpsing the sacred creatures. However, the afternoon had been more than an accidental sighting in some remote location. Quazon had planned and initiated close, intimate contact made all the more amazing because the request had been issued through an alien on their world.

Rodan rolled over and tossed aside the light sheet covering him. Leaving bed and walking toward a window, he pushed aside draperies to stare outside. Chikondra's silver moons hung suspended against the black velvet of night skies. He felt as if the two orbs kept watch over his world like ancient guardians. Warnach's fears echoed back at him from the far corners of his being. Silently, Rodan Khalijar's lips formed a prayer begging the Great Spirit to protect Chikondra in peace.

CHAPTER TWO

"Curt!" Sandra exclaimed excitedly as she threw herself into her brother's arms.

"Sis! It's great to see you!" Curt laughed heartily while returning his sister's enthusiastic hug. Gaiety sparkled in hazel eyes as he released her and looked toward Warnach. "Who's this shorty with you?"

As Warnach greeted Curt, Morcai bashfully hid his face against his badehr's shoulder. However, with a little nudging and gentle teasing, Curt finally gained the baby's attention. By the time the group reached the luggage claim area, he had made fast friends with his nephew and carried the tot from the passenger station to the docking tower.

Arriving at the Warner home, a happy and lively Morcai instantly won his grandmother's heart. Soon, jolly giggles erupted frequently as Mrs. Warner played the same games with him that she had played with her own babies. Shiny black curls bobbed as a delighted Morcai bounced and clapped his hands.

Although occasionally confused by the constant English, his sunny personality rapidly overcame any frustration.

Later in the day, as Sandra carried the baby downstairs following his afternoon nap, her father returned home from work. Involuntarily stiffening, she silently scolded herself. The last thing she needed was to communicate any tension to her son. Suppressing unwelcome inner qualms, she managed the last few steps and entered the living room where Warnach had risen to greet Dave Warner.

Dragging in a deep breath, Sandra approached her father and stretched upward to kiss his cheek. "Hi, Daddy. Mind if I introduce you to someone special?"

Dave Warner's jaw clenched as his features tensed. He reminded himself that an innocent baby shouldn't be blamed for the misdeeds of his parents. Forcing a smile, Mr. Warner waited.

"Daddy, I want you to meet Morcai." Giving her son a bright smile, Sandra said, "Morcai, this is your grandpa."

Mr. Warner grasped the baby's hand and gave it a gentlemanly shake. "I'm pleased to meet you, Morcai."

Huge brown eyes shifted. So far, Uncle Curt and Grandma Warner had been fun. Grinning at his mother, Morcai bounced within her embrace and laughed aloud. When his grandfather reached for him, Morcai leaned so far forward that Mr. Warner grabbed him to prevent a tumble from Sandra's arms.

By the time dinner was on the table, Sandra and her mother constantly exchanged amazed looks. Leaving Warnach to talk with Curt and Roy, Mr. Warner had lowered himself to the floor. As if no one else were around, he carefully held Morcai's hand during many clumsy attempts to string more than three steps together at a time. Several stumbles landed the toddler straight into his grandfather's lap. Resulting frowns and pouts were quickly chased away by his grandfather's cheerful encouragement to get up and try again.

After dinner, Warnach and Sandra started to get ready to take the baby for a short walk. Both were shocked when Mr. Warner suggested they leave Morcai at the house until he acclimated himself to Earth's environment. By the time they returned, Mrs. Warner had already bathed Morcai and changed him into colorful pajamas. Thoroughly contented, the baby relaxed against his grandpa's chest while Mr. Warner's fingers twirled silken curls into tighter spirals.

As days quickly passed, Dave Warner showed no change whatsoever in his behavior toward Warnach. However, Morcai had seemingly captivated his grandfather. Often, the two played in the small backyard or disappeared for their own private walks. Mischief glittered in dark eyes as chubby fingers sought to sneak away pieces of fruit or candy deliberately left within a little boy's reach. Evenings usually found Mr. Warner lying on the floor with Morcai sitting on top of his chest as they indulged in secret games only the two of them understood.

On the night before his daughter was to depart for Washington with her family, Dave Warner's blue eyes failed to mask sadness. Sitting in an old-fashioned rocker, he rocked back and forth as his grandson doggedly resisted going to sleep. Unexpectedly, Morcai wiggled upward and gave his grandfather a sloppy baby kiss.

Mr. Warner laughed softly. "You don't want to leave your grandpa, do you, boy?"

Morcai shook his head emphatically. "Empaw. My empaw."

Surprised and delighted, Mr. Warner grinned broadly. "That's right. I'm your grandpa."

Abruptly, Morcai threw his arms around Mr. Warner's neck and pressed his forehead against his grandfather's.

Sandra instantly leapt from the sofa and grabbed her son. "Morcai! No, baby! Grandpa doesn't know cerea-semi'ittá! You'll hurt Grandpa!"

Startled and frightened, Morcai puckered his lips and began to cry. Stunned by the electrical waves the baby had emitted in cerea-semi'ittá, Dave Warner shook his head several times. "Don't scold him," he muttered thickly. "He's too young to understand. Here. Give him back to me."

Concern flashed in Sandra's eyes as her glance darted quickly to Warnach and then back to her father. Almost fearfully, she placed her crying son back onto her father's lap. With Warnach hovering at her shoulder, she carefully watched the baby and his grandfather. What she saw was both shocking and endearing.

"Don't you cry, boy," Mr. Warner murmured as he held the baby close. "You sure caught Grandpa off guard, but don't you fuss. I'm not hurt." For a full ten minutes, Mr. Warner cuddled and consoled the baby with gentle nonsense meant to soothe hurt feelings. By the time he handed him back to Sandra, Morcai was fast asleep.

"He's absolutely adorable, Sandra. It's not difficult to see how he charmed even your father."

Evergreen eyes reflected continuing amazement. "Ange, if only you had seen them together. I still find it hard to believe that was really my father back there."

Returning to the Edwards family room after putting Morcai down for the night, Warnach settled on the sofa beside his lifemate. "Angela, Mr. Warner wasn't simply charmed. I always thought him to be distant and lacking the ability to show affection. Toward us, he was as reserved as ever. With Morcai, he seemed completely free of any inhibitions. Sandra's right. It was as if he transformed into a completely different person."

John leaned back in his favorite easy chair. "Maybe your dad's finally beginning to mellow."

"Please, Sandra, you must call me Eduardo."

Shy discomfort shone from eyes that noted the sincerity in his. "I'll try. You don't know how difficult it is for me."

With an encouraging smile, Warnach wryly commented, "Eduardo, don't worry. She once had the same difficulty with me. As I recall, I think she even managed to infer that I was an old man."

Blood colored her cheeks. With a comical grimace, she defended herself. "Minister Sirinoya deliberately misunderstood me."

Eduardo chuckled. "I'm glad that one ended happily. Now. Let's see if we can get comfortable enough to head this meeting to a similarly satisfactory ending."

"Do you honestly think my opinion is worth this much effort?" Sandra asked an hour later. "You're talking about six highly publicized speeches over the next two weeks. Public speaking isn't exactly my forte."

"I distinctly remember your speech the day your acceptance into CADS was announced."

John instantly agreed. "Eduardo's right. I believe that as long as you really believe in the goal, you'll give an excellent performance. Sandra, we desperately need every shred of help we can get, no matter how small it may seem."

Warnach, who had leaned against the dining room wall since checking on Morcai, moved closer to his lifemate. Dropping onto one knee, he grasped her nervously fidgeting hands. "Shi'níyah, you must remember what you told me when I was debating whether or not to attend the summit on Mijadka. The future ahead will affect all of us, including our Morcai."

Gazing into earnest black eyes, she swallowed. "Speaking to an audience is so different from a negotiation environment."

"Yes," Warnach confirmed. "You're right. However, your CADS acceptance speech was spontaneous and still well delivered. Here, you'll have ample opportunity to prepare. Beyond that, think of other times when you gave presentations at the academy. You have the ability. You simply need to decide that you'll do it. The rest will fall into place."

The left side of her mouth lifted in what fell short of a smile. "You sound so confident."

"I have every reason to be. The deputy minister assigned to me is among the very finest students who ever graduated from CADS. Once she realizes these speeches could yield essential protection for her minister and her family, I have no doubt that she'll excel in delivering meaningful and effective discourses that could very well alter the future."

His words caused her stomach to somersault with a nauseating lurch. However, his expression and the tone of his voice infused her with encouragement. He was right. Not one of them could fail with countless lives potentially at stake. Casting a hesitant smile at those around John's dining room table, she nodded. "I'll give it my best shot."

Firmly grasping her shoulders, Warnach stared into anxious eyes. "Remember. You've already earned respect and admiration as Earth's first citizen in the Alliance to earn a ministry title. Add your own special charm to that ministry status, and you'll do a wonderful job."

Wavering self-confidence showed in her smile. "How can you believe in me so much?"

Briefly, Warnach touched vibrating cerea-nervos to her forehead. "Remember. We share Ku'saá. Well do I know you, me'u Shi'níyah." He paused before leaving for his seat in the audience. "Do this for me and for our Morcai."

Standing behind a curtain, Sandra glanced upward at John, who stood just behind her right side. "Are you sure I look all right?"

Grinning, John nodded. "You look great, even if you do look like a Terran again. I'd gotten used to seeing you in Chikondran nashavris."

"I thought it better to project an image of pride for my Earth heritage. I don't want anyone to have a mistaken impression about how much I love this world."

"I agree. The image you project will add critical impact. Maybe you should consider a career change. Politics instead of diplomacy."

Groaning, she pulled a miserable face for him. "Never! I'd eat some of these politicians alive."

John barely avoided laughing out loud. "That's one way to get rid of some of these pompous idiots."

Minutes later, Premier Crister Carlsson finished a brief speech and leaned slightly forward over the podium. "Ladies and gentlemen, I have shortened my original speech tonight. My reasons for supporting Eduardo de Castillo are already well known. However, the career experiences of our next speaker give her an even broader perspective on why we must seek leadership from men and women like Mr. de Castillo. Please, allow me to introduce the Dil-Terra Interplanetary Alliance's Deputy Field Minister Sandra Warner Sirinoya."

In addition to her decision to wear a classic Earth-style suit, Sandra chose to avoid the formal Chikondran bow that had become almost second nature for her. Reaching out instead, she shook hands with Premier Carlsson before turning to smile at an audience comprised of political leaders from every continent on the planet. Many were cognizant of the Zeteron threat; some were uncertain and interested to hear more regarding interplanetary concerns holding high priority in de Castillo's campaign platform. Others were highly skeptical that the Zeteron Empire posed any risk at all to Earth or the Alliance.

While she waited for polite applause to subside, her fingertips briefly touched her Kitak. As her eyes swept the audience, she saw Warnach in his front-row seat as his fingers unconsciously stroked the Kitak circling his head. She felt the gesture as well as his confidence. With a steady voice, she greeted the crowd and launched a vibrant speech that quickly seized the interest of her audience.

"As a loyal citizen of Earth, I seek avenues to achieve lasting peace and provide a solid foundation for building long-term security on our world," she began summarizing her talk that had commanded rapt attention. "Peace within the Dil-Terra Interplanetary Alliance is essential to global prosperity so important to each of us here tonight. Closing our eyes to the Zeteron threat does not make it any less real. We must not only recognize the reality of Zeteron intentions; we must also stand ready to resist them.

"During its short Alliance membership, Earth has already earned critical influence. We must utilize our newfound status to continue peaceful initiatives. We must also deliver the powerful message that we will tolerate no action meant to destabilize and conquer our world or our Alliance. We cannot permit all we have accomplished to fall victim to the scourge of interplanetary war.

"We have far-reaching responsibilities to protect Earth for more than just ourselves. When you leave tonight, I remind you to look carefully at your friends and your families. Look at your children especially hard. Think of their children and generations to come. Our personal actions, beginning with upcoming elections, will determine the future for them, too.

"Based on personal experiences I've already described tonight, I firmly believe that Eduardo de Castillo merits the vote of every man and woman present. He possesses wisdom, integrity, strength, and the will to exercise leadership that, combined with the foresight and experience of Premiers Carlsson and Mazzini, will place Earth at the forefront of the Alliance's quest for a prosperous peace for all member worlds. I invite you to participate in securing a strong, stable future for Earth. Join me in giving wholehearted support to electing Eduardo de Castillo as one of the governing premiers of the Federation of Earth States."

Journalists milled around extremely late as they availed themselves of the rare opportunity to probe into the life of Earth's only active diplomat serving the Alliance's Ministry of Field Diplomacy. Exciting descriptions of her encounters on Tarmantrua and Simartis Major had elicited fresh interest in the dangers diplomatic envoys faced during their travels to worlds in conflict. Further inquiries arose concerning her life with Chikondra's famous Senior Field Minister Sirinoya. With adept patience and agile thought processes, she managed to relate many of her responses to the campaign for de Castillo's election.

By the time security teams whisked her and Premier Carlsson from the auditorium, she felt mentally exhausted. Arriving at Eduardo's home for a short meeting to recap the evening, she listened to analyses from experienced politicians. Crister Carlsson, normally staid and serious, appeared ecstatic. Early reactions indicated that Sandra's speech had depicted de Castillo as worthy of support from a broad spectrum of age groups. Furthermore, the body of her speech had woven her vision for Earth and her firsthand experience with forces threatening her homeworld into key points of Eduardo's campaign philosophies. From her opening comments, she had drawn the audience into often dire circumstances facing diplomatic ministers and their necessary reliance on strong, wise leadership from the Alliance's member planets.

"Sandra, I may be wrong, but I believe your delivery tonight will prove more than we hoped for," Premier Carlsson assured her. "You pushed emotional buttons that many are reluctant to acknowledge because the images are too harsh for them to confront. Combine that with the highly publicized courage you demonstrated while on actual missions... You have lent authority and validity that no one can contest."

Eduardo leaned forward in his chair. "I watched from my office at Division headquarters. I completely agree with Crister. What you bring to the campaign is a fresh viewpoint - one that defies people like Dorn to challenge the authenticity of what's happening around the Alliance. You can't begin to imagine the value of your contribution."

Her eyes moved from one face to the other. Her eyebrows lifted, and she sighed. "The value of anyone's contribution can only be determined after the election, don't you think?"

"Pragmatic as always, my dear." John's head cocked to one side as his eyes met Warnach's. "Are you too biased to offer an opinion?"

Warnach's jaw moved sharply from side to side as he mulled over comments offered by Eduardo and Crister. "I must agree with Sandra. Results will matter most. However, sitting in the audience, I actually felt the emotion she drew from listeners. She commanded their interest and, more importantly, challenged them to actively participate in developing the future. Even I was surprised by the quality of her delivery."

On the way to the Edwards home, she sank back into the contoured seat. With eyes closed, she remembered the crush of reporters and the following review session. She could hardly believe she had agreed to speak at five additional venues considered crucial to the final stages of de Castillo's bid for election as one of Earth's four premiers.

Arriving at the house, she pleaded fatigue to Angela and disappeared to check on Morcai. Gazing down at her sleeping cherub, she tried to imagine what it had been like for other mothers - ones who had watched their children die in wars. The very concept gave rise to crushing pain in her chest. Whatever the risk, whatever the price, she would protect her child with her life.

Exhaling a breath that marked her conviction, she suddenly realized Warnach stood just behind her. Touching Morcai's plump hand, she smiled and turned. "We have much to pray on," she whispered.

With an expression difficult to discern, he whispered back to her. "I know. Come."

By the time they left Earth, she carried a bolstered sense of self-confidence. Her speeches had received widespread acclaim, and Eduardo de Castillo's campaign had gained vital momentum. As a traveling diplomat, she had submitted her ballot early. Then, knowing she had done her best, Sandra embarked with Warnach on a ministry vessel headed to Frehatar. There, she would help Morcai grow accustomed to the specially trained I'imasah, who would care for him while his parents pursued the cause of peace.

After ten days on Frehatar, the Sirinoyas boarded the Curasalah with Morcai and the baby's new I'imasah, Hitara Nemizih. Dissension in the Dragar System was growing between the worlds of Marshimian and Eskarat. There was hope that early intervention could avert any eruptions of violence. In exchange for Warnach's agreement to accept the assignment, Farsuk Edsaka had dispatched his flagship to offer greater protection for the traveling minister's family.

Following the traditional welcome extended to boarding diplomats, Sandra smiled broadly and approached Captain Tibrab with open arms. "Forsij!"

"A personal welcome aboard to you," Forsij greeted in response to her affectionate embrace. "How wonderful you look."

Stepping back, she smiled into his amused eyes and laughed. "You tolerate my Terran ways so very well!"

Struggling to maintain a serious expression, he answered solemnly, "I accept that as a compliment." Lifting his head, Forsij admired the wiggling body Warnach carried in his arms. "How quickly he has grown."

Chuckling, Warnach nodded. "Too quickly, I fear. Already he wants down to practice walking. Unfortunately, his walking keeps me running."

Returning to his quarters that night, Forsij followed the routine he had practiced for years. Shoes were removed and placed on the base of a mobile rack inside a meticulously arranged closet. Removing his dark gray uniform, he hung it on the same rack that would be removed the following day for cleaning his personal attire. As he donned warm pajamas, his mind wandered.

Every moment he spent with Warnach Sirinoya served to reinforce a sort of disbelief. Years ago, he had been convinced that Warnach would devote his entire life to diplomacy. The changes wrought through unification were startling. Despite the demanding nature of his vocation, happiness shone from eyes that had held private torment for many years.

Invited into the intimacy of Warnach's family following dinner, Forsij had relaxed with the Sirinoyas in their quarters. Casting aside all dignity associated with rank, he had deposited himself on the floor and played with Morcai. The baby thoroughly entertained him with hearty laughter each time Morcai managed to catch the big orange ball Forsij rolled to him. Finally, Sandra had interrupted the game in order to help the I'imasah get the child ready for bed. Then, bathed, changed, and sleepy-eyed, Morcai had hugged Forsij goodnight and shared a tender cerea-semi'ittá with his badehr. How superbly content the Sirinoyas were with their miracle baby.

Hurriedly, Forsij whispered night prayers and, lying on his back in bed, stared at the ceiling. Memories of that desperate flight from Bederand flitted through his mind. Never had he seen a man so devastated as Warnach had been. Never had he dreaded more the possibility of an unsuccessful mission. Neither had he ever worried so much about maintaining his military image of emotional detachment. Receiving word that Badrik had delivered Warnach in time to save Sandra, Forsij had transferred command to his first officer. Returning to his private quarters that day, he had dropped to his knees. Intense longing for an understanding lifemate and family would continue unfulfilled. In prayer, he accepted consolation that his desperate efforts had helped preserve the happiness of treasured friends.

"Champagne for you, big brother," Sandra grinned happily. "We come home after six months of incessant travel and find you promoted to colonel and ready for fatherhood. I am so excited!"

Badrik flashed a wide grin. Setting aside his crystal flute, he took hers and handed it to Warnach. He then picked her up and swept her around in an exhilarating circle. "Little sister, I'm convinced you've been my good luck charm!"

Joyful laughter filled the room. "The hero and the charm! What a terrific team we make!"

Shaking her head, Araman laughed softly. "Badrik! One of these days, you're going to cause one of you to get hurt!" she warned.

"Relax, Mamehr! I would never hurt my little sister!"

With her feet firmly planted back on the floor, Sandra giggled mischievously. "Big brother, maybe we should try to settle down. You don't want to frighten your ki'mirsah or that little bundle coming your way."

Badrik's glittering eyes shifted to Farisa's glowing face. "Have I frightened you, dear one?"

Her expression reflected endearing indulgence. "Badrik, I'll be fine so long as you never pick me up that way."

Just before midnight, Sandra slipped into Morcai's room. Leaning over his crib, she couldn't resist smiling as she lightly stroked the silken spirals tumbled around his face. How peaceful he looked. For a moment, her heart swelled within her breast. How much she loved being a mother. Reflecting on the joy evident in Badrik and Farisa, she felt deeply thankful that God was granting them the gift of their own child.

Minutes later, as she curled herself next to Warnach, he extended his arm, tucking her closer. "I've never seen Badrik so happy as tonight."

"It took them so long to really find one another. He deserves to be happy."

"That he does," Warnach agreed, nuzzling his face into the curve of her neck. "He was right, you know."

"Right? About what?" she murmured while trying to resist coursing tremors created by his breath teasing her sensitive ear.

While allowing his hands more indulging liberties across the smooth expanse of her body, he whispered, "Right about you. You are a most unique good luck charm, especially for me."

"There. Read that part." Her manicured fingernail tapped against the monitor screen.

Rodan leaned forward over Warnach's left shoulder, and both men scrutinized the article. In an obscure publication, the journalist had detailed the chronology of recent conflicts. The galactic map she had drawn revealed frightening connections. Diplomatic ministers were being spread further and further from the Alliance's core planets. Carefully assessing the worlds falling into violence, she noted distinct patterns that pointed toward an elaborate master plan intended to isolate sectors rich in vital resources. In effect, future strategic blockades were being carved into the fabric of the Alliance.

Advancing the article, Warnach quickly studied detailed graphics compiled to justify the writer's ominous conclusion. Shaking his head slowly, he expelled a serious sigh. "Who wrote this article?"

"Her name is Deborah Levine. She's from the former Terran colony of Rehovot."

"Tell me. How did you come across this article?" Rodan asked.

"I met Deborah when I was in graduate studies on Earth. She had gone on a religious pilgrimage to Jerusalem before coming to Washington on business. Now, we correspond from time to time. She thought I might find the article interesting reading."

"Her writing is masterful. Why do you think she isn't better known?"

Shrugging slightly, Sandra perched on the edge of Warnach's desk. "I think journalism has, on an overall basis, become too image-conscious. There's a tendency to sway people's emotions and attitudes, but there's no stomach for digging into hardcore details and presenting them objectively. On the other hand, Deborah's brilliant, but she can be abrasive, especially when she's convinced people are afraid to face truth head-on."

Consternation shone from Rodan's eyes. "Mainstream journalists and politicians alike are reluctant to accept the idea that organized hostile intentions lie behind this growing tide of incidents. This Deborah points out what many of us in field ministry have believed for years."

"May I assume you refer to preying on pre-existing tensions to incite general violence?" Sandra asked.

"Exactly. Her analysis swells the risks to far greater proportions, and the evidence she compiled is startlingly clear. More and more political leaders completely avoid the issue if someone dares to ask a related question. That is what I fail to comprehend. Closing their eyes doesn't eliminate the danger. It actually heightens the risks."

Leaning far back in his chair, Warnach gazed at Rodan. "I think too many fear being perceived as weak or unsuccessful if they admit outside forces seek to destabilize the Alliance."

Sandra huffed in exasperation. "What do you think they'll say when armed Zeterons point lazon rifles between their eyes?"

"Let us hope the Zeterons give up before such a day comes."

A faint tide akin to nausea moved through Sandra's stomach, and her jaw tightened. Was it simply a sense of fear or a premonition that had sparked the uncomfortable wave? Quietly, she responded, "That, my ki'medsah, is among my most fervent hopes."

Wide eyes shone with awe as he stared at his mother. "Ba…by?"

Softly chuckling, Sandra bent forward and kissed him. "That's right. Baby. Careful, Morcai. You don't want to hurt the baby."

Farisa shifted her newborn son in her arms. Smiling serenely, she watched as Morcai's short fingers barely grazed the tiny infant's round cheek. "Very good, Morcai. You know how to touch the baby gently."

So fascinated he could barely smile, Morcai quickly looked from the baby's face to Farisa's several times. Leaning forward, he carefully touched his own cheek to the baby's face. Sitting up once again, he was plainly proud of himself. "Baby feels so soft. I like. He shines soft, too."

Shaking her head, Sandra dragged Morcai onto her lap and cuddled him. "You are such a funny boy, Morcai."

Happily, Morcai raised his arms around her neck and teased her with several brief touches of his cerea-nervos. An hour later, he napped in the corner of an enormous curved sofa in Badrik's lounge.

Farisa nursed the week-old Michahn while quietly conversing with Sandra. "I can hardly believe how much I love him."

Sandra nodded as, sitting on the floor beside her sleeping son, she caressed his nose. "As time passes, you'll find you love him even more. I suppose that may well be one of life's greatest mysteries."

Placing the infant against her shoulder and patting his bottom, Farisa gazed at Sandra and Morcai. Thinking back on the coldness between her parents, she finally dared to voice personal fears that had nearly stolen the life she now treasured. "You know, I'm so glad you gave me the courage to consider a family. I'm ashamed to admit how afraid I was of losing Badrik's affection. I was so wrong. He is thoroughly enthralled with this baby, but, as strange as it might sound, I think he never loved me more."

A lingering kiss came to rest atop straight black tresses. "Perhaps because I've never loved you more." Stepping around the chair, Badrik sat and kissed his son's tiny hand.

Dropping her face, Farisa smiled in embarrassment. "Must you always sneak around that way?"

Grinning broadly at Warnach, Badrik lifted his face. "My brother, help me with my confusion. Did she just say that I, Badrik Sirinoya, sneak around?"

"All right," Farisa laughed as she handed her son to his badehr. "Poor choice of words on my part. Now, be useful. Go change his diaper."

Rolling his eyes and shaking his head, Badrik quietly groaned. "The one parental task I could live without." However, with Warnach following close behind, Badrik quickly disappeared upstairs with Michahn.

After their visitors left for home, Farisa sank into the corner of the sofa where Morcai had slept earlier. Reaching behind her, she tugged a stuffed toy from beneath the cushion. Delicate eyebrows lifted as Badrik grinned. "Colonel Sirinoya, I suppose you'd better start getting used to things at home no longer conforming to precise military order."

Sitting down beside his lifemate, Badrik removed the stuffed animal from her hand and stared thoughtfully at the toy's embroidered eyes. "I'm certain I can handle a little chaos." He paused thoughtfully. When he spoke again, his voice held unusually low tones. "Farisa, what you told Sandra. Was it true?"

For the first time in the years she had known him, Farisa felt complete confidence in Badrik. "It seems to have taken me forever to overcome fears that you might reject me the way my own badehr did. I went from hearing that my parents were once passionately in love to Badehr saying he could never find happiness with just one woman. When he finally walked out on us, I blamed myself. Nothing could ever erase memories of hearing him accuse Mamehr of getting pregnant to force him to settle his life. He even accused me of helping keep him prisoner in a life he didn't want."

Badrik sighed. "Your badehr's character is extremely different from that of most Chikondran men."

Glancing upward, she managed a quick smile. "Explain that to a young girl whose badehr just broke her heart." Reaching for Badrik's hand, she grasped it firmly. "Shedding that kind of fear is a horrible process. How fortunate I am to have found a man patient enough to help me leave my sadness behind."

Badrik turned his head. Tears glistened along her cheeks. "Dear one, I have always believed in the woman beneath that professional demeanor you've always projected."

Leaning toward him, she rested her head against his chest. "I'm so very glad you did. Ci'ittá mi'ittá, Badrik."

She had never before mentioned the accusations her badehr had made. Emotionally, those cruel words had nearly destroyed her. Raising his arm to wrap around her, Badrik held her. Swallowing hard, he whispered across the thickness in his throat, "Me'u Farisa, ci'ittá mi'ittá."

Chapter Three

"Governor Lodarius, you do realize that circumstances beyond past differences already implicate you in the assassination of Governor Maijarus."

The aging Cosomond leader's head sharply tilted backward, and he stared blankly at the white ceiling. Broad shoulders lifted with his deep intake of breath. Finally, he met Minister Sirinoya's grave countenance. "As I review the evidence, even I agree it appears damning. During the years I served as judge on court panels, I would have had no difficulty convicting someone based on the details surrounding this case. The problem is that I know I had nothing whatsoever to do with the assassination."

Warnach's eyes momentarily darted toward Sandra's emotionless face. "If that's true, how do you suggest your authorities proceed with the investigation?"

The stout, older man stood and paced the width of Warnach's office. "Minister Sirinoya, I wish I could answer you. I had no great love for Maijarus. That is no secret. However, I did respect him. He understood his people, and he served them well. Believe me. If I had any idea who committed this crime, I would tell you now. There is nothing I want more than to avoid seeing Bederand embroiled in new hostilities. That's why I fled to request temporary asylum here. Lieutenant Governor Macabay will make every possible attempt to forestall any escalation of violence while we seek the truth."

Sitting outside that evening with a cup of tea in his hand, Warnach moodily stared across green lawns. Setting aside the half-full cup, he leaned forward and rested his forehead in his hands. He had trusted none of the Cosomond leaders, even though Lodarius had finally worked diligently to protect the truce negotiated by Deputy Minister Agaman. How could he ever support asylum for Lodarius?

"What really bothers you is that you know he's telling the truth."

Staring down at the textured stone tabletop, he didn't bother to raise his head. "How can you…? No. Forget that question."

Breathing deeply in and then out, Sandra lowered herself into a green chair with fat green and white cushions. "There's really no need to ask how. What matters is that I trust my own intuition. I don't like the man very much, but I'm certain he was telling the truth. You also believe that."

"So, you would have me march into Farsuk's office tomorrow morning and recommend that he grant asylum because you think Lodarius is innocent of plotting the assassination of his opposition's leader."

"Warnach, look at me."

The sharpness in her voice demanded his attention. Almost arrogantly, he cocked his head to one side. "Yes, *Deputy* Minister?"

Her mouth thinned into a stern line, and she brusquely stood up. "There's no need for sarcasm. If you decide you want to discuss this sensibly, let me know." She then abruptly pivoted and returned to the house.

An hour later, she looked up when her office door opened. Calmly, she pressed the panel button that lowered her computer monitor with a brief whirring sound. "Yes, *Minister* Sirinoya?"

Long hands flew up into the air. "I apologize. I should have never reacted that way. This whole situation turns my mind inside out."

Meeting his eyes with a no-nonsense gaze, she replied, "Apology accepted. Sit down. Let's see if we can muddle through this."

"Temporary asylum, granted on grounds that Governor Lodarius agrees to remain here under house arrest, will likely appease the Pifanamars for a while. In the meantime, Farsuk must find a way to convince neutral investigators to analyze the case."

"My recommendation is to recruit an independent team from Simartis Major, Earth, and, if possible, Rehovot."

"Rehovot? Home of your controversial journalist friend?"

Sandra scowled at him. "Acquaintance. I hardly know her well enough to count her among my friends. However, she is a perfect example of my reasoning for engaging Rehovot in any investigation. The people there are exceptionally tenacious. If truth is to be discovered, they'll find it."

Warnach considered her suggestion for a moment. If anything, renewed war on Bederand could be more devastating now than ever. He looked carefully at his deputy minister's expression. "Intuition aside, why are you so adamant that we pursue this rather than leaving it in the hands of Bederandan authorities?"

Meeting her lifemate's stare, she answered calmly, "A man's life is at stake, and I believe he's innocent of the crime. I'm also convinced that what we don't know is far too dangerous to ignore. Neither do I want you making a mistake concerning Lodarius because of the past."

His brow wrinkled, making his cerea-nervos appear more prominent. "The past? I don't quite follow you."

"It's simple, my ki'medsah. You still harbor suppressed anger because of his tactics when you tried to mediate the last major conflict on Bederand. You've never forgotten that, more than anyone else, he was primarily responsible for the lack of progress that delayed your return home and nearly cost me my life."

Mulling over her comments, Warnach grew extremely quiet. He couldn't begin to argue the point. Obstinate and hostile, Lodarius had been the major obstacle in developing a quick, workable accord. Deep down, Warnach recognized a truth he had not considered.

Her hand came to rest on his shoulder. "I'm going upstairs to check on Morcai and get ready for bed." Without another word, she disappeared.

Farsuk's head shook back and forth. "I must be out of my mind. Nolj Kirimaris and the Earth premiers will likely agree with no problem whatsoever. However, Prime Minister Shamir is a different story altogether."

"Farsuk, you must convince him. Rehovot detectives are indisputably the most successful in history. With them leading the investigation, odds greatly improve for us to quickly determine the truth and diffuse tensions growing in the wake of Maijarus' murder."

"Provided they agree to participate." Farsuk dropped heavily into his chair. "A personal question. To say you dislike Lodarius is an understatement. Why are you so eager to help him?"

Grimly, Warnach gripped the upholstered back of a straight-backed chair and leaned forward. "If this were merely a personal matter, I would leave him to his own devices. However, Sandra and I discussed the situation extensively last night. Unfortunately, I find myself forced to agree with her. I've studied currently available evidence. It's practically flawless. Blaming Lodarius for the assassination is a perfect ruse to revive old disputes and instigate new hostilities."

Farsuk considered an array of potential ramifications. "Considering Bederand has long been a world divided, are you saying you think the assassination represents a deliberate attempt to plunge Bederand back into civil war?"

Warnach's gaze dropped to the even pattern woven into dark green upholstery. "I believe it's a distinct possibility. We can ill afford not to further analyze so-called evidence. Remember. There's never been conclusive proof of who launched the attacks when I was on-mission on Bederand. Besides, Lodarius is far from stupid. I don't believe for a moment he would have left behind such a careless trail implicating him to the assassination."

"Do you suspect Zeteron involvement?"

Images of star charts from Deborah Levine's comprehensive article flashed through Warnach's mind. "I have some reading for you. When you finish, let me know what you think."

"I just spoke with Farsuk," Warnach said as he slid into a chair at the breakfast table and, without thinking, used his own napkin to wipe a trickle of green juice from Morcai's chin. "He wants me to go to Bederand while you act as his personal emissary to Rehovot."

"What!" Sandra exclaimed. "You can't be serious!"

"Momma! Juice, please!"

Surprised, Sandra stared at Morcai's cup that was suddenly on her lap instead of his tray. "Momma is so sorry, Morcai. Here's your juice." Summoning patience, she smiled and placed the cup in her toddler's waiting hands. Immediately, she looked back at Warnach. "Has Baadihm forgotten that you and I work together?"

"Morcai, stop blowing into your cup," Warnach admonished his son firmly before picking up a darkly toasted slice of bread spread with fruit jam. "He said that we would be working together, just on different angles of a major issue. Morcai! Please stop!"

Morcai's lower lip puckered. "Badehr mad. Morcai cry."

Quickly chewing and swallowing the bite in his mouth, Warnach reached out and tucked long curls behind the baby's ear. "Badehr is not mad. Morcai needs to remember. It isn't nice to blow bubbles in your cup."

A single tear emerged from the corner of Morcai's right eye. "Badehr mad."

Warnach glanced up at Sandra with a poorly suppressed grin before responding to the little boy. "Badehr is not mad, but Badehr won't be happy if you continue blowing bubbles in your juice. Be good now."

Morcai grinned mischievously. "Badehr love Morcai?"

Drawing in a deep breath, Warnach managed a smile. "Badehr loves Morcai very much. Will you be good now?"

"Morcai good boy." Giggling merrily, the baby bobbed his head up and down just before he started blowing a fresh barrage of bubbles through the straw in his cup.

"Not a word," Araman warned from the doorway. "At least he doesn't spit it clear across the table."

Coughing to conceal giggles, Sandra stared down at her plate and pressed her napkin against her lips. Meanwhile, Warnach's left brow shot up. "Mamehr, I didn't!"

"I have recorded proof. Would you like me to show Morcai today?"

Sandra laughed out loud as Warnach grimaced. "Mamehr, please. I can live without such favors."

On the way to Kadranas to meet with the chancellor, Warnach shot a glance at his lifemate. "I still believe he inherited his bad manners from his Terran ancestors."

"Ah, yes, those barbaric, meat-eating Terrans," Sandra replied smoothly. "No manners whatsoever. Unfortunately for you, your mamehr already showed me those recordings, complete with your direct shot of green najiniar juice into Master Sirinoya's face."

Warnach stared at the lighted panel of his transport while his jaw twitched from one side to the other. "How will we ever successfully mix parenthood with diplomacy?"

"Good question, my dear Minister Sirinoya. By the end of today, I think we may be forced to answer that question."

"Hitara, Lieutenant Douglas is in charge of security for you and Morcai. If you encounter any concerns, advise him immediately."

"I will, Deputy Minister." The young Chikondran woman handed the squirmy toddler to his mother. "He seems better today."

Evergreen eyes softened as Sandra kissed the child's forehead. "Does Momma's baby feel better?"

Morcai's expression was serious as his face drew into a pout. "Better, Momma. Morcai wants Badehr."

Sandra's lips rested gently against slowly pulsating cerea-nervos. "I know, baby. Momma misses Badehr, too. We have to be brave. He's trying to stop some bad things from happening. We'll try the com-link again later so you can talk to Badehr. All right?"

The little boy's arms circled his mother's neck and held her tightly. "Morcai stay with Momma."

Winking at the protective nurse, Sandra spoke softly, "I think Hitara feels bad, too. Maybe you can help Momma and take care of Hitara while I go do my work. Would you do that?" Sandra smiled and, as her son reached out to his I'imasah, considered how fortunate they had been to engage Hitara to care for Morcai.

Later, on the shuttle transporting the diplomatic party to the surface of Rehovot, Hitara Nemizih paused several moments before reviewing procedures yet again. Her thoughts echoed those of Morcai's mamehr. How fortunate she had been to find employment with the Sirinoya family.

Most families from Hitara's native region of Chikondra believed their role in the sacred mission of Meichasa had evolved to serve the diplomatic community by providing exceptional care for their children. Hitara had been born into one of those families. Entering official training at fifteen, she had excelled in all areas of her time-honored vocation. She had proven her skills to transition swiftly from playmate and teacher to fierce bodyguard. Despite that fact, she tended to be more open and fun-loving than most of her contemporaries. Her classmates had all secured positions within months after certification. After almost two years, her family had begun to wonder if their twenty-six-year-old daughter was unsuited to her heritage.

One cool autumn afternoon, Hitara had gone to her local Brisa'machtai. She understood well what Chikondran diplomats expected of the I'imasahs. What eluded her was why none could see her willingness to give all of herself to care for children either transporting across the Alliance or left behind when missions held too high a threat for danger. In prayer, she had pleaded for the Great Spirit's intercession so that she would not fail sacred heritage or disappoint her family.

Three days later, her mamehr knocked on her bedroom door, summoning her to take a call. Listening to the caller, Hitara felt her heart leap for joy and then plummet in fear. So far, a prestigious field service minister and his ki'mirsah had rejected five candidates. The couple would provide unique challenges for any I'imasah entering their service. Was she interested in meeting with them that morning?

Arriving at the center where she had studied, Hitara entered a large, sunny room. A doubtful placement manager introduced her to the Sirinoyas. Hitara's stomach jolted. Not just any diplomat. She would be interviewed by *the* Warnach Sirinoya and his Terran lifemate. Serving any field service minister was prestigious enough. The prospect of serving a member of the Sirinoya family was the source of dreams.

Marshalling her thoughts, Hitara executed formal bows to both the Sirinoyas. They gave her little chance to speak of her training. Instead, their interest focused on learning more about her character. They had even brought their baby with them. An hour later, she left for home in a despondent mood. Despite their kindness, their reserve had dashed her hopes.

The moment she walked through the door, she stopped in surprise. Her mamehr waited, and even her badehr had made a hasty trip home. Together, they proudly informed their daughter that she had honored them and her ancestors. The placement manager, sounding quite shocked, had called. The Sirinoyas had extended an offer for Hitara's services.

Landing on-world at Rehovot, Deputy Minister Sirinoya appreciated the quiet reception from Vice Premier Hamutal. She certainly had not expected to be received by such a high-ranking government official. On the other hand, she thought while smiling into the elderly gentleman's kind face, his world was likely much more alert to underlying provocations. His people's history was filled with many tragic lessons that had taught them never to relinquish their guard.

Reaching official transports, Sandra automatically shifted her gaze. Momentary tension eased upon seeing Morcai safe in Hitara's care.

"Deputy Minister Sirinoya, you have my personal assurances. Your delegation and your son are safe here."

Sandra smiled apologetically. "It wasn't lack of confidence in my Rehovotian hosts. I've simply conditioned myself to check on everyone all the time, especially my little one."

Chuckling, the vice-premier nodded sympathetically. "I fully understand. I feel exactly the same about my children and my grandchildren."

On Bederand, Warnach's mission suffered a rocky start. Public transports had been blocked from all flight streams along the route Minister Sirinoya traveled. Demonstrators, waving flags and angrily shouting, lined the streets of the temporary capital of Brullagin. Although protests were not aimed personally at Sirinoya, the Pifanamars were enraged that Chikondra had not immediately extradited Lodarius to face prosecution on Bederand.

Safely escorted into the government's provisional headquarters by a dozen military guards, Warnach strode rapidly through long corridors. Reaching a conference room, he was greeted by Secretary Ofjano Partizia.

"Minister Sirinoya, I wish I could welcome you back to Bederand under better circumstances."

"Mr. Partizia, despite the current crisis, I am grateful for being met by a familiar face."

"Our debt to one another is not one easily repaid, Minister Sirinoya."

Warnach's head dipped with respect. "I could not agree more."

Sitting, Secretary Partizia offered Warnach a beverage. Absently staring at condensation forming on his glass, the young politician's expression was grave. "Governor Maijarus was like a father to me. His death is a deep wound to the hearts of my people. If I receive you today, it is because he respected you." Light green eyes rose accusingly. "Why? Why does the chancellery in Kadranas extend asylum to a murderer?"

Warnach carefully controlled his expression. "That is a serious misunderstanding to be addressed before I broach a more difficult topic."

Distant and aloof, the secretary responded, "Explain."

Seeking direct eye contact, Warnach responded, "Asylum, as such, has not been extended. In truth, Governor Lodarius is severely restricted in all activities and kept under constant guard. He swears he knows nothing of the assassination plot."

Partizia remained calm. "He lies. He hated Maijarus and has long wanted him dead."

Carefully assessing the younger man, Warnach proceeded cautiously. "I'm well aware of the enmity between Maijarus and Lodarius. Quite honestly, I found Governor Maijarus to be much more responsible and compassionate. My feelings for Lodarius have required deep soul-searching during my long journey here."

Partizia looked puzzled. Minister Sirinoya's comment revealed emotional notes that sparked curiosity. "Will you elaborate?"

Knowing his biggest hurdle would be to instill confidence within Pifanamar leadership, Warnach explained, "During the mission to Bederand when you and I met, you undoubtedly recall the constant haranguing from Lodarius."

Receiving a nod in acknowledgment, Warnach continued. "Full explanation would be exceedingly complex, but his obstinate resistance delayed my return to Chikondra. Those delays nearly caused my lifemate to die a horrifically painful death. What she suffered would not have occurred had I been on Chikondra. My brother also risked his life by piloting a prototype vessel in hopes of getting me home in time to save her. Those memories remain fresh and clear in my mind. I will never forget what she suffered. I will always blame Lodarius."

Quietly, the Pifanamar considered Warnach's comments. Finally, he asked, "If what you say is true, why do you come on his behalf?"

Warnach breathed in deeply. "The truth? I don't come on his behalf. Although I take no pride in the statement, I wouldn't bother solely for his sake. However, I do come on behalf of Bederand's people - and because the lifemate I mentioned asked me to do so."

Blond eyebrows knit together. "I don't understand."

"At first, neither did I."

Deborah Levine's smile formed a sweet Cupid's bow. Hazel eyes glittered with sharp intelligence. "I must admit to following your career with great interest. After all, you're the only genuine field service diplomat with whom I'm on speaking terms."

Sandra smiled at the comment. "Perhaps that's because you haven't met the right ones. I know at least two others who are intrigued by one of your recent dissertations."

"*Divide and Conquer*?"

"Exactly. My lifemate went so far as to present it to Chancellor Edsaka."

The journalist's eyes widened. Her face, a study in sharp angles, appeared stunned. "Edsaka? He actually read what I wrote?"

When Sandra leaned forward, her eyes filled with fresh intensity. "He did. More importantly, he believes that everything you wrote is true. That's why I wanted to talk with you. I value your knowledge. I also want to ask for your help."

For more than two hours, the two women discussed the article and its frightful implications. They also talked about the Bederand crisis and how perfectly it matched the complicated hypothesis expounded in her article. By the time Sandra returned to her quarters for the night, Deborah Levine felt personally vindicated from years of skepticism and ridicule leveled by more mainstream journalistic organizations. She had also agreed to support Sandra's request for help from Rehovot's leadership.

Lying in bed, Warnach found sleep evasive. In four days, he had made no headway. Cosomonds were, of course, anxious to prove Lodarius' innocence and wanted to avoid reverting to the war-torn outbreaks that had so quickly demolished cities and killed thousands upon thousands. On the opposite side, Pifanamar leaders, trying to fill the void left by their governor's death, were confronted by a people in mourning. Anger seethed, and an explosion of that anger crept closer with each passing day.

He sighed, a slight smile tugging at his mouth. Her VM received that evening had delivered welcome news. Rehovot had already agreed to participate in any investigation. Her surprisingly quick accomplishment justified his faith in her capabilities.

Sandra had studied their history. Better than most Terrans, the people of Rehovot knew that wide-scale subjugation or annihilation of people began with small steps until evil assumed control of governments and lives. Dating back to Earth's ancient history, Rehovot's people had endured centuries of religious persecution, genocide, and ruthless attacks against innocent civilians.

In reaction and retaliation, their own leaders had fallen into a historical trap of tit for tat that perpetuated violence and killing in the ugliest of circles. As far too often occurred, vengeful politicians inadvertently adopted the tactics of their worst enemies. To be sure, they had not inflicted genocide; however, they had forgotten how it felt to lose everything one had. As a result, they extended little compassion to people who were enemies by random birth rather than by design and intent.

Despite the carnage and a heritage filled with unspeakable tragedies, intelligence and indomitable spirit had ultimately prevailed. Pioneers, desperate to break the circle, departed Earth after centuries of struggles and wars. Finding a beautiful, uninhabited planet, they called their new world Rehovot. Wide. The son of their ancient forefather had so named a well, saying, "At last, God has provided us ample space to increase in the land."

Building their new world had not dimmed their collective memory as a people. Citizens of Rehovot worked hard to maintain peace. However, they also recognized a disturbing truth. Peace at all costs was a most dangerous proposition. With malevolent powers always lurking and ready to snatch everything in sight, those desiring peace must never fail to be prepared to protect that which they valued most.

Closing his eyes, Warnach thought of his ki'mirsah and his bright-eyed son. How much he missed them. Rest, he whispered to himself. Rested, you'll think better on ways to resolve the current impasse. Then, you can go home to Sandra and Morcai.

Three days later, Lieutenant Governor Drufarza finally met with Warnach. Tension crackled inside Partizia's office.

The lieutenant governor raged over the protection afforded to Lodarius, insisting that the assassination was Bederand's sovereign issue. The Alliance had no right to interfere. Drufarza demanded extradition in order to force Lodarius to face justice.

Patiently, Warnach listened to the Pifanamars' long list of protests, most of which he could not contest. However, when their irate interim leader made a reference to truth, a possible new strategy popped into Warnach's mind. "Lieutenant Governor, one point you have stated multiple times is that you are committed to truth and justice. Am I correct?"

Stone-faced, the middle-aged Drufarza stared at Warnach. "You are correct. However, the truth is evident."

Pausing several prolonged seconds, Warnach rose and walked toward a window. The press of a button caused shades to rise. Still deserted, the haunting gray ruins of Mijirina were just visible along the horizon. Pivoting, Warnach straightened, and his expression commanded attention. "Were you in Mijirina during the attack that destroyed the city?"

"I was not." The lieutenant governor glared at Warnach.

"I was. Had it not been for Secretary Partizia, I probably would have died that day."

"How does that relate to the murder of Governor Maijarus?"

Deliberately leaving the shades up, Warnach returned to the center of the room. Leaning forward, he flattened his palms on the conference room table. "Specifically, it does not. However, that attack yielded crucial points to consider. Visual tracking and recordings of the attacks were studied. Crash debris was carefully analyzed. All of the attack ships bore Nelsiuan identification. Scanners from a fleet of Alliance vessels detected no evidence whatsoever that

Nelsiua launched the attack. Both Cosomond and Pifanamar investigators found no indication that either side had been responsible for the attack. Nevertheless, both Cosomonds and Pifanamars suffered great losses."

"The point you wish to make is?" Beyond impatient, Drufarza was clearly growing irritated.

Partizia suddenly rose from his chair. Pacing toward the window, he stared at Mijirina's ruins and remembered the choking clouds of dust and reverberating explosions. Following a tense pause, the secretary spoke in a subdued voice. "What he is saying is that we never discovered who attacked Mijirina that day. Because losses on both sides occurred in a mutually accepted neutral zone, Cosomonds and Pifanamars diligently searched for the truth. Together. In reality, the goal of both sides was to blame the other. Each was forced to acknowledge the apparent innocence of the other. That was why Deputy Minister Agaman's negotiated truce evolved into the final treaty that ended hostilities."

Drufarza's face drew into confused lines. "I fail to understand what that has to do with the crisis we currently face."

When Warnach would have explained, Partizia's eyes cautioned the minister to wait. "Cosomonds were furious that Nelsiuans had attacked. Pifanamar supporters on Nelsiua adamantly denied any involvement. Nelsiuan emblems were found to be counterfeit. Attack aircraft had been built from decommissioned ships and stolen parts. So-called evidence was later discounted. What had seemed glaringly obvious wasn't fact at all."

The Chikondran minister smiled gratefully at Partizia. "Lieutenant Governor Drufarza, the attack on Mijirina was intended to drive a permanently divisive wedge between

Bederand's two territories. Years later, investigators still search for whoever was responsible. I'm not saying that Lodarius is innocent. Quite honestly, I don't know. What I do know is that he is a keenly intelligent man who would be very unlikely to leave such an easily discovered trail."

Drufarza stared at his fingers as they drummed a quiet rhythm on polished glass. "What are you suggesting?"

Dropping into his chair, Warnach rested his hands on the table and gazed directly into eyes that had turned thoughtful. "Announce that Governor Lodarius is being detained under house arrest on Chikondra pending the outcome of further investigation. Emphasize the Pifanamar position that justice must be based on truth. Portray your people in the noble light they deserve. Then, accept a team of independent investigators who will come to Bederand to review the case."

"Independent investigators? Do you think the Cosomonds will agree?"

"Lieutenant Governor Macabay is anxious to resolve this matter peaceably. His people want to prevent renewed civil war as much as your people do. He has already obtained approval from the Cosomond cabinet."

When Drufarza fell into silent consideration, Ofjano Partizia asked, "Who would make up the investigative team?"

"Experienced detectives from Earth, Kurula, Simartis Major, and Rehovot."

Drufarza's eyebrows shot up, but Partizia continued, "What happens if they substantiate Lodarius' involvement?"

Warnach paused. For just a moment, he questioned whether or not he wanted Sandra's intuition to prove correct. "If that is the case, I will personally accompany the police detachment when they return Lodarius to Bederand for prosecution."

Chapter Four

Light breezes, practically undetectable on the ground, gently rustled towering tree branches. Blue skies stretched above them. The air smelled fresh and clean. Autumn was still too new for many leaves to have fallen. The warm afternoon had proven too glorious to resist.

"I'm still amazed by the differences. We were only apart four weeks."

Relishing the firm grip of his hand around hers, Sandra laughed softly. "His language skills are developing so fast that he surprises me daily. I can only imagine how you must have felt yesterday."

"Do you ever wonder what he'll do when he grows up?"

Looking ahead as they walked, her thoughts wandered. At last, she answered, "I suppose the thought has crossed my mind a time or two. Each time, I ask myself if I'm crazy. I don't want to rush his growing up."

On their way back to the house, Warnach suddenly stopped. Releasing her hand, he stepped off the well-worn path and peered into a thick stand of trees. A slight depression in the ground was covered by a thin layer of leaves freshly fallen from the treetops. Warnach glanced over his shoulder, his dark eyes dancing with mischievous invitation.

Her body shook with laughter. "You're joking, right?"

"Do I ever joke about wanting you?" he asked boldly.

Staring at his outstretched hand, she continued laughing. "I'm not so sure this is such a good idea, my dear minister."

Snatching her hand and dragging her toward the tree-sheltered spot, he kissed her. Lightly caressing her face, he questioned her as his expression reflected growing desire. "Why isn't it a good idea?"

Her eyelids drifted shut. His hands drew a long caress downward over her breasts until they stopped at her waist.

"Warnach," she whispered shakily, "I told you a long time ago. I'm positive this is the spot where we conceived Morcai."

"Mmm," he murmured as his teeth gently grasped the delicate tip of her earlobe. "Are you suggesting we might conceive another child if we make love here?"

Hot breath inside her ear caused her head to fall sideward. Her own breathing quickened. "I'm not sure what I'm suggesting," she muttered as her hands rose and tangled into the length of his hair.

Sensing imminent surrender, he continued torturously sweet caresses as his hands moved upward beneath her sweater. "Would having another child with me be so terrible?"

"Terrib..." Coherent thought failed.

The onslaught of his kisses and the heat of his caresses combined to enflame every inch of her body. Weak knees bent easily as he lowered them both to the ground. First tossing a light jacket over the thin bed of leaves, he quickly removed her sweater and support camisole. Within moments, his mouth clung to swelling flesh as her hands exposed his back to the heavens. Beneath nature's majesty, they lavished one another with fiery strokes and words of love until they breathlessly gloried in the satisfaction found only in their total union.

Their return to the house was quiet. Clinging to his arm, she felt infinitely happy. His lovemaking had filled her with warmth. The poetry of loving words had satisfied her heart as much as he had satisfied her body. Even as they walked, he dropped several quick kisses atop her mussed hair.

Just before they reached the back entrance, she stopped. Holding both his hands tightly and low at her sides, she gazed upward into his expressive eyes. Slowly, she touched her lips to his. "My dear Minister Sirinoya, have I told you today how much I really love you?"

His sensuous mouth spread into a smile. How much he loved times in the past when she had asked him that same question. Touching Kitak to Kitak, he kissed her nose. "I believe you just did, me'u Shi'níyah."

"Well, you look a bit on the grumpy side today."

Sandra wrinkled her nose disdainfully and lifted her arms. "I'm still going to hug you, even if you are mean to me."

Peter welcomed her embrace, then teasingly pushed her away. "Refresh my memory. I haven't just violated some sacred taboo about advocates hugging ministers, have I?"

Giggling, she shook her head. "You probably did. However, if it's any consolation, I can assure you that I long ago disintegrated that same taboo with my bad behavior."

"Right. I almost forgot. Is lunch still on?"

"You betcha."

Over dessert, Peter watched her thoughtfully. "You've heard all my tales about life on-mission with Minister Khalijar. Tell me now. How did you persuade our Alliance's reclusive Rehovot government to participate in the assassination inquiry on Bederand?"

Sipping hot tea, Sandra shrugged. "I'm not exactly sure. I'd like to take credit for understanding their history on Earth and doing my homework. Quite frankly, I think they had already decided to take on the investigation before I arrived."

"Why so?" Peter asked, genuinely curious.

"As a people, they've conditioned themselves to be more alert to impending danger than other Alliance members. It's almost as if their history has established an ancestral memory in their consciousness. Anyway, I think they sense more peril than many worlds in the Alliance are willing to admit. I saw definite signs that they're already installing stronger safeguards and defenses."

"Really?" Peter asked, straightening on his chair. "Have you informed Edsaka?"

"Of course," Sandra replied, staring into her cup. "He thinks the same. The problem is that convincing worlds in denial is so challenging as to prove nearly impossible."

The two sat in silence before Peter spoke again. "Are you okay?"

"I'm fine. Warnach left ten days ago on an unannounced trip to Bederand. He'll be back next week. Morcai gets fussy whenever his badehr is gone, and I never sleep well when he's away."

"No chance of a repeat performance of that time he went on-mission to Bederand when you were still at the academy, is there?"

A wry smile lit her face. "Thankfully, no. At least I hope not. Now, setting my whiney mood aside, what's new with you and Druska?"

"What's new?" he repeated as shadows crept into his eyes. "She's on-mission to Dargom with Minister Thapord. I haven't seen her in person for almost two months."

Sandra groaned. "That's tough."

"I miss her so much. It's like taking a walk through hell, especially with tensions so high on Dargom."

Sandra's forehead wrinkled. "Minister Thapord has done remarkably well under the circumstances. With him only covering for Minister Cordray, he's not as entrenched in his understanding of the problems there. Making matters worse, I think Dargom's conflict is based as much on a family feud as it is on political differences."

He nodded in agreement. "I received a VM from Druska yesterday. She looked exhausted."

"Encourage her. If you give her positive encouragement, you'll make things a lot easier."

Peter's blond head jerked sharply away. "That isn't easy when I don't think she should be out there in the first place."

Sandra's voice assumed firmness. "Peter, you can't deny her the opportunity to do what she spent years preparing to do. You know that would be completely unfair."

Grinding his teeth together, Peter looked back into Sandra's eyes. "I'm so afraid for her. I wish I could explain. It's like something gnawing away at my insides."

Sandra's lips pressed tightly together. "All the more reason to encourage her. If your worry is more like a premonition, she needs your support more than ever. It will help her remain energized and alert. Knowing that you're waiting for her will be added incentive in case of any incidents."

A knot swelled in Peter's throat. His eyes met hers. "How do you and Minister Sirinoya do it?"

Sliding her hand across the table, she grasped Peter's. "We make every minute together count. There's nothing more anyone can do."

"Shi'níyah, are you all right?" Warnach rose on his elbow and leaned over her shoulder.

Twisting onto her back, she expelled a frustrated breath. "I'm so tired of not being able to sleep. There's just too much light in this room."

"Sandra," he said in a soothing voice, "there's no way to make this room any darker. There are padded stops in front of the doors, and you covered the display on the clock. You even installed dark film over the windows. Outside, it's too cloudy to see either moon. There's no light in here!"

Pulling covers all the way over her head, she groaned. "I still see light. Where the hell is it coming from?"

Gently, he pried the comforter loose from her hands and uncovered her face. "Shi'níyah, forgive me. Desperate measures are needed here." Rising above her, he pinned her shoulders into the depth of the mattress and lowered his face to hers. For long moments, his cerea-nervos poured tranquilizing energy into her. Sensing change, he shifted back onto his pillow. Relieved that she was finally asleep, he snuggled under the covers. Tomorrow, weekend notwithstanding, he would send her for an eye exam.

The following weekend, she looked up from the sofa where she sat reading to Morcai. Male voices were filled with laughter as Badrik, Rodan, and Warnach strode into the spacious family lounge.

Badrik quickly crossed the shadowy room and picked up his nephew. "Is your mamehr still keeping you in the dark?"

"Momma, not mamehr," Morcai boldly corrected his uncle. "Not so dark, either."

Kissing Sandra's cheek, Warnach closed one eye and stared at her. "How can you see to read with drapes drawn and no lights on?"

"There's plenty of light. How did you do in pafla?"

Rodan laughingly shook his head. "Your ki'medsah trounced his brother and me."

"Not surprising," she grinned proudly. "Can I get you gentlemen some snacks or something to drink?"

Badrik knelt onto the floor, setting Morcai on his feet. Glancing upward, he nodded. "I would appreciate that very much. With Farisa and Michahn away visiting her maméi-mamehr, I feel lost. Food is the only thing that fills the loneliness."

Morcai reached out and touched his uncle's cerea-nervos. "You look sad. Your light's not so shiny today."

Halting her walk from the lounge, Sandra turned and fixed puzzled eyes on her young son. "Morcai, what did you just say?" she asked gently.

Morcai shrugged his shoulders. "His light isn't bright today. He's sad because Michahn is gone."

Warnach exchanged a puzzled glance with Rodan and then looked at Sandra. "What is he talking about? This isn't the first time he's mentioned someone's light. I find that especially odd considering your current fixation with darkness."

Sandra scowled affectionately at her lifemate. Walking back and sitting on the sofa, she beckoned to Morcai. "Come, little one. Let's talk. Tell me about this light."

"Everybody has light. You don't see it?"

Calmly, she shook her head. "I don't think I see it the way you do, so you have to help me. Let's start by telling me about Badrik's light."

"Oh," Morcai answered before grinning at his uncle. "I like Derma'ad Badrik's light. Bright and big all the time. Except today. His light isn't so big. Looks sad."

Sandra's eyebrows rose. Patiently, she continued questioning the child. "What about Baadihm Rodan? Does he have light, too?"

Morcai's reply wasn't quite so patient. "Momma, I told you already. Everybody has light."

"I apologize. You're right. Can you tell me how you see Baadihm's light?"

Tentatively, Morcai walked over to Rodan, who knelt on the floor. Small hands cupped his baadihm's face. "Baadihm has pretty light. Happy light. I like it. Blue like the sky and bright."

Fascinated, Warnach dropped onto his knees at the end of the sofa. "Morcai, come to Badehr."

Soulful brown eyes gazed into Warnach's. "Badehr's light is soft when he holds Morcai. Feels good."

Thoroughly perplexed, Warnach smiled and hugged his son. "Maybe Badehr's light feels good because he loves his Morcai."

The child's expression was almost too serious for a boy of three. "Badehr's light is real bright when he hugs Momma. Momma's light is real bright, too."

Warnach chuckled as he quickly glanced at his lifemate. "Badehr loves Morcai's Momma, too. Do you think that's why her light gets bright?"

Thinking for a minute while the adults exchanged amazed looks, Morcai nodded. "I think so."

Leaning far enough forward to kiss her son's forehead, Sandra smiled encouragingly. "Morcai, I think we don't see people's lights the way you do. Can you tell me about Badehr's light? Do you see what color it is?"

"Momma, I like to talk about your lights."

"My lights? Do people have more than one light?"

Quite earnestly, Morcai strode around the room. Curiously, he tilted his head from side to side as he studied first Badrik, then Rodan. Stopping in front of his badehr, he stared thoughtfully before looking back at Sandra. "Only one light."

Climbing onto the sofa, he placed his palm against his mother's cheek. "Except Momma. Momma's light so pretty here. But here…" He moved his hand to her stomach. "New light is very bright. Too white. Sometimes it hurts Morcai's eyes."

Badrik and Rodan rose almost simultaneously. Both stared at Warnach, whose head jerked around. Facing Sandra, he gazed intently. "Do you know what he's talking about now?"

A dumbfounded expression transformed her face as a smile played at the corner of her mouth. "It's like he already knows. I…I'm pregnant again."

"Pregnant?" Stunned, Warnach reached for her hands. "Are you sure?"

"Momma? Momma!" Morcai tugged insistently at his mother's sleeve. "Pr..." Unable to pronounce the word, he started again. "What's that? What does it mean?"

"Come with me, little one," Badrik said, lifting Morcai into his arms. "I think some of us need to go to the kitchen for a snack, and your badehr needs to talk with your momma."

Setting his tea mug on a matching coaster, Warnach stared blankly across the kitchen. Although he had asked for Nadana's advice, serious reservations filled him with worry.

"Warnach, I wouldn't make the suggestion if it were merely a matter of seeing auras. The fact that he's so young is astounding enough. Think. Not only does he see auras, but he also differentiates colors, size, and brightness. Then, he discerns emotional changes based on how he sees the auras. I believe we would be doing him a great disservice by not taking him to a Luradrani for formal evaluation."

Warnach's shoulders rose and fell. "Nadana, I know what you say is true, but I also know my son. He is sensitive and very young. I fear the evaluation is more than he's mature enough to handle. He's only three."

Nadana's expression softened. "Luradrani Fuhlamnad is very wise and kind. I'm positive he would exercise every precaution to avoid frightening Morcai."

Thoughtfully, Warnach tipped his mug for another drink of strong tea. "I fear more than just frightening him. Sandra and I worry about something else. Even though Morcai looks Chikondran, he's still half Terran. That alone makes him different. This newly discovered capability makes him even more unusual. Neither of us wants to overwhelm him."

"Warnach, I can't discount your concerns," Nadana replied. "On the other hand, appropriate assessment and compassionate guidance will strengthen his ability to cope. I cannot stress how strongly I feel about this."

"Sister," Araman interjected as she refilled cups, "you've never had children of your own. I understand Warnach's hesitance. In his place, I don't think I could send away a child so young."

"Araman," Nadana countered, "the time would be short. A matter of only a week or two."

Listening just outside the doorway, Sandra finally decided to make her presence known. "Excuse me for eavesdropping on your conversation." Going to the table, she kissed Araman's cheek and then stood behind Warnach with her hands resting on his shoulders. "Nadana, you know how much I love you. I also respect you, but I will not allow the Luradrani to evaluate Morcai away from this house."

The Simlani met Sandra's stern eyes. "I mean no insult, child. You know how I feel about you. You must understand that this could be a very critical time in Morcai's life. You've always been so open in the past to our rituals and traditions. Why do you now resist?"

Sandra's grasp tightened on her lifemate's shoulders. "The other times felt right to me. Sending my baby away, especially to strangers, doesn't. With all due respect, I won't allow it."

Warnach's right arm lifted across his chest, and his hand covered his lifemate's. "Nadana, I believe with all my heart that you have the best intentions. However, neither my ki'mirsah nor I will consent."

Araman gently placed her hand on her daughter's arm. "Child, you had very little for breakfast. May I fix you something to eat?"

Forcing a smile, Sandra sat down beside her lifemate. "Toast and a vitamin shake didn't last long. I'd love something if it isn't too much trouble."

Tense minutes later, she lifted a spoonful of creamy soup to her mouth. As she swallowed the bite, her eyes moved from one solemn face to the other. "It may not fit in fully with tradition, but there could be a possible compromise."

Interest flared in Warnach's eyes, but he said nothing. Nadana was the only one to respond. "What do you suggest?"

Popping a piece of warm, crusty bread into her mouth, Sandra met Nadana's direct gaze. "Please correct me if I'm wrong. The old tower. It was once a Brisajai and is now registered as a historic site and holy relic. Correct?"

"Yes," Nadana answered slowly. "And?"

"What if a Luradrani comes here? He could stay in this house and perform daily evaluations of Morcai at the tower. We would be nearby, and Morcai would have his family and familiar surroundings in the evenings."

"Sandra, the Brisa'machtai contains extensive areas for meditation and prayer. There would also be more opportunities to observe his unique behavior."

"I see," Sandra said. Moments passed as she finished her food and thanked Araman once again. Thoughtfully, she continued, "If the Luradrani is as sensitive as you say, he can interact with Morcai here. He would have privacy in a consecrated place. That is the best I can offer. Otherwise, the matter is closed."

Rising, she carried her dishes from the table and put them inside the dish sanitizer. Turning around, she smiled. "I have some work to do in my office while Morcai is asleep. Excuse me."

Nadana glanced at Warnach once Sandra was gone. "You will not speak to her?"

Warnach leaned forward and took his aunt's wrinkled hands. "Nadana, Morcai is her son, too. Especially now that she's pregnant again, I will do nothing that might upset her. Besides, her suggestion to use the old tower far exceeds any offer I would have made."

A month later, Warnach responded to a request from Master Barishta for a meeting in Farsuk's office. He was surprised to find Governor Lodarius also waiting. Eyes filled with questions met those of his baadihm as he lowered himself into a comfortable chair.

"Minister Sirinoya," Governor Lodarius was the first to speak as he twisted in his seat. "I owe you the debt of a lifetime." The Bederandan noted Warnach's inquiring glance toward the chancellor before continuing. "Chancellor Edsaka just informed me that the lead investigator from Rehovot announced the existence of falsified evidence. Newly discovered details were presented to a joint panel of judges representing both Pifanamars and Cosomonds. The vote was unanimous. The panel will recruit a new team of detectives and further investigate the assassination. They are determined to learn who is really responsible for the murder. In the meantime, I've been exonerated."

Warnach released a heavy sigh as his face dropped. He had not erred in trusting her intuition. Without smiling, he again faced Governor Lodarius. "Sir, in this case, justice negates any concept of debt."

"Minister Sirinoya, that isn't the way I feel. My people will hear how this came to be. I also intend to do all in my power to unite peoples of Bederand. Our internal strife and disagreements may never disappear completely, but I'm confident our people will join forces to prevent outside entities from dictating our future through subterfuge."

Farsuk stood up. "Governor Lodarius, I regret that Deputy Minister Sirinoya isn't here today. If any debt exists, she's the one to whom it is owed. She raised the convincing arguments that resulted in the independent inquiry. She is also the one who convinced Rehovot to manage the investigation."

Lodarius also stood, but he directed his comments to Warnach. "I extend my deepest regards to your wife, Minister Sirinoya. She must be an admirable woman."

Warnach's head tilted slightly. "My ki'mirsah is the most remarkable woman I know. I shall be pleased to give her your regards."

After Master Barishta escorted the Bederandan governor from the chancellery, Farsuk turned thoughtful eyes to his godson. "You could have been more congenial."

Warnach gazed steadily at his baadihm. "I'm pleased the investigation brought out the truth. I addressed him respectfully. What more would you have me do?"

"Do you still resent me as much as you resent him?"

The question prompted no change in Warnach's expression. "At times."

"So I thought. I would do anything to regain your full trust."

"Farsuk, I will do anything I can for you. Most of what I once felt for you is restored. However, that does not include what was once unquestioning trust."

Sadness crept into Farsuk's eyes. "Warnach, I proved that I'm fallible. I believe I've also proven the extent to which I'll go to earn back your faith in me."

"Had she died, I would have lost her, my son, and this new child she carries. I would suggest you content yourself with Sandra's total forgiveness. I still work on mine. Is there anything else you care to discuss?"

That evening, Ifta Edsaka left her lifemate alone inside the Brisajai of their home. Deep in meditation, Farsuk prayed. Danger insidiously threatened the far corners of the Alliance in which he believed. He worried for the many peoples whose lives could be turned upside down by war, and so he prayed for them. He also prayed for strength to guide the Alliance wisely until the end of his term. More than anything, he prayed that Warnach and Badrik would someday forgive him for the mistake made years earlier that continued to divide them.

Chapter Five

Morcai clung to his badehr. Tears brimmed in his eyes. "Badehr, you come back soon?"

Warnach's heart lurched. "As soon as I can, Morcai. Until I do, I want you to take care of Momma."

"Empaw will help me. Empaw is big and strong."

David Warner placed his hand on Morcai's shoulder. "That's right, boy. Empaw is strong. We won't let anything happen to you or your momma while your badehr is gone."

Arms tightened around his son one last time before they released the baby to his grandfather. While Morcai buried his face against his grandpa's leg, Warnach rose from the floor and pulled Sandra into his arms. Holding her tightly, he dreaded leaving more than ever. "Ci'ittá mi'ittá, Shi'níyah."

"I know," she whispered. "Be careful."

"I promise I will. Security will be tight, and the Rahpliknar will stay in orbit in case of emergency."

Pulling away, she smiled. "Everything here is organized. I'll do whatever possible to assist you, even if it is long distance."

Drawing her closer, he felt against his body the swollen evidence of his unborn child. Holding his ki'mirsah, he looked directly into David Warner's blue eyes. "Please. Take care of them until I return."

Mr. Warner's square jaw set firmly. "She's my daughter. No one will hurt her or my grandson as long as I'm around."

Watching the shuttle lift into the air, Sandra fought disconcerting nausea. Circumstances on Dargom had worsened and were teetering precariously on the verge of war. A waiting shuttle would carry Warnach to the Rahpliknar. There, he would join Rodan for the voyage to Dargom to provide additional support to Minister Thapord, Minister Wang, and Chikondran Master Vahmindra. Turning dry eyes to her father, she inhaled deeply and reached for Morcai. Cuddling her son close, she whispered into his ear, "Don't you worry, Morcai. Momma promises. Badehr will come home."

At her parents' house, Sandra accessed secure data banks to complete some research Warnach had requested. Delving into archives occasionally proved time-consuming as she narrowed search criteria to target specific topics. Reviewing the newest list, she sighed and tried another option. Unfocused concentration slowed her progress.

Turning at the sound of Morcai's voice, she laughed at his grimy face and dirty clothes. "What have you been up to, you rascal?"

Little arms flew up into the air. "Gempaw took me to the park. We play. Morcai has new friend, too."

Tipping his cap off, she planted a noisy kiss on his sweaty forehead and then pinched her nose closed. "We've graduated to Gempaw, eh? Well, Momma needs to talk to Gempaw about letting you get so dirty! And stinky!"

Dave Warner grinned. "He's a boy. He's supposed to get dirty when he plays."

"Right," Sandra responded with a laugh. "Well, he won't be dirty long."

Her father's blue eyes glittered mischievously as he winked at Morcai. "Don't worry, boy. We'll just do it all again tomorrow."

Time dragged as she responded to requests from the ministry team on Dargom. Warnach and Rodan had reached the struggling planet five days after their departure from Earth. Three weeks later, despite concentrated efforts of a council master and four experienced diplomatic ministers, practically no headway had been made in settling compounding disputes.

Meanwhile, the mission team labored under extremely threatening conditions. Communications were already complicated by natural planetary alignments that restricted open transmissions. Sandra's decision to work from her parents' home proved an unexpected boon because Earth's location allowed her to act as a relay point for information flowing between Dargom and Chikondra.

Finished with last-minute updates to a report just before dinner one evening, she waited for approval of security codes before submitting her latest transmission. Leaning back in a chair, she felt weary. Her sleep continued to be unsettled by inexplicable perceptions of light. Warnach's absence only added to her restlessness. Morcai's close relationship with her father provided welcome distraction.

Tones sounded. Security codes were confirmed. While entering final commands to transmit reports to ministry headquarters in Kadranas, she turned at the sound of her name.

"He shouldn't be gallivanting around space with you in your condition." Her dad's expression was almost as stern as his voice.

So much for happier distractions, she thought. "Daddy, he's doing what he does hoping that war doesn't keep spreading to overtake Earth or Chikondra."

"I never took off when your mommy was expecting. Don't tell me he doesn't have a choice."

A quick look at the monitor showed the transmission was complete. Signing off the system, she stood up and stretched. "I'm too tired to argue the subject right now. Where's Morcai?"

"Outside with Roy. And I wasn't arguing. I was merely stating a fact."

Shrugging, she shook her head. "Argue. Discuss. Stating. Doesn't matter, Daddy. Warnach never does anything that meets your approval. If you'll excuse me, I'm going to help Mom with dinner."

Later that evening, she was reading a story to Morcai when her mother interrupted. "An official call is coming through on the com-link. You go. I'll bring Morcai down in case it's his father."

Setting aside the book, she shifted her legs off the edge of the bed. Hurrying downstairs, she swung into the desk chair and activated the monitor.

"Deputy Minister Sirinoya?"

"Yes. You have a link?"

Earth's interplanetary communications center confirmed connection of a secure call and prompted her to wait. Within less than a minute, Warnach's tired image appeared. "Shi'níyah, how are you?"

He sounded so anxious. "I'm fine, my ki'medsah. I visit the doctor later this week. However, not only am I as healthy as a horse, I'm starting to look like one."

He laughed in response. "That I shall be glad to see for myself. How is Morcai?"

"He's fine except for missing you." Twisting slightly, she took Morcai from her mother and settled him on her lap.

"Badehr! Badehr!"

Heartened by the sight of his son, Warnach smiled. "How is my Morcai? Are you being a good boy?"

"Yes, Badehr. I play at the park. Gempaw takes me."

Moments later, with Morcai cuddled in his grandmother's arms, Sandra gazed at the blank screen. Warnach had just started to say something when the sound garbled, and the picture scrambled and disappeared. Frustrated, she signaled the communications officer who advised he was unable to re-establish a clear frequency.

After an hour, she contacted the communications center again. Transmissions reconnected, but some sort of space interference had continued to break up the signals. Filled with aggravation, she thanked the patient comm officer before disconnecting and leaving with her brothers for a short stroll to ease her tension.

On Friday, she kept an appointment with the physician regularly consulting with her doctors on Chikondra. After an encouraging exam, she decided to visit the park where Morcai went with his grandfather for their afternoon romps. Stopping behind an enormous tree, she eavesdropped on the conversation between her father and two other women.

"He's such a beautiful little boy," commented a young woman who was overdressed for an afternoon on a playground. "It's a shame he's got those scars on his forehead. I'm surprised your daughter hasn't had them corrected. Are they from an accident, or are they some type of birth defect?"

The other woman, clad in black slacks and yellow shirt, turned. "Arlene, that's a terrible thing to say."

Dave Warner's face reddened. Oh, God, Sandra thought. Her dad felt embarrassed by the woman's thoughtless remarks. Just as she started to approach, she saw her dad's fists clench. Pausing, she listened.

"I don't suppose either one would matter. He's as smart a child as I've ever seen and a good deal better mannered than some other children who play around here. By the way, to set the record straight, you're wrong. No scar. No birth defect. He looks just like his father, who just happens not to be from Earth."

The lady named Arlene looked shocked. "You mean that little boy is half-alien?"

For just a moment, Mr. Warner glanced around to check on his grandson. "Morcai! Stay where Grandpa can see you!" Facing the two women again, he glared. "The boy's father is from Chikondra, and his mother is my daughter. Half-alien or half-human doesn't matter much, does it? He's still a little boy."

"Well, I'm surprised you have the nerve to bring him to play with normal children. From what I've read about Chikondrans, he could hurt one of these youngsters with those things on his head. Don't you think you're being rather careless with the safety of innocent children?"

Before Dave Warner could answer, the other woman spoke up. "Arlene, it's my opinion that you're being extremely ignorant as well as rude. The only regular child around here who ever hurts anyone is your little bully that you won't discipline. Personally, I don't even like for my daughter to play with your son, and I certainly don't want her exposed to your bigotry. What a disgrace you are."

Suddenly, two other mothers and a father joined the discussion. Angrily, they all expressed disgust with Arlene's comments and agreed that she owed Mr. Warner an apology. Acting affronted, she called to her little boy and stalked off. In the meantime, the others assured Mr. Warner that their children were happy having Morcai as a playmate and that he should ignore Arlene's insults.

One by one, the other parents excused themselves only after Mr. Warner promised to bring Morcai back to the park the next day. However, the first woman to speak out remained. Grim-faced, she forced a smile. "I almost punched her in the mouth." She then added, "Did you say his father is Chikondran?"

Mr. Warner appeared calmer. "Yes, I did. My daughter's staying with us while her husband's away - for his job."

Curiosity transformed to surprise as she repeated the last name. "Warner. It never occurred to me before. Your daughter isn't the same girl who's in Alliance diplomatic service, is she?"

Mr. Warner's face tensed. "That's my daughter, Karen. The well-known Deputy Minister Sandra Sirinoya."

"Wow! Wait until I tell Brad! He's going to faint when he finds out his little girl's favorite new playmate is the son of Warnach Sirinoya! Morcai is all she talks about. If that's not enough, Brad is fascinated with current events, and he admires Sirinoya more than anyone else in the Alliance. He also says Minister Sirinoya's wife may turn out to be even better in diplomacy than her famous husband."

David Warner stared at her. "You're kidding."

"Absolutely not! Wow! I didn't even have a clue! You must be so proud of your daughter! I can hardly wait to tell Brad!"

Pretending she hadn't heard a word, Sandra nonchalantly strolled forward. "Daddy! There you are! I thought I'd stop by to see where you keep disappearing with my baby!"

That night, having her usual problems falling asleep, Sandra got up, dragged on a robe, and went downstairs. Helping herself to a glass of milk, she decided to go outside. The autumn night was beautiful, with clear skies. Looking heavenward, she gazed at twinkling stars.

"Can't sleep again?"

Startled, she swung around. "Daddy!" Catching her breath, she looked embarrassed. "I'm sorry if I woke you up."

"I heard noises and came downstairs. Are you feeling all right?"

"I'm tired but not sick or anything."

"Your mommy said you got a VM today. Is something wrong?"

Finally, she smiled. "No. It was Badrik. He's constantly checking on Morcai and me."

"Well, take some advice. Drink your milk and then try to get some sleep. You need to take care of yourself."

Hours later, her eyes opened abruptly. Squinting against brilliant light, she looked at the clock on the nightstand. Three-fifteen in the morning. Dragging herself into a sitting position, she squeezed her eyelids tightly shut. Unconsciously, her fingers splayed over her pregnant abdomen. Words formed inside her brain. Confused images raced through her mind. Comprehension blew like mighty winds throughout her entire being.

Scrambling out of bed, she hurried to check Morcai. Lovingly, she touched her little angel's smooth cheek. Thank God, she thought to herself. She knew she could trust her parents to take good care of him.

Within minutes, she dragged luggage and clothing from the closet. Quickly and efficiently, she organized everything and packed. Her mind raced. The packets for her vitamin drinks were in the kitchen. She mustn't forget them. Toiletries she could get later. Hurrying, she stepped into the shower. Within half an hour, she had dried her hair and dressed.

Downstairs, she heated water for tea and prepared her shake. Sipping the vitamin-laden beverage essential for her new baby's proper development, she sat down with cell-com in hand and entered a code.

"John? John! Wake up. It's Sandra."

The sleepy voice at the other end responded thickly, "Sandra? What the…? The baby! Is something wrong? Are you all right?"

"The baby's fine. I'm fine. John, listen. You need to get up and take care of some things for me. It's urgent."

Just as she disconnected the call, lights flashed on. "Sandra? What are you doing down here in the dark?"

Glancing around the room, she looked slightly confused. "Mom, I'm sorry. I didn't notice it was dark." Rising quickly, she went to her mother and took her hands. "Mom, I need to ask a huge favor."

"What kind of favor?" her dad asked, sleepily walking in behind his wife.

Drawing in a deep breath, Sandra forced a calm, controlled demeanor. "I need you to take care of Morcai. There's a problem with the mission on Dargom. I've already packed, and I'm ready to leave for Washington."

Dave Warner shook his head several times. "What? It's not even five in the morning!"

Only the tight curling of her hands revealed burgeoning anxiety. "I know it's sudden, Daddy. The problem is that I'm the only Alliance official in four sectors with authority to assess and deal with the situation."

Mrs. Warner recognized steely determination in her daughter's eyes. "Sweetheart, do they know what's happened?"

So much in a hurry, Sandra realized she hadn't put on her Kitak. "Not exactly. I don't think they even know yet."

"Excuse me?"

Shaking her head impatiently, she breathed in sharply. "Daddy, if I explain, it still wouldn't make sense. I just have to go. Please. Please, say I can rely on you and Mom to take care of Morcai."

Mrs. Warner embraced her daughter. "You know we'll take care of him the best we can. What can we do to help you?"

"I already ate, and I've got my nutrition packets here on the table. I'm going to run upstairs to get my things so I can leave. If you could call someone to take me to the transport station…"

"If you're dead set on this insanity, I'll take you," her dad said. "Give me time to get dressed, and I'll bring down your luggage."

In her room upstairs, Sandra mouthed a prayer as she slipped her Kitak into place on her head. Sensitive fingertips touched the cool rafizhaq ring. "Warnach, be careful, my ki'medsah. Be careful."

"Momma?"

Entering the room that once belonged to her sister, Sandra was surprised to see her son sitting up in bed and reaching for her. Lowering herself onto the mattress, she pulled him into her arms. Showering his face with kisses, she whispered over and over in Chikondran how much she loved him.

Stopping her for a moment, he gazed at her in semi-darkness. "Momma, are you bringing Badehr home?"

Puzzled, Sandra stared into his eyes. "How did you know?"

"We talked."

"Talked? With whom?"

He smiled enigmatically. "You know, Momma. The light."

"The light," she repeated blankly. "Then you know Momma may have to be gone for a long time. Grandpa and Grandma will take good care of you. I'm also going to send a message to Derma'ad Badrik and Maméi-mamehr. They can come and take you back home to Chikondra."

"I wait here, Momma. You bring Badehr back. I wait."

Once again, she held his little body tightly. Choking back a sob, she kissed him and repeated how much she loved him.

"Are you ready?"

Her father's voice interrupted her. Nodding, she kissed Morcai a final time. "You be good, little one. I'll come back as fast as I can."

Although his expression was serious, her son smiled. "Momma, don't forget."

Standing by the door, she paused. "Don't forget what, baby?"

"Don't forget. Listen, Momma. *Listen to the light.*"

Digging deep within her soul, she found sufficient fortitude to smile back at him without starting to cry. "I promise. I'll remember. I love you, Morcai."

At the transport station, diplomatic identification gained personalized attention that had her fare secured and her luggage on its way to an express transport in record time. Turning around, she smiled at her dad. "The Arrowspeed boards in ten minutes." She stopped and sharply sighed. "Thank you, Daddy, for helping me, especially with Morcai."

Her father's eyes assessed his daughter's expression. His stomach pitched and rolled. Something told him he was better off not knowing her real intentions. "Morcai is a delight to have around. I swear I'll refuse any responsibility if he's totally spoiled when you get back."

She managed what almost passed for a laugh. "Too late. He's already spoiled, and I know exactly who did it."

When they reached the boarding area, an attendant had already been alerted and was waiting to personally escort her to the air transport that would reach Washington in half an hour. As Sandra smiled at the uniformed young woman, her father's hand firmly grasped her arm. When she looked around, she saw blue eyes glazed with worried tears.

"Whatever you do, don't make me spend the rest of my life regretting that I brought you here this morning."

Her chest swelled with a heavy breath. "Daddy, I have every intention of watching my baby grow up. Both of them." Suddenly, she threw her arms around her father's neck and held him desperately.

"What?" she practically shouted as she walked so fast that John trotted to keep up with her. "Why the hell wasn't I notified?"

"I don't know, but we will be getting answers."

"You're damned right we'll be getting answers! And they'd better be the right ones, or I'll personally send heads rolling!"

An hour later, Sandra sat in an austere conference room at Earth's Command Center for Extraterrestrial Communications. Major Carmen Ortiz faced her squarely. "Deputy Minister, I can't say yet who withheld reports from you. General Manzoor's orders were clear that you be advised immediately in the event of any irregularities."

For a moment, Sandra studied the military presence of the woman across the table from her. At last, she asked, "Major Ortiz, is the general informed yet?"

The officer looked uncomfortable. "No, I hoped to identify the source of the problem first."

Evergreen eyes reflected angry frustration as they briefly met John's. "Major Ortiz, that is yet another problem. General Manzoor's orders have not been followed, and now you tell me he doesn't know about a major breach. I find that completely unacceptable. Implications related to this failure could far exceed the safety of ministry personnel on Dargom. Within fifteen minutes, I expect confirmation that the general is fully briefed on this matter. I then expect his response within the hour."

After the discomfited major departed, John appraised Sandra's expression. He could almost see thought processes inside her mind drawing analyses and plans to address extremely complicated circumstances. Clearing his throat, he quietly remarked, "Sandra, I commend you for how calmly you reacted. I'm stunned by Ortiz's inaction on what is clearly spelled out in procedures."

"It's more than carelessness. I'll leave her to her superiors. In the meantime, I want to speak with Manzoor immediately."

She breathed in deeply to calm an underlying case of nerves. "Do you know if either of the premiers is available yet?"

"Mazzini and Dorn are on their way."

"Dorn?"

"Unfortunately. I fear he may try throwing up roadblocks to any action you may suggest."

The corner of her mouth twitched as she considered the hours ahead. "I will let no one stand in my way, not even an Earth Premier."

Following several tense moments, John broke unnerving silence. "Sandra, how did you know there was a problem?" When her eyebrows lifted, he saw her smile for the first time that morning.

"How? Let's just say a little light went off inside my head."

"Deputy Minister Sirinoya, I'm appalled. Major Ortiz has been relieved of duty and restricted to quarters pending full investigation of this incident. There's no excuse for not reporting a matter of this magnitude. I know how critical it is to monitor scheduled MSR beacons from field missions. I would have reacted after the second missed beacon. Failure to report nearly three days of missing beacons is, in my estimation, criminal negligence."

"Or outright treason. General Manzoor, I leave actions related to your officers in your hands. Our more urgent task is to determine the status of the Rahpliknar and ministry personnel on-mission."

"Deputy Minister, I've already called in top intelligence officers. They'll begin immediate analyses on all communications and any other factors that could explain the missing MSR's. In the meantime, if you have any questions, I will personally assist you."

Smiling, she nodded. The general, who was of Middle Eastern heritage, exuded efficiency and reliability. "Sir, your advice is something I could use at this moment. We need to dispatch a starship to Dargom immediately. I believe our mission team is in serious jeopardy and that expeditious launching of a rescue mission is imperative. Do you have recommendations for me?"

The general's black eyebrows lifted high. "A starship?" He shook his head. "On that point, I'm not the best to advise you. If you'll excuse me, however, I will get the person most qualified to provide answers."

Twenty minutes later, the general's personal aide escorted John and Sandra to Manzoor's office. Waiting for them were the general and Admiral James Mswati, chief commander of Earth's formidable space fleet. Already briefed on current details regarding the interruption of status transmissions from the Dargom mission, Admiral Mswati wasted little time on introductions. Quickly, they discussed the situation at hand and what action Sandra advocated in the face of the mission team's undetermined status.

"Deputy Minister, I am a careful man with the fleet entrusted to me. Forgive me if I ask too directly this question. We've confirmed that no MSR's have been received from the Rahpliknar for the past sixty-four hours. If we did not, how is it that you knew a problem existed?"

Deliberately, Sandra raised her hand to her Kitak. "Admiral, perhaps my answer will not suffice for those unable to grasp concepts and realities that cannot be explained with neat mathematical equations. However, the Kitak I wear gives me a unique bond to Minister Sirinoya. Through this ring, I know much about whatever he faces, even when he is worlds away. Some would call it telepathy. I only know what I know."

Brown eyes set in a dark, chocolate-brown face studied her. Her demeanor revealed strength and thoughtful composure that inspired trust. His instincts prompted immediate support. Worried and thinking ahead, Mswati despised Premier Dorn and expected resistance. Experience prompted words of caution. "I warn you, Deputy Minister, for your own good. Premier Dorn opposes any involvement of Earth's military forces in what he refers to as Alliance affairs. I believe Adnan here will agree. Dorn will resort to whatever tactics necessary to prevent sending a starship to Dargom. In your shoes, I would anticipate accusations regarding your state of mind."

"My state of mind?" she repeated. Suddenly, she understood. "You think he would actually accuse me of being emotionally unstable and incapable of making decisions because of the hormonal balances of a pregnant woman?"

Sitting behind an enormous, highly polished desk, Manzoor leaned forward. "Something is amiss within the communications center. I believe you were right earlier when you said it smells of treason. For that reason, and others of our own, Admiral Mswati and I support your position. That is why we advise you on what to expect from Dorn."

Nodding, Sandra forced a confident smile. "Gentlemen, I believe that starting now, I owe you both a debt of gratitude. Find me a starship. The fastest, best-equipped available. I suspect we may also need tactical support. You ready the military side. I will secure whatever diplomatic approval is required to proceed."

Leaving the CCEC, John firmly held her arm. "I'm taking you home now."

Turning her head, she glared at him. "Home? I have emergency arrangements to make."

Blue eyes held no patience for resistance. "Pay attention, young lady, and trust me."

Irritation faded as she stared at him. John was one of very few who had never failed her. "All right."

Entering the family room at the Edwards house, Sandra appreciated John's earlier demands. Lunch and a nap had refreshed her. Now, with a cup of tea in hand, she lowered herself onto a chair across from him. "Okay. I'm ready. Fill me in on Dorn."

Depositing himself on the sofa, he stared at the floor until Angela broke the silent lapse by offering him coffee. Straightening, John leaned back and looked directly into Sandra's eyes. "You're already aware that Dorn advocates what he calls an independent Earth."

"Go on."

"In my personal opinion, I see him as arrogant, power-hungry, and interested in changing the entire structure of the federation. I'm convinced his reasons are fueled by personal ambitions. He loves to compare himself to historical revolutionaries who accomplished change for the good of their respective nations. Going up against opponents, he excels at debasing them while promoting his self-image of integrity."

Pensively, Sandra stared at tiny leaves scattered around the bottom of her cup. "Do you believe he advocates secession from the Alliance?"

John smiled. "Not exactly. That's the strangest thing. He sees the economic value of relations with the Alliance. His position is that Earth is subject to too many laws and restrictions written into the Alliance charter. He claims Earth needs complete sovereignty over its policies."

Breathing out a heavy sigh, Sandra rested her hands atop her abdomen. "For the moment, I see no reason to delve further into Dorn's political philosophies if, indeed, they are philosophies and not ambitions. In fact, I need only secure the approval of one premier. Does Mazzini have the guts to defy Dorn?"

John shook his head. "I can't be positively sure. Dorn will place highly visible pressure on Mazzini and focus on recent shortcomings within his administrative scope. Mazzini does, however, staunchly support the Alliance. We'll have to approach with caution."

Rubbing circles over her stomach, Sandra stared blankly across the room. Finally, she returned her gaze to John's waiting face. "There's no time for caution. Dorn may well be the one who gets a taste of his own tactics tonight."

That evening, John escorted Sandra into a conference room at the relatively new Department of Dil-Terra Interplanetary Affairs he had headed since Eduardo de Castillo's election as premier. Her practiced eye scanned every angle, every corner of the room.

"It's clean. I promise you."

Without hesitation, she smiled. "I believe you. Years of conditioning are too ingrained at this point."

John chuckled. "How soon before you take over Alliance leadership altogether?"

She actually laughed. "That's one job I definitely don't want!"

Later, after dominating the conference for more than fifteen minutes, Premier Langston Dorn practically shouted as he shot accusing blue eyes around the room. "This is absurd! You are all sitting here, admitting to me that you're willing to endanger the crew of an entire starship based on the unsubstantiated emotional whims of a pregnant woman who probably just misses her husband!"

When John would have defended her, Sandra motioned him to stop. Despite seething anger that Dorn had finally slipped into his predicted pattern of personal insults, she stubbornly maintained cool self-control. Rising from her chair, she took several steps backward as Dorn continued his diatribe. "Excuse me, Premier Dorn."

Ignoring her, Dorn shook his head disdainfully. "After I finish what I have to say."

Sharp and clear, Sandra's voice rang out. "You are finished - *now*."

Eyes around the table darted quickly from Sandra's face to Dorn's stunned expression. General Manzoor's eyes met those of his old friend, James Mswati. Rarely did anyone openly challenge Dorn.

"Now that I have your attention, Premier Dorn, it's your turn to listen to me."

"Mrs. Sirinoya, I have no interest in anything you have to say."

"Deputy Minister Sirinoya," Sandra firmly corrected. "My attendance here is based strictly on my capacity as a fully recognized official of the Dil-Terra Interplanetary Alliance, of which Earth is still a member in good standing. I suggest you remember that before you embark on any additional personal insults. The only one I have seen this evening who has lost emotional control is you, sir. Further, your slurs before witnesses have been unethical, derogatory, and discriminatory. As I understand, Earth law has not changed since I left to enter diplomatic service."

She turned a grim smile to Manzoor's aide. "Captain Antonakis, you possess a legal degree, do you not?"

Respectfully, the captain rose. "I do, Deputy Minister."

"Please confirm if I am correct. Statements just made by Premier Dorn, especially while in a professional capacity, fall into a category of discrimination and are subject to full prosecution, are they not?"

Manzoor bit into his cheek. It was quite apparent that Deputy Minister Sirinoya had earned her growing reputation for sharp analysis and swift ability to efficiently disarm unwary opposition. The slightest nod of the general's head signaled approval for his aide to respond.

Captain Antonakis replied assertively, "Such behavior and blatant comments in a professional environment are expressly not tolerated by Earth law. Furthermore, they are grounds for prosecution, fines, and under certain circumstances, incarceration."

Sandra's expression revealed no emotion whatsoever. Her eyes, however, glittered more threateningly than the words that followed. "Premier Dorn, you disgrace your position as a leader of our noble world. I assure you that once the current crisis is adequately addressed, we will meet again in a court of law."

"You wouldn't dare," the premier hissed back.

"Do you think not?" she asked, her expression finally assuming a challenging smile. Leaning forward, she rested her weight on hands flattened against the glass-topped conference table. "Official entry to meeting records," she spoke clearly to the computer recording the conference. "Under security level one, all statements made by Premier Langston Dorn regarding Deputy Minister Sirinoya and the deputy minister's responses are to be extracted, duplicated, and immediately transferred via secure link directly to the Federation Bureau of Legal Affairs in Brussels for formal complaint and litigation. Entry authorized by Deputy Minister Sandra Sirinoya, Division of Diplomatic Field Services, Dil-Terra Ministry of Inter-Alliance Affairs." Stern eyes questioned those of Premier Mazzini.

Suppressing an admiring smile, Premier Mazzini cleared his throat. "Litigation request and entry witnessed and confirmed by Mario Mazzini, duly elected Premier of the Federation of Earth States."

One by one, boldly defiant, John and every officer present added their identities as witnesses to the entry. Finally, Sandra straightened. "Entry complete. Transmit - now." Coldly, she stared at the infuriated premier. "As you can see, sir, I make no idle threats. The time I waste with you is time that could cost lives on Dargom. You are now free to remain in this meeting, or you may go."

Thwarted but unwilling to leave, Dorn sat down. Ignoring icy glares meant to intimidate her, Sandra turned to the others and assumed direction of the meeting. "There is no dispute regarding the prolonged breach in receipt of MSR beacons. Neither is there any argument that I am the sole Alliance official present with authority to initiate a mission to Dargom. It is incumbent upon us to determine the status of the Rahpliknar and make every effort to secure the safety of diplomatic personnel on-mission. I prefer to proceed with the approval of all here. However, according to governing statutes, the authority of only one member of Earth's top leadership is necessary. Do I have that authorization?"

Mario Mazzini nodded. "I hereby authorize immediate deployment of whatever military support is deemed appropriate and necessary by Admiral Mswati and Deputy Minister Sirinoya."

By the time Sandra walked through the door of John's house, she could no longer hold stress and exhaustion at bay. Swiftly, she crossed the family room to where Angela had risen from the sofa. Wrapped in the arms of her dear friend, she surrendered to a torrent of tears. Much like a wintry afternoon years earlier, John and Angela Edwards provided refuge and comfort to the young woman who seemed destined to face life in one head-on confrontation after another.

Chapter Six

In sheer disbelief, John stared across the table at her. "You have to be out of your mind!"

Draining the last of her vitamin shake, Sandra plucked a slice of apple from her plate and popped it into her mouth. Recovered from her crying jag the night before, she said, "If you think this is something I want to do, you're mistaken. Unfortunately, I have no choice."

Huffing several times, John searched for words. "What if the Tecumseh reaches Dargom and comes under attack? Then what?"

Dropping her hands, she rested them against her abdomen under cover of the tablecloth. For mere seconds, her eyes closed. When she answered, her tone was soft without losing its edge of decisiveness. "If I don't go, everyone there on-mission may be lost. John, we've got the equivalent of four mission teams out there plus Master Vahmindra. Rodan, Peter, and Druska are there, too." She paused. "I can't just sit safe and tidy when

Warnach's life is at stake when I might be able to save him. I can't, and I won't."

Tossing his napkin onto the table with an angry snap, John stalked out of the room. Five minutes later, he returned and said to his wife, "Angela, could I impose on you to pack for me? If she's going, I'm going with her."

Startled, Angela frowned at her husband. "John?"

Snapping eyes met Sandra's aloof expression. "Young lady, if you get me killed, I'm going to chase you from one end of heaven to the other."

Knowing it was useless to argue, Sandra smiled sweetly. "Can we stop at church to light candles and pray before we head back to CCEC?"

Entering a dimly lit chapel, Sandra walked straight to a bank of flickering candles. Kneeling, she paused and thought of Chikondra's matching custom of dispatching prayers. Crossing herself, she whispered the Lord's Prayer that was so precious to her heart and then begged protection for the mission team and those preparing to embark on the voyage to Dargom. Finally, after Sandra formed a final sign of the cross, John extended his hand and helped her stand.

Smiling yet wordless, she felt inexplicably drawn toward one of the church's many antique statues. Walking along a side aisle and stopping without any idea why, she gazed upward. Cool stone had been carefully carved into features strong and beautiful. Long ago, some devoted follower had lovingly embroidered a wide sash of red silk that circled the waist of the early Christian martyr. Atop her head rested the virgin's crown and a circle of candles. Serenity marked Sandra's expression as she sensed the divine message.

Later, striding swiftly through broad corridors of CCEC, Captain Antonakis escorted John and Sandra into General Manzoor's office. Rising to greet them, the general smiled kindly. "We've still received no beacons or any other communication from Dargom or the Rahpliknar. Admiral Mswati is on his way here with the commander of the Tecumseh."

Within minutes, the admiral briskly entered Manzoor's office. Close behind him followed a tall, powerfully built man in the blue, sveltely tailored uniform of a starship captain in the Earth Space Fleet Command. Blue eyes that were sharply intelligent quickly assessed Sandra's appearance as introductions were made.

Straight and to the point, Captain Timothy McAllen addressed Sandra. "Deputy Minister, it's highly unusual to have a pregnant woman, especially a civilian, onboard a starship when the vessel is on a potentially dangerous mission."

"Captain McAllen, although I do understand and appreciate your concern, I am the only accredited ministry official available for this mission. I assure you that my health is excellent, and my condition will pose no undue difficulties."

Shifting his gaze, the captain looked at John. "Secretary Edwards, I understand you also intend to board my ship for this mission."

John responded with a nod. "I will accompany Deputy Minister Sirinoya to offer whatever official assistance I can."

The captain's square jaw set. Although he often wondered about the common sense of decisions made by ground-based commanders, never would he have expected Mswati to allow a pregnant diplomat to board a starship on such a mission. Revealing none of his doubts, he stood. His erect posture enhanced his finely cultivated image of command. "When can you be ready to depart?"

John responded. "Our luggage is already stowed in a transport standing by to take us to the military shuttle. I believe Deputy Minister Sirinoya needs to finalize a briefing for relay to Chikondra. We can leave within half an hour."

"Half an hour, then."

Rays of sunlight bounced blinding reflections off the silvery metallic surface of the starship Tecumseh. Turning her face from the shuttle window, Sandra listened to instructions to prepare for entry to the hangar deck and subsequent disembarking.

"There's still time for you to go back. Are you sure about this?" Anxiety saturated John's voice.

Eyelids closed over evergreen irises. "I told you. I have to go. They'll all die if I don't."

"Can you at least tell me what you think has happened?"

Her voice dropped to a whisper. "Nothing yet."

"Excuse me?"

Finally, expressive eyes opened and held his questioning gaze. "Trust me, John. Please. All I ask is that you trust me."

Two days into the journey, the Tecumseh was close enough for direct com-links with the Rahpliknar. However, hailing over all frequencies yielded nothing except static and unexplained interference across both standard and emergency channels. The Tecumseh's communications officers were at a loss to explain the problems unless there was no Rahpliknar to contact.

McAllen was troubled by the necessity of informing the deputy minister. Despite the calm military manner of an experienced command officer, he was a compassionate man who was keenly aware of the worrisome burden resting upon his ship's guest. Finding John in a lounge reserved for special passengers, McAllen inquired regarding where he might locate Sandra.

Resolute, he marched toward the ship's chapel. Silently, he entered the sanctuary utilized by crewmembers of various faith persuasions. Reaching the front row of seats, he stopped. With her head down and her hands tracing circles over her rounded stomach, she looked far too vulnerable to have undertaken such a journey. When her hands stopped and she looked around, she seemed far too young to be a diplomatic officer.

"Captain McAllen, please, sit with me. I need to talk to you."

Accepting her invitation, he smiled gently. "I came to talk to you."

She nodded. "I know. You still can't establish contact with the Rahpliknar. However, you are in contact with the Excalibur, are you not?"

Curious, he nodded. "Yes, on both counts."

"Contact the Excalibur. I know she carries scout ships as fast as Chikondra's Cuseht 1T. Dispatch scouts to both the Malambar and the Zichapatan Systems."

"Those systems are on opposite sides of our course. Why?"

"If you follow my instructions, I believe you'll find that your unexplained interference is deliberate."

Stunned because she had not been on command deck and completely confident she could not have overheard any careless conversation, he studied her closely. "How did you know about the interference?"

"The same way I know that Captain Trifehrian refuses to desert the mission team that believes it's close to a solution on Dargom."

"That still doesn't explain how you know."

"Captain McAllen, if I tell you the truth, you will likely restrict me to quarters for psychological evaluation. You don't know me personally, but John Edwards does. He'll tell you. I do not act irresponsibly. You can trust me." She paused. "Captain, warn Excalibur's pilots to be alert to the possibility of attack."

After joining John for a light meal and discussion regarding McAllen's inquiries, Sandra retired to her quarters. She needed peace and quiet. After the passage of months, she was almost accustomed to the nearly constant perception of light inside her mind. For several hours, she slept.

Chimes sounded. Groggy with sleep, she got up, pulled on a robe, and went to the door. After she pressed a softly glowing pad, the panel door slid open with a quiet swish. Waiting in the corridor were Captain McAllen and John Edwards. Without a word, she invited them inside. Her voice was husky with lingering sleep. "I take it you discovered the source of the interference."

For some inexplicable reason, McAllen wasn't surprised. "As we speak, tactical squadrons are surrounding uninhabited planets in both systems. Deputy Minister, the lives of many fine pilots could be at serious risk. I need to ask again. How did you know?"

Glancing up at John with drowsy eyes, she turned and went to sit on a contoured lounge. Tucking bare feet into folds of her warm velour robe, she breathed in deeply. "Captain, many of my dearest friends are on-world at Dargom. Minister Sirinoya is there with them. I swear to you. I love him more than what most people can begin to understand. I wouldn't be doing this if they weren't all in such danger. Neither would I deliberately endanger the lives of any of your pilots or crew."

"That doesn't explain how you seem to know what's going on when no one else does."

John went to the lounge and crouched down beside Sandra. "Sweetheart, please. You can't blame the captain for worrying about the crews of the Tecumseh and the Excalibur. He also doesn't know you like I do. Think. What would you do in his position?"

The monotonously steady hum of engines and life-support systems filled the background. Her brain stalled. Slowly, she pushed her fingers through tangled, shoulder-length tresses. Breathing in deeply and then sighing, she began a quiet explanation. "Captain McAllen, you can verify through your ship's libraries. Chikondrans are well known for highly developed intuition and certain psychic tendencies. I, too, possess those tendencies. I can't explain how or why. That doesn't lessen the reality of their existence."

Noting skepticism in his eyes, she continued, "If I've spent unusual amounts of time in the ship's chapel, it's because I've been meditating. I can see more clearly the images that first alerted me to the disrupted MSR beacons. Contact Mswati and Manzoor. They'll confirm that I was the one who alerted High Command to an irregularity that had continued unreported for sixty-two hours."

"So," the captain ground out, "I'm hurtling through space on the basis of some crazy hocus-pocus?"

"Hocus-pocus?" she shot back. She then stood and, despite her sleep-mussed appearance, exuded the same resolute strength she had shown Langston Dorn. "I would laugh at your choice of words if this mission weren't so critical. Captain, if I'm wrong, I face complete ridicule and the loss of a career I've worked for my entire life. Believe me. That is not a sacrifice I would make for some frivolous exercise of authority. If I'm right, we might save the lives of the diplomatic staff on Dargom and, quite possibly, even the Rahpliknar. Is it worth turning around when you've been forewarned of the danger?"

The captain's handsome, ruddy complexion flushed bright red. "I have no option but to obey orders. However, I warn you. Don't play games with the lives of my crew."

Tears brimmed in her eyes. "Lives on board your ship and on Dargom are already in danger, Captain. That same danger threatens the baby I'm carrying. I wouldn't be here if there were any other avenue to resolve this matter. I must try to save my colleagues on-mission." As the captain pivoted sharply on his heel and angrily left, she whispered to herself. "I must try to save my ki'medsah."

Four hours later, Sandra again sat inside the chapel. When Captain McAllen approached her, there was a decided difference in her posture. He swallowed nervously when he realized she was crying. Slowly approaching her, he knelt in front of her, and all harshness left his voice. "Deputy Minister Sirinoya? Are you all right?"

When she lifted her face, dim altar lights revealed swollen lips. A flood of tears coursed down her cheeks. Without thinking, she reached for his hands. Her chin quivered as she murmured, "The attack is already underway. Warnach. He's trapped. I can feel it. He's trapped in darkness."

Not knowing quite what to say, the captain's gaze held steady. "Deputy Minister, our pilots disabled four unidentified bases. They were broadcasting signals that interrupted communications across this entire sector. I came to advise you that we're hailing the Rahpliknar and to see if you wanted to join me on deck."

Swallowing several times, she nodded. Forcing back tears, she looked at him with the saddest eyes he had ever seen. "Do I have time to wash my face?"

Within ten minutes, he escorted a much calmer deputy minister onto his command deck. John, already seated on the spacious deck, directed a worried look at her just as the senior communications officer announced that security transmissions were complete. They had established contact with the Rahpliknar.

Anxiously, Sandra clutched John's hand as she sat beside him. The familiar voice of Captain Trifehrian sounded across the Tecumseh's command deck.

"Captain McAllen," the Chikondran officer's accented greeting began, "I cannot tell you how relieved I am to hear from you."

"Captain Trifehrian, we're requesting permission to enter Dargom's orbit. We should arrive within fifteen hours."

There was a tense pause. "Captain, do not wait for authorization. A major attack is underway on the planet's surface. Scanners detect heavy bombing." Again, he stopped. "The latest is that the complex where negotiations were being conducted has sustained several hits. We have no means of determining the condition of mission personnel."

"Captain?" Sandra's voice was subdued but steady. Receiving silent approval from McAllen, she rose to her feet. "Captain Trifehrian, have you identified the origin of the bombing?"

Startled for only brief moments, the Chikondran captain responded, "Deputy Minister, scanners are picking up the general area, but signals from the surface are distorting scanner images."

"Captain Trifehrian, hold your position as long as you consider reasonable and continue your scans. I will contact you shortly."

Onboard the Rahpliknar, Captain Trifehrian ordered the link with the Tecumseh to remain open. Aware of Deputy Minister Sirinoya's pregnancy, he silently questioned how she could possibly be en route to a hostile destination. Despite unanswerable questions, he prayed thanks to the Great Spirit. Help was coming, and he would not be forced to abandon a mission team in crisis.

An hour later, Sandra tightly pressed her hand against her stomach as her eyes rapidly scanned graphic maps on one of the Tecumseh's library monitors. As John watched without her knowledge, he puzzled over repeated whispers. "Show me, little one. Show me."

Abruptly, her back straightened. "There!" Spinning around in her chair and practically leaping upward, she stumbled into John, who was close behind her. Gasping and gathering her wits, she dragged herself away from him and ran from the library.

"Sandra!" he called out, running after her.

"Hurry, John! No time!"

Dozens of eyes stared as she arrived on deck, flushed and panting. "Captain McAllen!" She gasped for air. "Is the link to the Rahpliknar still open?"

Startled as much as his crew, McAllen stood up. "Yes, it is."

"May I speak to Captain Trifehrian?"

Shrugging slightly, McAllen nodded to his comm officer, who instantly signaled the Rahpliknar. Within moments, Trifehrian acknowledged the open link.

"Captain, listen carefully. The interference signals and bombing come from a stretch of caverns seven kilometers due north of a mountain called Dimu Graj. Train your scanners on that location. Once precise coordinates are established, that area must be neutralized immediately. Unless we stop the attack, we have no hope of rescuing the mission team."

The captain switched to Chikondran. "Deputy Minister, are you certain?"

For the sake of the Tecumseh's crew, she answered him in English. "Captain Trifehrian, remember. Minister Sirinoya and I share Kitak in Nivela-Ku'saá. My perceptions are accurate."

Instantly understanding her intent, Trifehrian reverted to English. "Acknowledged. My problem is that the Rahpliknar carries no ships suitable to conduct such an operation."

McAllen interrupted. "Eight Hawk attack fighters are launching now. They'll reach orbit in one hour. Just secure those coordinates for my pilots."

With orders issued, McAllen escorted Sandra to an officer's lounge. "Sit down."

Without protest, she followed his command. "I would really appreciate something cold to drink."

After an orderly swiftly served a glass of icy lemonade, McAllen stared at her. "Hocus-pocus aside, what are Kitak and Ku'saá whatever you said, why did Trifehrian immediately accept your explanation, and what the hell does that have to do with this mission?"

Sucking refreshing liquid through a straw, she considered how to answer his questions. She started by pointing to the engraved ring encircling her head. "This is Kitak. Trifehrian accepted my explanation because he understands that Nivela-Ku'saá is what you might consider a unique form of Chikondran hocus-pocus. What does it have to do with the mission? All I can say is that Chikondran hocus-pocus may very well prove to be salvation for the lives of Alliance diplomats trapped on Dargom. Now. I thank you for the lemonade and ask that you excuse me. I need to rest."

Once she had gone, McAllen downed two double shots of espresso. What was it about that woman that infuriated him one minute and made him extremely uncomfortable the next? Unable to answer his own question, he left to monitor the Hawks already heading into their approach to Dargom.

At the conference center attached to Dargom's Department of State Affairs, hospitality had included an array of teas, water flasks, and trays of fruit and pastries. Someone was obviously serious about extending a more welcome ambiance. Warnach cradled a mug of hot tea between his hands as he leaned back against a long table. His eyes studied the two young men standing before him. Both were uneasy. In defiance of their fathers' political divisions, they had sent a request to meet with Alliance diplomats who had decided that the crisis had reached a point beyond their ability to mitigate.

Short and stocky, Calvin Riley initiated the discussion. "Minister Sirinoya, we wanted to talk to you and Minister Khalijar privately, before Master Vahmindra and our fathers arrive. Yes, we both understand the differences between our two clans. We also believe that people on both sides are sick of the hostilities. This is no way to live."

"Calvin speaks the truth," added Craig Brennan. "History shows our people came united to Dargom before this damned feud ever began. This feud was settled but then revived after seventy years. No one understands why. Our fathers don't even want to know why. They just want to stir up old grudges and fight it out."

"Gentlemen, why did you wait so long to come to us?"

Brennan's face filled with regret. "Minister Sirinoya, we were hoping our fathers would decide to try working with some of your recommendations. When we heard the news about your departure today, we realized we were wrong. I love my father, sir, but he is not rational about this. It doesn't help that several small towns have suffered deadly raids over the past few days."

Rodan watched Riley's face harden.

"Sir, I know this sounds crazy, but Craig and I both believe the attacks are not being planned or executed by either clan."

Warnach and Rodan exchanged curious looks. Just as they began to question the young men further, Master Vahmindra joined them. Acknowledging his arrival, the Chikondran ministers greeted Master Vahmindra with formal bows. Introductions had just begun when powerful vibrations shook walls and floors.

"We're under attack!" Rodan shouted. Before he could make another move, lights flashed on and off. The building creaked. Following a mighty groan, ceilings started crashing in on top of them

For what felt like an eternity, the roar of breaking concrete and the screech of twisting steel filled their ears. Thick, powdery dust swirled through the air, burning eyes and choking throats. Screams penetrated the pandemonium and shafted through their minds. Then, while their souls reeled in the face of imminent death, all grew eerily quiet.

Lying in darkness, Warnach freed his hands. With a low groan, he shoved aside a heavy piece of debris that had fallen across him. Sharp, jabbing pain instantly halted his attempt to move. Moments passed. He caught his breath. "Rodan!"

No answer. "Master Vahmindra!" An agonized moan sounded far away.

Muffled voices called his name. "Minister Sirinoya! How badly are you hurt?"

Brennan, he thought. "I'm not sure," Warnach answered in a hoarse voice. "Broken ribs, I think. You?"

"Calvin and I are all right. This part of the center has a reinforced structure that prevented total collapse. It's impossible to see anything. There's no light at all."

Concentrating, Warnach clutched his arms over his ribs and tested his legs. Shattered ceiling tiles and chunks of concrete clattered when he moved. Bruised and probably bleeding but not broken, he thought. Staring upward, he realized they were indeed engulfed by total darkness.

Darkness. Why did that word dance tauntingly inside his dazed mind? Suddenly, he remembered. They had teased her mercilessly about her constant avoidance of light. As a joke, she had given him an engraved cylinder containing a powerful flashlight so he wouldn't lose his way coming to bed at night. Before he left Earth for the trip to Dargom, she had slipped the cylinder into his pocket and laughingly warned him to keep it with him at all times. Sliding his arm downward and tugging at his long coat twisted beneath him, he plunged his hand inside a pocket. Circling his fingers around the slender metal case, he withdrew it from his pocket.

"Can you see the light?" Warnach called out.

"We see it! You're about three meters away."

"Do you see the others?"

"Not yet. Can you raise the light higher?"

With an involuntary groan of pain, Warnach dragged himself upward by gripping a sturdy table with tubular legs that, by some miracle, had not completely buckled. Sitting up, he cast the light around with shaking hands. He couldn't find Vahmindra among piles of fallen ceiling panels, broken light fixtures, and pieces of concrete that continued their tumble from above. However, nearby, he glimpsed Rodan's hand beneath another stack of rubble.

"Minister Sirinoya, we see him. Shine the light toward him."

Carefully crawling over jagged metal spikes and unstable chunks of building material, Brennan and Riley reached Rodan within minutes. Working on hands and knees, they moved away debris that had fallen across Rodan's upper body.

"He's alive!" Riley called out as Rodan tried to move.

"Minister Khalijar, don't move. Not yet," Riley warned as Brennan helped lift and shove away part of a fallen beam.

When a heavy hand fell against his left shoulder, Rodan cried out in pain.

Without any apology, Riley bent forward and felt around the shoulder. "Sir, I can't tell if it's broken or out of socket. Tell me what you feel."

Hoarse from dust he had breathed in and swallowed, Rodan rasped, "Pain. My head is throbbing. Everything else is all right. I think."

Glancing around, Brennan dragged a service tray from a nearby pile. "Here," he said, handing the tray to Riley. "This might work. Slide it under his shoulder. Hold it steady and press your other hand against the front. I'll help him up from this side."

Minutes later, Rodan sat with his back against an overturned table. Brennan, trained as a paramedic, had unexpectedly jerked on the minister's arm, popping the dislocated shoulder into place. Unfortunately, the ulna on that same side was broken. Warnach balanced the precious flashlight on a large chunk of concrete to give steady light while the Dargoman fashioned a crude splint to stabilize Rodan's fractured arm.

Deciding a bloody gash on Rodan's head was superficial, Brennan asked Warnach to shine his light to the far right. Thinking he had heard something, he inched his way over piles of debris. "Here! Point the light here!"

Master Vahmindra lay beneath a beam that had plunged through the ceiling. Within seconds, it was evident that the steel was too heavy for them to move, and insufficient space made it impossible to create a lever to lift the beam aside. Critically injured, Vahmindra drifted in and out of consciousness.

Onboard the Tecumseh, Sandra listened carefully as Captain McAllen conducted a briefing that was also being transmitted to Earth. Hawks had returned to the now orbiting Tecumseh. They had quickly located the caverns, but it had taken hours to end the bombing and destroy the transmitter responsible for scrambling communications from Dargom. Initial reports indicated widespread destruction and power outages on the planet's surface. With nightfall fast approaching, little in the way of rescue efforts could be undertaken.

Following a painfully long night, Sandra watched distractedly as a crewmember stowed two pieces of luggage into the hold of a small, armed shuttle. Lifting her face, she told John, "You don't have to come. I'll be okay."

"If McAllen is right about losing his mind, then I'm completely insane. However, you're not going down there without me. Besides the fact that Warnach is my friend, you're like my own daughter."

A faint smile crossed her face. "What would I ever do without you?"

Hawks screeched through the air as they guarded two shuttles landing on Dargom. Once on-world, teams from both orbiting spaceships traveled via land vehicles armored with lightweight, super-strong alloy. Reaching a building that had escaped the bombing with only minor damage, the arriving delegation was escorted inside by armed members of the Riley clan.

Captain McAllen watched as Deputy Minister Sirinoya introduced herself to Daniel Riley. Disciplined and efficient, she quickly dispensed with friendly formalities. Informing Riley that her immediate concern was the status of the mission team, she made very clear her expectations that domestic hostilities would cease until she had accounted for the diplomatic team. Remembering the pathetic face he had seen in the chapel, the captain almost wondered if he could be seeing the same woman.

MERR teams from the Rahpliknar quickly established secure communications and a central command kiosk inside what usually served as a government administrative center. Trifehrian's first officer assumed military command. Before noon, fourteen mission members had been located in nearby lodgings and safely transferred to the buzzing rescue control center. Hearing that Minister Wang's advocate was among them,

Sandra immediately hurried from the more secure basement to meet arriving survivors.

"Sandra!" The tall Chikondran woman ignored formalities and threw her arms around her former classmate. "Eyach'hamá eu Yahvanta!"

"Ziaman!" Sandra took a backward step. "How glad I am you're all right! Come inside. We need to talk."

Wrapped in a blanket and nursing a cup of Tzitua, Ziaman responded to Sandra's questions in hopes of clarifying the situation. Minister Wang had asked her to stay behind and oversee final collection of equipment housed in quarters used by the mission team. He had then departed with Master Vahmindra to meet Warnach and Rodan, who had left at dawn for a hastily arranged, last-minute meeting. With formal negotiations suspended, ministry personnel then planned to transport to the Rahpliknar. The bombing then began, leaving her stranded with several technicians and security officers. She wasn't certain how many members of the mission team were inside the conference building when the attack began.

That afternoon, after technicians from both spaceships had assembled equipment and temporary triage kiosks, rescue workers pulled the first victims from the bombed conference center. Two Terran officers had been crushed to death. A third was critically injured. Watching video links, Sandra grabbed her coat and headed out of the command center. Jerking to a stop, she swung around.

"Where the hell do you think you're going?"

Her eyes flashed fire. "Captain, I'm in charge of the diplomatic side of this operation. Those are my colleagues out there, and I'm going to them. Care to join me?"

Sidestepping bomb craters and debris, they hurried toward the main triage kiosk erected at the far side of the wide boulevard. Rushing into the shelter, she watched doctors and medics tend the injured man. Approaching the moment a medic moved aside, she took the victim's hand in a comforting grasp. "You're in good hands now, Lieutenant."

Barely able to speak, the young man clung to her hand. His mouth formed a pain-contorted smile. Seeing him trying to whisper, she leaned closer. "Deputy Minister…so many inside. We ran back. Got trapped. So cold. Dark. Thank you - for coming."

"Shsh," she murmured. "We have two starships and a battlecruiser here. You rest while we take care of everything else."

Stepping out of the way, she smiled as a doctor whispered to her. This man would survive. Facing McAllen, she managed a grim smile. "You don't understand the bond mission teams share."

Despite possible dangers, he respected the courage that had brought her to the triage unit. "I suppose I don't. However, I just received advice that the head of the Brennan clan has arrived at the center. I think your diplomatic skills might be more valuable there."

Inside the command center, tensions were palpable as a veritable standoff appeared to divide the enormous room in half. A tall, slender man shouted obscenities at President Riley. The shorter man stood his ground and bellowed countering insults and accusations.

Finding she couldn't shout loud enough to be heard by either, she looked up at Captain McAllen. Placing himself between her and the arguing men, McAllen jerked his head in signal to his officers. Then, pointing a lazon pistol downward, he seared a straight, narrow line across the floor between them.

"Gentlemen! Lower your voices! You're free to kill one another, but not until after our rescue mission is executed."

"Thank you, Captain," Sandra said with unsmiling approval. Her voice turned sharp as she focused her attention on the presidents. "What was that all about?"

When the men erupted into a fresh round of shouting, Sandra lost her temper. "Stop it! If you two don't stop this minute, I'll have you both bound and gagged."

Brennan snarled, "And who might you be, Miss High and Mighty?"

Protectively pinned behind two security officers, John choked back a snort of laughter.

"Miss High and Mighty here just happens to be Deputy Minister Sandra Sirinoya. Miss High and Mighty here is also very close to losing all civility after barely two minutes in your company. A warning, gentlemen. I'm in no mood for any more of your arguing or your obscenities. You either talk in civilized tones while you're here or else. I want an explanation. Now!"

While both men glared furiously at each other, an older woman stepped forward. "Deputy Minister Sirinoya, I'm Glenda Brennan. My husband is angry because we were delayed getting here. President Riley accused him of staging the delay until the bombing stopped. He also accused him of ordering the bombing."

"Why were you late?"

Tears filled the woman's eyes. "We were searching for our son. He has disappeared."

"My son's the one who's gone, and filthy Brennans took him! I demand to know what they've done with him!"

Sandra fixed an icy cold gaze on the belligerent president. "Riley, shut up. This is your last warning."

Another woman stepped forward. Fear clouded blue eyes. "They're not exactly missing. I know where they are."

Observing the woman's distress, Sandra approached and clasped her hand. "You are?"

"Eleanor Riley." Eyeing her scowling husband, the woman sobbed quietly. "My Calvin made friends with Craig Brennan. They're both fine young men who've tired of watching this world destroy itself for no good reason. They went to the center for a secret meeting with the Alliance diplomats. I know they're trapped inside that building. I know it."

"Mrs. Riley, why didn't you let us know sooner?"

"My husband left early this morning with his bodyguards. Afterward, I had a terrible fight with two of his cousins. I had to sneak out of my own house. I just got here." She smiled at Sandra. "You're pregnant. You shouldn't be here in the middle of this."

"Mrs. Riley, Minister Sirinoya is my husband." How awkward that word seemed to her. "I came because of him."

"Some of us don't understand what's happening."

"Shut up!" Riley yelled at his wife.

"You shut up and let her talk!"

When a new shouting match ensued, Sandra threw her hands up in the air. "Damn it! That's enough! Captain McAllen, I want those two men gagged, and I want their right hands cuffed and then chained to each other. Give them no more than a meter slack."

McAllen's eyebrows lifted in shock. "You want me to do what?"

"Do you want me to order the MERR commander…?"

Unable to resist a grin, McAllen shook his head. "No, I think I can handle it."

Once the two presidents were secured and seated back to back, Sandra walked a circle around them. "Gentlemen, I invite you to file whatever complaints you deem necessary once we leave Dargom. However, there is desperate work to be done, and until you decide you can work together like civilized human beings, you'll remain as you are, bound and under guard. Now, excuse me while I try to locate your sons, my friends, and my husband."

That evening, while Sandra rested on a cot in a nearby small office, John shook his head. "She's not afraid of unusual tactics when necessary, Captain."

"Please. Call me Mac. Unusual tactics is quite the understatement. I don't think I've ever heard of anything so outrageous."

"You didn't argue the point."

Mac grinned. "How could I? Not only did she effectively shut them up, she's forcing them to cooperate. Ingenious, don't you think?" He paused. "She's really in love with Minister Sirinoya, isn't she?"

John nodded. "They're incredible together. They've overcome tremendous adversity. I honestly don't know what will happen to her if…"

"She loves him that much?"

"If you'd ever seen them together, you'd understand what I mean."

Warnach sipped a little water from one of the half dozen or so bottles Riley had salvaged. He then offered Rodan another drink.

"No, my friend. We may need it later. How's Master Vahmindra?"

"Breathing. Unconscious. I'll check on him again in a while."

Closing his eyes, Rodan rested against the wall. "Do you wonder what's going on out there?"

"It's hard to say. With no responses to the MSR beacons, we should have left two days ago."

"Master Vahmindra always pushed. He doesn't believe in defeat. It isn't entirely his fault. We both agreed to meet Riley and Brennan."

Falling silent and resting his hand against his temple, Warnach closed weary eyes. "She feels so close," he mumbled.

Rodan sighed. "I miss Mirah, too. I hurt every time I think about them telling her..."

Oblivious to his friend's subdued monologue, Warnach fell into exhausted sleep.

Midday sun did little to banish the chill of early spring on Dargom. Huddled inside her coat, Sandra watched as four survivors were carried into the triage unit. Recognizing a shock of blond hair caused her heart to leap. "Peter!" she cried out.

Dirty and unshaven, Peter sat upright and pushed helping hands away. Wrapping his arms around her, he held her close. "So, you're the angel come to save us!"

"Hardly an angel. Thank God they got you out! How badly hurt are you?"

Impatiently, he shook his head. "Scrapes and bruises I can deal with. It's starvation I can't stand!"

Hugging him tightly, she nodded. "If it's food you want, food you'll get. Let me get out of the way here and check the others."

Peter's eyes darkened fearfully as he refused to release her. "Druska?"

Sadness swiftly replaced her smile. "We haven't found her yet. Neither have we located Warnach or Rodan."

Peter's face dropped. "It's so cold in there. How long has it been?"

"Best estimate is fifty-three hours."

Peter met her eyes. "Sandra, I'd give anything you hadn't needed to come. Still, knowing you're here, I can believe they now have a real chance."

Having appointed himself Sandra's personal bodyguard, Captain McAllen tucked yet another cryptic remark into his collection. Besides direct observation of the deputy minister, he had watched Chikondran officers treat her with exceptional deference. Secretary Edwards was extremely protective. Now, this young man's odd comments. Watching as the deputy minister shared encouraging words with newly rescued mission staff, McAllen marveled at both her energy and her presence.

Late afternoon brought with it the discovery of additional survivors and several bodies. Pale and resisting fatigue, Sandra had clung to Captain McAllen's arm for support and again doggedly made her way to the triage kiosk. Once there, she sadly watched as three more bodies were placed inside sanitary body tubes.

A Chikondran security guard, gasping for breath, was transferred to a gurney. Seeing Sandra, he reached out. Tears glazed her eyes. Instructing the doctors to tend the other patient coming in, she leaned forward. Gently stroking the young officer's cheek, she repeated sacred words and received his final prayers.

Straightening, she forced herself to check the new arrival. The ashen face and blood-caked hair prompted a lurch inside her chest. "My God!" Desperation crossed her face. "Is…?"

"Scanners indicate severe head trauma. She's also suffering hypothermia and dehydration. We need to transport her immediately."

Barking orders regarding the transfer, a doctor moved just enough for Sandra to bend over. "Druska," she whispered brokenly. "It's Sandra. We're taking you to the Tecumseh. Hold on, Druska. If you don't, Peter will never forgive you or me. Hold on." Hastily placing a kiss against her friend's cheek, she stepped backward while Druska was moved out for emergency transport to the Tecumseh.

On the way back to the library, Sandra stumbled. Caught by an alert Captain McAllen, she raised tearful eyes. "How many more?" she sobbed and, desperately in need of comfort, welcomed strong arms that wrapped around her.

Gritty pieces of pastry and bruised fruit provided little substance to placate growling, empty stomachs. Sips from the precious few salvaged bottles of water were hardly sufficient to soothe dry, dust-coated throats. Cold air barely eased the stench of urine, excrement, and death. Occasionally, loose pieces of the building fell around them, creating eerie echoes.

Clumsily negotiating his way to Master Vahmindra, Warnach stroked the distinguished statesman's feverish forehead. Glazed eyes opened for mere seconds. Suddenly, a crack resounded, and more rubble crashed into the room.

"Warnach!" Rodan shouted his friend's name into fresh billows of blinding dust. Ignoring shards of glass and twisted metal intent on jabbing him, the senior minister dragged himself toward the small flashlight that had rolled from Warnach's hand. Riley and Brennan followed close behind. Frantically, the three men pushed and tugged at pieces of the building's collapsing skeleton.

"Warnach! Warnach!"

"Rodan," Warnach mumbled. "My leg. It's pinned. Can't…"

Inside the library, Sandra mechanically lifted a bite of food to her mouth. "Mac suits you."

"I haven't decided if your name suits you." He teased gently, hoping to ease a little of her tension.

"What would you suggest?"

"Good question. While I think of an answer and you eat, tell me something." With her mouth full, she could only nod. "Have you always been so unorthodox?"

She shrugged and swallowed her bite. "Maybe. As traditional and conservative as I am, I always seem to find myself in the middle of controversy or extenuating circumstances of one kind or another. No one tries to avoid trouble more than I do."

"And no one finds it better than you?" He noted fleeting sparkles in her eyes.

"What about you? Handsome, dashing starship captain."

"Boring starship captain, actually. Married beautiful girl. Beautiful girl needed more attention." Sadness crept across his features. "She divorced me a few years ago. Does everything she can to keep me from my son."

"I'm so sorry, Mac. That must be awful."

"Worse than awful. You're more interesting. How in Heaven's name did you end up married to a Chikondran diplomat?"

Dozens of images marched through her mind, and she laughed. "I'm not always sure myself."

They chatted amiably while she slowly finished her dinner. Leaving the table, they walked toward the command consoles. Thoughtfully, Mac gave her a sideways glance. How he wished Melinda had loved him as much in a single day as Sandra loved Minister Sirinoya every single minute.

Hearing arguments break out on their way to the kiosk, they quickly turned and headed toward the room housing the bound presidents. McAllen barged in first. Several of his officers were scuffling with two men who had apparently tried to free Riley. Mrs. Riley lay sprawled on the floor with Mrs. Brennan kneeling beside her.

Additional guards rushed in and subdued the intruders. Ten minutes later, the men were identified as distant cousins of President Riley. The more aggressive man demanded to be set free. He also threatened formal complaints about the abominable treatment of his cousin.

Unaware that Sandra had followed him, McAllen was startled when she gripped his arm. "Mac, trust me. Have your men secure their hands. Behind them."

Once they were bound, she crossed the room and studied the two of them. She then walked over to Riley. "If I remove your gag, can you promise you'll speak civilly?" Wide-eyed, the man nodded. Promptly, she uncovered his mouth.

"President Riley, these men claim to be your cousins. Is that true?"

"It is."

"Are you certain, Mr. President?"

Curious, McAllen signaled his men to hold onto their captives.

"We found them half-dead in a town settled by my own parents. A rampage by the Brennan clan destroyed the town and everyone else in it. I brought these men to live with me years ago."

"May I assume eleven years ago?"

"About. Any more questions, Miss Deputy Minister?"

Ignoring his sarcastic barb, she answered, "Yes. Did you know either before you rescued them?"

"No, I didn't know them, but they're family just the same."

Turning her back to the president, she once again approached the intruders. Breathing in deeply, she spoke to Mac's officers. "These men are to be kept under constant guard. Scan them from head to toe. Search for any signs of poisons, especially Zinocamitoxin."

Spinning on her heel, she met Mac's questioning gaze. "These men aren't related to the Rileys. The Riley clan originated in the Earth state of Ireland. Terrans through and through. The men your officers are holding right now are infiltrators."

"Infiltrators? I don't understand."

Instead of answering, Sandra stared down at the red-faced President Riley. "I don't know how many more cousins like these you have, sir, but I guarantee they're the reason you and the Brennan clan are at war. Those two men are Zeteron."

On the way back to the command post, Mac questioned her. "How can you be so sure?"

"I'll explain later. Medical scans should bear me out. After that, we train some of your officers on how to identify them."

Baffled, Mac shook his head. Reaching the consoles set up to monitor rescue efforts, he immediately requested updated status. Leaning forward, one of the officers raised a hand for quiet. At the same moment, Sandra's hand flew to her Kitak.

"Warnach!" she screamed out. "Oh, dear God! Warnach!" Staggering drunkenly, she grabbed onto Mac's arm.

"Get a doctor!" Mac commanded in a loud voice. Quickly, he drew her against him for support. "Sandra! What's wrong? What happened?"

Terror-stricken eyes shone with tears. "The building! They've got to work faster to stabilize it! It's starting to cave in!"

Abruptly twisting around, the officer at the console stared in amazement. "Sir, she's right. Sensors just recorded a shift in the wreckage and a collapse at the building's rear."

Unsteady with fear, Rodan brushed debris from his friend's face. Within filthy, cramped confines, there was no space to maneuver the heavy block that now rested across Warnach's left leg. "Warnach, can you hear me? Warnach?"

Heart-pounding seconds later, Warnach stirred. "Sandra?"

"Who's Sandra?" Brennan whispered.

Rodan fought invading desperation. "His lifemate."

"He may be hurt worse than we thought if he's delirious."

Warnach's head rolled toward Rodan. "I feel her, Rodan. I feel her so close."

The air Rodan breathed in held scents of blood and fever. His heart felt death all around. If he died comforting his closest friend, then perhaps the Great Spirit would speed their souls' journey back to their beloved Chikondra. Exhausted, Rodan lay down in thick, cold dirt and huddled next to Warnach.

Arrow straight and bright, the tiny beam of light did little to make foreboding darkness more bearable. Warnach's eyes followed the slim ray, and he smiled. "She made my life worth living, Rodan."

"I know," came the muted reply.

"She's so strong. On Bederand, I heard her. Rodan..." Breathing hurt so much. "She saved me there. I know she did. Right now, she feels so strong that it's almost as if I could reach out and touch her." Suddenly, he was overcome by a fit of coughing. Excruciating pain proved stronger than his will, and he surrendered to welcome unconsciousness.

Chapter Seven

Kneeling on the floor, John was worried as he tightly clutched her shaking hands. "Sweetheart, you've got to sleep. Just a little. If not for yourself, you've got to think of your baby - Warnach's baby. You know they're doing everything in their power to rescue anyone still trapped inside."

Blankly staring over his shoulder, she shook her head. "He's hurt, John. Badly. What if they don't find him in time? What will I do? How will I go on?"

McAllen knelt beside John. "You've got to believe he'll make it. Heaven only knows how, but you brought us here in time to save so many lives already."

Evergreen eyes, the most beautiful he'd ever seen in his life, shifted to look at him. "Mac, I don't understand. Not any of it."

"Sandra," John continued gently, "I know you. Sweetheart, you've got to trust your instincts. No matter what, you've got to take care of yourself for the sake of your baby. Listen to those inner voices you always talked about."

Expressive eyes looked puzzled. "Listen." Her voice dropped to a whisper. "*Listen to the light.* Dear God. Now I understand what Morcai meant. Listen to the light." A faint smile crossed her face. "John, all right. I'll rest here for a while."

Outside, McAllen's compounding concerns were evident. "Do you know what she was talking about? She isn't - isn't losing..."

"Losing her mind?" John shook his head. "Honestly, I don't know what's going on, but I have an odd feeling she's working it out right now."

Hours later, she still sat in solitude inside the drab office commandeered for her use. Sitting Indian-style on a low cot, she had gazed down at her protruding middle. Gently, her hands had drawn rhythmic circles. With intense effort, she had finally accomplished a kind of meditative detachment from the crisis playing out beyond the closed door. Light flooded her mind with awareness, vivid and beautiful. Her face remained sober as she fulfilled Morcai's reminder. *Listen to the light.*

At dawn, she stopped on the way to the command center to mix a vitamin drink that she quickly gulped down. Hurried steps then carried her toward the shift of technicians monitoring communications, sensors, and scanners. She spoke to the Chikondran officer controlling the probe threading its way through the maze of destruction. "Please, let me sit here."

Mild surprise crossed the middle-aged officer's face, but she gave no protest. Once Sandra held the controls, she felt the light's presence flow into her hands then through the controls to invade the collapsed building. Quietly, she ordered everyone away except one technician working the scanners. Then, she ordered all overhead lighting extinguished.

Minutes later, summoned by one of the displaced technicians, Captain McAllen hurried to the command area. "What's wrong here? Why is it so dark? Sandra! I thought you were resting!

"I did rest," she answered calmly. "Nothing's wrong with the lights. I need them off so I can see."

"See what?" he demanded. "What the hell are you doing now?"

"I'm going to save my ki'medsah. Please, Mac. Let me concentrate." Refocusing her attention, she closed her eyes and manipulated instruments guiding a sophisticated probe while the technician at her side redirected scan devices.

Awakened by one of the Terran officers on duty, John had also risen from his makeshift cot and joined McAllen.

"What the devil is she doing?" Mac hissed into John's ear.

With a curt shake of his head, John whispered back, "I have no clue. My advice is to let her do it her way. It's been so long already. There's very little left to lose."

Time crawled with nerve-shattering slowness. The tearful face Mac had seen earlier had transformed into an emotionless mask of pure concentration. Occasionally, he heard her whisper words that made no sense.

"Left. A bit more. Show me, little one. Light the way for Momma. Right. Keep going. There?"

Abruptly, all sound in the room stopped. Sandra sat motionless for several seconds. The technician beside her rapidly reviewed and analyzed data received from scanners. Thick metal reinforcements had blocked or deflected earlier signals. Spinning in his chair, the technician shot an urgent glance toward McAllen. "She found what appears to be a relatively sizeable void. Scans are detecting signs of life."

Despite huddling together to conserve body heat, cooler air seemed to be penetrating more rapidly than before. Exhausted, the Dargomans slept. Adjusting his position, Rodan wondered if he had ever felt so cold in all his life.

"Rodan?"

"Warnach, try to rest."

"There'll soon be time for nothing else." Clearing his sore throat, he continued, "It seems odd. My thoughts should be of reconciling myself with the Great Spirit. Instead, I think only of Sandra and our children."

Rodan marveled at the fact he could still smile. "We face cold and lonely deaths. Memories of my Mirah and our little Kaliyah remind me of the blest life I've led."

Quietly, Warnach agreed. "What hurts is when I think of never seeing or holding my new baby. How much I want to watch my children grow and, perhaps, have children of their own."

"To see Kaliyah flower into womanhood is both dream and terror."

Warnach managed an ironic chuckle. "Ah, yes. The badehr who must surrender his daughter to another man." The thought echoed inside his mind. "Despite everything, Sandra's father still refuses to accept my role in her life."

"I can almost understand."

"Perhaps. What should matter most is her happiness. Rodan, I've made mistakes where she's concerned, but I swear

I've done everything possible to make her happy. How I wish for one final chance to tell her how much I love her."

"My friend, that she knows already. Your ki'mirsah exudes happiness. In that, you claim your greatest success in life."

Weakly, Warnach dragged his hand toward his Kitak. Pressing fingertips tightly against the rafizhaq ring, he moaned low in his throat.

"Warnach? What's wrong?"

A sob escaped of its own volition. "Rodan, I keep sensing her presence. As impossible as it sounds, I can almost hear her voice."

"Warnach, you mustn't torment..." Rodan paused abruptly. "Shsh. Quiet. Do you hear something?"

Calvin Riley suddenly rose on one elbow. With his free hand, he nudged Craig's shoulder. "Listen! I hear it, too! Voices!"

Delirium perhaps? Hallucinations? Rodan dragged himself into a semi-sitting position. Straining, he heard the clatter of metal, as if something had been tossed aside. Echoing through the skeletal remains of the conference center were voices not their own.

Firmly, joyfully, he grasped Warnach's hand. "Keep heart, my friend. I think the Great Spirit may grant us the miracle for which we prayed."

Lights inside the large room flashed on. Highly skilled technicians swung back into their chairs and started guiding rescuers and their robotic tools through narrow passages and across perilous obstacles. Technicians and rescue workers alike knew that survivors had been trapped for a dangerously long time. The delicate balance of caution and speed offered tentative hope that they might yet save more lives.

Painstaking work cleared a path, and powerful equipment supported sagging ruins, providing just enough space to extricate survivors. Dargom's red sun had just risen high above the horizon when a rescuer's voice broke the tense silence. "We just spotted a speck of light. We're almost there."

Pushing her way past John and Mac, Sandra dashed into her little room, grabbed a coat, and hurried back. Reaching out and snagging her hand, John exclaimed excitedly, "I'm going with you!"

Anxious feet carried them outside and across the broad boulevard with its charred, broken trees until they reached the triage station. Medical teams had already arrived and were setting up emergency equipment to treat any new survivors pulled from the bombed ruins.

On tiptoe, Sandra strained to see as the first stretcher was maneuvered out of the building. Stopping on the rock-littered sidewalk, rescue workers transferred a red-haired man to a larger hoverbed. Blond hair crowned the head of the next evacuee. She realized instantly that each was alive. Although grateful for the life of each survivor, her heart sank beneath indescribable weight each time her lifemate did not emerge from the ruins.

Her breathing quickened. Too much time was passing. Her fingers constantly rose to her Kitak. Continuously, her lips formed unheard words. Her soul refused to surrender its call to him. Frightened, she looked to John for reassurance. "Why is it taking so long?"

"Sweetheart, it can't be easy in there. There's little space to work. We also don't know the condition of the survivors." Captain McAllen, who had just joined them, encircled her shoulders, hoping to offer some measure of encouragement through his presence.

Suddenly, rescuers signaled doctors waiting outside the building. They were bringing out a critically injured survivor. Together, John, Mac, and Sandra watched as the stretcher appeared from the narrow opening. Desperation showed on dirty faces as, once more, a victim on a hoverbed was rushed to physicians who scrambled to stabilize the patient. The medical staff's voices and rapid movements revealed their patient was in crisis. Rescue operation coordinators were requested to arrange urgent evacuation of Master Vahmindra for HAU treatment onboard the Tecumseh.

Swallowing hard, Sandra whispered prayers as the venerable master was guided past her to a waiting transport. Fear sucked at her energy. Without thinking, she leaned against Mac. Minutes later, another signal called for a hoverbed. As the newest victim entered the tent, she gasped and tugged herself free from McAllen's grasp.

Typically black hair was powdery gray with pulverized concrete. The head turned. Black eyes widened as they peered between bodies of doctors and medics initiating emergency treatment. A dirty hand reached out. "Sandra! I don't believe it!"

One medic moved aside, allowing her to get closer. Her hand curved around his fingers, and she leaned over, kissing his cheek. "Rodan! God be praised!"

Tears, sliding from the corners of his eyes, carved muddy streaks through the dirt on his face. "Sandra," he murmured while squeezing her hand. "The Great Spirit sent you to be our miracle. Eyach'hamá eu Yahvanta. Eyach'hamá eu Yahvanta." Finally surrendering to pain and exhaustion, he smiled and closed his eyes.

When her eyes questioned the doctor standing over Rodan, the woman smiled encouragement. "Scanners show he's in remarkably good condition to have been in there so long. We'll take care of him now."

Dragging steps carried her back to John and Mac. "They say he'll be fine."

Mac reached out, grasping her arm. "He's your friend?"

"Rodan Khalijar. He's my son's godfather." Pausing, she fought tears. "He didn't mention Warnach."

"Sandra!" John's voice held a note of excitement. "Look! They're bringing someone else out!"

Spinning, Sandra saw rescuers bending forward to help draw yet another stretcher from the low tunnel. Almost immediately, her hand flew up and touched her Kitak. "Warnach!" Reacting instantly, she started running.

"Careful!" Mac shouted, grabbing her and helping her over a pile of broken marble from the building's façade. "Let me help you!"

Frantically, she clambered over stones and started running again. Rescuers were carefully positioning the stretcher onto a hoverbed, already waiting to receive the newest survivor. Controls weren't functioning correctly. As someone worked to manually adjust the hoverbed's height to ease transfer to the triage shelter, Sandra sidestepped around people and debris to reach Warnach's side.

Too afraid to cry, she reached for the hand nearest her. Curling her fingers around his, she lifted them to her lips.

Desperate eyes roved over every grimy feature, seeking some sign of life, some reassurance that she hadn't lost him.

Fluttering eyelids opened. Eyes accustomed to darkness squinted against midday sun. For several prolonged seconds, Warnach stared at the image before him. For a moment, he thought he had died. When her lips moved in fervent prayers against his stiff, cold fingers, he felt the inundation of energy. "Shi'níyah," he whispered hoarsely. "Rodan..."

Looking into his eyes, she smiled. "Rodan's safe."

"No," he croaked, rolling his head once. "Not - what I meant."

As the hoverbed began to rise, she straightened and stroked her fingers through long waves of grit-stiffened hair. "What, then?"

"I told Rodan," Warnach whispered. "I felt you. I knew you were close. He couldn't believe it, but I knew."

Stepping backward into arms waiting to steady her, she watched as her ki'medsah was moved to waiting physicians for evaluation and emergency care. With Mac's help, she navigated the obstacle-strewn distance one last time. Once Warnach's condition was assessed and treatment started, she stood again by his side as they waited for the next transport. Tenderly, she caressed his cheek. Several times, she bent forward and kissed his temple.

Warmth generated by the trauma blanket seeped into his chilled body. Gentle strokes across his eyebrows soothed his aching head. Soft, sweet words drove away earlier fears. Opening his eyes again, Warnach managed a feeble smile. Weakly lifting his hand, he rested it over her rounded stomach. "My beautiful Shi'níyah," he whispered. "How are you? And our baby?"

Firmly, she covered his hand with hers. As she did, they both felt the baby turn inside her womb. Smiling, she said, "She knows your touch. She wants her badehr to know she's well."

His eyelids fluttered yet again. Utter weariness proved a mighty foe. Still, he so wanted to drive frightened shadows from eyes he adored. "Ci'ittá mi'ittá, me'u Sandra."

Unable to resist, she placed trembling lips against his. Feeling his mouth produce a faint smile in response, she stood. Lovingly, she watched over him as he drifted off to sleep.

Crew members secured the final victims before transferring them to the shuttle that had just landed. Keeping close watch from the corner of her eye, she talked with John. "Are you certain?"

John nodded reassuringly. "I'll stay just long enough to be sure they both still intend to transport to the Tecumseh. Now that they know they've been dragged into war by spies in their midst, they may decide to band together to search for more Zeterons on Dargom."

"Make sure you have sufficient security, all right? I really don't want to come back here and rescue you, too."

Captain McAllen chuckled as the two men watched her head toward Minister Sirinoya. "Is she always like that?"

John's eyes rolled heavenward. "Always."

Mac's gaze froze for a moment. Sirinoya had awakened again and reached for the woman by his side. Emptiness cascaded through his being as he observed the tender yet very powerful connection between the two. Turning back to John, he sighed. "She's amazing. I'm astounded by what I've seen since we departed Earth. Minister Sirinoya is an incredibly lucky man."

Half an hour later, Sandra reclined into her seat on the shuttle. So much left to do. At the last minute, Mac boarded. Quietly, he advised her of his immediate return to his ship. A coded transmission from the Tecumseh had advised that the Curasalah was preparing to enter orbit around Dargom.

Arrival on the Tecumseh's flight deck ushered them into a fresh flurry of activity. Medical technicians were organized into efficient teams reviewing scans and whisking patients to Med-Deck. Uniformed crewmembers monitored instrument panels or secured transports and equipment. Glancing around, Sandra swayed slightly.

Strong hands swiftly steadied her. "What you need is rest. Real rest."

Wincing, she grinned. "You're right. Unfortunately, I don't have time. I need to verify the condition of the mission teams and then check on Warnach and Rodan."

Mac's face assumed command expression. "I think you've done quite enough already. Since I've already figured out how stubborn you are, I'm willing to offer a compromise. One of my officers will escort you to Med-Deck to check on our newest patients. I'll meet you there with a status report. Then, I intend to personally escort you to your quarters so you can get some sleep. And no arguments. These are direct orders from the ship's captain."

Her face dropped, and she laughed. A delightful blush colored her cheeks when she met his gaze again. "You don't suppose I could fit in something to eat between Med-Deck and my quarters, do you?"

Blue eyes glittered when he laughed back. "I shall see to it."

On the medical deck, one of two Chikondran physicians onboard reassured her. Scans had revealed that Warnach had several broken ribs and some internal bleeding that would be addressed immediately with specialized micro-surgical techniques. His left leg had suffered multiple fractures and would require invasive surgery. They would deal first with the effects of dehydration and then perform microsurgery to properly position ribs and stop any bleeding. A surgeon on the Rahpliknar would transfer vessels the next day to operate on Warnach's leg.

How much had she hated leaving him, but fatigue was too strong to resist. With assurances from the medical team, she had kissed her sleeping lifemate and forced herself to go. While eating, she listened to a briefing regarding the mission team. Minister Wang had died inside the building. Minister Thapord had been extracted. His condition remained critical. Master Vahmindra was in deep coma, and physicians held little hope for his recovery. Druska Zenitsky also remained unconscious.

On the planet below, eighteen Dargomans and thirteen mission members had perished inside the conference building. Dargoman hospitals were flooded with bombing victims. With so many casualties straining the world's medical resources, there was no possibility of surface hospitals offering care for patients from the Alliance's diplomatic delegation.

Of twenty-four mission survivors rescued from the conference center, seventeen were in serious or critical condition. Complicating matters was the fact that most were Chikondran. The Rahpliknar's four HAU's were operating non-stop with the critically injured. The Tecumseh's larger Med-Deck contained ten HAU's, but only two were calibrated for Chikondran physiology. The surprise announcement that the Curasalah would soon arrive provided minimal encouragement because so many victims were in such poor condition.

Emotionally, food held no appeal whatsoever. Intellectually, she understood the need for nourishment for both herself and her unborn child. Eating mechanically, Sandra mentally assessed the scope of the disaster. Somehow, she needed to separate herself from the staggering losses and get some sleep before tackling emotional circumstances in the hours ahead.

Once inside the silence of her quarters, she moved around slowly. Flipping up an ornate golden latch, she opened a velvet-lined case. Pausing, she removed her Kitak and placed it onto the molded form within the box. Then, she unfolded the towel wrapped around Warnach's Kitak. With loving reverence, she lifted the engraved ring and rested it against her cheek.

A faint smile widened the line of her mouth. His whispered request had been so touching. She had promised to reconnect the two rings. Then, she had assured him she would later bring the rejoined band to his bedside so that they could resume their cherished tradition of placing Kitak on one another.

After changing for bed, she opened another case and removed a leather pouch. Crystal beads gleamed iridescently beneath soft lights. Beside the bed, she knelt and closed her eyes. Her fingers slid along cool glass as she recited beloved prayers. Blessed had she been thus far with strength to face resistance and then actual crisis. Gratitude filled the heart that had pursued the rescue of dear friends and the love of her life. So much had happened in so little time. Fervent prayers that offered thanks also requested wisdom and perseverance to complete the trying mission set before her.

✧✧✧

Nurses and physicians showed signs of strain and fatigue. Availability of only two HAU's suitable for Chikondrans created frustration in men and women dedicated to caring for sick and injured. Emotions churned at the sight of innocent people hurt in an unwarranted attack.

Doctor Prihmazar forced a tired smile. "The microsurgery went well. The ribs are repositioned. Internal injuries were worse than first expected. However, the bleeding has stopped for now. Healing will certainly improve once we can get him into an available HAU."

"When is Doctor Hehfrari expected to transport from the Rahpliknar?" Sandra asked, trying to mask anxiety.

"In about three hours. He needed some sleep before undertaking the surgery on Minister Sirinoya's leg."

Nodding thoughtfully, she failed in her attempt to smile. "May I see my ki'medsah?"

"Of course," the young doctor replied. "He's sleeping with the aid of neuro-sedation, but I'm certain he'll sense your presence."

Reaching Warnach's side, she bit into her lips to avoid crying. Now that his face had been cleansed, she noticed angry red scrapes and scratches marring his cheeks and neck. His breathing was shallow. His leg was encased in a sleeve of inflated air and suspended above the bed. How inconceivable it seemed that her ki'medsah, so strong and vital, could appear so fragile and helpless.

She reached for the limp hand wearing a wide band of gold and held it against her heart. Standing beside him for long minutes, she couldn't even find the wherewithal to pray. Swallowing back a solitary sob, she shook off the urge to succumb to hurt swelling within her.

Leaning forward, she gently kissed his cheek and whispered into his ear. "I love you. I'll be back later. Ci'ittá mi'ittá, me'u Warnach. Ci'ittá mi'ittá."

A little later, she accepted Rodan's fervent one-armed embrace. Following their brief visit, he struggled with one hand to adjust a pillow beneath his still aching head. Eyes stared blankly upward.

Questions collided inside his mind. Images of Quazon leapt through his head. A nurse had chatted with him earlier. At first, most believed Deputy Minister Sirinoya had used her pregnancy to overstep her authority. Among themselves, the nurse had said, the Tecumseh crew's new topic for discussion centered on the marvel and the mystery that had brought them to Dargom when the mission team needed them most.

Finally, Rodan closed his eyes. "Sandra, my wonderful friend," he thought, "*who* are you?"

✧✧✧

Gently, she placed her hand on Peter's left shoulder. He looked up at her with a tear-stained face. Rising, he drew her into his arms. Holding her tightly as moments crept by, he found comfort in her closeness.

"No change?"

"None," he answered gloomily. "Even HAU treatments haven't improved her condition."

"What about you?"

Peter shook his head. "Cuts and bruises. How I was so lucky, I'll never know. What about Minister Sirinoya?"

Her lips formed a hesitant smile. "Multiple fractures in his leg. Broken ribs. Internal injuries. He underwent microsurgery last night. We're waiting for an orthopedic surgeon to transport over from the Rahpliknar to operate on his leg." She sighed. "So far as I know, the prognosis is good."

"I'm scared, Sandra." Peter glanced around at Druska's pallid features. "I'm scared to death she's going to die."

Sidestepping him, Sandra went to Druska. Delicately, she stroked her friend's cheek. An odd sensation washed through her. Prompted by something inexplicable, she repeated the tender gesture. Perhaps it was imagination. Perhaps not. She was sure she had seen light trail behind the path of her fingers.

Smiling, she turned back to Peter. "Have you eaten?"

"My stomach's roaring, but I can't bring myself to leave her."

Reaching out, she affectionately tousled blond hair. "I'm starving. If I promise Druska will be all right, will you go and have breakfast with me?"

Blue eyes squinted. "Sandra, how can you..." Words abruptly died. He had overheard rumors about how the Tecumseh had come to Dargom along with stories about the mysterious behavior exhibited by Deputy Minister Sirinoya ever since their departure from Earth. Behind her waiting gaze lay certainty. Inexplicably reassured, he accepted the invitation.

Accompanied by an officer assigned to escort the deputy minister, they sat down at a table in an officer's dining room. Colorful artwork was displayed inside lighted niches in light gray walls. Several tables boasted white tablecloths and low centerpieces with the clean, sweeping lines of abstract sculptures. Peter and Sandra sat down after entering their breakfast orders.

Minutes later, Peter added sweetener to coffee and watched as Sandra stared into a glass of juice. "Do you mind if I ask you something?"

"Such as?" she asked back, pausing to smile at the steaming omelet just placed before her.

"Why aren't you wearing your Kitak?"

An odd expression crossed her face, and she smiled uncomfortably. "I left it connected with Warnach's in my quarters. I promised to leave them together until..." She paused, unsure exactly how to phrase her answer. "He wanted us to be together when we put them on again."

"Oh," Peter mumbled as he bit into a crisp slice of buttered toast. Swallowing, he shrugged. "No insult intended, but you look kind of strange without it."

She couldn't help but laugh. "Not half as strange as I feel without it."

Drinking from his cup, he took several bites before speaking again. "Another question?" Her brow creased, but she nodded, and he continued. "I overheard some odd comments. Rumors are that the Tecumseh is here because you declared a diplomatic emergency. I even heard you knew there was a problem with the MSR's before CCEC did. Is that true?"

Distractedly, Sandra spooned strawberry jam onto toast. "All true," she said after a prolonged pause. "If you heard any other weird stories regarding the rescues of Warnach and Rodan, they're also likely true."

Peter sat back and drank slowly from a cup of fresh coffee. "You're saying we're all alive because of your intuition."

"No," she answered, shaking her head. "It has little to do with intuition. I hope you'll forgive me if I can't explain."

Peter leaned forward. "Hey, we're friends. You don't have to say a word unless you feel like it. I just want you to know that I appreciate the hell you must have gone through to get here and then deal with the Dargomans *and* the rescue."

Just as she started to respond, a hand grasped her shoulder. "Hello there. Feeling better?"

Twisting her head around, she grinned wryly up at Mac. "Better. Amazing what sleep and good food can do for a person."

Straightening, Mac smiled. "In that case, someone is waiting to speak to you."

Placing her napkin beside her plate, she slid her chair backward and rose. "Now is as good a time as any, I suppose." Tears instantly sprang into her eyes, and she rushed forward.

Powerful arms enfolded her, providing the kind of relief she hadn't realized she needed so much. Unwilling to admit to anyone else how emotionally and physically drained she felt, she drew immense comfort from their unique closeness. With eyes squeezed tightly shut, she buried her face against Badrik's broad chest.

Badrik's heart ached for the pain he felt pouring from her. When he stepped back and lifted her chin, he frowned. Tears glazed her eyes. Strained features held worry and sadness. "Little sister, I thought you might need me."

Her arms flew up and around his neck. "Oh, Badrik, you were so right."

Shortly afterward, with Mac acting as escort, they arrived at Med-Deck. Sandra's steps slowed for a moment before she again hurried into another pair of outstretched arms. "Baadihm!"

"Dear child," Farsuk Edsaka greeted her with a fond but troubled smile. "We came as fast as we could. How are you?"

Captain McAllen's eyebrows shot up. Mac had long been acquainted with Chikondrans. Since Earth's entry into the Alliance, several had served under his command. Exemplary officers they had been, but personal reserve and self-restraint had marked their behavior. The obvious closeness of her relationship with Colonel Sirinoya had been surprise enough despite family ties. Now, he watched in awe as Chancellor Edsaka embraced Sandra, kissing her cheek and stroking her hair as if she were a beloved daughter.

"Baadihm, I had no idea you were coming! Besides, it's too dangerous for you here."

Farsuk smiled and kissed her forehead again. "You were responsible for reawakening my awareness of the importance of meeting oaths made long ago to Morcai and Araman. I had to come. We can talk later. For now, while I visit the others, I suggest you go see your ki'medsah. I left him awake and asking for you."

Quietly, she approached the bed where Warnach lay with his eyes closed. Bending toward him, she lightly kissed his lips. Heavy lashes lifted, and a weary smile crossed his face. "Shi'níyah," he whispered.

"I stopped earlier. You were asleep, so I went for some breakfast. Look who I brought back with me."

Rolling his head on the pillow, Warnach managed a short, breathy laugh. "Badrik," he said as his brother firmly grasped his hand.

Badrik's usual levity was absent. His face, framed by his meticulously groomed beard, exposed lingering anxiety. "My brother, you have no idea how deeply glad I am to see you."

Warnach gave a nearly imperceptible nod. "At this moment, life and family hold altogether new meaning for me. It feels so good to see you again."

They had little time to talk. The surgeon from the Curasalah had transported to the Tecumseh to operate on Warnach's leg. Badrik and Sandra accompanied the nurse who guided Warnach's hoverbed toward the operating salon. Drowsy from sedation, he still managed to wink at his brother. "Can I rely on you to take care of her?"

Badrik smiled encouragingly. "Always. Remember. She's the only sister I have."

When the nurse disappeared, Sandra breathed in deeply. Looking up at Badrik, she forced a smile. "Why don't you go see Rodan for a while? I want to visit some of the others."

Leaving the bedside of a woman technician who had lost an arm to one of the bomb explosions, Sandra's thoughts turned again to the useless loss and carnage created by war. Countless times had she pondered why and how war could be glorified. Almost always, the conclusion was the same. Throughout history, those clamoring for war rarely faced its ugliness firsthand. Those who dictated the bloodletting and perpetuated the scourge were evil, heartless creatures.

"Deputy Minister Sirinoya?" A Terran physician named Dunn approached her. "We need your help."

Matching the doctor's quick stride, Sandra faced new tension. Master Vahmindra had regained consciousness, but his physical condition continued to deteriorate. Brushing past medical technicians inside the sterile care unit where the Alliance master lay, she cautiously lowered herself into a chair beside his bed. Gently, she took the statesman's hand into her own.

"Sandra," he mumbled thickly. "Help me. I - remember. You know them. "

Her heart ached as she calmly said, "I know the prayers. I will accept them and deliver them home for you." She then received Master Vahmindra's final messages and repeated sacred prayers while an uncomprehending doctor and two nurses looked on. Reassured that his prayers would be delivered home to his family, Vahmindra no longer resisted, and a peaceful mask of death settled upon his face.

With Dargom's sun on the planet's far side, evening plunged four orbiting ships into deeper darkness. Thoughtfully, Mac tried to relax inside his quarters. When he last saw her, she had been alone, kneeling inside a chapel. Not wishing to disturb her, he had lingered in silence for only moments before heading to the hangar deck where Chancellor Edsaka was boarding a transport departing for the Rahpliknar. Mac had then personally escorted Colonel Sirinoya to private quarters.

Getting up from a sleek chaise, Mac paced several times. Finally, he poured himself a shot of whiskey and downed the fiery liquor in a single gulp. Sitting again on the edge of the lounge, he leaned forward with elbows propped on knees and face buried in hands. How could this have happened? He demanded of himself the answer to an impossible question. How could he have fallen so helplessly in love with the pregnant wife of another man? Struck by the absurdity, he released a hollow laugh filled with self-loathing.

Rising again, he went to his small desk. His index finger pressed a button. A monitor rose and came to life. Briefly, he looked at photo images of the son he rarely saw. Next, he entered a series of commands. Archives produced a variety of pictures of Deputy Minister Sirinoya. Finally, he returned the monitor to its niche and went to lie on his bed. Life had never seemed so empty.

Following a restless night, Sandra reached Med-Deck very early and headed directly to Warnach's room. Surgery the day before had successfully reconnected fragmented bones in his legs. Later, he would begin a series of HAU treatments. Within four weeks, the bone should heal enough for him to start walking with the aid of a cane. With continued treatments and therapy to hasten recovery of muscle strength, he should fully recover before the birth of their baby.

He looked up with a drowsy smile the moment she walked through the door. "Good morning, me'u Shi'níyah."

Saying nothing, she approached on the side opposite his injured leg. Carefully, she sat on the bed's edge. With speech eluding her, she stretched out her fingers and caressed his face.

Sensing her emotional strain, he mentally resisted aftereffects of medication and earlier neuro-sedation. Grasping her hand, he lowered it and gazed at her wedding rings. "We have so much to discuss. Yesterday, Farsuk briefly told me how you initiated the rescue mission and orchestrated the rescue itself. How did you know?"

Her eyelids fell, and her free hand lifted to rest over her stomach. "I'm not sure you would believe me."

"Try me," he prompted gently while noting the play of shadows cast on her features by dim lighting.

"Maybe we should discuss this another time. When you're better," she said evasively.

"Shi'níyah," he responded in a slightly firmer voice, "I see how much weighs upon your heart, and I have nowhere else to go. Neither can I think of anything I'd rather do right now than listen to you."

So much had happened. So much did she want to explain. How she needed his wisdom. Tired in ways impossible to understand, she studied his waiting expression. Pangs of guilt assaulted her. Still, she just couldn't keep holding it all inside.

"Warnach," she began tentatively, "I honestly did everything I could. If I had understood sooner, I might have prevented any of the mission team from being in that building complex. We arrived too late to save everyone, but I did the best I knew how. I was terrified of losing you."

"Shi'níyah, you must help me. What was it you could have understood sooner? Were there communications you feel you didn't decipher or analyze quickly enough?"

"Not exactly," she muttered.

Patiently, he asked a new question. "Will you tell me exactly what, then?"

Nervously, she slid from the bed and walked away. With her back to him, she spoke in a tremulous voice. "Back on Earth, I spent days trying to clear away what I can only call mists clouding my thoughts. Finally, I figured things out."

"And what was it that you figured out?"

Slowly turning, she looked directly into his eyes. "I know exactly how unbelievable this is going to sound. What makes it even stranger is that even Morcai knows. He knew before I did." Noting Warnach's puzzled frown, she went on. "Sooner or later, you'll hear it all. Missing MSR beacons. Hidden bases blocking communications from Dargom and the Rahpliknar. Locating sites where the bombs originated. Most especially, finding you, Rodan, and the others in that building. Warnach, I knew because…" Her voice trailed off, and nervous hands tracked circles around her swollen abdomen.

"Me'u Shi'níyah, come," he beckoned. Clumsily, he scooted further to the side and patted the bed. "Sit down and tell me."

Her jaw trembled. Taking his hand, she placed his open palm against her body. As if in response, the baby shifted position. "I was able to do those things because our baby showed me the way."

Long, silent moments passed between them. Warnach's eyes studied his ki'mirsah's expression. Clearing his throat, he ventured carefully. "Sandra, how could she show you?"

Sandra's face fell. Hidden were fears he would think her insane. "Before I left Morcai with Mom and Dad, he asked if I was leaving to bring you home. I didn't want to frighten him, so I simply told him that you might need my help. He said he already knew. Then, he told me to listen to the light."

"Listen to the light?" Warnach asked, clearly confounded.

"I still didn't understand completely. Not until they were ready to give up hope of finding more survivors. I tried to get some rest. That's when I realized this baby is the light he mentioned. I meditated, and ideas formed inside my mind. Not my ideas. Hers. That's when I went to the command console and, with my eyes closed, guided probes until they located you."

Again, silence. Her revelation chased from his mind all vestiges of medically induced fog. He knew her too well to consider for even a moment that she wasn't telling the truth. As he searched for something to say, he again felt movement beneath his hand.

"Sandra," he asked gently, "how did the baby show you?"

"It's so difficult to describe. It was as if she drove away the darkness so I could see what needed to be seen." Sandra looked into brown-black eyes. "I went to church to pray before I left Earth. Maybe it was coincidence, but I found myself in front of the statue of a saint I always admired." For a moment, she looked embarrassed. "Especially after all that's happened, I want to name our baby in honor of that saint."

Warnach's head tilted slightly upward as memory prompted a smile. "Will you tell me now or make me wait as you did with Morcai?"

She carefully wriggled herself until she could lie next to him on the narrow bed. How wonderful it felt to be near him. "I want to name her Lucia."

"Lucia," he repeated softly. "That sounds very beautiful. Do you know what it means?"

"It's from an ancient language no longer spoken on Earth. It's derived from a word that means light."

While lying beside him, every confrontation, worry, and fear from the past two weeks swelled into a flood she could no longer resist. Sharing closely guarded secrets about their baby had collapsed the dam holding back her feelings. Suddenly, she surrendered to uncontrollable tears. Emotionally spent and tired beyond belief, she cried herself to sleep with her head resting against her ki'medsah's shoulder.

He glanced upward when the door opened. Captain McAllen had brought Badrik for a morning visit. Unwilling to disturb her, Warnach lifted his index finger to his lips. Understanding the unspoken message, the visitors silently closed the door and left.

Chapter Eight

Forcing swollen eyelids open, she lifted her head and slowly realized that Warnach had shifted his position. Embarrassment instantly snapped her brain awake. Careful not to jar him, she sat up and looked at him, her face reddening. "I'm so sorry. I never meant… You must have been so uncomfortable."

Slightly adjusting his body, Warnach shook his head. "Not another word."

Dismayed, she bit into her lip and turned away. "I can't help it. I shouldn't have…"

"Sandra," he cut her off abruptly. His expression immediately gentled. "Shi'níyah, I can hardly imagine what you've endured these past weeks, especially that you're pregnant. Please, never apologize for coming to me with your burdens."

Mutely staring at his elevated leg, her thoughts stalled. Feeling his hand against her back, she closed her eyes. "I needed to be near you again."

"As I needed you close again, me'u Shi'níyah," he responded with a tremor in his voice.

Arrangements to transport mission victims to home planets were undertaken with urgency. Critical Chikondran patients were transferred from the Tecumseh to the Curasalah. Escorted by the heavily armed Excalibur, the flagship broke its three-day orbit and struck a direct course back to the seat of the Alliance's government.

Before the Curasalah's departure, John Edwards accompanied Dargom's two presidents onto the Tecumseh. Following difficult meetings with Chancellor Edsaka and Deputy Minister Sirinoya, the two agreed to release Zeteron prisoners into Alliance custody. Although their domestic conflicts were not fully resolved, Brennan and Riley decided to focus on ferreting out other Zeterons who might still be waiting to foment additional violence. Once their mutual enemy was contained, they would concentrate on extending the current truce into meaningful negotiations.

Leaving Dargom's fate in the hands of its people, the Rahpliknar exited orbit for the journey to Chikondra. The Tecumseh also quickly departed, hurtling through space with dead and injured Terrans, a recovering Chikondran field minister, and the Terran deputy minister whose thoughts turned from diplomatic tragedy to the small child she missed so much.

"May I join you?"

A wide smile lit Sandra's face. "Mac! Of course."

Setting down a tray holding a large salad and hot bread, the captain lowered into a chair directly across from her. He grinned teasingly. "Where's that overly protective brother-in-law of yours?"

"Badrik?" She laughed. "With Warnach. By the way, be careful. He long ago declared himself my big brother and accepts no other title. Except hero, of course."

Mac took a bite of salad. "Hero?"

"Long story. Bottom line is that he risked his life to save mine."

"I see," Mac replied. "That does make him a hero. By the way, just so you know, everyone on board this ship considers you quite the heroine."

Her expression grew solemn. "That's hardly a title I deserve."

"A lot of people would argue that point. You can include me among them."

Looking downward, she played with colorful chunks of fruit on her plate. "Thanks."

"Hey, I didn't mean to upset you. I just admire the way you've conducted yourself since I met you on Earth. What you did took guts. Starting with Dorn."

"You know about that?" she asked with a grimace.

"Mswati and I've known each other for years."

"I see. Well, all I can say is that Dorn underestimated me, especially with Warnach's life in danger."

Blue eyes thoughtfully assessed the steely glint in her eyes. The more he observed, the more he truly admired her. "Does Minister Sirinoya know what a prize he has in you?"

Pursed lips failed to hold back a wry laugh. "I don't know if he would call me that." Her eyelids fluttered, and her expression softened. "On the other hand, he really loves me, so I'm the one with the best prize of all."

After final duty rounds, Mac retired to spacious quarters and changed into comfortable lounging attire. Serving himself a drink from a well-stocked bar, he was drawn to his ship's massive library archives. Curiously, he looked up biographical information describing Warnach Sirinoya. Drifting to archival data regarding Sandra Warner Sirinoya, his interest was far more satisfied. Standard Alliance bio-briefs contained dry facts. However, accounts from Tarmantrua and Simartis Major fascinated him. Photographs captured his prolonged attention.

Twisting uncomfortably, he could hardly believe the aching stiffness in his neck. Raising his head, he realized he had fallen asleep at his desk. Angrily punching buttons to retract the monitor displaying a picture of the Sirinoyas together, Mac got up and went to bed. As he lay awake, questions bombarded him. Finding no answers to satisfy his longing, he resorted to long-practiced military discipline and forced himself back to sleep.

"Shi'níyah, I don't understand your opposition. You know Nadana loves you."

Standing in front of the observation deck's enormous window, Sandra stared into the star-spangled vastness of space. After long consideration, she responded without turning around. "You know how she wanted to take Morcai for evaluation. She'll be even more insistent on taking them both if we tell her. I'd rather not even mention it."

HAU treatments had advanced Warnach's recovery to the point he could move around with the aid of crutches. Shifting his weight on the padded bench, he moved his immobilized leg to a more comfortable angle. "And if Morcai says something? Or if she perceives this on her own? Then what?" He watched her shoulders lift in a shrug.

Finally, she turned. "I'll face her then, but I'm telling you now. I won't let her take my children. I won't."

"No one will take our children anywhere without your consent. That I promise. On the other hand, you must face facts. Morcai has already demonstrated a unique gift. What you've experienced with this baby exceeds mere intuition or clairvoyance. I'm only asking you not to close your mind entirely to the idea that we may need special advice in the future."

Approaching him, she pensively gazed into solemn features. Kneeling between his legs, she rested open palms against his chest. "I do understand your concerns. I just feel so strongly about protecting our babies. Especially now."

Bending his head, Warnach kissed her lightly. "No one would do more than I to protect Morcai and Lucia. You and our children are everything to me. Still, we must both remain open to circumstances beyond our current scope of understanding. Erecting walls could deny Morcai and Lucia opportunities to develop gifts granted by the Great Spirit."

In silence, she considered the depths of her trust in her ki'medsah. At the same time, softly echoing Quazon voices sounded inside her mind. She heard no words, understood no thoughts. However, a sense of comfort touched her heart.

"I'll try," she finally whispered as her arms snaked around his waist. "I can hardly wait to reach Earth tomorrow. I miss Morcai so much."

With his head tilted, Warnach's cheek lay against the crown of her head. He also missed his little son. Terribly. Holding his lifemate, he pondered growing mysteries surrounding his children while savoring the blessing of their mother within his embrace.

Sandra rocked back and forth. Morcai slept peacefully in her arms. Their reunion in the middle of the living room floor had been one of kisses, laughter, and tears. He had wanted to know about his badehr. She had asked if he had been good. More hugs and kisses until Grandma Warner had insisted that they get off the floor and sit someplace more comfortable.

Yawning, Dave Warner stood and stretched. "Why don't I carry him upstairs to bed?"

Weariness still penetrated every muscle in her body. Offering no objection, she let him lift her sleep-heavy son from her arms. Standing, she twisted her body, hoping to drive away deeply entrenched kinks before following her dad upstairs.

After he had tucked Morcai into bed, Mr. Warner reached out. Hugging his oldest child tightly, he wanted to tell her how deeply relieved he was to have her safely home. Relief tonight. Sadness tomorrow when she would leave for Washington with the little boy who had stolen Gempaw's heart. Never a man good with words, he kissed her cheek and left.

The next day, sunshine bathed them in golden light. Chubby hands framed Dave Warner's ruddy cheeks. "Morcai will miss Gempaw. Gempaw, come see Morcai."

Chuckling as he shook his head, Mr. Warner replied, "Gempaw isn't brave like Morcai and his momma. Gempaw is afraid of spaceships. I'll have to wait for Morcai to come back."

Morcai's long curls flew in the air with the wild swishing of his head. "Gempaw not be 'fraid. Come see Morcai. Morcai will take Gempaw to see big trees."

"Okay, that's enough, young man. Maybe Gempaw will come someday, but your badehr is waiting right now. We have to go." Farewells were then laden with hugs and promises for their next visit.

Inside an official transport, a pilot waited to fly them to Washington. Badrik, who had accompanied Sandra to her hometown to get Araman and Morcai, stood outside with a patient smile. Once underway, Araman turned fond eyes to her daughter. "Although I would have preferred different circumstances, I'm glad I finally had the chance to meet your parents."

Sandra's eyebrows lifted as she handed Morcai a new book. "Mom's a sweetheart, and my dad can be when he wants."

"Your mother is a delight. Your father is more of a challenge. He holds much in reserve." Araman silently recalled Mr. Warner's tension every time a news report mentioned the Dargoman crisis. Also remembering his reactions, she smiled to herself. "What I noticed most is how devoted he is to Morcai. The two have an amazing relationship."

Sandra sighed. Words escaped. If only her dad would try to build a better relationship with Warnach.

Standing in front of a full-length mirror, Sandra's nose wrinkled, and one eye closed while she twisted to see herself. Watching her from the long bench at the end of their bed, Warnach laughed. "What are you trying to do?"

When she turned to face him, her expression comically blended a sarcastic scowl with a pained pout. "I was trying to see if my hips really look as big as they feel."

Rising, Warnach limped slightly as he approached her. Firmly grasping her upper arms, he glared at her sternly. "I want you to listen well, Deputy Minister Sirinoya. Your hips are absolutely perfect. Besides, as long as you waddle, I don't feel so conspicuous with my limp."

The scowl he earned quickly dissipated into laughter. "That was awful!"

His lips delicately touched her nose. "The part about the limp or the part…"

"Badehr! Derma'ad Badrik is here! Time to go!"

Teasing lights danced in dark eyes as Warnach snatched a brief kiss. "They're waiting downstairs."

A wide smile followed a grimace of feigned disdain. "They'll just have to wait."

Leaning over his ornately carved cane and striking a jaunty pose, Warnach grinned. "Me'u Shi'níyah, Chancellor Edsaka and a host of dignitaries from around the Alliance are gathered in Kadranas for today's ceremony. Do you really intend to make them wait?"

Drawing glowing features into a mask of overstated haughtiness, she nevertheless managed a sweet smile. "Me'u ki'medsah, I'm eight months pregnant. They can wait much more easily than my bladder." Executing an elegant turn and holding her head high, she gracefully waddled toward the bathroom.

An hour later, Sandra shot a smiling glance toward Hitara. Firmly holding onto Morcai's hand, the I'imasah carefully guided the small boy through a forest of legs for a final trip to the restroom before the Sirinoya family would head for the auditorium's front row. Assured her son was in safe hands, Sandra turned at the sound of Warnach's voice.

Smiling but paying little attention to his conversation with Earth Premiers de Castillo and Mazzini, her eyes wandered around throngs of dignitaries and guests waiting to be escorted to reserved seats. Top leaders from many worlds had come to join members of the Alliance's Council of Masters for the ceremony. The gathering represented interplanetary leadership from as far away as Rehovot.

"Sandra?" Warnach's expression was gentle as he sought her attention.

An embarrassed shake of her head accompanied an apologetic smile. "I'm sorry."

Indulgence marked his expression. "Eduardo and Mario just left, and I must also go. I shall see you later at the reception."

Nodding, she leaned forward to receive his kiss on her cheek. For a moment, their gazes locked. Despite being in the center of a crowd, she surrendered to the urge to circle his neck. Quietly, she whispered into his ear, "My dear Minister Sirinoya, have I told you today how much I really love you?"

He gave a low, husky laugh and pulled back. His eyes held honest regret. "Have you any idea how much I'm going to miss hearing you say that?"

Handsome in formal dress uniform, Captain Forsij Tibrab accompanied Sandra to the center section of front-row seats in the crescent-shaped auditorium. Adjusting the gold sash received at graduation from CADS, she lowered into the velveteen-covered seat next to Morcai and grasped his small hand. Hitara sat in the aisle seat beside him in case the precocious child became too fidgety. Araman sat on Sandra's left with Nadana. Next to her were Badrik and Farisa.

As the lights of three crystal chandeliers dimmed, ceiling-high curtains sounded a satiny swish as they drew open. Graduated levels of platforms crossing the back of the stage displayed colorful floral arrangements. Suspended high above polished wood floors hung the Alliance flag. Embroidered on a field of royal blue trimmed with gold, its bold design of intertwined silver swirls represented united star systems. The center boasted a diamond-shaped emblem made of a flexible silver sheet upon which lasers had carved the finely engraved words "Peace through Unity" in all major languages spoken across the Alliance. On stage, many Alliance officials, including Senior Field Ministers Khalijar and Sirinoya, sat in two rows of upholstered chairs arranged in a semi-circle.

Distinguished in knee-length coat and wearing a diplomatic sash studded with service awards, Chancellor Farsuk Edsaka approached a carved podium that had witnessed centuries of such ceremonies. Observing an initial moment of silence, Edsaka initiated the afternoon's first speech.

Closing her eyes, Sandra listened to the occasionally poignant, always riveting discourse. Several times, she peeked at Morcai and rewarded his wide grin with a proud smile of approval for his good behavior. Redirecting her attention to the stage, she watched as Baadihm Farsuk invited eighteen members of the Council of Masters to stand.

In practiced unison, men and women from nearly a dozen planets rose to their feet. First, the chancellor executed a bow and introduced each by name. Then, he formally addressed them as a group. "Esteemed Masters of the Alliance Council, I ask each of you for renewed affirmation of your acceptance of Senior Field Minister Khalijar and Senior Field Minister Sirinoya into the elite council responsible for overseeing the Alliance General Assembly and the ultimate well-being of all member planets."

One by one, each master's voice rang out with the ritualistic response, *"I do so affirm."* Following the unanimous Affirmation of Masters, Chancellor Edsaka invited Rodan and Warnach to cross the stage and stand before him. Carefully, he removed the first of two pins from silk-covered boxes resting on the podium. With great dignity, he secured the pin onto Rodan's gold sash.

"Rodan Khalijar, receive the insignia pin of the Alliance Council of Masters." Repeating the action with his own godson, Farsuk exuded undisguised pride. Stepping backward, he formally addressed both men. "On behalf of my respected colleagues, I welcome you, Master Khalijar, and you, Master Sirinoya, to your new roles in our great Dil-Terra Interplanetary Alliance."

Farsuk Edsaka bowed to each man, and each, in turn, bowed to him. Then, they pivoted and saluted the other masters with yet another bow. When they turned around, the audience had risen at Farsuk's signal and applauded as the two newly inaugurated masters bowed a final time.

Crystalline tears eased down Araman's cheeks. Her heart swelled with pride as she watched her elder son receive a Master's pin identical to the one her ki'medsah had earned many years ago. How proud the first Master Sirinoya would be of both their children.

Peripheral vision caught Araman's expression, and Sandra reached for her hand. Their fingers laced together as they both watched the ceremonial reception of two newly acknowledged leaders of the Alliance.

A rush of muted sound filled the auditorium as privileged guests sat down for the next phase of the ceremony. Sensing the right moment, Farsuk again addressed his audience. "As an experienced politician and an old man, I've learned to recognize when the time has come to step aside so others may speak. That time is now as Masters Khalijar and Sirinoya assume the podium for their first official acts as Alliance masters."

Warnach stood just behind his friend's right shoulder after Rodan moved directly behind the podium. Rodan's thoughtful eyes swept the expansive sea of people waiting for his first formal words as one of the highest-ranking officials in the entire Alliance. He then turned slightly, and Warnach nodded a signal to proceed.

"Ladies and gentlemen, this day marks dramatic change in my career and that of Warnach Sirinoya. Throughout most of our lives, we have dedicated ourselves to achieving reality for the lofty concept expressed on the center of the flag above our heads. Peace through Unity. As members of the Council of Masters, we will now seek new avenues to strengthen and expand the foundation of peace that provides stability, safety, and prosperity throughout the Alliance.

"One point upon which we both agree is that governing bodies of this Alliance must never forsake the men and women who devote themselves to field service diplomacy. We must never take for granted the invaluable work performed by field ministers and their advocates, technicians, and security personnel, or the military support assigned to the diplomatic fleet that transports them from planet to planet. Each of these dedicated professionals faces danger and sacrifice in what is truly a sacred labor, no matter the origin of the individual."

Rodan paused. Vital richness in his voice captured his audience's rapt attention. Dropping the volume of his words, he continued, "Master Sirinoya and I are truly the privileged ones. Present today are many who shared with us recent life-threatening events on Dargom. Family members of respected colleagues who died in noble pursuit of peace are also here."

A lump in his throat momentarily choked him. "I lost a valued friend and mentor when Master Vahmindra succumbed to injuries sustained on Dargom. Our Alliance not only lost a wise council master, but it also lost two experienced diplomats, Minister Thapord and Minister Wang. Each of them recognized the value of field service missions. As Master Sirinoya reads the names of others who perished on the Dargom mission, I ask you to stand and show respect for their total sacrifice."

Allowing time for quiet reflection once the final name echoed through the vast chamber, Rodan continued, "The greatest tribute to those who have died is life - the lives of friends and family and the lives of those who persist with peace missions despite the risks. Master Sirinoya and I now have the honor of acknowledging those who were fortunate enough to return from Dargom with their lives."

They first announced that a prized special service pin would be awarded to surviving support staff of the mission team. Each pin was engraved with the site and date of the mission and was set with a small diamond. Pins for those who had been injured were also set with rubies.

Warnach exchanged places with Rodan before inviting John Edwards, Captain Trifehrian, and Captain McAllen onstage. Each man had demonstrated courage and persistence in efforts to rescue the trapped mission team. Alliance Meritorious Service Medals were suspended from white satin ribbons around each man's neck.

After the three men returned to their seats, Rodan asked a uniformed officer to escort Peter Collins on stage. Nodding toward his advocate and the audience, Rodan finally smiled. "Advocate Collins was one of the lucky few to have escaped the collapsed building on Dargom with only minor injuries. I have watched him develop his skills and assume more complicated tasks on several recent missions. I am now pleased to announce that Mr. Collins has earned his new title of Deputy Minister."

As Sandra leapt to her feet, ministry staff joined her with rousing applause accompanied by laughter at Peter's stunned expression when Rodan attached both service pin and a deputy minister's pin to his sash. Managing stuttering thanks, Peter then took an unoccupied seat on stage.

"Momma? Momma!" Morcai tapped his mother's hand to gain her attention until she leaned sideways to listen. "People happy about your friend. You, too?"

Kissing his head, she whispered, "Momma's happy, too. Especially that you're being so good. They're almost done now. Let's be quiet while Baadihm Rodan finishes."

After order resumed, Rodan's expression grew solemn. "On Dargom, I spent days in oppressive darkness while my best friend and I waited for death in the bowels of a bombed building. Cold, hungry, and suffering cuts and broken bones, our thoughts inevitably turned home to beloved families left behind. At times, I feared being the last to die, especially when Master Sirinoya began to insist he felt his ki'mirsah near. I was convinced he suffered delirium caused by pain and impending death.

"When rescuers pulled me from the ruins and carried me into a mobile triage station, I was stunned to see the familiar and beautiful face that, from my perspective, belonged to an angel. That angel was Deputy Minister Sandra Sirinoya."

Sandra's brow creased upon hearing her name. Her heart lurched as Araman squeezed a hand that suddenly began to tremble. Her frown deepened. Her plans were for this day to be a celebration of Warnach's accomplishments.

"My friend had been right. Although trapped beneath collapsed beams and stone, his spirit had connected to his ki'mirsah's presence. Since then, without her knowledge, we have listened to accounts from technicians, military officers, and, as well, Dargom's presidential leaders. The stories were consistent and, in many aspects, astounding.

"The facts, however, are simple. She exercised her authority to organize and launch a daring rescue mission. Under demanding and dangerous circumstances, she directed rescue efforts while coping with the effects of a mid-term pregnancy. Not only that, her final effort successfully located the last victims in the ruins of a collapsing building. Master Sirinoya and I were among those final survivors."

Rodan paused and breathed a sigh. "Her mission didn't end there. While watching over her seriously injured ki'medsah, she constantly monitored the condition of all mission staff undergoing medical treatment. During the rescue aftermath, she also engineered a temporary truce between Dargom's divided factions. What we learned only yesterday is that Dargoman leadership signed a treaty that includes an aggressive peace initiative for their world."

On cue, Colonel Badrik Sirinoya stood up and walked over to Sandra. Staring into her pale, shocked face, he gave a slight nod of his head and offered her his hand. "Deputy Minister, may I have the honor of escorting you?"

On stage, shaky legs barely supported her as she stood a short distance from the new masters. Unsure what was in store, she waited nervously.

Warnach exchanged places with Rodan. Expressive eyes clearly mirrored the complexity of what both senior diplomats had shared. "Master Khalijar will agree that no words can describe the thoughts and feelings we experienced as we lay in darkness, believing we would die on Dargom. Had it not been for the intuitive vision and expertly executed actions of Deputy Minister Sirinoya, many more on that mission would have died.

"The Dargom incident wasn't the first time we had witnessed the deputy minister's abilities to analyze and address life-threatening situations. Neither was it the first time she had saved lives of field ministry staff, including our own. In recognition of her actions, the masters already sitting on Council voted to bestow upon her the rare honor of the gold medallion of Supreme Meritorious Valor."

Warnach turned to watch Rodan place the gold chain and medallion around Sandra's neck. Noting her fleeting smile, he looked back at the audience and signaled for continued silence. "At the request of President Brennan and President Riley of Dargom, Master Khalijar will now present her with the emerald cross of the Order of Dargom. The cross is awarded in appreciation for the lives of that world's citizens she saved, and for what I understand was an enlightening lesson on cooperation that will long benefit both their parties."

Finally, Warnach stepped away from the podium. Reaching out, he firmly grasped her sash to attach one final pin. Simultaneously, Rodan invited the audience to rise and join them in congratulating the newly appointed Field Minister Sandra Sirinoya.

"Minister Sirinoya?"

Sandra glanced over her shoulder. Her frown melted into a smile. "I thought we dispensed with titles on Dargom."

"So we did." Mac's expression was curious. "I thought I'd visit Chikondra's fabled Miferasud Park before the Tecumseh departs tomorrow. I certainly didn't expect to find you here."

"I love it here. Especially when I need time to think."

"You're here alone?"

"Not for long. Warnach had a meeting this morning in Kadranas. He should be coming back for me in half an hour or so."

"Brave man, leaving you here alone in your condition."

Sandra laughed. "The baby's not due for another two weeks. Besides, I have my cell-com and..."

"And?" Mac asked, his eyebrows lifting above amused blue eyes.

Laughing self-consciously, she stared at the ground. "Let's just say that my dear lifemate knows that when I need to do something, I do it."

Strolling along a wooded path, she pointed out locations that were even more beautiful in early summer. Listening to her, Mac felt nearly certain that something weighed on her mind. Her voice sounded unsteady. Several times, it seemed she distanced herself from everything around her.

Reaching the observation point she had visited on her first trip to Chikondra, they leaned against sturdy fencing. Gazing out over the panoramic breadth of the park, she grew very quiet.

Fixing his eyes on a river winding through the valley, he wondered aloud, "How sad you seem today. Is everything all right?" Surprised by the sound of his own voice, he shut his eyes in disbelief.

Sandra didn't notice. Sighing, she continued to watch rain clouds sail across gray sky. "I don't know."

Mac peeked at her serious profile from the corner of his eye. "That's a cryptic response."

Her face dropped. "You're right, and, no, everything isn't all right."

"It might help to talk about it."

She smiled down at what she could see of her feet. "It's nothing horrible. I - I guess I still feel stunned about being named a full minister, especially now."

"Why?" Mac asked.

Her face lifted as she blindly faced a panorama she ordinarily loved. "That ceremony was for Warnach and Rodan. They've spent years working in field diplomacy - years facing conflict and real risks. I wanted the ceremony and the reception afterward to be perfect for them. I never dreamed of actually becoming part of the celebration. I felt like a fraud. I still do."

Mac shook off confusion. "A fraud? Because you received awards and a promotion? Excuse me for disagreeing, but you are the real thing, lady. I watched you from the time we left Earth until we got back. You demonstrated solid thought processes, determination, and rare courage."

Stepping away from the railing, she plunged her hands into the deep pockets of her blue raincoat. "It wasn't like I did everything myself. Mac, as crazy as it sounds, I acted on messages I only received - inside my head."

He took her by the arm and led her back to the fence. It actually hurt seeing her troubled features. "Sandra, I don't know exactly what you mean, although I think I could hazard a guess. Whatever the case, I suggest you look at things from a different angle. For argument's sake, let's say you received these messages, as you call them, from some deity or other psychic source. Fine. The source gave you valuable information. What makes you worthy of recognition is the way you interpreted and then acted on the information. You could have sat on Earth, wringing your hands and crying that you couldn't do anything because of your pregnancy. We all know what you did, from making Dorn stand down to operating those probes. You were willing to open yourself to the messages and then take action. Hell, you even forced Earth's government and military to react, and it's a damned good thing you did."

Following an uneasy quiet punctuated by several frustrated sighs, she turned to him, tears brimming in her eyes. "Mac, do you honestly believe that?"

His mind reeled from a nearly overwhelming desire to hold her and kiss away her doubts. "I do. I can't see why you don't."

"Nothing seems clear to me right now. Maybe I should chalk everything up to hormones and so much recent stress. I don't know. I guess I'm not making very good sense."

Mac's eyes shone with gentle lights. "You went through hell on Dargom, but you delivered the souls of a lot of fine people. You have a right to muddle for a while."

Her eyes shifted away. "I had no choice. Down to the farthest corners of my toes, I realized that losing Warnach would be the one thing in life impossible for me to bear. Mac, I almost lost him there. Just thinking about Dargom still terrifies me."

Reaching out, Mac caressed her cheek. "Dear Sandra, I wish I could wipe every shred of that fear away, but I can't. You've got to focus not on what could have happened but, instead, on what did happen. Master Sirinoya's life was saved because of courage born of your love for him. In my opinion, no man could ever receive a greater tribute."

"And no man could ever appreciate such a tribute more than I."

Sharply lifting her head, she looked both shocked and chagrined. Her voice quivered. "Warnach?"

"Master Sirinoya," Mac acknowledged Warnach with a slight tilt of his head. "I apologize. It must be getting late."

"Captain McAllen, it's good to see you again." Warnach's voice greeted McAllen, but his gaze fixed on his ki'mirsah.

Nearing her and lifting her chin, he gazed steadily with solemn eyes that imprisoned her. "Me'u Shi'níyah?"

Without a word, Mac nodded goodbye to Warnach before departing. Meanwhile, Sandra received her lifemate's undivided attention. Tenderly, he tucked strands of windblown hair behind her ear. "Why did you not share your feelings with me?"

Unable to answer, she would have turned away, but he stopped her. Grasping her upper arms, he held her in place. "Although it wasn't my intention, I'm glad I overheard your conversation. The captain was right. You deserve the recognition you received."

"The day was yours, Warnach. Not mine."

"Sandra, every day I live belongs to both of us. We each know how hard it was for me to accept the master's title and leave fulltime field service. However, I understand that the time has come for me to be at home. More importantly, I want to be here. For Morcai, Lucia, and you."

"Where's all this going to lead?"

He shook his head. "That I do not know, Shi'níyah. It doesn't matter. Not as long as I have you beside me."

Clutching tightly to the curved handrail, Warnach swung outward, skipping the last two steps and landing firmly on two good legs. "Mamehr! Mamehr!"

Emerging from a corridor on the far side of the lounge, Araman appeared with a frown. "Warnach! Quiet. Hitara's working with Morcai on a book."

Warnach sucked in a deep breath. "Tell Hitara we're leaving. Sandra's contractions are coming closer together. Dr. Walters is already waiting for us."

Araman laughed. "Calm down, will you? One would think you've never done this before."

Long hair swung back and forth across his face. "Mamehr, with Morcai, I had no time to get nervous. Remember?"

"Men," Araman muttered with a sharp tilt of her head. "Go help Sandra down the stairs."

Two hours after their arrival at the hospital, nurses guided Sandra's hoverbed into a waiting delivery room. Unlike the night Morcai was born, lights were already dimmed, and relative calm replaced prior chaos. Doctors and nurses moved around with quiet efficiency while Warnach clung to his lifemate's hand and encouraged her.

Dr. Walters lifted his masked face. "Push again. The baby's crowning."

An irritated question flashed through her mind at the speed of light. She wondered what else he expected her to do under the spell of pure, unadulterated, primal instinct. Yet again, the irresistible urge usurped all cognitive power as her body pushed and pushed.

"Sandra! Look!" Warnach's excited voice claimed her attention.

While a nurse wiped beads of sweat from her brow, her sight fixed upon the perfectly formed baby girl who had just drawn her first breath. A loud wail filled the room. With heart pounding and blood throbbing inside her temples, Sandra's eyes followed the nurse who carried the baby to pre-warmed blankets before introducing the infant to her parents.

Warnach's eyes glowed with pride as the nurse turned and winked, indicating that all appeared well with the newborn. Lovingly, he smiled at his tired ki'mirsah and leaned forward, kissing her forehead. As sensitive lips lingered against damp, slightly salty skin, he felt an abrupt change. Tension first. Then, she seemed to shove her head down into the low pillow beneath her head. Jumping backward, he heard a scream that turned his blood cold.

"Quickly!" Dr. Walters commanded one nurse. "Get Master Sirinoya out of here! The baby, too! Call in another surgeon! We have an emergency! Hurry, people!"

Too stunned to move after two nurses practically dragged him from the delivery room, Warnach stared at doors that were barriers between him and his lifemate. His stomach pitched and rolled, and his heart pounded so hard within his chest that it literally hurt. Her scream had been one of sudden, horrific agony.

"Master Sirinoya?" The voice belonged to one of the nurses who had led him from the delivery room.

Shock prevented speech. Mutely, he stared at her with questions he feared to ask.

The Terran woman's expression held compassion. "Master Sirinoya, your family is down the hall. I'm going to take you there to wait."

Swallowing repeatedly, he rediscovered his voice. "Wait. For what? What happened?"

"Dr. Walters and Dr. Waite are performing emergency abdominal surgery," the nurse answered calmly. "Because of extensive hemorrhaging, they haven't determined the extent of damage yet, but initial scans indicate that Minister Sirinoya's uterus ruptured."

Attempting to digest the woman's words, Warnach stared at her. His mind protested. "How can that be? She's so strong. Everything went so well. My daughter…"

"Master Sirinoya, all indications are that your baby's fine. You'll be able to see her shortly. As for the rest, there's nothing you can do except wait and remember that your lifemate is in excellent hands."

Grasping the doorway for support, Warnach staggered into the waiting room. Badrik, who was sitting near the door, jumped to his feet. Grabbing his brother's arm, he held him firmly and guided him to a sofa. Crouching low, he gazed into Warnach's stunned face as Nadana and Mamehr hurried to them. "Warnach?"

The only reaction was a stupefied stare. "Warnach!" Badrik demanded. "The baby! Is the baby all right?"

"Baby. My baby girl. She's so perfect. So beautiful."

Araman's arm stretched behind her son's shoulders, and she pulled him close. "Warnach, tell us. What about Sandra?"

"Sandra," he repeated. Suddenly, he choked on a gut-wrenching sob. "They don't know. Something happened. She screamed. Blood everywhere. The doctors are performing surgery." Abruptly, he leaned forward, burying his face in his hands to cry.

Chapter Nine

Inside the private nursery, a uniformed nurse carefully placed a white and yellow bundle of swaddling into Warnach's waiting arms. Only his daughter's face and hands were visible. Tiny fingers opened like delicate flower petals. Whimpers sounded simultaneously sweet and sorrowful. Lifting her upward, he tenderly touched his face to the feather-soft down of her cheek.

Instinctively, he responded to her whimpers and brought her forehead to his. Mystified, he could hardly bring himself to break the bond formed through their cerea-nervos. For the very first time, he fully comprehended Sandra's constant difficulties with light from the beginning of her pregnancy.

"Warnach?"

Forcing himself to part from his daughter, he noted the peacefully sleepy expression that caused tiny eyelids to flutter and close. Lifting his face, he whispered, "She's so beautiful, Mamehr."

Araman dropped to her knees. With slender fingers, she caressed the baby's face. "She's exquisite. Have you settled on a name for her?"

"Weeks ago." A thought flitted through his mind. How appropriate the baby's name seemed. "Her name is Lucia."

Araman's eyes met Nadana's, and both women shrugged. "A Terran name?"

He nodded. "A Terran name. Sandra told me it means light."

Nadana's face froze. "What did you say?"

Warnach frowned for only a moment at the unexpectedly sharp edge in his aunt's voice. "Lucia means light."

"Child called Light." Araman and Warnach both watched as Nadana's lips silently formed the words.

"Sister, what's wrong?" Araman inquired, worried by the sudden drain of color from her sister's features.

Nadana forced in a calming breath. "N...nothing," she stammered. "Just a strange thought."

Badrik entered the room, effectively ending the odd exchange. "Warnach, a nurse just advised that Sandra's out of surgery and being transferred to an HAU. Dr. Walters should be out in a few minutes to speak to you."

"Araman, why don't you go with Warnach to talk with the doctor? I'll stay with Lucia until you return."

The nurse nodded approval. Desperation to know Sandra's condition failed to diminish Warnach's reluctance to leave his newborn daughter. After giving the sleeping baby to his aunt, he drew his fingertips across Lucia's cerea-nervos in a lingering caress. "We shouldn't be long."

Accompanied by Badrik, Warnach and Araman reached the waiting room just as Sandra's doctor arrived. "Dr. Walters. My lifemate? How is she?"

The middle-aged physician sighed wearily. "The good news is that her condition has stabilized. We transfused her with blood replacement serum equivalent to a third of her normal blood content. Internal bleeding has stopped. We plan to keep her in an HAU for three hours tonight and then three hours a day for the next four days."

"The rest?"

"Master Sirinoya, I wish I could explain what went wrong. Scans indicated no problems whatsoever up until moments after the delivery. I've ordered a complete review of all readings as well as the equipment itself. I've also requested an immediate analysis of damaged tissue."

"Damaged tissue?" Warnach's jaw tensed as he awaited the doctor's response.

"The uterine wall essentially exploded. We were forced to perform an emergency hysterectomy and repair damaged abdominal blood vessels. We were able to save her ovaries. Physically, she can look forward to a strong recovery. Psychologically, this will come as a terrible shock. You should prepare yourself. She'll likely need a great deal of patience and emotional support."

After Dr. Walters left, Warnach leaned with his back against enameled walls. Dazed, he hardly knew what to think, let alone say. What would he tell her? How would he comfort her? Why? Why did this happen to her?

"My brother." The pitch of Badrik's voice was low and compassionate. "Your daughter needs her badehr. Go to her for a while. Then, I'll take you home. You need to get some sleep."

Eyelids remained closed. "I can't leave her, Badrik. What if she wakens? What if she needs me?"

Badrik's voice remained gentle but firm. "She *will* need you. Her strength has never failed you. Now the time has come when you must be strong for her."

"Badrik is right," Araman said. "We love you both, and we'll help in every way possible. Still, in the end, you're the one she'll need most. You need to rest."

Warnach paused at the nursery doorway. Holding tiny Lucia, Nadana exuded a protectiveness he had never seen before. Smiling despite his own shock, he gathered the baby into his arms and cradled her close to his chest. How fragile she appeared. How utterly precious. Lifting her to his face, he whispered against her forehead. "Your momma loves you, little one. Soon you'll see. Until then, know that your badehr loves you as much as anyone ever will."

Subtle tones of blues and greens, wallpaper trim, and warm woods created a soothing ambiance in the private hospital room. Vertical blinds cast long shadows across the interior with only tiny slits of light peeking through to chase away lonely darkness. Crisp, clean-smelling sheets enfolded her. Heavily weighted, her body refused to move.

Sounds crept into her waking consciousness. Pad, pad, pad. Swish, swish. Sounds of motion. Someone walking. Someone breathing. Focusing her concentration, she opened her eyes. A young woman in a light blue coat studied a handheld medical scanner.

"Who are you?" The question emerged as a hoarse whisper.

A surprised face smiled. "I'm Dr. LaRue."

Stiffly, Sandra stretched her legs. Unexpected pain prompted a gasp. Catching her breath, she grasped protective rails on the side of the bed. "What happened? Why am I here?"

The young physician's features grew cautious. "You don't remember?"

"Remember," Sandra's voice echoed emptily. "Remember what?"

"Minister Sirinoya, why don't you rest? Dr. Walters should arrive shortly. He'll explain everything."

Distant eyes later focused on a picture across the room. Her physician's explanation had been thorough and kind. Nevertheless, learning of her surgery and the results had come as an unexpected, heartbreaking shock. Tears that filled her eyes quickly disappeared. Maybe it was just a bad dream. Clutching a plump pillow against her tender midsection, she turned slightly. Her heart told her otherwise.

"Shi'níyah?"

Drowsy eyelids lifted at the hushed sound of his voice. She managed a smile at the sight of him, seated beside her on the edge of the bed. Awkwardly, she pushed herself upward. Weak arms circled his neck as her suddenly tear-drenched face sought comfort against the firmness of his chest.

Despite the sanctuary's spacious dimensions, darkness seemed to draw in walls painted a deep wine color. Stone pillars of varying heights were scattered throughout the room. Atop each was a gold-based pedestal holding a burning ivory candle. Randomly strewn around carpeted floors were thick, tasseled cushions. In the room's center was a drifpatihl, a broad, low chair piled with silk-covered pillows.

Robed in lavishly embroidered robes of black satin, Camudahmni Lobrihm completed an ancient prayer before he opened private discussion with Simlani Nadana Kimasou. Rarely did any of Chikondra's seven Camudahmni grant such exclusive interviews with avowed religious guides. Although Camudahmni conducted regular instruction for both Luradrani and Simlani, they dedicated most of their reclusive lives to intense personal meditation on the teachings of the Great Spirit. However, Nadana's life had been one of exemplary service, and her unusual request had arrived at a most unique time.

A week earlier, for the first time in his one hundred twenty-five years, Lobrihm had received a vision during nighttime meditations. The vision had since revisited him each night. In midnight's velvet depths, that same vision had finally spoken, leaving the religious leader thoroughly mystified.

The final vision had been startling. A man had appeared within clouds of dazzling white. Steady breezes had rippled his shoulder-length hair, causing it to flow in silver waves. Lobrihm had discerned a dark face, bearded in white. The eyes had astounded him. Black irises shone with pupils that burned with golden flames. Muscular arms had reached out from the tall, lithe body attired in loosely wrapped garments swept about by the same wind blowing through the figure's hair.

Anxious, Lobrihm had straightened, turning a keen ear to catch words tossed upon swift currents of air. The striking figure had come to deliver a message of crucial importance. "Darkness foretold approaches ever more quickly. Turn your eyes from the mundane. Seek wisdom from one who labors as guide to your people's spirits. Only then will you discover truth as the Great Spirit reveals fruition of promise and prophecy."

The image lingered in Lobrihm's mind long after he had centered. Exhausted, he had lain awake for hours. Words replayed themselves inside his mind. What did they mean? Had an aging man's mind begun to fail too soon?

Rising at dawn, he walked beneath skies donning rose-hued stripes. Glancing upward, he glimpsed the flaming tail of what he thought at first to be a meteor. Not so uncommon, he had thought, until the fiery ball swung in a broad circle before returning to the heavens from which it had come. Stunned, Camudahmni Lobrihm dropped onto age-stiffened knees that did not feel the chilly, damp ground upon which they had heavily come to rest. Reverently, the Camudahmni gratefully acknowledged the sacred sign and, through prayer, begged wisdom to recognize the significance.

"I bid you look at me, Respected Simlani."

Slowly, Nadana raised her bowed head. Glowing faith surrounded her. Peace flowed from her. According to custom, she extended her hands, and the religious leader held them for long seconds.

Revealing none of his current personal contemplations, he released her hands and spoke. "The urgency of your request was quite unusual. What counsel might I offer you, Respected Simlani?"

Time for hesitation had passed. Quietly yet firmly, Nadana addressed him. "Esteemed Camudahmni, I shall not dishonor the time you share with banalities. I believe that Chikondra quickly approaches the trial of dark times predicted in the ancient Word."

"Do I assume you also saw the sign?"

"Sign?" Nadana asked. "What sign?"

"In the sky. It happened this morning at dawn. I heard murmurings. Others secluded here also saw it."

A smile tugged the corner of Nadana's mouth, and she shook her head. "Such sign I did not see. However, shortly after midnight, I am convinced that I held in my own arms the gift intended to turn away the darkness."

The vision's haunting words echoed anew inside the Camudahmni's mind. Carefully, he controlled his expression. He dared not give encouragement if he wished to glean truth. "Explain, Respected Simlani."

With an elegant nod, Nadana continued, "For years now, I have carefully noted and studied events which constantly amaze me. I said nothing for fear my observations were more hope than fact. However, after rereading accounts of the Mi'yafá Si'imlayaná, I am convinced the legend is prophecy."

Lobrihm's forehead creased. The account of Chikondra's Guardian of Light was widely regarded as a charming fairy tale, more imaginative poetry than divine foretelling. At the same time, some learned theologians believed sacred writings augmented the beloved story first discovered inside crypts near the caves of Efi'yimasé Meichasa. Swiftly, the Camudahmni recalled long-ago teachings from those religious scholars.

"Respected Simlani, will you explain more precisely?" His voice sounded appropriately emotionless.

Before Warnach's unification, Nadana thought, she would have been far too nervous about approaching someone like Lobrihm. Revitalized courage and strengthened conviction empowered her to continue. "Esteemed Camudahmni, several years ago, a Terran woman came to Chikondra. I met her at the home of my nephew, Warnach Sirinoya."

"Warnach Sirinoya?" The holy man's mind swiftly sifted through the legend. Fierce warrior. Guardian of peace. Perhaps the legend's defender spirit and guardian warrior?

Attentively, he listened. As Nadana Kimasou unraveled her experiences with Warnach and his Terran ki'mirsah, Lobrihm felt the continuous prickle of standing hair along the column of his neck. In silence, with eyes closed, he concentrated on fine details. Sirinoya's scandalous deviation from faith practices followed by unparalleled reaffirmation. Lonely sadness described by the Simlani. Helper spirit from a faraway star. Sandra. Helper of mankind. Fresh, clean light. The Terran who had celebrated Shi'firah and proudly wore the diamond-studded Kitak. Faithful guide. Morcai, the son who should not have been.

When Nadana lapsed into uncertain silence, Lobrihm's contemplative eyes opened and fixed upon her features. Her appearance was the kind to inspire confidence. So far, however, he saw only a list of convenient coincidences.

"Respected Simlani," he began in a kind voice, "I must agree that, superficially, what you say is consistent with the legend. However, as you must understand, I find key links missing. The story speaks of acceptance by the angels of Meichasa and a second child."

Nadana's face dropped. She had expected an easier explanation. She could not fail to gain the wise leader's guidance.

Hushed words resumed. "Esteemed Camudahmni, there is more. Beginning with Sandra's first visit to Chikondra, she has communed with sacred Quazon."

"Communed?" Silken robes whispered as the Camudahmni shifted his position and leaned forward. "What do you mean by commune?"

Nadana could not restrain the smile of treasured memories. "I've seen her with them three times. They come to her and even invite her touch. They also show delight in touching her. Occasionally, they instruct her to invite certain people to join them in the water. I carry with me the sacred honor of having actually touched Quazon."

"Nadana Kimasou, are you absolutely sure this is all true?" Unwavering eyes bored into his soul until he shivered.

"I know what I saw. I even questioned her. Her communication with them occurs telepathically. She offers no reasons for the contact but always speaks of them with deep respect and gratitude. Unless otherwise allowed by Quazon, she also speaks of them only with those in our family who guard this incredible gift."

Despite the astonishing revelation regarding Quazon, Lobrihm remained skeptical. "There is still the issue of the child."

Serenely, Nadana returned the holy man's waiting gaze. "Yes, the child. She was born at midnight last night. Her mamehr claimed to see bright light from the beginning of her pregnancy. Morcai, the brother, spoke of the new light so bright that it sometimes hurt his eyes. Privately, the mamehr insists that her unborn child showed her the way to save dozens of lives."

Drawing in a breath fully expanding her lungs, Nadana exhaled slowly. "The child's name is Lucia."

"Lucia?"

"Lucia. Its origin is from ancient times on Earth. The name means light."

"Where is the child now?"

"She's in hospital. Her mamehr must stay for a week. Moments after the birth, her uterus ruptured, forcing the physicians to surgically remove it."

Lobrihm sank heavily backward into the drifpatihl. Again, echoes inside his mind. Child called Light. Guardian of Light. In muted tones, he recited from memory. "Tho' the portal would be closed by brilliance unrivaled…"

Nadana's head tilted sharply. That part of the account she had failed to consider. Noting Lobrihm's stunned expression, she ventured onward. "With all that happens throughout the Alliance, I believe the Zeteron threat looms as the prophesied darkness. The future is too difficult to accurately predict, but I do not doubt that the time has come to prepare ourselves."

Lobrihm's eyes closed. The vision's words roared through his brain. "Discover truth. The Great Spirit reveals fruition of promise and prophecy."

Nadana waited until she wondered if the aged Camudahmni had perhaps fallen asleep. Growing uncomfortable, she shifted. The quiet rush of yards of gray satin robes broke the silence.

Lobrihm opened his eyes. "Family Sirinoya will observe the first anointing in celebration of life?" Receiving Nadana's puzzled nod, he smiled. "It is many decades since this old man last enjoyed the simple pleasure of attending Ohmtra'ame eu Si'im. Today, I shall join the family in this special rite."

A downward glance sent light into clouded corners of Warnach's heart. Inside the glassed elevator rising to the hospital's chapel, she sat in a hoverchair with her face nestled against Lucia's. Unconsciously, he reached out to caress his lifemate's temple. Her responding smile reflected the tender glow of new motherhood.

Reaching the hospital's Brisajai, they found Badrik waiting outside the door and holding Morcai's hand. Morcai tugged loose and hurried to lean over the right arm of the chair. "Momma!" he exclaimed in an astonished voice. "My baby sister?"

Affectionately, Sandra stroked her son's smooth, plump cheek. "This is your sister, Morcai. Her name is Lucia."

Little fingers tentatively stretched out and touched a balled fist. Lucia's hand opened like a flower bud with slender petals immediately curling snugly around her brother's index finger. Marvel glittered in Morcai's eyes as he looked from his sister to his mother's face. "She holds my hand! My sister loves me!"

Warnach chuckled as he squatted and wrapped an arm around his son's shoulders. "I think you're right, Morcai. Now, we must go into the Brisajai, just as we did when you were born. Lucia needs her first blessing from the Great Spirit. You must pray with us."

Morcai's animated features highlighted his excitement. "I pray hard, Badehr. I want Momma and Lucia to come home."

Entering the Brisajai, Warnach abruptly stopped. Expanding their role to be godparents to both Warnach's children, Rodan and Mirah waited. Farisa sat in a chair, attempting to quiet a squirming Michahn while Farsuk and Ifta stood with Araman, whose puzzled face failed to dim joy in her eyes. The expression of every adult inside the Brisajai mirrored the odd look Badrik had given him minutes earlier.

Suppressing swiftly rising curiosity, Warnach guided the hoverchair to the front of the intimate chapel and made certain that the hover function was disengaged. Transferring Morcai's hand back to Badrik, he turned to help Sandra stand. Securely holding her with his arm around her waist, he matched her shuffling steps as they approached the altar. Once there, he took Lucia and, after pausing long enough to bestow a tender cerea-semi'ittá, placed the baby in a hammock made of embroidered, quilted satin.

Gently, Warnach loosened Lucia's snugly wrapped blanket. He stepped backward and formally bowed. Mirah then came forward to stand at Warnach's left, and Rodan approached to stay at Sandra's right. Despite weakness following the delivery and surgery, Sandra had insisted she was strong enough to honor the tradition of standing through the relatively brief ritual. She did so with Warnach and Rodan both having an arm around her in case she faltered.

High above the altar, a curtain of air served as barrier against an invasion of cool air from outside where cloudy skies concealed afternoon sun. Flickering candles bathed the Brisajai in subdued light. A single cone of Efobé emitted purplish-gray plumes laden with fragrance.

With Camudahmni Lobrihm standing beside her, Nadana serenely regarded all from the altar. Bowing her head, she recited the traditional opening prayer of Ohmtra'ame eu Si'im.

"Sacred Great Spirit, unto You we come. In joy this day, we present this sacred gift of new life. We humbly seek many blessings. Present are parents, Warnach and Sandra, who ask Your strength and wisdom to guide this new child in holy faith. Rodan and Mirah stand with them and request that You help them be godparents to this baby. Surrounded by family, all join prayers for good health and a lifetime of blessings for Your tender and precious gift. Eyach'hamá eu Yahvanta."

When Nadana stepped aside, Camudahmni Lobrihm moved to the altar's central point. Both watched as the baby girl stretched and opened curious eyes. Each wondered if this child might indeed be Mi'yafá Si'imlayaná. As questions echoed through both their minds, Nadana reached for an elegantly shaped cup crafted of gold. Turning, she held it respectfully high while Lobrihm chanted ancient prayers invoking Yahvanta's spirit to consecrate freshly pressed virgin oil so that the sweet oil might soak blessings into the newly anointed child.

Winds above sounded a mournful moan. Disregarding the eerie cry and continuing the quiet chant of sacred prayers, Lobrihm firmly grasped a solid gold Kaa'michinah. Dipping it into golden oil, the holy man opened the child's gown and touched the gleaming rod to her chest, just above her heart. Cold metal startled Lucia, but she didn't cry. Ever so carefully, the Camudahmni dabbed oil onto the baby's lips, on her ears, and beneath her eyes. Finally, as he touched final drops onto her forehead, a brilliant shaft of sunlight pierced dark clouds and invaded through the open skylight, momentarily shining upon the child's face.

Many startled sets of eyes darted around the intimate chapel. Although no one spoke, the odd occurrence provoked a shared memory. Recalled was the day Warnach and Sandra had celebrated Meu'yah ezhá Kitak. Just as Warnach had placed Kitak upon his new ki'mirsah's head, an unexplained breeze had swept into the Brisajai at the Sirinoya home. Immediately afterward, rays of sunshine invaded with golden glow.

Unaware of the incident at the Meu'yah ezhá Kitak, Camudahmni Lobrihm noted the newest anomaly but hesitated only moments. His voice held none of its usual quavers born of advancing age. Instead, as Lucia began to whimper, he prayerfully reminded those inside the Brisajai never to veer from faith and always to guide their children according to the Great Spirit's teachings.

That evening, Warnach tucked Morcai into bed and watched as the toddler drifted off to sleep. Then, after wishing goodnight to Hitara, he returned to the family lounge. Depositing himself on a sofa beside Araman, he held her hand.

Sensing his questions, Araman rested her head against her son's upper arm. "Before you ask, Nadana has said nothing to me. I remain as surprised as you."

Tilting his head backward, Warnach closed his eyes. Fingertips nervously traced circles on his mamehr's arm. "I still cannot comprehend why a Camudahmni would preside over the anointing of a newborn. Even Farsuk is dumbfounded."

"As we all are." Intuition teasingly insinuated itself into her mind. While she wondered if she even dared ask Nadana, Araman also believed it best to say nothing to Warnach. At least, not yet. She again reminded herself of Sandra's advice that some matters were best left to unfold with time.

"I was just trying to remember if I've ever even seen a Camudahmni in person."

"Once. You were about Morcai's age. You were fascinated and afraid at the same time."

"Afraid? Why?"

"I never knew. We watched as a Camudahmni walked past you at the Brisa'machtai in Tichtika. I remember you started crying, but no one understood a word you said."

"Hmmm." Warnach sighed as his thoughts changed direction. "Sandra looked completely drained when I left tonight. All things considered, I almost wish she'd reconsider nursing Lucia."

"I understand your concern, but your ki'mirsah does what's best for your children."

Tiredly, he sighed again. "I know. I just want her to get better."

"She will, Warnach. She will."

At midnight, Warnach impatiently tapped his foot as he waited for the com-link transmission to complete. Hoping his timing was right, he received confirmation that the connection was successful. Surprised, he stared for a moment at Dave Warner's face. From long-instilled habit, he nodded respectfully. "Mr. Warner, I hope my call hasn't disturbed you."

David Warner shook his head. "I was up already. How's my daughter? Did she have the baby?"

"She did. We have a beautiful little girl. Sandra named her Lucia."

Mr. Warner looked visibly relieved, but his voice held little warmth. "I'm glad everything's all right."

"Mr. Warner…" Warnach practically choked on the growing knot in his throat. "I… I need your help."

Suddenly suspicious, Mr. Warner's expression changed. "My daughter. Is she all right?"

Struggling for words, Warnach dropped his face for several moments before he trusted himself to speak. When he finally faced the monitor, tears tracked unashamedly down his face. "Mr. Warner, the delivery went fine. However, immediately afterward, there was a rupture. The doctors can't explain what happened, but they rushed Sandra into surgery."

Impatient, Mr. Warner demanded again, "Is my daughter all right?"

Drawing in a deep breath, Warnach forced himself to answer. "The doctors were forced to perform an emergency hysterectomy. Physically, she'll be fine. It's just..."

After the com-link terminated, Warnach dropped his aching head onto arms folded atop his desk. For the first time in his life, he had begged. He had pleaded with Sandra's parents to come to Chikondra. Utilizing every argument he could think of, he had tried to persuade them to visit their daughter. He insisted that her recovery would be much faster with comfort from her parents. She needed help coming to grips with the reality inflicted by the surgery. In the end, all he had received was a request to give her their best wishes.

Frustrated, he no longer resisted burgeoning anger. His voice had risen. Sharp words had erupted and hurled through space. Spent, he had furiously disconnected the link.

Angry tears scorched his eyelids. Bitter bile seared his throat. With his eyes closed, he pictured Morcai and Lucia. He would dare the heavens themselves to reach his children if ever they would call to him in need. And Sandra. His love. His life. Never would it be possible for him to comprehend how callously her parents behaved with her. Never.

Morning sun was determined to brighten his bedroom. He had managed to climb the stairs and fall asleep across the bed without undressing. Surrendering to the new day, he groaned and dragged himself from bed to the shower. Dressing casually, he went downstairs and found Hitara playing with Morcai.

Picking his young son up from the floor, he treated them both to cerea-semi'ittá. He then carried Morcai into the Brisajai for morning prayers. Once breakfast was out of the way, he left Morcai again happily playing with Hitara. Donning a sweater, he turned in response to Araman's voice.

"Warnach, you have a call. They're transferring a com-link from Earth."

Dark features tensed. He thanked his mamehr before hurrying to his office. Swinging into his chair, he accepted the link. Surprise etched deeper lines into his worried face. "Mr. Warner?"

Dave Warner's eyes opened and closed several times. A heavy sigh accentuated his grim expression. Seconds passed before he finally spoke, beginning without greeting, without preamble. "My wife and I have talked. Neither of us is happy about this situation, and neither of us wants to leave home. However, I've convinced Lee to see a doctor about ways to cope with her travel fears.

"On the other hand, I don't know anything about traveling away from Earth. Tell me what I need to do, and we'll come to our daughter."

Stunned for mere seconds, Warnach recovered quickly. "Mr. Warner, you need do nothing beyond packing and assembling appropriate identification. I'll arrange special diplomatic status and have someone contact you to finalize all travel arrangements."

Minutes later, Warnach instructed his office staff to organize details immediately and keep him informed. During the short trip to the hospital, he felt bewildered by the abrupt change. Still, he resolved to say nothing to his lifemate. With her family's long history of disappointing her, he could not risk piling more hurt on her. If her parents did indeed come, the surprise would be a happy one.

Inside her hospital room, she questioned him about Morcai while doting on Lucia. They discussed the previous afternoon's ceremony for the baby, and she asked curious questions about the Camudahmni's participation. Together, they enjoyed time to better acquaint themselves with their new daughter. He felt intensely relieved that her mood was subdued but far from somber.

By the time he returned home, Warnach's head still ached. Knowing too well Sandra's sensitivity, he started worrying that she might be suppressing inner turmoil. He feared that she suffered denial since she avoided speaking of the operation. Longing for her homecoming grew. There, they could speak more frankly. At home, their Kitak could be rejoined, and his senses would more deeply connect to thoughts and feelings that would be captured within the ring of rafizhaq.

A day earlier than scheduled, he accompanied her to his waiting transport. Impatient as usual with confinement, she had demanded release. Insisting that the HAU's had substantially advanced healing and that her body was quite capable of completing the process, she had practically bullied the staff into releasing her. Having observed irrevocable decision in her eyes, Warnach had exacted a promise that she would rest and follow Dr. Walters' orders before assuring the physician that they would both benefit from giving in to her.

True to her word, she claimed a sofa in the lounge as her downstairs domain. From there, she watched over both her children while resting according to doctor's orders. Hitara good-naturedly played fetch by retrieving Lucia from her cradle for feedings and cuddling. While the baby slept, Sandra lavished time on Morcai by keeping him close to read, play simple games, or just to talk.

Several days after her return home, Warnach took both children upstairs and tucked them into their beds. Returning to the lounge, he was surprised to find Sandra gone. He first checked her office, his music room, and then the kitchen without success. As he passed the Brisajai on his way back to the lounge, peripheral vision caught the golden glow of a single candle.

Stopping, he rested a hand against carved wood framing the doorway. She had returned to the tiny chapel after earlier family prayers. Inside, on her knees, she prayed aloud. Her voice trembled. His heart quickened in response.

"Holy Father, help me bear this sadness without making it weigh upon my ki'medsah. I want so badly to cry and scream and demand to know why. I feel angry because this all seems so unfair. Then, each time he smiles at me or I hold our children, I remember that I have more than I ever believed I'd have. All my answers lie within my love for my family and my faith in you. Help me. I don't want to fail them, but I don't feel like being strong anymore. All I really want to do is cry."

From behind, he watched as she formed a cross over her breast. By the time she rose to her feet, he had reached her side and drew her into protective arms. His legs bent. In unison, they sank to the floor. Within his arms, grief overtook her as brokenhearted weeping initiated the cleansing of sorrow from her soul. Patiently, he held her close as he once again became her refuge, her perfect place to be.

Sporting a pink flannel pad over his shoulder, Warnach held Lucia and patted patiently until she burped. Tenderly kissing her head, he then transferred the infant to Sandra's waiting arms. "I think she needs a change."

"Great timing," she teased.

Despite the attempted humor, shadows still lurked in her eyes. Smiling, he briefly touched cerea-nervos to her forehead and noted her instantaneous shiver. "I love it when you do that."

She grinned in response. "You're going to be late. Your visitors arrive in forty-five minutes."

"I won't be late. As soon as I get them to their lodgings, I'll be home. All right?"

"In time for the next diaper change?"

He laughed. "Let's hope not."

Later, hearing voices from inside the foyer, Sandra's forehead wrinkled. Letting Morcai hold the book they'd been reading, she glanced at Araman, who stood beside Lucia's cradle. "I wasn't expecting him to bring anyone home with him."

Araman hoped her smile wasn't too revealing. "Something unexpected must have happened. Perhaps you should greet him. I'll stay with the children until Hitara comes back downstairs."

Wondering what had prompted Warnach's change of plans, Sandra stood and smoothed her nashavri. Sighing, she left the lounge. Reaching the foyer, she halted abruptly. Her chin dropped, and evergreen eyes widened in utter shock. "Mom? Dad?"

Seeing her daughter frozen with surprise, Lee Warner approached with open arms. Tears slid down tan cheeks as she kissed Sandra's face. "Warnach told us what happened. We - we wanted to be here for you."

Pulling slightly away from her mother, an expression of stunned disbelief gave way to torrents of tears as Sandra excitedly hugged both of her parents. "I can't believe it! I can't believe you're really here!" she exclaimed between sobs.

Minutes later, Warnach feared she might collapse from excitement. His hand came to rest on her shoulder. "Shi'níyah, perhaps your parents would like to come in and see the children."

She stepped back, and her cheeks flooded pink with embarrassment. "I'm so sorry. I…" Unable to speak, she started crying again.

Blue eyes brimmed with tears as Dave Warner chuckled and wrapped his arms around her. "Hey, it's okay. We thought you might need us."

"Oh, Daddy, I did…I do… Oh! What do I say?"

Above her shoulder, her father's eyes met Warnach's. When Warnach had advised the Warners of Sandra's surgery, the com-link had ended bitterly. He had first asked why they refused to come to their daughter when she needed help from everyone who loved her. Angrily, Warnach had declared that for his own children, he would traverse the entire galaxy if ever they needed him. He had gone so far as to accuse her father of having no compassion at all for Sandra, no real love.

Furious words had finally shamed David Warner into an honest evaluation of his relationship with his oldest child. Reluctantly, he faced the truth. No matter what wrong she committed, Donna received all the attention to the detriment of her brothers and older sister. Although his sons had also suffered, Sandra had borne the brunt because she was so different from the others. While consoling the daughter in his embrace, Mr. Warner nodded slightly. Reluctantly, he acknowledged that his son-in-law's wrath had opened his eyes to his own shortcomings as a father while finally clearing a path for him to rebuild relationships with all his children.

Twelve days flew by in a blur. Never had Sandra communicated so freely with her parents. Everyone spent hours playing with Morcai and cuddling the newborn Lucia. Talk about friends and family helped her catch up on events back on Earth. Comfortable temperatures provided perfect opportunities for leisurely walks outside where she and her father discussed differences and similarities of flora and fauna on Earth and Chikondra.

All the while, Warnach watched with quiet reserve. His instincts had been accurate. His ki'mirsah had needed the healing touch best given by mothers and fathers. However, he remained vigilant, fearful that her father's unpredictable moodiness might resurface and undo all the good.

The day before her parents were to return home, Warnach walked outside to retrieve toys Morcai had left. Surprised to see Mr. Warner leaning against a tree, he smiled. "The day is beautiful."

Dave nodded. "I was just wondering if I could take a long walk without getting lost."

Warnach's wide eyebrows arched as he sensed his father-in-law's odd mood. "If you don't object, I'll take these in and join you."

Rounding a corner more than half an hour later, Mr. Warner slowed. Carefully stepping down a sloped embankment, he stopped at the edge of the broad stream crossing the Sirinoya estate. He sighed heavily as Warnach reached his side. "You have a beautiful piece of land here."

Crouching down, Warnach dipped his fingers into clear waters. "This place has belonged to my family for many generations. It's always been my home."

"Home," Mr. Warner repeated. "I'm anxious to get back to mine, but I also hate leaving my daughter so soon. You were right when you said that she needed us."

Drying his hand on his slacks, Warnach lifted his face to sunny heavens. "Sandra is very strong. She would have gotten better eventually, but your trip here hastens her recovery. I also believe that your coming has finally brought healing to old sadness. For that, I shall always be grateful."

Dave Warner extended his hand, and, although he needed no help, Warnach grasped it and stood. Staring into his father-in-law's face, Warnach wondered what thoughts churned through Mr. Warner's mind.

Finally, with snatches from an accidentally overheard conversation ringing inside his mind, Dave spoke uneasily. "Being here, I see how close your family is to her."

"Mamehr adores Sandra. My brother loves her so much that he risked his life for her."

"From what I've seen, I don't doubt he'd do it again." Dave paused as years of regrets filled him. "I've said a lot of ugly things about you and to you. There's no way to take any of them back. It's obvious to me now that you're providing her with a good home and a lot more things than I ever could. She was right when she told me she loves you in ways I can't understand."

Uncomfortable with words, Dave walked over to a large stone and sat down. "I'll always be afraid so long as she keeps traveling on these missions. She's almost gotten herself killed a couple of times already. If you love Morcai and Lucia as much as you say, you've got to understand how I feel."

Quietly, Warnach replied, "I do have new empathy on that point. I've also shared your fear for Sandra's life. Losing her would destroy me. That's one of the reasons I accepted the Master's Chair on the Alliance Council. Besides, our little ones deserve having both their parents at home."

"You're quitting field service missions?"

"Not entirely, but my role will change. As head of the diplomatic ministry, my presence on missions will be occasional and mostly to review already negotiated treaties for formal approval."

With jaw shifting thoughtfully from side to side, Dave said, "Sandra told me you thrive on field ministry missions. Won't that be a hard change for you?"

Breathing in deeply, Warnach expelled a sigh. "Very hard. Many years before I met her, I swore I'd never leave active ministry a second time. On the other hand, after learning what she faced on Dargom, I vowed never again to place her or one of my children in that kind of danger." The veil of memory fell over his expression. "My career on-mission seems a small price to pay to ensure my ki'mirsah's safety."

Swallowing hard, Dave studied his son-in-law's expression. "She said you're both dedicated to diplomatic missions."

Warnach aimed a steady gaze at his father-in-law. "That is true. Our task now is to discover new ways to contribute to peace initiatives."

Nodding, Dave stood and started uphill toward the path. The two men walked until Mr. Warner again broke contemplative silence. "Leaving field missions is a huge sacrifice for you."

Warnach could not lie. "It is."

"Do you really love my daughter that much?"

The crunch of footsteps echoed through the woods and punctuated the long pause following Dave Warner's question. Finally, Warnach responded pensively. "In a very literal sense, your daughter saved my life several times. What few know is the depth of personal despair I lived through before I met her. Her love lifted me from depression and brought me incomparable joy. As I told you when we first met, she restored meaning to my life. So, to answer your question, I do love her that much."

Dave Warner could hardly ignore the truth suffusing Warnach's words. "When I decided to come, it was more out of angry pride. I wanted to prove what you said about me was wrong. I understand now why you felt the way you did and how right you were that she needed us. Admitting mistakes isn't easy. I just want you to know I believe you now. I also want to thank you for bringing Lee and me here. I could never have afforded it on my own. You also have my respect and my gratitude for what you're doing to keep her from harm's way."

Warnach stopped for a moment. Without conscious thought, his right hand lifted. For the briefest moment, his fingertips stroked his Kitak. "Mr. Warner, you cannot know how much that means to me."

Further discussion would be meaningless. As their walk wound back to the house, both men silently considered the importance of Sandra in their lives and the newfound peace between them.

PART THREE

To have faith is to truly love...

To have faith and love is
to truly live...

Chapter Ten

Kneeling, Sandra brushed hair away from her daughter's eyes. Sometimes, it seemed impossible to believe Lucia was almost ten years old already. "Remind Badehr to use your headbands while I'm away. I want those beautiful eyes of yours to stay healthy, all right?"

Lucia smiled despite sadness that her mother was leaving on-mission. "Momma, you know that Maméi-mamehr and Hitara will make me even if Badehr doesn't."

"You're right," Sandra laughed as she hugged Lucia tightly. "I also want you to remember how much I'll miss you because I love you so much."

As Lucia looked back at her mother, her smile faded. "I'll miss you, too, Momma. Don't worry, though. I'll be fine. Someone has to stay and take care of Badehr."

Affectionately, Morcai tousled black curls that spiraled to his sister's waist. "Don't worry. I'll help with Badehr, too!"

Standing, Sandra pulled her son closer. Holding him snugly, she kissed his cheek. "I love you, too, young man. You know Momma hates the idea of leaving you."

Morcai's eyes grew solemn. "We know, Momma. Your light shows us."

For a moment, she wondered if she would ever grow accustomed to her children's ability to see auras. "I honestly don't want to go, but many people need help."

Lucia reached for her mother's hand. "We understand, Momma. Badehr says you carry the mission for all of us. We'll be waiting when you come home."

"Absolutely." Warnach's voice sounded just behind her shoulder.

Spinning on her heels, she smiled. In the years since she'd met him, it seemed he had aged hardly at all. "Is that a promise?"

Black eyes adored her. "Must you really ask?"

Swallowing hard, she moved forward and wrapped her arms around him. "I do hate leaving," she whispered.

"I know," he replied in a hushed voice. "No one will miss you more than I."

Minutes later, she hugged her children a final time and shared a lingering farewell kiss with Warnach. Turning, she headed into the tunnel leading to the shuttle that would carry her to the orbiting Rahpliknar.

Once onboard the diplomatic starship, she settled into mission mode. On the rare off-world missions she had accepted since Lucia's birth, she found work her greatest ally in the battle against longings for home and family. Several times throughout the years, she had considered resigning her ministry post altogether. Warnach had offered support but, based on personal experience, had warned her to consider the decision carefully. Each time, events somewhere in the Alliance had required her services, causing her to postpone any final decision.

Now, on the way to Rehovot, the history of a neighboring star system provided distraction. Emerging from war decades earlier, Ashapat had begun rebuilding with assistance from Rehovot. Its leadership had also responded favorably to Rehovot's requests to consider Alliance membership. During a worldwide referendum, the planet crossed paths with an enormous meteor storm after the unexpected explosion of a massive comet passing nearby. Resulting destruction had killed hundreds of thousands and devastated vast areas of the planet.

At Rehovot's request, a fleet of Alliance ships was en route with humanitarian supplies and equipment to assist survivors. Because of her organizational skills, Warnach and Chancellor Meyahfra had decided Sandra could best direct personnel and relief efforts during the initial phases of disaster recovery. Despite her reluctance, duty and compassion had prevailed. The people of Ashapat urgently needed help.

Six weeks after Sandra's departure, Warnach sat on a patch of thick grass at Miferasud Park. Nimble fingers tucked long curls beneath the elastic band securing Lucia's hair away from her face. Bounding to her feet, his daughter smiled brightly. "Thank you, Badehr!"

Across a broad field, Lucia spotted Morcai practicing with a soccer ball he'd gotten on the family's most recent trip to Earth. Swiftly, she ran and snatched the ball with a swipe of her foot. Both laughed while challenging one another for possession. Grinning wickedly, Morcai raced toward his sister. Slipping on slick grass, he slid across the ground. His toe caught the ball and sent it flying through the air.

Morcai's eyes grew wide as the ball grazed the shoulder of someone strolling along a nearby path. Startled, the woman turned around. Leaning over and picking up the ball, she stared at them. "Is this yours?"

Lucia trotted toward the lady while Morcai sat motionless on the grass, nursing wounded pride and dreading explanations to his badehr. "Miryah," Lucia said contritely upon reaching the stranger, "we're very sorry. My brother slipped on wet grass and accidentally kicked the ball too hard."

Sad eyes stared into young, innocent features. "If your brother is the one who kicked it, don't you think he is the one who should apologize?"

Smiling beautifully, Lucia nodded and turned. "Morcai! You need to apologize, too!"

With a sheepish expression, Morcai joined his sister. For just a moment, he had to force himself not to look at the woman's aura. "I'm very sorry, Miryah. I was careless, but I certainly didn't mean to hit anyone."

As the lady handed him his ball, she closely studied his features. "I accept your apology. Did I hear correctly that your name is Morcai?"

"Yes, Miryah," he answered proudly. "I was named for my badeí-badehr. He used to be on the Chikondran High Council. He was an Alliance master."

The woman's dark features softened. "Morcai Sirinoya?"

"Yes," Morcai responded, not fully comfortable with the woman. "Do you know of him?"

For the first time, the lady smiled at the children. "I do. I was once friends with his son, Warnach Sirinoya."

"Lucia! Morcai!" Both children started at the unusually sharp tone in their badehr's voice. "Gather your things and go back to the other side of the field. Immediately!"

Without protest, the children picked up the ball and headed toward their transport. Warnach turned and watched until they disappeared. Pivoting, he glared coldly. "What were you doing with my children, Lashira?"

Blood drained from her face, making her features appear more tired and sad than ever. "We only talked. Their ball flew my way, and I gave it back to them."

"And since when did you start coming to parks? You always said they were boring and lifeless."

Lashira swallowed nervously. "Warnach, there's no need for anger. I wasn't stalking you or them. I needed a quiet place to think. I swear. Our encounter was accidental." Seeing skepticism on his face, she managed a weak smile. "I just left the clinic in Kadranas. I don't know if you've heard. Badehr is very ill. The doctors say he has only a matter of days left."

His gaze held steady. "I didn't know. I'm sorry. Your badehr is a good man."

"Too good." Tears stung her eyes. "I wish I'd realized sooner how very good he is. I would have spent more time with him."

Uncomfortable in her presence, Warnach nodded. "Excuse me, Lashira. I must check on my children."

Regret shone from almond-shaped eyes. "They're beautiful children, Warnach. Really beautiful. You must feel very proud."

Warnach's sensually shaped mouth curved into a smile for mere seconds. "I am proud. I must go now. Please, give my sympathy and my regards to your brother."

Watching him turn to leave, Lashira felt her heart sink beneath the weight of sorrow. "Warnach?" When he turned, she tried to smile into features that remained devastatingly handsome. "Does she still make you happy?"

His brow dipped. "Lashira, Sandra makes me far happier than you can imagine. I love her more now than ever."

Watching as he disappeared, Lashira stood without moving. Her mind drifted. All those years ago, she had been unfaithful to satisfy a selfish ego and make him jealous. She had denied him the stability and family he had wanted, and she had mocked his faith. She had played games, confident he loved her so much he would always return. Angrily wiping tears from her face, she questioned if she would ever stop paying for mistakes that had destroyed Warnach's love and driven him from her life.

After dinner, Warnach followed Lucia into the family lounge. At her request, he sat on one of the long sofas while she stood before him, her expression earnest. "Have I done something wrong?"

Dark brown eyes gazed into his. In a voice far too solemn for a child her age, she said, "Not really. I just wondered if I could ask you about today."

Warnach's stomach lurched. He often found his daughter's intuitive perceptions challenging to answer. Despite unease, he valued Sandra's wisdom about always openly facing their children's inquiries. "You know you're always free to ask me anything."

Thoughtfully, she nodded. "Badehr, that lady in the park. She was so beautiful, but Morcai and I saw her light so small, like it wanted to stop shining. Her heart was very sad. When you came, your light was different. Bright and red like fires. You were mad, Badehr. Why?"

How to answer? Warnach sighed. Reaching out, he pulled his daughter onto his lap. As she rested her cheek against his shoulder, he combed fingers through long locks of hair. "It's hard for Badehr to explain, Lucia."

"She told us you were friends. Is that true?"

"Not exactly." He searched for words. "A long time ago, years before I met your momma, I lived through a troubled time. My work was hard, and I felt very lonely. For a while, I thought I was in love with that lady. As a result, I made some terrible mistakes. The good thing is that I saw my mistakes in time. Your badeí-badehr taught me to pray again, and the Great Spirit forgave me. Then, Yahvanta helped me find your momma."

Lucia's right hand slid upward until she placed her open palm against his face. "Badehr, I think the lady still loves you very much."

"Unfortunately, she did too many bad things. That's why she's so unhappy. Now, she lives a lonely life. I didn't mean to be angry. I just remembered all the bad things she did, even to your momma. Lucia, I don't wish sadness for her. I really don't. I feel sorry for her."

Lucia straightened in his lap. Intently, her eyes studied his face. "You miss Momma more than ever, don't you?"

Not wanting her to see the shame in his eyes, Warnach hugged his daughter tightly. "Whenever I think of bad times, she makes my sadness go away."

Lucia grasped her badehr's hand and kissed it. "You know the Great Spirit brought Momma to you because He knew how much you'll always need her."

"You sound very sure of that."

Lucia closed her eyes and squeezed his hand. "I am sure. Quazon told me."

"Mac!" Sandra exclaimed delightedly as she greeted him with a hug. "I never expected you here!"

Bright blue eyes sparkled with dancing lights upon seeing her again. "I received an unusual assignment for a captain in Star Command. It seems there's a Terran minister stranded on Ashapat. My orders were to drop in, escort her to my ship, and deliver her home to Chikondra."

She invited him to sit at the large table where she was working. "I just finished final recommendations for aid to Ashapat. Those people lived through absolute hell, but they're so appreciative of every single effort the Alliance has made on their behalf."

"I hear you've organized a pretty aggressive recovery plan."

She nodded thoughtfully. "On some parts of the planet, destruction is unimaginable. Initial deliveries of emergency supplies have already allowed us to organize sanitary services, food distribution, and housing construction. The rest is up to Council Planetary Services. After fourteen weeks, I'm ready to turn over long-term management and go home."

"Don't you think you're a little old to be homesick?" he teased gently.

Laughing lightly, she wrinkled her nose. "I have a son and daughter who might forget me, and an extremely handsome lifemate who may attract sly predators. If homesick takes me home, then homesick I am."

Depositing his tall frame into a chair, Mac watched as she closed her sleek computer and pushed it aside. Time had touched her gracefully. Her complexion remained smooth and clear. She wore glossy hair in a longer style that curled around her shoulders. Her figure remained trim and femininely enticing. Beyond all else, expressive eyes beamed with inner joy.

"You look particularly thoughtful today."

His smile quickly concealed private assessment. "I was just thinking that it's been ten years since we met, and you look like you might have aged ten days. Care to share the secret?"

Her wide smile reflected delight. "Thanks for the compliment. I don't know any secrets beyond taking care of myself and staying ridiculously deep in love."

Mac grinned wryly. "Ridiculously deep in love, eh?"

Her features gentled. "Yeah. I thank the angels every day for bringing Warnach and me together."

Brown eyebrows lifted. "Angels?"

Soft laughter held a mysterious note. "Yes, angels. It's a long story. "

The following morning, she boarded the small military transport that would depart Ashapat's solar system for the sixty-hour voyage to Rehovot. Once there, Mac would escort her to the orbiting Tecumseh for the journey back to Chikondra. After leaving personal belongings inside her private quarters, she made her way through narrow corridors to the officer's mess for lunch with Mac and the transport's captain.

As a young man cleared plates from the table, she gazed thoughtfully into her coffee mug. "I thought it odd that a military starship came for me rather than a diplomatic vessel."

"Attacks on outposts from Mitrakt to the Shawav systems have everyone on edge. Chancellor Meyahfra issued an immediate recall of all diplomatic ministers. Although other Alliance vessels were closer to Rehovot, the Tecumseh received orders to transport you."

"Have attackers been identified?"

Captain Wright nodded. "All indications point to Zeterons."

Mac's expression hardened. "In my opinion, the Zeteron Empire recognizes that Meyahfra isn't nearly the leader Edsaka was. Meyahfra is a decent man but much too tentative. Edsaka was smarter, stronger, and capable of making quicker, more effective decisions."

Sandra sighed. She and Warnach had discussed that very same point. "Baadihm Farsuk is among the best leaders the Alliance ever had. There's been talk about trying to convince him to seek re-election to the chancellor's post."

"You're close to him, Sandra. Do you think he will?"

"Hard to say," she replied, sipping her coffee. "At a hundred-twelve, I'm sure he wonders if he'd be considered too old to shoulder the responsibility, especially now."

Captain Wright met her gaze. "My opinion is that Meyahfra spells doom for the Alliance. If Edsaka doesn't reconsider, our only hope of avoiding outright war with the Zeterons is to find a new leader with the same strength of character. I can think of only two or three who fit the necessary profile."

Sandra's eyes moved from one face to the other. Their thoughts were frighteningly transparent. Unwilling to give voice to their ideas, she shrugged. "Let us hope the Alliance finds someone with the necessary courage to face what promises to be a rocky future."

Pressing the command pad, Warnach repeated the VM received two days earlier. How satisfied she looked with the results of her mission to Ashapat. How happy her voice sounded when she talked of being en route to the Tecumseh and on her way home. Her expression reflected longing she felt free to express since she had sent separate messages to the children. "I can hardly wait to be home, me'u ki'medsah. I hope you'll be ready for me to show you exactly how much I've missed you."

If only she knew how ready, he thought. How much he needed to make love to her again. Just as his eyelids slid closed and sensuous memories invaded, tones sounded. The ministry com-link in his home office demanded immediate attention.

Half an hour later, his transport nosed into a reserved spot at the ministry's docking tower. Exiting quickly, he ran through the garage, accompanied by military escorts. Just outside an enormous briefing room, Badrik waited, and the two men whisked inside. A wall-sized screen soon filled with images of debris floating through space. Silent, the two brothers stared at a dark, crippled shuttle that was the only recognizable image captured by the Tecumseh's visual scanners.

From onboard the starship, Commander Dietrich's voice sounded on the decoded transmission. "Analysis of debris collected indicates the York was fired upon by L Category lazon cannons, the same type used during recent raids against outposts in the Medron sector. The shuttle sustained damage attributed to a strike at its rear. We have no explanation for its otherwise intact condition since neither survivors nor bodies were located onboard."

By the time the transmission ended, Warnach's head pounded, and his stomach pitched with nausea. Shocked disbelief flooded him. The attack on the York represented bold deviation from usual Zeteron tactics. Implications for the Alliance were staggering. From a personal perspective, he asked himself how he would possibly survive.

"Minister Sirinoya! Hurry!"

Grabbing the long strap of her attaché, Sandra swiftly looped it over her head and across her shoulder. Dashing from her cabin, she ran behind the ensign assigned to evacuate her from the listing York. Upon reaching the hangar deck, Mac hurried her aboard an emergency shuttle. Inside, he barked commands to the crew of five as he jumped into the pilot's seat and urgently initiated sequences to launch the craft.

Sandra's heart beat rapidly as she secured safety restraints. Blood throbbed painfully at her temples. Lights inside the cabin dimmed. Engines hummed louder. The ship shifted into motion. Tension gripped those aboard. Captain McAllen and a navigator skillfully maneuvered the shuttle when the deck level changed angles as the damaged York lurched drunkenly in space.

The shuttle had barely cleared the large transport when a new volley of lazon rays streaked through space. Explosions were seen tearing through the damaged vessel. As McAllen accelerated shuttle engines, a blinding flash marked the disintegration of the York and her crew. Those ordered to evacuate their ministry passenger were the only ones who escaped.

McAllen concentrated on control panel readouts while piloting the shuttle and curtly ordering a technician to power defensive force shields. To his left, he saw a long, sleek ship veer. Desperately, he shoved his weight into manual controls, rolling the shuttle to one side. Sustaining a hit, the craft shuddered. Lights flickered on and off. While an engineer scrambled from his seat to assess damages, McAllen struggled with the vessel's failing guidance computers.

"Captain! Main power systems failing! Diverting to auxiliary power!"

Abruptly, another vessel appeared from seemingly nowhere. Within seconds, the first ship changed course and, pursued by yet a third ship, shot past them into deep space. Cursing, McAllen slammed his fists against the dimming control panel. Their shuttle, captured by tractor beams, was being drawn into the yawning mouth of an unidentified craft.

With a jolt, the shuttle stopped. Anxious eyes shifted from face to face. The engineer's voice cut through tense silence. "Auxiliary power plant now failing. Estimating life-support sustainable for two hours. Emergency equipment will extend survival one additional hour."

Captain McAllen spun around in the pilot's seat. "Is anyone hurt?" Relieved there were no injuries, he twisted forward again and angrily stared through polymer windows. A track of lights shone down from the ceiling of the compartment where their craft now rested. Uniformed figures scurried across the deck. All wore black helmets with lowered face shields.

Mac studied their movements at length. "Ladies, gentlemen, it seems we have an armed reception party waiting to greet us. Do scanners have sufficient power to detect the atmosphere?"

The engineer, Ensign Brinker, said, "Atmosphere oxygen-rich and satisfactory to sustain humanoid life. Ambient temperature is twenty-six degrees Celsius."

Mac faced Sandra and his crew. "We have no idea what to expect outside this ship. Unless we wish to suffocate, there is no option but to release hatches and face our captors. Comments or recommendations?"

With eyes closed and fingertips pressed tightly to her temple, Sandra's lips moved in what appeared to be silent conversation. As Mac watched changes in her expressions, he recalled the eerie conversations he had witnessed on Dargom. From someone otherwise so practical and analytical, he could hardly fathom her strange lapses. "Minister Sirinoya?"

Blinking several times, she finally returned his gaze. "Mac, open the hatches slowly. I'll go out first."

"You know my first inclination."

Her smile was nervous. "Duty first. Protect the diplomat. I know. Open the hatch and lower the ramp."

Dargom had also taught him that she allowed nothing to stand between her and decisions made under pressure. Slowly, so as not to provoke waiting captors, he switched remaining power and opened the main exit. Upon opening, the hatch admitted an influx of fresh air. Next, he pressed in the command to extend the ramp. Glancing to his left, he saw dark uniforms tighten ranks in front of the open hatch. "Sandra, wait. I don't want..."

Spinning and simultaneously rising from his seat, he saw his warning was too late. She already stood directly in the center of the doorway. With arms extended and palms upward to show she was unarmed, she slowly took one step forward onto the ramp. Outside, weapons were raised. No one moved.

Encouraged, she slowly proceeded down the sloping ramp to the deck. Not once did she lower her face. Not once did she look away. Instead, she faced their mysterious captors and waited. She swallowed nervously as one stepped forward.

Uniformed in dark gray, the slender figure in charge raised a gloved hand to the helmet's face shield. Slowly, the shield lifted and revealed a woman's face. Black eyes glittered angrily. Full lips pulled into a taut line. She stepped forward and pointed toward the shuttle's hatch.

In response, Sandra nodded and pointed. She then signaled those inside to disembark, one at a time. Joined by the shuttle crew, then flanked by several guards, Sandra acknowledged the woman's signal to follow.

Expecting to be led to holding cells, she was surprised when they reached what appeared to be a small briefing room. Inside, she heard the female officer speak for the first time, apparently ordering one guard to remain on alert before leaving with the others. Sandra listened carefully, her forehead crinkled in concentration.

Minutes later, the woman reappeared. Without her helmet, her expression appeared nearly as severe as that of the man who accompanied her. During a rapid verbal exchange between the two, Sandra's evergreen eyes widened with questions as she strained to listen to their conversation.

Mac whispered into Sandra's ear. "Am I wrong, or are you thinking what I'm thinking?"

"I believe so," she replied, staring at the two captors.

Suddenly, the woman pointed and motioned Sandra forward. Quickly, Mac sidestepped in front of her, effectively placing himself between her and their captors.

Resting her open palm against Mac's back, Sandra spoke softly. "It's okay, Mac. Let's see if we're right."

She then approached the man and woman. With deliberate slowness, she bent her elbows and raised her hands, placing palms together. Pointing straight from the level of her heart, she bent forward while simultaneously rotating her hands upward to touch her forehead. When she straightened, she noted two shocked expressions just before the man and woman repeated the solemn salutation.

Sharply, the man spoke. Shaking her head, Sandra raised her hands with palms downward, hoping he would understand her request to speak more slowly. Again, he addressed her. This time, his speech was more distinctly enunciated.

Uncertain, Sandra smiled at them while her brain raced backward in time. She had first heard that cadence, that speech pattern, the night Warnach and she had celebrated Shi'firah. How difficult it had been for her to fully comprehend the complicated, old form of Chikondran Nadana had used during the ritual. Since then, her only exposure had been during religious rites or when she had struggled to read the Mi'yafá Si'imlayaná legend. Was imagination playing tricks on her? Again, she smiled at them, noting nervous pulsations of cerea-nervos.

An idea struck as she gazed at the woman's puzzled expression. Thank heavens she hadn't yet removed her Kitak before heading to work out in the York's gym. She pointed her index finger to the ring of rafizhaq circling her head. In a firm, clear voice, she spoke. "Kitak."

Visibly startled, both the man and woman touched the matching rings around their heads. In unison, they responded, "Kitak."

Sandra expelled a relieved sigh and placed her hand over her heart. Slowly, in Chikondran, she spoke again. "My name is Sandra Sirinoya."

The woman took one step forward. Her eyes narrowed suspiciously. Copying Sandra's gesture, she inclined her head and gently grasped the man's coat sleeve. "I am Isrina Kimasou. This is our captain and my ki'medsah, Sidrihn Kimasou."

Sandra's eyebrows lifted in undisguised surprise. "Oh, my God!" she exclaimed softly.

"What? Sandra! What happened? What did she say?"

The man boldly approached Sandra and pointed toward her face. His observation led to the obvious question.

"Bear with me, Mac. This isn't easy. They're speaking an ancient form of Chikondran that I hardly know." Smiling back at the man, she reverted to Chikondran. "My home planet is called Earth. I live on the world of Chikondra. My ki'medsah is Chikondran. His name is Warnach Sirinoya."

The man stared at her skeptically. "Sirinoya? Our forefathers told of the Sirinoya who protected the true faith of Chikondra. This is only legend."

"Neh-ohm," Sandra said, shaking her head. "Chikondra is real. The Sirinoya are real." She paused and swallowed. "On

Chikondra today, Sirinoya blood runs strong together with blood of the Kimasou."

Each side struggled to comprehend the other. Communication was difficult and would require time and patience to clarify. However, for the first time since initial explosions had rocked the York, Sandra sensed purpose in the madness. Patience alone would reveal the origins of these people and how they had come to rescue the sole survivors of the doomed York.

Somberly, Warnach held his children's hands as they mounted steps to the Brisa'machtai where he and Sandra had celebrated their unification. Accompanied by his family and Sandra's two brothers, he walked through the crowded chamber toward front-row seats. Twenty minutes later, he barely heard the Catholic priest who had graciously agreed to deliver words of his lifemate's faith to those gathered for her memorial. When Luradrani Fuhlamnad stood to address mourners, Warnach's eyes closed as his arms encircled the shoulders of his son and daughter. While both religious leaders spoke of faith, Warnach delved into his soul and severely doubted his ability to withstand the test now set before him.

Before final prayers, Badrik solemnly walked to the altar to take the podium. Now a general, his uniform declared him a man of skill and strength. Beneath that uniform beat the heart of a sensitive brother grieving for the sister he loved. Delivering a heartfelt eulogy, he recounted ideas and concepts she had shared with him over the years.

Unashamed of tears sliding down his cheeks, he gazed directly at his family. His voice trembled. "To my brother, I can barely imagine the scope of your sorrow. However, you must go forward with her memory as comfort and her children as evidence of the love you shared. Sandra would tell you to live your life in faith and cherish your children." Badrik paused before forcing himself to continue. "As long as you do so, she will live within you."

That evening, a single lamp did little to illuminate the spacious lounge. Earlier, Warnach had tucked his children into bed after kissing tears from their faces. He had then come downstairs and said goodnight to Curt and Roy. Feeling disconnected, he had no energy to climb the stairs to his master suite. The memorial had driven into his heart and soul the final nails of certainty. He had lost the most precious part of himself.

"My son, here. Drink this."

Glancing upward, he managed a slight nod. Mamehr's eyes were as worried as they were sad. "Tea?"

"Yes. Something soothing." She gave him the cup and watched him wrap his hands around it before she sat beside him. "Warnach, I wish I could bear this pain for you. I know fully how horrible you feel."

Staring into steaming gold liquid, he wondered if he might strangle on the knot in his throat. "Mamehr, I feel lost - as though my feet don't know how to take the next step and my lungs have forgotten what to do with the next breath. How do I go on? How do I face tomorrow?"

Tears filled Araman's eyes. Her son's questions rekindled the all-encompassing grief she had confronted after her own lifemate's death. "Warnach, I won't lie to you. You face the greatest difficulty of your life. My advice is to cling to her wisdom as much as to her memory. The love you shared is something that will not die. You will need that. You know as well as I that terrible times lie ahead for all of us."

Long after she said goodnight, he finally forced himself upstairs. Mechanically, he undressed for bed. Standing in front of a mirror on the dresser, he started to remove Kitak. His heart throbbed. His spirit resisted the separation. He staggered into bed. Lying on top of blankets, he stared into silent, oppressive darkness. Around his forehead, he detected distinctive tingling much like what he had felt during the time he lay trapped on Dargom. Perhaps Badrik had been correct. If only he could continue to live without losing faith, she would also continue to live within him.

Chapter Eleven

Mac comfortingly massaged her neck and shoulders. "Sandra, your ability to communicate with them has been our salvation. You can't blame them for not going back yet. In their place, what would you do?"

Hiccupping on an unrestrained sob, she buried her face into her hands. "I know, Mac. Just like I know we have to help them. It's just that it's been so long. My own children need me, too. And Warnach… My God, his grief is killing me."

Coming around, Mac knelt down. He knew better than to repeat his earlier suggestion that she remove her Kitak so that she wouldn't be so sensitive to Sirinoya's emotions. "Hey, everything's going to be okay. You've got to pull yourself together. Remember. We need you, too. You're the only one who can communicate with them. That means you're the only one who can get us all home."

By mealtime, her eyes were still red and puffy. Her stomach ached with emptiness. Despite very little appetite, she forced herself to eat. Taking a bite from a slice of spicy vegetable loaf, she glanced up as Isrina Kimasou approached. Worried shadows clinging to the woman's tired expression prompted feelings of guilt when Sandra thought of her own children safe at home on Chikondra.

After the escape shuttle was jettisoned and the starship again hurtled through hyperspace, the tedious task began to learn about the people who had saved the shuttle's crew. According to Isrina, they lived on a planet far beyond the outer limits of the Alliance.

Their ancestors had been scientists who had embarked from their homeworld of Chikondra on a mission of exploration. Caught in an inexplicable energy storm, one ship in the group was destroyed, but two others emerged despite extensive damages. The voyagers had valiantly held their ships together until they reached a habitable world not identified on any of the star charts contained in their vast computer banks. Salvaging everything possible from their vessels, they had shuttled back and forth until both crews were safe on the uninhabited world they called Yezabrá Chikondra.

Survivors concentrated on constructing shelter and establishing means to provide basic requirements for life. The world they had discovered was rich in resources and natural beauty. Their collective consciousness accepted Yezabrá Chikondra as home. Religious rites continued, but origins were lost. The format of their language froze in time. As centuries passed, the history of the old world was relegated to the stuff of legend and fairy tale.

Isrina then explained how her ki'medsah had stumbled upon an ancient city long abandoned. While exploring the site, the Chikondran settlers discovered amazing, functional technology. They also found massive underground caverns concealing four starships. Brilliant minds studied, analyzed, and deciphered. They quickly realized their discovery provided means to move into space and far from the planet they called home.

Although they taught themselves to pilot the ships around their own star system, they had seen no need to utilize their incredible discovery until a strange ship landed on Yezabrá Chikondra. Leaders from that ship had demonstrated friendly attitudes but had received wary welcomes. Within days, the alien officers recognized the potential value of their discovery. With no knowledge that natives had access to interstellar travel, they attacked a school and abducted many children, including the two sons of Sidrihn and Isrina Kimasou.

Sidrihn had immediately taken action. The starships were launched. Perfectly preserved uniforms were donned by families desperate to retrieve abducted children. With highly advanced sensors and scanners locked onto energy trails, they pursued the rogue ship, determined to rescue their children.

Mechanical problems that had brought the enemy ship to Yezabrá Chikondra recurred, causing it to slow upon reaching the Ashapat system. Spotting the York as it emerged from hyperspace, the vessel fired multiple rounds on the military transport in hopes of distracting tenacious pursuers. Reentering hyperspace, one of the Chikondran ships continued the chase while the second stopped long enough to retrieve the ill-fated shuttle piloted by Captain McAllen. After bringing survivors safely on board his starship, Captain Kimasou had discarded the useless shuttle and doggedly resumed his original course. He focused on a single goal, the recovery of his two sons.

✧✧✧

Chancellor Meyahfra addressed Warnach sympathetically. "You cannot advocate war simply because your ki'mirsah was killed in a fluke attack in a remote solar system. This Alliance is comprised of countless citizens who would suffer from war."

Warnach glared furiously at the chancellor. "Excellency, my lifemate did not die in a fluke attack. Your memory obviously fails if you have forgotten attacks in the Medron sector and the more recent assaults near Nipapwa and Iquasht. Zeteron forces grow bolder with each day that passes. I would never advocate war except as a last resort. However, I demand that we immediately implement powerful defenses to protect those citizens for whom you claim to be so worried!"

Meyahfra stood up and leaned forward. "You have no right to demand any such action, Master Sirinoya. This decision resides within my scope of power, and I will not allow it."

Master Khalijar jumped to his feet as several colleagues murmured to one another around the Circle of Masters. "I agree, Excellency. You do hold decision power. You are also charged with responsibility to protect this Alliance. As a member of this circle, Master Sirinoya has every right to demand that you exercise that responsibility!"

"Gentlemen," Meyahfra said, raising his hands, "calm yourselves. The two of you are reacting more from personal loss than sensible consideration."

Master Devorius stood. Pale blue irises widened with angry regard. "Excellency, I have exercised my own responsibility by discussing this matter privately with every council master present, except for Masters Khalijar and Sirinoya. Not one agrees with you. The Zeteron Empire has grown tired of unsuccessful attempts to destabilize this Alliance. They now initiate forays to test our will to defend ourselves. Delay invites doom. Since you are unwilling to accept the advice of this Council, I hereby move that we adjourn for one hour. When we reconvene, I shall call for a vote to initiate your removal from an office with responsibilities you refuse to fulfill."

Joining Master Devorius, Master Barishta added his voice. "With due respect, Honorable Master Devorius, I suggest there is no need for an adjournment. I move that we place this matter on the table for an immediate vote."

Meyahfra's face reddened with fury. "How dare you? I am the duly elected leader of this Alliance! I want peace, not war!"

"I dare, Chancellor Meyahfra, because you turn your back on the safety and the future of this Alliance. Although not a single master present wants war, each recognizes that only the strongest defensive measures can hope to stave off galactic catastrophe."

Barishta leaned across the table and pointedly looked from face to face around the table. "Fellow Masters, we face the most threatening crisis our Alliance has ever encountered. There is little time for hesitation. I call now for a vote to hold a referendum to remove Chancellor Meyahfra from office."

One by one, eighteen robed masters stood. "Ashay." One yes after another. Only one, a close friend of Meyahfra, declined. The majority prevailed.

"You will not humiliate me with your damned referendum!" Meyahfra declared furiously. "You have my immediate resignation!"

Meyahfra stormed from the Circle of Masters. The remaining masters viewed Meyafra's unresisting departure as justification for the decision to oust him from the chancellery. Dreading consequences of their unprecedented action, they faced their next task: the selection of a new leader, one capable of facing trials ahead.

Camudahmni Lobrihm studied script on the yellowed pages of an ancient tome. The eerie hush of rustling satin robes claimed his attention as he looked upward to see Nadana Kimasou approach. With a tranquil smile, he invited her to sit and noted sadness in tired eyes. "If the prophets were truly inspired, Respected Simlani, this is no more than another sign bidding us prepare more quickly for coming tribulations."

"I don't understand," she replied.

"Are you aware that there is a final sign omitted from the better-known versions of the legend prophesying the Mi'yafá Si'imlayaná?"

Nadana's gaze intensified. "A final sign?"

"Yes," the wise old man nodded. "We shall soon know if our silent wait and careful teachings of your nephew's children were naught but unnecessary precaution."

"Esteemed Camudahmni, what sign do we await?"

The wise elder pointed to a spot on parchment opened before him and read aloud. "Children of faith will cast their eyes to Yahvanta's heavens. Tears from the guardian warrior's eyes will dry when his wandering helper's light returns, borne by children lost. Given the sacred sign, the wise ones will know the time is at hand to prepare all children of Chikondra for the darkness that will surely befall them."

Nadana mulled over scriptures shared with her alone. What did those ancient writings mean? How much did she believe? Had she possibly seen signs where none existed? Could she dare to hope?

Before she had time to voice her doubts, the Camudahmni placed the sacred book aside. "I am not certain how this could come to pass. The advice from this old man is to shed sadness and guard strength. The time of prophecy is closer than either of us thought."

Nadana's head inclined respectfully. "And the children?"

"Watch over them, Respected Simlani. Say nothing. When the time comes, they will say all."

Concealed by heavy undergrowth, Mac and Sandra watched in tense silence. About two dozen children huddled together before a glowing outdoor furnace. Many looked sick or hurt. Younger ones whimpered. Older ones offered comfort. With repairs hastily underway on the damaged ship, guards either scolded the Yezabrá children in words none understood or harshly struck them.

Sandra's eyes reflected grave determination as she readied herself. A sidelong glance caught Sidrihn's signal. From twenty meters opposite them, a series of high-pitched screeches filled the night. Birds squawked in protest. Animal moans rose above the forest floor. Zeterons and children alike were felled by the ear-piercing signals. With their ears protected by special plugs, Mac, Sandra, and others from the York fired deadly rays directly at the open hatch of the Zeteron ship. Meanwhile, courageous Chikondrans snatched up the children and raced back into the protective cover of tall reeds and brush.

Swooping down from a cloaked orbit, one of the Chikondran ships fired at the enemy vessel. For people who had never known the violence of war, their aim had been deadly accurate. The Zeteron ship would never again attack unsuspecting victims, nor would it steal innocent children.

Weeks later, Captain Kimasou reviewed star charts contained in the small computer Sandra had grabbed before she fled her quarters on board the York. As she translated, he and Mac discussed the safest way to enter Alliance space without provoking an attack. Despite technology advanced even beyond that possessed by the Alliance, the Chikondran starships were incapable of voice transmissions.

Afterward, Sandra wearily headed toward the ward set up for the children. Many had been beaten. Others were seriously ill. Isrina raised hopeful eyes to her strange ally. Her younger son was among the sickest. "Are you certain there is hope for my baby?"

Sandra's expression masked doubt with hope. "I believe so. Our hospitals have special machines that accelerate healing. I pray we arrive in time."

"Captain, are you sure?"

"Positive, sir. Vessel configurations are unlike any in our archives. They just suddenly appeared on scanners and are on a direct course to Chikondra."

"Are any hostile intentions indicated?" Badrik listened attentively as he initiated orders bringing all of Chikondra's military forces to full alert status.

"None, sir. Fighter squadrons intercepting…now."

"Do not fire without my command. We may be nearing war, but we will not engage unless we know those ships are hostile."

Tension swiftly heightened. A steady stream of reports crossed lighted displays. The unfamiliar starships slowed their speed on their continued approach toward Chikondra. Badrik monitored all transmissions. He also prayed.

"Damn it, Brinker! Reconnect the circuit!" Mac grew impatient. "If we don't make some kind of transmission, we can't be sure they won't attack."

"Done. Let's just hope this works, sir."

"Sandra, I hope you know what the hell you're doing. Otherwise, we may all die today. We're entering orbit around Chikondra, and an entire fleet of starfighters surrounds us."

Breathing in, she nodded. Deftly, her fingers started tapping codes into the crude transmission device. Once. Twice. She repeated secret ministry codes a third time. Sitting back, she waited.

Voices buzzed inside the air command center near the capital city of Kadranas. A communications officer spun around in her chair. "General Sirinoya! We're receiving a transmission!"

Leaving his seat and rapidly approaching the younger officer, Badrik leaned over her shoulder. "What sort of transmission?"

"Some sort of code. Analyzing now." Colored lights flashed across the console pad. The comm officer pressed her hand against slim earphones. She lifted shocked eyes to the general. "The computer identifies it as an Alliance security code, sir. A field ministry code."

"What? Are you sure?" With a surprised nod, Badrik then unceremoniously shoved the officer aside and swung into the chair in front of the control panel. Holding the earphone close to his ear, he listened to the computer analysis. Quickly, he keyed his secret code to unlock secure ministry archives. As seconds passed, his breathing quickened.

The emotionless computer voice responded. "Code identified and confirmed as issued to Minister Sandra Sirinoya."

Disbelief instantly gave way to frantic action. Badrik keyed codes requesting repetition of the transmission. Seconds again spanned what felt like an eternity. The coded transmission repeated. One. Two. Three. Closing his eyes, Badrik swallowed hard. Dared he try? He keyed a private code he had given her in case of an emergency. He held his breath. A pause. A third transmission.

"Eyach'hamá eu Yahvanta!" he exclaimed, bolting from the chair. "Captain, notify our starfighters to guide those vessels for a landing on this base! Tell them to sustain top alert status but advise them there's an Alliance ministry official onboard one of those ships!"

Badrik issued a rapid succession of orders to command officers, including the dispatch of a military pilot to Alliance Central Headquarters. He then ran to his office, slamming the door behind him. It required several attempts before he was able to calm himself. Quickly, he breathed a fervent prayer that there was no mistake. He then pressed the code to his brother's private office and waited.

"Warnach?"

"Badrik? What's happening? This entire complex just went on high alert and is undergoing security lockdown."

"Warnach, listen. Leave your office immediately and go to the rear security exit. A military escort is on its way to bring you here."

"Badrik, are we under attack? If we are, I'm leaving to get Morcai and Lucia."

"No, we're not under attack. I praise Yahvanta that there's no sign of any attack underway across the Alliance."

"Then..."

"Warnach, starfighters are escorting two starships to the base here. Origin and design of the alien vessels are unknown. However, they're transmitting valid codes - field ministry security codes."

"Field ministry codes?"

"Yes." Badrik paused, again praying he wasn't wrong. "Warnach, the codes belong to Sandra."

For a moment, Warnach felt faint as he stared at her photograph on his desk. Lifting sensitive fingertips to his Kitak, he gasped. Was it possible? Gulping in a deep breath of air, he propelled his chair backward and leapt forward into a headlong dash from his office and through corridors leading to the exit to meet the escort sent by his brother.

Surrounded by soldiers and aides, Badrik rushed outside. Bright sunshine was blocked by the hulking size of a silver-skinned starship descending onto the specially constructed landing pad. Armed troops assumed strategic positions as starfighters crisscrossed the skies. At safe distances, ambulance transports gathered.

Badrik continuously barked commands into the tiny mouthpiece connected to the slim band circling his head. A jumble of communications streamed through his earphone. Impatiently, he waved aside aides who insisted that he seek protective cover. He observed attentively as the mysterious vessel settled onto slim support beams that had extended with a whir.

Hundreds of armed soldiers tensely waited. Starfighters continued streaking above the base. A smooth, mechanical hum sliced through heavy silence. From a broad opening, a ramp of shining metal mesh lowered. Badrik's breath grew ragged. His heartbeat raced. Raising his right hand, he signaled gathered forces to stand ready.

"Wait for my signal, Mac. We need to be sure they know there's no danger." She smiled encouragingly at Isrina. "Patience, my friend. I promise. We'll get those children to hospital."

Cautiously, Sandra took one slow step at a time. Wearing a borrowed black uniform, she realized how menacing she must look. Pausing before descending all the way, she stared at the statuesque figure standing about twenty meters ahead. Taking final steps onto solid ground, she smiled shakily and called out, "Badrik!"

Seconds later, abandoning all semblance of military reserve, Badrik joyously wrapped her in his arms. Finally, disbelieving eyes stared into tear-stained features. "My sister! We thought…"

"I know," she whispered. "Badrik, I'm fine, but we need help. Desperately. Come."

Hurriedly advising his aides to stand by for further orders, he followed Sandra into the strange ship. Immediately recognizing Mac, he inclined his head. "Captain McAllen."

"Badrik," Sandra said quietly in Chikondran, "I want you to meet our rescuers. This is Captain Sidrihn Kimasou and his ki'mirsah, Isrina."

Quickly masking bewilderment, Badrik bowed in a formal salute returned by the strangers. "I am General Badrik Sirinoya. I welcome you to Chikondra and the Kadranas Air Command

Center. Forgive my boldness, but have I heard correctly that you are Kimasou?"

Sidrihn nodded seriously. "My family is Kimasou, from the old world of Chikondra."

"The old world? It seems we have much to discuss since my mamehr is also Kimasou. However, that must wait. My sister says you require help."

Isrina nodded. "People called Zeterons abducted children from our planet. Your sister and her friends helped us rescue them. Many are sick and hurt. They need medical care our ship is not equipped to provide."

Within minutes, Badrik's officers initiated rapid coordination of efforts to care for the Chikondran children. Medical transports formed lines at the end of the ramp as paramedics examined patients and swiftly organized their transfer to base hospital facilities also on alert. Several adults, including Isrina, were allowed to accompany the victims.

His expression worried, Sidrihn stood outside and watched as transports lifted and veered away from his starship. He turned grateful eyes to Badrik. "Your aid will not be forgotten."

Badrik smiled. "Captain, you have saved the life of my sister and brought her home. Since it seems we are likely tied by blood, I would say this is what families do for one another."

Sidrihn choked back growing tightness in his throat. How incomprehensible this all seemed. Sandra firmly grasped his arm. "Our doctors are exceptional. They will do everything possible to help your children."

"Sandra?"

Turning her attention from Sidrihn, Sandra noted Badrik's forward nod. Looking around, she saw a small transport land about forty meters away. As the door lifted, Warnach hurriedly exited the vehicle and stared anxiously toward the crowd of people near the ramp of the alien ship.

Bursting through a throng of aides, soldiers, and visitors, Sandra shouted Warnach's name. Launching into a dead run, she raced across the landing pad until she leapt into his arms.

Overjoyed, Warnach clutched her so tightly she could hardly breathe. "Sandra! Me'u Shi'níyah! Eyach'hamá eu Yahvanta!" His voice broke. "I thought I'd lost you! Eyach'hamá eu Yahvanta! You're alive! You're alive!"

Simultaneously laughing and crying, she pressed her face against his chest. "Yes, me'u ki'medsah, I'm still alive! Ci'ittá mi'ittá, me'u Warnach."

Emotion-laden minutes passed before he could bear to loosen his embrace. Still, he found it impossible to release her. With his right hand raised, he pressed her face against the firmness of his shoulder. His tears wet her hair. Trembling lips whispered her name.

Finally, she gently pushed against his chest. Gazing into beloved black eyes, she caressed his damp cheek. "Me'u Warnach, come. I know how shocking this is, but you must meet the people who saved me."

By mid-afternoon, after stunning introductions and revelations, Sandra felt confident leaving arrangements for her rescuers in capable ministry hands. After promising to meet Sidrihn and Isrina at the hospital the next morning, she excused herself to go home for a reunion with her children.

Piloted in an official ministry transport, Warnach and she clung to each other during the entire trip home. Arriving at the estate, she drank in the sight of the house and grounds. How wonderful home felt. Holding her hand as if he feared she might evaporate into thin air, Warnach led her through double doors.

Inside the foyer, he dared to kiss her for the first time since her return. Reluctantly, he dragged hungry lips from hers. A shaky smile spread his mouth. "Wait here, Shi'níyah. Badrik said there's a news blackout. I think it best to prepare Mamehr and the children."

"Hurry, Warnach. You can't imagine how much I want to hold my babies."

When he entered the kitchen, Araman looked up with a puzzled expression that mirrored surprise on the faces of Morcai and Lucia. "Warnach, you're home early," Araman began, studying his odd look. "Would you care to join us for our afternoon treat?"

Shaking his head, Warnach hurried to the table and knelt between his two children. Smiling at his mamehr through fresh tears, he then looked from Morcai to Lucia. "I think if you two go to the foyer, you'll find a much more delightful treat waiting for you." Rising with the children, he prompted them with a broad grin. "Go. I think you'll both be very happy."

As the children left while casting doubtful glances over their shoulders, Araman approached her son and took his hand. "What?"

"A miracle, Mamehr. A true mira…" Joyous screams echoing from the front of the house interrupted him. He turned glistening eyes to Araman. "She's home, Mamehr. My ki'mirsah has come home."

Unabashed excitement calmed slowly. Stories of mystery and rescue followed an onslaught of questions and lasted through dinner. Laughter then mixed with tears when they connected an emotional com-link to Earth. Evening prayers assumed fresh dimension and profound meaning. Bedtime was late coming with neither child wanting sleep to separate them from their mother.

Finally, the house quieted. Lifting Sandra's hand to full lips, Warnach's eyes fixed upon ivory features. Drawing her close, he felt rejuvenating energy flood every part of his body. Numbness that had afflicted him disappeared. In her presence, he discovered resurrection for his soul.

Without a word, he led her upstairs to the suite where he had retreated during the sixteen weeks he had believed her dead. In silence, he lit dozens of candles scattered on decorative columns around the room. After lighting several incense cones, he turned. Watching as she pulled down the bed's silk comforter, he felt every muscle in his body sharply contract with need.

Going to her, he bent forward and captured delicate lips. What began as a gentle kiss suddenly flamed into full possession of her mouth. Tasting the inviting sweetness just beyond her parted lips only whetted his appetite for more. Desperate hands removed her Kitak and set it aside on the night table. Long fingers tangled in her hair, deepening the kiss until he could no longer bear the feel of clothing separating them.

As his shaking fingers undid buttons on the shirt worn beneath her Yezabrá uniform, she took his Kitak and, twisting, joined it to hers for the first time in months. Undressing him, she gasped when their bodies finally touched. The heat of his skin against hers far exceeded the effects of any aphrodisiac known to the galaxy. Guided backward onto the bed, she clung to him as her need grew exponentially with his.

For hours, yielding to unleashed passions, they were each conqueror and conquered. Words were saturated with expressions of love. Pleading whispers. Soft moans. Lingering caresses and powerful strokes. Bodies in constant motion, fueling the physical manifestation of their unified love. Dazzling explosions of overwhelming sensation.

With candles finally extinguished, he lay with his face cushioned against her breast. Her presence had calmed raging grief. Her touch had erased overwhelming sorrow. Her love had once again restored peace.

His thoughts wandered as he lay beside her. Outside their nighttime haven, times grew more unsettled. Threats loomed, enveloping the future in clouds of doubt. Events imprinted sharp talons upon life itself. He realized that her strength and her love were his safe place to escape. Changing position, he snaked his arm beneath hers and held her until he fell asleep.

Farisa's expression was grave. "I wish I could give them some cause for hope. Only the younger ones are affected. All suffer from unidentified, rapidly reproducing parasites. Treatments to slow the process have been useless."

Sandra bit into her lower lip. Her heart broke for Isrina, whose son was very young and among the sickest. Thanking Farisa, she grasped Lucia's hand and headed toward the quarantined rooms. Before knocking on the door to speak with Isrina, she knelt and looked into Lucia's eyes. "I think it's better if you stay out here."

"Momma, the parasites won't hurt me."

"They won't if they can't get to you, sweetheart."

"I want to see the boy. His mamehr saved you. I can talk to him and make him feel better."

Farisa had said only children under five had been affected. Sandra feared for Lucia but decided to relegate any risk to God's care. "You're right. His parents did save my life. Maybe we can help a little. You can go in for a few minutes, all right?"

Inside, little Ehmrihm fussed. His face glistened with perspiration. His mother's face shone with tears. "My baby is dying," she whispered brokenly.

Sandra encircled the distraught mother's shoulders. "We came to be with you."

Isrina looked down and braved a smile. "You must be Lucia. You shouldn't be here, little one."

To Sandra's surprise, Lucia responded in the same old form of Chikondran spoken by Isrina. "It is my place to be here. Momma and I came to help."

Seeing that Isrina was near a breakdown, Sandra suggested Lucia talk to the little boy for a few minutes. In the corridor outside, a nurse offered Isrina a cup of tea just as blinding light flashed from Ehmrihm's room. Sandra spun around and, with Isrina and the nurse at her heels, ran back to the room. "Lucia! Lucia, what happened?"

Serene and wide-eyed, Lucia said quietly, "Nothing, Momma. Ehmrihm and I were talking. I think he feels better now."

"Ehmrihm!" Isrina gasped, rushing to her son's bedside and pulling him to her breast. "My little one! What happened? Are you all right?"

Weakly, the child smiled. "Mamehr, may I go to sleep? Lucia made me feel better. I'm really tired now."

While the nurse inspected lighting and equipment, a doctor joined them and scanned the little boy. Her forehead creased into confounded lines. "Nurse!" she ordered briskly. "Bring me another scanner! Hurry!" Turning to Sandra, she asked her to step aside with Isrina.

Terrified, Isrina watched as the physician reviewed results from the second scanner. Her eyes quickly moved from the room's special care monitor to two handheld units. Readings were identical.

"Ladies," she explained five minutes later, "I shall request another full examination, but as unbelievable as it sounds, scanners indicate that something has neutralized the parasites. Essentially, they're disintegrating and already moving through his bloodstream with other substances for elimination. I have no medical explanation."

With a shocked smile, Isrina leaned over Ehmrihm. Her mother's eyes instantly noted differences around his eyes. Blotches were already slowly fading from his skin. Sensitive lips detected a slightly lower temperature. With a sob of relief, she climbed onto his bed, pulled him onto her lap, and rocked him back and forth.

In disbelief, Sandra clasped her daughter's hand. Leading Lucia to a waiting area, she sat down. Bewilderment shone from her eyes as she gazed at the girl. Not wanting to frighten her, she caressed a smooth cheek. "Sweetheart, all of us in the hall saw a brilliant light from Ehmrihm's room. What was it?"

"I didn't see any light, Momma."

Sandra's head fell forward, and she drew in a calming breath. "Lucia, something happened in there. We all saw a very bright light, and now Ehmrihm is suddenly better. How could you not have seen such a light?"

Tears brimmed in Lucia's eyes. "Momma, there are other sick children. I want to help them, too."

"Oh, baby, we all do, but we don't know how."

Lucia swallowed and swiped a tear from her cheek. "Momma, I know. I can tell you, but you must promise to keep the secret. You can't even tell Badehr."

"Secret? Lucia, what kind of secret?"

"Momma, you have to promise first. Then, you have to help me."

Observing almost frightening intensity in her daughter's eyes, Sandra struggled to stay calm. "I promise, Lucia. I'll never tell anyone unless you say so. Did the light make him better?" Receiving the slightest of nods, Sandra pressed ahead. "But, baby, you said you didn't see any light."

"I didn't, Momma." Lucia reached out with arms that circled her mother's neck. She then whispered into Sandra's ear. "I didn't see the light, Momma. I *was* the light."

Shaking off initial shock, Sandra's embrace around her daughter tightened. In truth, she should have known. Glancing upward, she saw Warnach appear in the wide doorway. Questions filled his eyes. Reaching them, he knelt on one knee and lovingly combed fingers through waist-length curls.

"We were with the older Kimasou boy when nurses came for Sidrihn. When we got there, they said I'd find you here. What happened? Are you two all right?"

Closing her eyes, Sandra placed a kiss against Lucia's hair. "We're fine. We were just stunned to hear about Ehmrihm's abrupt recovery. We needed a private celebration of our own."

Stretching out his hand and cupping his palm against Sandra's face, Warnach smiled. "Two miracles in as many days.

I believe a celebration is in order. I left Morcai with Gehrnach. I'll go get him, and we can go home."

"Warnach," Sandra said softly as he stood, "please, stay with the boys until I come. I promised to help Lucia with something."

Narrowing eyes looked puzzled. Sensing an odd tone in her voice, he gave a slight shrug. Without argument, he nodded and left.

Watching her lifemate disappear, Sandra held Lucia away and gently lifted her chin. "We must hurry, baby. Those children are very sick, and it may not be easy for Momma to get the doctors and nurses out of the way."

"Here, me'u Shi'níyah. A lovely glass of wine."

"Mmm, Chilean. My favorite," she said with a smile.

Joining her on the sofa, Warnach turned and leaned sideways against the thickly cushioned sofa back. Drinking from his glass, he swirled rich liquid around his mouth before swallowing. Lowered eyelids concealed burning curiosity. "You must admit. Today was more than a little strange."

Evasively, she said, "No more than most I've spent recently."

Warnach's eyebrow cocked high. "No? You don't think six miraculously cured children are stranger than an encounter with displaced Chikondrans?"

Sandra sniffed her wine and took another sip. "Warnach, since we met, extraordinary events have become quite the norm."

Several moments passed in speculative silence. "Me'u ki'mirsah, I love you with all of my self. I also know when you're holding back. All of those children were near death and then suddenly got better after you and Lucia visited. Please, tell me what happened today."

Setting aside her glass, she shifted in order to gaze directly into his eyes. "Me'u Warnach, if I really knew what happened today, I'd tell you. Since I don't, I think you should take me upstairs, because I need some of my Chikondran lifemate's magic touch."

Grinning wryly, he shook his head. His eyes darkened. A sultry, amorous expression transformed handsome features. "Clever diversion."

She leaned forward. Her lips captured his lower lip and tugged slightly. She murmured in a deliberately sexy voice, "Clever doesn't matter. Only success counts."

Low-pitched laughter emerged from his throat as he gladly surrendered. "Come then, me'u Shi'níyah. Let's go upstairs and explore your concept of success."

Chapter Twelve

The Yezabrá Chikondrans remained in Kadranas for ten days. Meanwhile, they learned about changes on their ancestral world during the centuries since the fateful mission of their forebears. Bonded by tradition and blood, they forged strong friendships with their hosts.

As a guest in the Sirinoya home, Sidrihn Kimasou observed his younger son with Lucia. "They seem to have formed a strong friendship very quickly," Sidrihn said as he and Warnach sat outside on a spacious patio.

Warnach smiled while watching Lucia patiently roll a ball across a wide expanse of thick, emerald green grass. "I must agree."

Picking up a tall glass, Sidrihn sipped a chilled drink. His voice carried hesitation when he spoke again. "News of more attacks in the Medron sector is troubling. Are you certain war for your Alliance is imminent?"

As his smile faded, Warnach's eyes darkened. "War is much closer than most wish to believe. I fear a lack of readiness on many Alliance worlds."

"On Chikondra, as well?"

Warnach shook his head. "I would like to believe Chikondra is safe, but prophecies tell of a dark time. My personal belief is that the predicted darkness is close at hand. Chikondra has ready military defenses, but our people are not warriors."

Pensively, Sidrihn responded, "Chikondra is far from the attacks. Surely these Zeterons would not penetrate this far into your Alliance."

Discussions with Badrik rolled through Warnach's mind. "My assessment of Zeteron strategy differs from that of most politicians and Alliance military intelligence. The Zeterons are patient, cunning adversaries. They're also unpredictable. We know too little about them to rule out anything."

After a prolonged pause, Sidrihn spoke again. "We must leave tomorrow to return the children to their homes and families. However, Isrina and I have discussed the situation your Alliance faces. The ships we brought were our fastest and, therefore, more suitable for pursuit. Two more starships remain on our world. Those ships were designed for war. The prospect is frightening because we have always known peace. However, considering all your scientists have learned from our vessels, Isrina and I believe Chikondra might need the others even more if war truly lies ahead. We have decided to assemble a crew of volunteers and return with those ships."

"You would do that?"

Sidrihn stared ahead. "Your ki'mirsah risked her life helping us save our children. My son lives because of this world. To leave and never look back would be poor repayment."

Warnach gave a heavy sigh. "What she did came from her heart. Remember. You delayed your rescue mission to save her and the crew with her. I see no debt owed by anyone."

Sidrihn finally smiled. Recalling Badrik's words the day the Yezabrá ships landed, he finally looked around. "Then, let us say our return to help is what families do for one another."

Although worry lines did not vanish from Warnach's face, his expression reflected gratitude. "My cousin, although I sincerely hope to be mistaken, I believe your assistance will be needed and heartily welcomed."

Four days after the Yezabrá Chikondrans departed, Sandra strolled through midsummer woods. With slender arms, tall grasses reached skyward for the sun. Dense foliage on trees fluttered and danced, allowing teasing peeks of sunshine to sneak through and dapple stone pathways with light and shadow. Clearings wore jewels of yellow, blue, red, and purple wildflowers. Rich soil and nature's wealth combined to saturate fresh air with the fragrance of life.

Finally, while sitting on a patch of grass, her rambling thoughts converged. Past months seemed almost bizarre. Had the attack on the military transport not occurred, she would never have encountered the Yezabrá Chikondrans. The Yezabrá would have continued their mission without Mac's strategic guidance that had aided the rescue of the children. Even if the Yezabrá had successfully recovered the children, several would have died without Chikondra's HAU's or…

Again, her thoughts jumbled. Six children had survived because of Lucia's direct intervention. Sandra's brain strained to grasp the concept, let alone the reality. Her thoughts still reeled from the effect of Lucia's simple declaration that she had been the saving light. What did that really mean? How could she possibly explore the subject with a ten-year-old who accepted what she was without understanding herself? Sandra's head shook as if she could shake the puzzle pieces into proper position.

"Me'u Shi'níyah, you look troubled."

Glancing upward, she couldn't quite manage a smile. Seeing her hesitation, he came closer and dropped onto the ground in front of her. His hand reached out and caressed her cheek. "How glad I am to have you back. I would be happier yet if I understood those shadows in your eyes."

"Not shadows exactly. Questions, I think. Understanding everything that's happened recently turns my mind upside down."

Quietly, he plucked at sturdy blades of grass. "I continue to sense conflict through Kitak. I'm not wrong when I say you don't tell me all on your mind."

How desperately she wanted to explore with him their daughter's strange explanation for the otherwise inexplicable healing of the Yezabrá children. She exhaled heavily and shifted position so she could stretch out on the grass with Warnach's muscular thigh for her pillow. Closing her eyes, she could think of no words to say. Instead, she escaped into delightfully tingling sensations created by his fingers stroking through her hair.

Minutes passed. "Why do you not confide in me?" His tone of voice conveyed concern and, perhaps, an edge of reproach.

Swallowing, she forced an answer. "Me'u ki'medsah, I made a solemn promise. If you only knew how much I wish I didn't have to keep that promise."

Warnach's fingers tracked along the edge of her Kitak. Her distraction was so intense. His thoughts involuntarily drifted to a brief, private encounter that morning with Captain McAllen before the Terran's departure from Chikondra. "Are you concerned about an incident or a person?"

"A combination." Pausing, she grasped his hand and kissed his fingers. "Warnach, don't be upset with me. You know I'd tell you if I could."

His tone lowered. "My past often makes me wary of secrets."

She stiffened slightly, then sat up and stared into his eyes. "Secrets? Like the beautiful woman you met in the park while I was away?"

Startled, he stared back. "The children told you?"

Her lips pursed together. "Morcai mentioned it."

"It was a chance encounter. Nothing more."

"Yet it makes you question me as if I've done something wrong," she countered in a wounded voice.

"If that is your reaction, I apologize. You know I trust you."

Reaching out, she touched his hair. "Warnach, you know how I feel about keeping promises. I vowed a long time ago that my love for you would never falter. After all we've lived through together, you surely must know that promise is even stronger now."

Although he wished differently, he knew his expression reflected relief. Diplomatically, she said nothing. Instead, she drew him closer. Guiding his head onto her lap, she lovingly caressed dark features with her eyes. Her lips formed words that reminded him that his life was again his.

"Ci'ittá mi'ittá, me'u Warnach. Ci'ittá mi'ittá."

"How long it's been since I took time to go to the beach!" Farsuk exclaimed in a jovial voice. Affectionately, he tugged at the length of Morcai's hair pulled back into an elastic band. "Be kind enough to help an old man with his things."

"With pleasure, sir." Morcai's eyes glittered with good humor as he hoisted the tote over his shoulder and headed toward the beach house.

Farsuk smiled approvingly at Warnach and Badrik. "That young man does his parents proud." Glancing toward shore, he saw Michahn and Lucia already on hands and knees, scooping white sand into mountains that would become fantasy castles. "As do those two."

Badrik nodded. "My brother and I are both blessed and relieved that our children aren't as troublesome as we were."

Farsuk grinned happily. Years had passed since Badrik had spoken to him with so little reserve. Neither godson had forgotten the near-tragedy of Sandra's brush with death during Ku'saá. However, while tensions with Warnach had eased because of his lifemate's influence, Badrik had remained aloof and distant ever since. His casual mood this day delivered sparks of joy to his godfather's heart.

As the day passed, Araman and Ifta prepared lunch while Farsuk relaxed by watching boisterous games of volleyball and admiring whimsical sand creatures crafted by imaginative children. Several times, he leaned forward beneath his broad beach umbrella to cheer aggressive players charging the game net. Frequently, he trotted across the sand and knelt to study unique shells discovered by Michahn and Lucia. For a while, with an arm around Morcai's shoulder, he walked along the shore and talked of odd facts related to ancient ocean travel.

Lunchtime began with a prayer and ended with rowdy competition for hammocks swaying invitingly in afternoon breezes. Naptime overtook adults and children alike as the ocean rolled soothing lullabies on shore and drew them back into softly rushing waters.

Children were first to awaken and leave their hammocks. Bare feet kicked up clouds of sand as they hurried back to shore. Somewhat disappointed, Michahn soon returned. Farisa was leaving early for Kadranas to drop her son off at a friend's house for a birthday party. Badrik would stay behind to enjoy the remainder of the afternoon.

While Ifta and Araman retired inside the house for the comfort of cooler temperatures, Farsuk remained on the bungalow patio with Warnach, Badrik, and Sandra. Conversation avoided current political maneuverings and turned toward the astounding discovery of the Yezabrá Chikondrans. Especially curious, Farsuk questioned Sandra about her experiences onboard their spacecraft.

Laughingly, she described attempts to communicate in the modern, contracted version of Chikondran while her rescuers spoke the more protracted form from centuries past. In her typically animated style with hands flying every direction, she described odd misunderstandings and embarrassing blunders.

Abruptly, in the middle of relating a hilarious encounter with the solemn Captain Kimasou, she stopped mid-sentence. Seconds later, Morcai appeared on the patio. "Momma?"

Farsuk's brow knitted together as he noted unspoken communication between mother and son. Sandra's response to Morcai's single word puzzled him even more.

"I know, sweetheart. I hear them. I'll join you in a minute."

Casting glances toward Badrik and Farsuk, she grasped Warnach's hand and smiled. "Excuse me. We have visitors," she murmured.

Feather-soft breezes whispered from the open ocean onto the shore. Standing motionless at the point where stiff grass met white sand, she gazed at her children who were staring out toward the horizon. Her mind registered the voices of the marine friends calling her name along with those of Morcai and Lucia. The fact that all three could hear Quazon voices still astounded her.

Sensing imminent arrival of the Quazon, Sandra trotted forward. Holding hands, mother and children moved out into shimmering waters and, within moments, were greeted by a wave of splashes. The lacy tunic Sandra wore over her swimsuit was quickly soaked. Lucia, dressed in a pink bathing suit, giggled at playful antics while Morcai surrendered any attempt to maintain a more dignified demeanor and joined in the fun fracas.

As play subsided, Quazon swam close to them and welcomed affectionate caresses. Sensing invitation, Lucia grasped a large fin and, straddling a Quazon adult, clung to the gentle creature for a smooth glide across the waters. Keeping careful watch, Sandra asked Morcai to summon his badehr and to bring Badrik and Farsuk.

There was no need for her to turn around. She felt Farsuk's stunned eyes upon her. Instead, she continued to concentrate on her visitors as Morcai joined the new game of riding the waves while holding onto the strong Quazon.

Glancing over her shoulder, she smiled as Warnach reached for her hand.

Badrik joined them with a jolly exclamation. "Sister! Tell your friends how glad I am to see them again!"

Laughing out loud, Sandra shook her head. "You just did! Do you think they don't understand?"

Tentatively, Farsuk edged closer to his godsons. His eyes were wide with childlike wonder. His aging features drew into a frozen, disbelieving smile. Not once had anyone mentioned Quazon since the day Sandra had told him the sacred angel spirits had asked her to forgive him. If memories of that day invaded, he usually dismissed them as a peculiar dream. Now, in their presence, he felt completely awestruck.

Suddenly, one of the smaller Quazon swam toward him and, with an acrobatic twist, landed a broad tail against the ocean surface, sending a spray of water into his face. Sandra laughed aloud. "He just said hello!"

The venerable statesman laughed nervously. "What should I do?"

Bounding across swelling tides, Sandra grabbed his hand. "Here! Like this!"

With her hand wrapped tightly around his wrist, he watched as she drew his fingers across slick, silvery skin. Again, she repeated the action. Suddenly, with a broad grin, he bravely stroked the sleek hide of one of the adults gliding past him. As reward, he received a face full of saltwater.

After the last Quazon disappeared, Badrik and Warnach led their godfather back to shore. Araman awaited them on the beach with Ifta, whose shock kept her speechless. While Farsuk chattered as excitedly as a child, Warnach turned his eyes back to the sea. His family stood close together in foaming tidewaters. Although he could see none of their faces, their very posture belied earlier levity. Instead, they listened to voices only they could hear, and he wondered what it was those voices were saying.

Chapter Thirteen

Sitting cross-legged at the foot of the bed, Sandra plucked at the folded silk comforter. Her eyes stared blindly at smooth, cream-colored sheets. Free from the restraints of Kitak, shining brunette hair fell in a concealing cascade. "I'm not sure what to say."

Leaning forward, Warnach stretched out his bare arm and, with just the tips of long fingers, tilted her face upward. "Shi'níyah, you know potential dangers as well as I. Farsuk and I have discussed this from every angle. The Alliance needs solid, experienced leadership. No one can fulfill that need better than Farsuk."

"But for you to leave your ministry post. What about the added responsibility? Have you fully considered the impact on our family? Morcai and Lucia are at ages where they need you more than ever."

"I know. I expect sacrifices, but I promise to make time for all of you."

She turned her face away from his touch. "I don't know, Warnach. Something doesn't strike me as quite right."

Firmly grasping her shoulders, he pulled her toward him. Gentle lips kissed her hair while he cradled her close. "Shi'níyah, Chikondra is my home - our home. I feel deeply the need to protect this world and its people. However, you are my heart. If you feel the decision is not right for us, I will advise Farsuk in the morning."

Resting her face against the warm expanse of his chest, she traced nervous paths along the outline of his well-defined bicep. Anxiety unfurled penetrating tendrils into the pit of her stomach, making her feel queasy. At the same time, she trusted in his strength and his foresight. Tilting her face upward, she murmured against his throat, "I'll back you every way possible."

Morning in the Sirinoya household bustled more than usual. Hitara urged Morcai and Lucia to hurry so they would not be late to school. Araman gave last-minute instructions to caterers for the formal luncheon Warnach would later host. Sandra inspected her lifemate's appearance with a keen eye, noting nothing more than a stray hair across his shoulder. Teasingly, she pulled it away. "Obviously mine."

Capturing her lips for a moment, he wrinkled his nose in mock disdain. "Behave."

At the impressive headquarters of the Chikondra High Council two hours later, Alliance masters and representatives milled outside the enormous conference hall and waited for escorts to guide them to reserved seating. Many diplomatic guests were accompanied by aides. Also in attendance were members from various Alliance ministries as well as officials serving Chikondra's domestic government.

"It's extremely rare to see so many high-ranking dignitaries in one place."

With a smile, Sandra nodded. "A bit nerve-wracking, I think. It's a shame Druska couldn't make it."

Peter frowned. "Danny was still fussy this morning."

"You would be, too, if you'd broken your arm just yesterday."

"Such is life with a five-year-old who thinks he's part monkey." Peter's grin faded. "You look tense."

Shrugging, she could hardly deny his remark. Neither could she rid herself of swelling apprehension that had plagued her ever since Warnach had informed her of his intentions. "Too much is happening too close together."

"I suppose you're insider enough to have the whole scoop."

Before she could respond, an official usher approached them. "Minister Collins, may I show you to your seat?"

Nodding at the escort, he turned a tentative smile toward Sandra. "Are you all right?"

Her voice lowered. "I'm not sure, Peter. I just feel so uneasy."

Almost by reflex, Peter cast a look around. "I learned a long time ago to trust your instincts. Don't worry. I'll help you keep watch."

"Thanks," she replied sheepishly. "Maybe I'm just getting too old for all this."

Just then, three Alliance representatives and their aides passed by her. Automatically, Sandra's head turned. Staring long moments at the robed Gazzumans, she turned back, but Peter was already gone. In fact, nearly everyone had entered the crowded auditorium.

Hurrying, she crossed the outer hall and addressed one of several Chikondran guards. Following his directions, she rushed down the corridor to her right. Reaching the security office, she rapped insistently on the door. When the sliding door swished open, she barged past a sentry. "Lieutenant! Is General Sirinoya here yet?"

A surprised officer turned around so sharply that his long hair swung in front of his face. "Minister Sirinoya, the general is just arriving. Is something wrong?"

"I'm not certain." Her breath quickened as her head shook sharply. "Yes. Something is wrong. Notify your people to go to high alert status. We have intruders."

Bending over, she pulled off her shoes. Spinning around, she then raced out the door and back through the corridors to the main entrance. She reached Badrik and his aides in the main hallway leading to the auditorium.

"Little sister!" he exclaimed, grabbing her by the arms and staring as she gasped for breath. "Tell me! What's wrong?"

Taking in a quick breath, she bobbed her head up and down. "Badrik, thank God. I hope I'm wrong, but I think we have a big problem."

Badrik's aides immediately tightened ranks around their commander. Calmly, he addressed her. "Catch your breath and tell me."

Closing her eyes, she concentrated on slowing her breathing. Nothing could stop her heart from pounding or blood from pulsing erratically through her veins. "The Gazzuman delegation… they passed me close on their way into the auditorium. There were Zeterons among them."

Badrik's eyes hardened. "Are you sure?"

"Badrik, especially after Dargom, I'll never forget that scent."

Rapidly, Badrik issued instructions to his aides to have additional security officers begin assuming strategic positions inside the auditorium. Clutching Sandra's arm, he headed toward the chamber's grand entry. Uniformed attendants flanked open doors, and guards stood at attention. Otherwise, everyone else was inside, already listening to Farsuk's opening words.

"Perhaps they're only here to observe, sister," Badrik whispered as he escorted her through the door. Still, his eyes scanned the sloping floor on the near side of the crescent-shaped gallery.

A slight nod indicated hopeful agreement. "Maybe I'm just too jittery after recent attacks. I'll cross to the far side and go to my seat."

"We'll keep watch." Badrik's hand grasped hers for just seconds before discreetly passing her a hand weapon. "Just in case. By the way, maybe you should put your shoes back on."

Farsuk's voice carried through the acoustically dynamic gallery. He was a gifted speaker, and his richly intoned words were as inspired as ever. As always, he spoke of the value of cooperation in achieving shared goals throughout the Alliance.

Advancing nearly halfway down the far aisle toward her reserved seat, she stopped. Curving behind Farsuk was the polished wood table where masters of High Council sat during presentations and speeches to various departmental officials. Rodan and Warnach, who served both the Alliance and the Chikondran government, sat side by side amongst the twenty-four masters who directed Chikondra's state-level departments. By habit, she noted the position of every master, every guard, every piece of equipment, and furniture. Quietly, knowing what Farsuk was preparing to say, she stopped to avoid disturbing others.

Pausing, Farsuk smiled at his audience. Then, he announced his resignation as Master Paramount of the Chikondran High Council. Moments later, as he announced to the audience that he had accepted interim responsibilities as Alliance chancellor, a disturbance arose in the center section.

Without conscious intent, Sandra's right hand flew to her Kitak. Jerking her head sideways, she glimpsed what she had feared most. "Baadihm! Warnach! Get down!" she shouted.

Instant chaos accompanied her desperate warning. Brilliant rays crisscrossed the auditorium with sizzling screeches. Panic seized many, prompting them to run, making themselves easier targets. Avoiding rays aimed in her direction, she dropped to carpeted floors, kicked off her high-heeled shoes, and rushed toward the podium.

An anguished groan filled her ears with horror. With a darting glance, she saw a man behind a seat on his knees, taking aim. Snatching Badrik's gun from a pocket in her nashavri, she rose and fired. Bumped by a fleeing spectator, she fired her first shot ceiling-high. Her second shot eliminated the threat.

Dodging people frantically trying to escape pandemonium, she pushed and shoved her way forward. Reaching the lower center floor, she dived forward. Rolling sideways, she clenched her hands into scorched, blood-soaked fabric and, with feet flat against the floor, shoved herself backward along with her burden.

Shouts, screams, and piercing lazon screeches continued for what seemed like forever. Suddenly, terrifying quiet. Hardly daring to breathe, she raised her head. Chikondran soldiers grappled and subdued three attackers. Staring ahead, she saw a head rise. When a weapon cleared the top of a seat, she quickly aimed and fired. This time, her first shot struck its target.

Dragging herself into a sitting position, she pulled Farsuk's head onto her lap. "Baadihm!" Tremors filled her voice. "Baadihm! Stay with me! Don't leave me!"

Eyelids opened, revealing pain-glazed eyes. "Sandra," he mumbled weakly.

Tears streamed down her cheeks. "Baadihm, help is coming. Stay with me."

Scrambling on hands and knees, Warnach reached her side. Fingers swiftly and deftly sought to pull burnt fabric from seared skin. A weakly shaking hand grasped his wrist. "Warnach, stop. It does no good. Let me touch you."

Leaving prisoners and evacuation of wounded to his aides, Badrik ran to his brother's side. Kneeling beside Warnach, he reached out and stroked Farsuk's sweaty brow. "Baadihm, you must fight. Medics are almost here."

A faint smile lit agonized features. Farsuk's gaze focused on his godsons. "You must both watch after Ifta for me. And Chikondra. Our world I leave in your care."

Badrik's voice broke. "Baadihm, we need your wisdom! Truly we do! You mustn't die! Not like this!"

Warnach swallowed back tears. "Baadihm, we will not fail you or Chikondra. You know that."

Farsuk's face turned toward Sandra. "Child," he whispered, "I love you as my own daughter. Thank you for guiding me to Quazon."

"Baadihm," she sobbed, "they were the ones who came to you."

"I love you, child. I have since the moment I met you. You…don't know…" A wheezing gasp escaped. Dark, suddenly lifeless eyes stared at the gold-leafed medallion on the ceiling.

"Baadihm?" The name escaped in a strangled whisper. With tears coursing down her face, Sandra cradled Farsuk's face to her breast and surrendered to body-jarring sobs wrenched from her very soul. Rocking him back and forth, she cried out over and over, "No, Baadihm! No! No!"

At some point, she opened swollen eyes and watched as strange hands respectfully arranged Farsuk's arms and prepared to remove his body. Her lifemate's voice, in unison with his brother's, chanted ancient prayer. In keeping with tradition, they accompanied their baadihm from the building. Stiff and in shock, she remained motionless on the floor.

At some point, her head lifted. Strong hands had grasped her shoulders, insisting she stand. Familiar arms surrounded her. Fresh tears blurred her vision. "Oh, Peter! Thank God you're all right! How did this happen? How?"

He felt tremors traverse the length of her body as he tightly held her. "Let's not talk about that now. Let's get out of here. Come on."

Trembling legs resisted walking. Pulling away from Peter, she looked from side to side. Where the masters had sat, tables were overturned and chairs toppled. Paramedics urgently tended two victims. In the general seating section, people were still being helped up from where they had fallen or been knocked over. Moans evidenced others awaiting medical attention. The bitter smell of scorched flesh hung in the air.

Frightened eyes appeared startlingly prominent in the blanched face that turned back to him with countless questions.

"We don't know how many yet. Right now, I think Master Sirinoya needs you, and I need to let Druska know that I'm okay."

For a moment, she felt paralyzed. Her stomach lurched. Finally, she looked into her old friend's face. "Do you know what this means?"

So quietly spoken were her words that he barely heard them. Her posture straightened. Her expression changed. Peter recognized those changes from the past. He shuddered, knowing well the subconscious signs of steely preparation. "I'm not sure."

Evergreen eyes held his. "This, Peter, was a declaration of war."

Hours followed in a jumble. The number of dead would mount to include three masters of Chikondra's governing High Council. Seven Alliance representatives, including two Gazzumans, two diplomatic ministers, and seven Chikondran officials had been killed. Many more had been trampled and injured, some seriously, while attempting to flee the chaos. Journalists already jockeyed for position to update a stunned public as details poured in.

Sandra swiftly collected her wits. With composure restored and Peter at her side, she moved through a crowded, heavily guarded hallway until she found one of Badrik's aides. "Colonel Nerefimah, where is General Sirinoya?"

Curtly waving his hand, the colonel signaled several junior officers to remain on guard. Respectfully, his head dipped. "Minister Sirinoya, the general went outside to oversee the transfer of Master Paramount Edsaka's body for burial preparation."

"Will you be kind enough to have someone escort us through the crowds? I need to be with my ki'medsah and my brother."

Sandwiched between six soldiers, the two Terran ministers were led past dazed witnesses to the shocking assassination. Armed guards ceremoniously opened gleaming, brass-framed doors to grant the ministers exit from the building.

Beneath sunny skies, an honor guard had hastily assembled. Farsuk's body was carefully guided into a body transport. Sandra watched as Warnach was finally forced to release his godfather's hand. Sensing her arrival, he lifted his grief-stricken face, and his fingertips touched Kitak.

The rafizhaq band around her head vibrated faintly, allowing her a direct sense of the emotions awash within her lifemate. Her heart ached for him. She wanted so much to reach out to him, to hold him, to console him. The time was not yet right. For the moment, her presence alone would have to suffice.

Rodan, who had been slightly wounded by a glancing shot to the shoulder, joined Badrik and Warnach. Somberly, they escorted deceased council masters, one by one, to arriving body transports. Finally, Rodan departed in a heavily guarded ambulance, and the parade of transports for dead and injured ended. Badrik led Warnach across the street and sidewalk to the stone-paved oval where Sandra waited.

Nearing her, Warnach reached out and drew her to him, pressing her face against his shoulder. Bleary eyes gratefully acknowledged Peter. "Thank you for staying with her."

Peter nodded once. "I'll go back inside. I need to give a statement and let Druska know that I'm safe."

For mere seconds, Warnach watched Badrik and Peter disappear inside the building. He murmured shakily as his arms convulsively tightened around his lifemate, "Me'u Shi'níyah, yet again have you saved my life."

His words made no sense to her. Her mind rejected everything beyond the feel of his body and the sound of his voice. She felt so abominably weary. Her hands locked behind his waist. "Me'u ki'medsah," she wept bitterly, "please, never let me go."

Alliance masters had intended to recall Farsuk to head an interim government until elections could be organized. Instead, Edsaka's assassination forced them to move quickly to place interim leadership of the galactic union into the capable hands of Master Devorius and Master Barishta. Perilous circumstances required decisive action. Alliance leaders also opted for temporary relocation of principal government operations. Immediate arrangements were undertaken to transfer the seat of power to Earth because of its more strategically sound location.

Plunged into mourning, Chikondra had little choice but to proceed with haste to bury its dead and reconstruct its government. Farsuk had intended to announce the High Council's decision to name Warnach Sirinoya to the post of Master Paramount. Surviving masters, including Rodan Khalijar and others recovering from serious injury, unanimously agreed to continue changes advocated by their fallen head of state.

While Araman and Nadana protected Ifta in relative seclusion on the Sirinoya estate and Badrik assumed control of the planet's security, Warnach directed a government facing a crisis unlike anything ever encountered by his world. Supported by dedicated staff, he also planned funeral services for his slain godfather.

The funeral for Farsuk Edsaka took place under the highest state of defensive alert Chikondra had ever known. Memory of the Gazzuman delegation had initiated uncomfortable awareness of vulnerabilities. Alien dignitaries readily agreed to whatever security scans were deemed necessary so they could attend the ceremony for the revered former chancellor. Despite the potential danger, many were willing to risk personal safety to pay respects to the Alliance's most influential champion ever.

Lying in state for three days and three nights, Farsuk was honored by thousands from many worlds. Massive pillars, standing at each end of his bier, held broad, shallow bowls continuously lit with leaping flames. Mourners pressed forward, straining to touch the pillars. Many cried openly. Others prayed aloud. Everyone demonstrated respect for a man who had lived a life devoted to peace and welfare for all.

On the seventh day following the assassination, Farsuk's body was encased in a carved wooden chest placed on a hand-rolled cart. Accompanied by family and cherished friends, his body was transported to a Brisa'machtai. At the sacred temple, Chikondra's seven Camudahmni congregated in a rare joint appearance to perform the rituals they believed would dispatch Farsuk's soul into the Great Spirit's presence.

Despite many objections, Ifta requested the private service. Other more public memorials could follow. Heartbroken, she wanted final farewells conducted in the presence of spiritual guides and those close to her ki'medsah. With Warnach and Badrik holding her on either side, she approached the chest holding Farsuk's body. She lovingly laid two enormous, royal blue, ci'ittá-shivayah flowers atop the cool wood. Bursting into tears, she collapsed beside her dead lifemate's coffin. Seven days later, Warnach and Badrik somberly watched as she was laid to rest inside a small tomb beside her beloved Farsuk.

Word of her early warning had reached a press hungry for details regarding the historic murder. Following the assassination, an official statement was issued. As bad as it had been, a government spokesman confirmed the attack would have been wholesale slaughter had Minister Sirinoya not alerted security. Several witnesses had also described her part in the fray, including how she had neutralized two assassins. Sandra quickly became prey for reporters and photo-journalists seeking details of the deadly assault in Kadranas. As Terran heroine and spouse to Chikondra's new Master Paramount, gaining an interview with Minister Sirinoya dangled as a coveted prize.

Finally, weary of avoiding reporters at every turn, she contacted Earth. The father of Morcai's childhood playmate on her homeworld had begun a career as a knowledgeable political commentator. Trusting him to treat the subject with respect, she offered him the prize. An exclusive com-link interview launched his career into high gear while the exclusivity dampened ambitions of most others.

Craving return to some semblance of normalcy, she was glad when schools finally reopened. Sandra sent Morcai and Lucia off to the welcome distraction of classes at schools discreetly surrounded by armed security. Mamehr left with Nadana for a few days in Tichtika. Warnach had spent the past three nights in Kadranas. At home, she felt isolated and alone. Even the quiet seemed deafening.

Restless, she walked outside to the patio. Hugging herself tightly, she stared at soaring treetops. Cheerful songbirds sounded strangely out of sync with reality. Sunshine cast brilliant rays upon green grasses when it seemed the whole of Heaven should be crying over the loss of a great man. Sighing, she breathed in deeply and went back inside.

Within thirty minutes, she stood outside the door of Peter's and Druska's apartment. She barely made it to the lounge sofa before tears surfaced. Patiently, Druska encouraged her to talk. Slowly, Sandra spoke about the attack itself, describing the fears and horrors she had seen that day. She also expressed lingering guilt that the outcome might have been less severe had she reacted differently. That concept gnawed at her insides. However, with so many funerals and so much work necessary to stabilize the government, she had hardly even seen Warnach, let alone had any time to explore the swelling tide of personal reproach.

As morning wore on, self-recriminations grew more embittered. She cried harder and harder until Druska found herself on her knees three times, rubbing Sandra's back and shoulders while her friend vomited into the bathroom bowl. The petite blonde finally convinced her best friend to lie down in a guest bedroom. Placing ice pack and pain-relieving electrodes to Sandra's head, Druska stayed until her friend fell asleep.

Within an hour, Druska stood outside the offices of Chikondra's Master Paramount. She was in no mood to deal with bureaucracy and layers of protective executive insulation.

Despite her tiny frame and delicate beauty, blue eyes shone like ice as she glared at one of Warnach's aides.

"I told you already. If I didn't have proper credentials, I would never have been permitted on this floor. I also don't have a damned appointment, but if you think you're man enough to stop me from marching through that door this very minute, get ready to prove it."

Indignant, the aide stood up. "Deputy Minister Collins, Master Sirinoya is extremely busy. I cannot allow you to disturb him."

"Call security then. I'll wait inside."

When the aide would have restrained her, Druska easily evaded his grasp and swung through the office door, slamming it behind her. Warnach's head jerked upward, and he stared at her in surprise. "Druska?"

Calmly, Druska stepped aside and flung the office door open to admit one angry aide and four security guards.

"Nifthat, it's all right. Deputy Minister Collins and I are old friends." Standing, he dismissed everyone except Druska. Giving her his undivided attention, he looked both puzzled and exhausted. "Please, Druska, sit down. I was just trying to contact Sandra, but she isn't answering her comm."

Druska's jaw tensed. "That's because she's at my house, hopefully still asleep. I asked Peter to go and stay with her so I could come here."

"Your house? Asleep? I don't understand."

Druska's head shook impatiently. "She came over this morning to talk. Mostly, she cried until she got so sick that all she did was throw up. Warnach, I can barely imagine the responsibilities you're facing right now. However, your family needs you, too."

Wearily, Warnach rubbed his eyes. "Druska, do you think I don't want to be home with them?"

She cast him a sympathetic smile. "I know you do. I also know how much you've always relied on Sandra. What you don't seem to realize is that she can't always be the rock beneath you. For a while today, I was honestly afraid she might have a complete breakdown. She's hurting, Warnach, through and through. Not only is she grieving, but she's also finding a million ways to blame herself for not stopping the assassination. She even went so far as to wonder aloud if you're avoiding her because even you blame her."

"Druska, that's craziness. She saved my life! She knows that. I even told her so."

"Intellectually, she probably does know. Emotionally, she's on overload. You seem to forget that it wasn't so long ago that she witnessed the destruction of that transport and the deaths of almost a hundred crewmembers. She was nearly killed herself. After that, she was part of the raid that saved all those children from the Zeterons. Now, this. Warnach, she hasn't had time to process and deal with it all.

"As friends, Peter and I can listen and console her. That's not the same as having you to help her work through her fears and doubts. We love her dearly, but it's not the same as when you remind her that you still love her. If you can be so strong for your whole world, surely you can spare a little of that strength for your ki'mirsah."

Warnach stared at Druska. Tears glistened in blue eyes and formed narrow tracks along ivory cheeks. Sandra had dedicated so much time and energy to her friend's slow recovery from brain injuries sustained on Dargom. His ki'mirsah had joyfully celebrated Druska's tiniest triumphs. She had encouraged her friend through difficult HAU treatments until the day Druska had run through a hospital corridor, thrown her arms around Sandra's neck, and screamed out, "I love you!" for all the world to hear.

Personal exhaustion no longer mattered. Warnach recognized his shortcomings. Crestfallen, he could barely face Druska. At the same time, he was thankful his lifemate had such a friend. "She's always made it too easy to rely on her resiliency and strength," he murmured.

Druska stood and, going around the desk, placed a comforting hand on his shoulder. "She still possesses that strength and resiliency. She just doesn't realize it right now. She needs you to help drive away her inner demons."

Moments later, Warnach pressed the intercom button on his desk's console pad. "Nifthat, I have a family matter that needs immediate attention. I wish not to be disturbed unless there's an emergency. Advise Master Khalijar that I'll contact him later today." Glancing upward at Druska, his mouth formed a grim smile. "Shall we leave?"

Entering the lounge behind Druska, Warnach forced a wan smile. "Peter, Druska told me you came home to stay with Sandra. Is she still here?"

"I haven't heard a peep. My guess is she's probably worn out."

"We all are." Warnach grimaced. "That's still an unacceptable excuse for the way I've neglected her."

Druska grasped his arm. Compassion softened her expression. "You look like you could also use some rest. She's in the guest room. You're welcome to join her."

His sigh sounded sad. "We won't be inconveniencing you?"

"Not at all," Peter said. "Besides, you should have fewer interruptions here."

Thanking Peter, Warnach followed Druska to the bedroom door. Pausing with his hand wrapped around a crystal handle, he looked sideways into Druska's eyes. "There's no way to thank you. I'll always appreciate what you've done today."

"Just take care of her. And, Warnach, rest well."

Inside, vertical blinds blocked early afternoon sun. On the bed, Sandra lay on her side with knees drawn toward her chest. Glancing around, he saw no sign of her Kitak. How upset she must have been to leave it behind. Unfastening the wide mehshtra around his waist and placing it on a chest at the foot of the bed, he removed his long coat and dropped it on top.

After leaving his Kitak with his coat, tired steps carried him around the bed, where he stepped out of shoes and lay down. Carefully, to avoid disturbing her, he draped his arm over her. "Me'u Shi'níyah," he mouthed silently against her hair, "I'm so sorry. I love you so much."

Slowly, she rolled toward him. Eyelids barely lifted. "Warnach?" she mumbled.

His fingers gently caressed her forehead. "I'm here, Shi'níyah."

"No." Her voice, although very low, cracked. "I'm only dreaming."

Moist lips pressed against her forehead. "Then, dream, Shi'níyah, and I shall dream with you."

"Dream... I keep - dreaming you'll come home and forgive me. I just want you to love me again."

"Sandra," he whispered brokenly, gathering her closer. "I've never stopped loving you. Not even for a second." Burning tears crept into his eyes. "I love you, Shi'níyah. I always will."

Sandra awoke. Her headache had faded, but her eyelids felt stiff, her eyes scratchy, her stomach empty. Sensing strangeness in her surroundings, she started to sit up. Something restrained her. A sleepy sigh sounded behind her. Memory of the morning sifted into her consciousness. Druska had left her in the guest room. Alone.

Sliding her legs over the mattress edge, she slid off the bed to the floor. Although disoriented, Warnach instantly sat up and looked around. Seeing her above the side of the bed, head down, filled him with a renewed tide of remorse. Silently, he slid over and onto the floor beside her.

"Shi'níyah?"

Dull eyes revealed surprise. "Warnach? What are you doing here?"

Tenderly, he tucked untidy hair behind her ear and kissed her nose. "Trying to get some much-needed rest with the woman I love."

"But..."

"Druska came to my office this morning. In my defense, I was trying to call you when she barged in. On the other hand, she made me realize something. I depend on you so completely that I often forget about the part of you that tends to find ways to blame yourself whenever things go wrong. Emotionally, we've all been through so much lately. In so many ways, though, you've faced the worst."

Her lips quivered, and she began to weep. "I'm so sorry. I didn't mean for Druska to…"

"Shi'níyah, you've no reason to apologize for anything. Ever since I met you, it seems you've always borne the brunt of challenges we faced. Only the Great Spirit knows how much I hope that won't always be the case. There's so much uncertainty right now. Druska was absolutely right in coming to me. She reminded me that, whatever lies ahead, you're my most devoted and most valuable ally. I need to be more sensitive to your needs."

Her face twisted away, and she stared at the door. "Don't you see, Warnach? It's like Daddy always used to tell me. I always foul things up. If I'd been more decisive when I first sensed danger..."

"Sandra, stop it." He immediately regretted his sharp tone and softened his voice. "There is no question that many more would have died had you not alerted security. Everyone seems to know that except you. Even your father now realizes what a capable, wonderful woman you are. You've got to forget what was said in the past. You've proven your worth again and again. If anyone is at fault for anything, I am. For years, I've immersed myself in Alliance affairs in ways that always caused you unfair burdens.

"Shi'níyah, I need you more than ever. Terrible times are upon us. I fear decisions waiting to be made. Without your support, without your strength, I'm nothing."

She swallowed several times. "Warnach, I tried to save Baadihm. Honestly, I did. I killed two Zeterons in the process. I actually killed two men. Knowing I had no choice doesn't make that fact any easier to face."

Pulling her toward him, he lowered her head to his lap and caressed her hair. "Shi'níyah, I should have realized how much that hurts you. Have you…"

"Ever since the attack on Simartis Major. Most of the time, I can forget. Sometimes, I feel haunted. My life's goal is to save lives, not take them."

"My sweet Shi'níyah," he sighed. "I wish I'd known. Even with Kitak, you kept that from me."

Her hand rested on his knee. "I keep telling myself I did what was necessary."

He searched for words. "What you did was necessary. It also doesn't necessarily conflict with your goal of saving lives."

"How can you say that?"

"Sandra, those Zeterons chose violence as means to kill and take what isn't theirs. Your actions went well beyond self-defense. They would have killed more people had you not stopped them. Your courage and skill saved my life more than once. My life. Rodan's. How many other lives did you save? You need to see that perspective."

She flattened her hand against the floor and pushed herself upward and reached toward him. Her fingertips traced the full line of his lower lip. "Are you so sure?"

He smiled reassuringly. "I have not a single doubt."

Chapter Fourteen

"There. That's the last of your china." Sandra cast her eyes around Druska's nearly empty apartment. "I'm going to miss you so much."

"You think I won't miss you? Or Chikondra? This has been home since I started at the academy."

Sandra smiled sadly. "Staying in touch might not be so easy, but try, will you?"

"You know it, girlfriend!" Druska secured the clamps on crates of crystal she had preferred to pack herself. Her perkiness disappeared as quickly as it had surfaced. "I hope the Zeterons can be deterred from attacking."

"I have the feeling nothing will stop them. I'm just glad there's time to evacuate Alliance personnel to safer worlds."

Worry darkened Druska's expression. "What about you and the children?"

Sandra shook her head. "I'm not sure what we're going to do. Morcai and Lucia are more Chikondran than Terran. This is their home."

Over tea a few minutes later, the two friends sat on the kitchen floor. "I don't know what I'd do in your shoes."

"I can't see Warnach leaving Chikondra. I can't see myself leaving him. Neither do I want to send my children away."

Druska sipped her tea. "I pray things never get so bad."

Déjà vu. The very worst kind. Sandra secured the packing bin containing fine china. Quickly, her mind raced through the household inventory. Paintings. Artwork. Antiques and artifacts. Everything valued as family heirlooms was either being transferred to secret underground vaults or transported to Earth. Only ordinary household items and furnishings would remain.

Quietly, Sandra entered the lounge used most often by the family. Araman stood by the window, somberly staring outside. "Mamehr? Are you all right?"

"Not really, daughter. I never once dreamed I'd be forced to flee this house."

Sandra draped her arm around slim shoulders. "I probably need you more now than I ever have."

"We need each other. Morcai and Lucia will need both of us."

Sandra smiled through a film of tears. "I'm not sure I agree. I think we're the ones who need them. The way they're coping amazes me."

Araman took Sandra's hand and kissed it before leading her to a sofa. Gazing into eyes as sad as any she'd ever seen, she smiled encouragingly. "You know this decision torments him."

Biting into her lip, Sandra murmured, "I know. It torments him, but it's killing me. Mamehr, I don't know how I can just leave him behind."

"You have his children to protect. Warnach belongs to all of Chikondra now. As much as I hate the truth, I firmly believe he's our world's best hope."

"Mamehr, the Zeterons are closing in. I understand Alliance strategy to form defensive lines for protecting the concentration of heavily populated worlds between here and Earth, but Chikondra needs protection, too."

"We aren't being deserted. It takes time to move so many forces from the Medron sector and others that suffered all the initial attacks. Some of those regions are months from Chikondra."

"We could argue valid points all day long. It doesn't change the fact that Chikondra will essentially be left alone to face the initial onslaught of Zeteron invasion."

"Yes, and our people must withstand that onslaught until sufficient assistance can arrive."

Exasperation with the situation forced her to sigh sharply. "They mean to annihilate this world."

Araman met Sandra's gaze. "Yes, they do. That's why Warnach needs you so much. You must be his voice on Earth. Rodan is a brilliant orator and a convincing negotiator, but the fact that you're Terran will be crucial to securing necessary backing. Warnach will also be free to act here knowing that you have his children safe on Earth."

"Mamehr, my mind knows how right you are. My heart just refuses to accept."

That night, the Sirinoya family gathered outside for dinner. Hands joined around the table. Warnach recited grace as though all were well. The children kept dinner conversation light by talking about seeing Grandma and Grandpa again. Morcai speculated on his chances to earn a spot on an Earth soccer team while Lucia asked about visiting ancient pyramids she had read about. Michahn joined his cousins and wondered aloud how long it might take him to learn English without the distinctive Chikondran accent.

After dinner, parents helped children get ready for the following morning's trip to Kadranas. Pauses for hugs and kisses were many. When the family finally gathered inside the Brisajai, night prayers assumed nearly tangible intensity. Lucia and Morcai comforted Michahn, who had never been away from Chikondra. Adults prayed for fortitude and the safety of friends and family.

Birds heralded dawn's arrival. Waking, Sandra turned onto her side and ran her fingers along the length of Warnach's bare back. Her lips followed suit. They had made love the night before. She desperately wanted him again. Within moments, she succeeded in waking him and arousing him.

As their bodies joined, she escaped into a different existence. His voice, whispering her name, filled her ears. His skin, smooth and supple, tantalized sensitive, questing fingertips. His lips, moist and hot, kissed her mouth, her neck, and her mouth again. Her body writhed, seeking unending union with him and the overpowering pleasure he created for her. Then, quaking at the pinnacle of shared passion, she gasped for breath and clutched him tightly, terrified by their impending separation.

"Me'u Shi'níyah," he whispered as his cheek rested against her shoulder, "swear that you'll always love me like this."

Her lips trembled as she kissed wildly straying black waves. "I've always loved you like this. I always will."

"If only you could know how deeply I dread this day."

Breath caught in her throat. "If only you could know how much I wish you'd let me stay."

With sunshine invading to chase away the night, birds sang louder. Faint sounds of a waking household reached their ears. Quietly, they lay together, jealously stealing every second of a day that would part them as the wave of war threatened their home, their world, and his life.

Showers. Clean clothes. Bed-making. Morning prayers. Breakfast. Anxious touches. Last looks. Nadana arrived from the nearby Brisa'machtai. Personal bags were stowed onboard official transports. Soldiers helped women and children inside. Warnach and Badrik joined them.

Lucia sat on her badehr's lap and leaned against his chest. Morcai sat on one side, his head against Warnach's shoulder. Sandra reclined sideways on the seat, her fingers delicately caressing his hair, face, and beard. Nadana held her sister's hand. Inside the second transport, Badrik encouraged Michahn and Farisa about the upcoming journey.

Arriving at the Kadranas Air Command Center, the family alighted from transports and headed directly for the shuttle ready to transfer them to the orbiting Curasalah. No one moved quickly. No one wanted to go.

Following farewell embraces, Badrik escorted his own family, Araman, and Nadana on board before returning to the shuttle pad. Warnach tarried with Morcai and Lucia, needing just one more hug, one more kiss, one more promise. Finally, he allowed Hitara to usher them to the ship before she would bid her charges farewell.

Finally, reluctantly, he turned to Badrik. "My brother, I know you disagree with me, but you understand your mission. No one knows more than you about our world and its defenses. Yours will be the leadership I trust to guide help when it becomes available."

Badrik embraced him. "Warnach, I need my brother. Don't get yourself killed."

"I have no such intention." Warnach's arms tightened around his brother, and he whispered, "Take care of them. Especially Sandra."

Badrik stepped back, his gaze locking on his brother's anguished eyes. "We all will. May the Great Spirit watch over you and keep you safe."

Warnach turned. His ki'mirsah stood alone and silent. He approached her and framed her face between long, slender hands. "Me'u Shi'níyah, I see your hurt. Can you not leave me with the memory of your smile?"

Her eyelids fluttered as she made a weak effort to satisfy his request. Her arms encircled him, and she held him close, breathing in his scent and savoring the warmth of his body. "Me'u Warnach, I feel like I'm dying."

"So do I, Shi'níyah. Think of all that must be done so we can live. I trust no one more than you to find the solution to save us. I promise to do everything possible to hasten our reunion."

Feeling the shudder that ran the length of her body, Warnach's eyes closed. He felt like his guts were being ripped from his body, centimeter by centimeter. His heart thudded painfully. Watching his children disappear inside the shuttle had shaken him. Sending his beloved ki'mirsah away was surely the hardest decision he had made in his entire lifetime.

Her face raised. Glazed eyes moved quickly, memorizing anew every feature. Her lips parted. She wanted to drown in the kiss that followed. A hand on her shoulder drew her away from the man she loved.

"Sister, we must leave. Come."

Mechanically, she turned. Fingers reluctantly slipped from her ki'medsah's hands. Short, hesitant steps carried her to the carpeted boarding ramp. She stopped, unable to move forward another millimeter.

"Sandra." Badrik's voice was gently insistent. "Come."

Abruptly, she pivoted. Desperation drove her back to Warnach. Throwing her arms around him, she nearly strangled on the flood of sobs erupting from her soul. "Warnach! Please! I beg you! Don't make me go! Don't send me away! Please! I can't leave you! I can't!"

"Shi'níyah!" His arms enfolded her tightly, and he cried with her. "Me'u Shi'níyah, you must go! I have to know that Morcai and Lucia are safe! You have to take care of them. Oh, Sandra, please. Try to understand!"

She shook off Badrik's hands. "I'll never understand! You're part of me! Warnach, ask me anything but not this! Oh, God! Warnach! Not this! Don't send me away!"

He felt her body succumb to uncontrollable quakes. Her sobs progressed to wailing as she begged him to let her stay. Her knees began to buckle, and he sank with her onto the shuttle platform. "Shi'níyah," he pleaded, "you must understand. I can't let you stay. You know I can't risk your life. I can't!"

"Warnach, I love you. I swear it! I love you too much to desert you. Let me stay. Mom and Dad will take care of Morcai and Lucia. Damn it, Warnach! You're a peacemaker, not a soldier! Don't make me go! Don't!"

Her tears flowed with such force that he felt their heated wetness soaking through his clothes. He had expected a sorrowful farewell, but even he had been unprepared for the near hysteria gripping her.

Quickly, he dropped his face. Cerea-nervos, pulsating rapidly, pressed against her forehead. His head snapped back. The force of energy she projected into him sent shock waves roaring through his body. He gulped in a breath of air and focused intensified control. Again, his cerea-nervos pressed against her forehead. The energy exchange was startling, but he finally succeeded in concentrating sufficient power to tranquilize her. Her sobs subsided. She quieted, and her body went limp.

Struggling, he dragged her into his arms and, with Badrik's help, stood up. Holding her high against his chest, he wondered whether his legs could support them both. He nodded gratefully as Badrik steadied him.

"Brother, what happened?"

Warnach breathed rapidly. "Cerea-semi'ittá. Like nothing I've ever experienced."

"From a Terran?" Badrik muttered in disbelief. His glance narrowed. His throat tightened. "Perhaps you should reconsider sending her away."

Grief shone from Warnach's eyes. "My brother, especially now, I can't let her stay. If something would happen to her, I could never survive for our children."

Badrik swallowed. "Here. Let me take her." Gathering her into his arms, he glanced at Sandra's sodden features and then looked up at his brother. "The greater question may well be whether she'll survive the separation."

Warnach bent forward and kissed Sandra's Kitak and her temple. "She will, Badrik. Just never let her forget how much I love her."

Chapter Fifteen

Moaning, Sandra shoved gentle hands away. Heat suffused her face. Her body vibrated with familiar tingles she related to some of Warnach's more amorous cerea-semi'ittá. Drunkenly, she swayed while trying to sit up. Dizzy, she collapsed sideways onto a pillow. Shaking her head sharply to clear thick fog, she sat up again. Forcing her eyelids open, she waited impatiently until her vision cleared.

"What hit me?" she muttered.

Farisa smiled, relieved to see signs of recovery. "I'm not quite sure. How do you feel?"

Shaking her head again, Sandra consciously assessed her body. "Hot. Thirsty. Tingly."

"No pain?"

She suddenly remembered going to pieces. "Only my broken heart. Where are we?"

"Onboard the Curasalah. You've been unconscious for hours."

Drawing legs up, Sandra placed elbows on her knees and covered her face with her hands. "Warnach?"

"On Chikondra. We promised to connect a com-link as soon as you felt up to talking."

"Morcai. Lucia. Are they all right?"

"They were a little frightened when Badrik carried you onto the shuttle, but we explained that their badehr got a little carried away with his last cerea-semi'ittá."

Straightening, Sandra spun her head in a circle. Even her neck felt stiff. "I feel like I ran through the middle of a power generator."

"More like the power generator ran through you."

With one eye shut, she looked at Farisa questioningly. "Meaning?"

"Here, drink some water. Slowly." Setting aside the half-emptied glass, Farisa gazed sympathetically at her sister-in-law. "As far as your question, I don't have an answer. As I understand, you returned Warnach's cerea-semi'ittá with so much force that you both nearly collapsed."

Vague memory seeped into her clearing mind. Never had she experienced anything comparable to what she had felt on that shuttle pad. Not her lifemate's kiss. Not his electrifying cerea-semi'ittá. Not a single thing.

Cautiously, she stood on wobbly legs. "Farisa, we've got to steady these legs. I need to apologize to Warnach. He must think his lifemate turned into a raving lunatic."

"Lunatic? Chikondran translation, please."

Sandra blinked her eyes several times. "Maybe later."

"Talk as long as you want." Forsij quietly left his quarters.

It seemed forever before the com-link connected and his image cleared. "Me'u Warnach," she blurted out tremulously, "can you ever forgive me?"

Despite his depressive mood, he smiled. "Forgive you? You've always told me, but this morning, you finally managed to show me exactly how much you love me. I'm still reeling."

"You're angry."

"Quite the opposite. Shi'níyah, I must ask. How did you learn to project your energy with such force?"

"I don't know. Badrik and Farisa told me. Maybe you taught me, and I never before realized."

"You amaze me." Tension in his face eased slightly. "You also gave me quite a shock." He paused. "Shi'níyah, I need to know you'll be all right. I... I've always asked so much of you. Say you can get through this."

Her eyelashes lowered, and she swallowed uncomfortably. "I'm honestly not sure, but I'll try. I don't want to fail Morcai and Lucia." Her eyes opened. "I can't fail you, either. I…" She paused and breathed in deeply. "I won't fail you. I love you too much."

Her words soothed some of the raw ache in his soul. "I don't know how many more times we'll be able to talk. In all honesty, I don't even know if I'll ever see you again. No matter what happens, me'u Shi'níyah, never forget that I've loved you more than any woman has ever been loved. Remember that. Always."

His obvious pain deeply hurt her. "I know, Warnach. Me'u ki'medsah?"

"Yes?"

"I've always kept my promises to you, haven't I?"

A smile played at the corners of his mouth. "Always."

"It's time to tuck one more promise into your heart. I don't care how far I have to go or how long it takes. I promise you now that I will find a way for us to be together again."

"Sandra…" For a moment, he thought how unrealistic that promise might prove to be. Even as they spoke, Zeteron warships were approaching faster than earlier projected. Staring directly into the monitor, he imagined he was actually gazing into those beautiful evergreen eyes. She had always kept her promises. Many times, she had turned impossibilities into reality. Even if this time the promise proved an unreachable dream, he could cling to it, knowing how much she meant it.

Finally, he smiled. "When you do, I promise to hold you and kiss you as never before."

Adoration glowed from her otherwise sad face. "Remember that promise. I intend to remind you in person."

It took nearly two days to fully recover from the electrical charges her body had projected and received as a result of the farewell cerea-semi'ittá she and Warnach had exchanged. Spending much of the time in bed, she rested while making plans with Morcai and Lucia for their stay on Earth. Especially dreading the first long night, she convinced her children to sleep in her bed. Trying to accept the wisdom of Warnach's decision, she loved his children more than ever and kept them close. Their quiet breathing was calming. Their presence eased her aloneness. Sleeping between them reminded her of how very sweet and powerful had been the love Warnach and she shared.

Feeling better, Sandra set aside time daily to study every available report on Alliance reorganization. Master Devorius had made tremendous strides in organizing relocated Alliance ministries while Master Barishta dedicated his attention to military issues. Reviewing official communiqués, she offered recommended responses to coded transmissions. With astonishing calm and concentration, she attended briefings conducted by Forsij and Badrik. Initial skirmishes had already occurred between Zeteron scout ships and Chikondran starfighters. War had been delivered to a world that had always stood at the forefront of peace.

By the time they reached Earth, her sense of purpose had returned. Within a week, she had settled into a comfortably large apartment not far from her parents' home. Opting for the hour-long commute to Washington, she felt her family's closeness would help Morcai and Lucia transition more comfortably into Terran schools. Nadana chose to stay with her while Araman moved into the same Washington apartment as Badrik and Farisa.

Confident that her children were adjusting to their new environment, Sandra began the daily commute to Washington. Organizing a routine that allowed her to stay abreast of developments across the Alliance proved difficult. Demands were challenging when she refused to sacrifice time with her children.

Worsening circumstances on Chikondra made transitioning back to life on Earth far from easy. So many factors required her attention. Fearing possible confrontation because of her children's blended heritage, she checked in regularly at the schools Morcai and Lucia attended. Dietary considerations for Nadana would be managed in terms of Earth foods. Lucia comfortably adhered to vegetarian alternatives, but Morcai readily widened his tastes to include meats. Daily prayers continued but without the gentle, reassuring sense of routine from home. Forced exile from her adopted world and separation from Warnach sank into her a nearly unbearable despondency.

News from Chikondra grew sporadic. Zeteron warships greatly outnumbered Alliance vessels in the sector. A blockade was quickly being established. Zeterons were aiming attacks from orbit. Regrouping, the Alliance Council focused on ways to manage the crisis politically, logistically, and militarily.

"Momma?" Morcai's face was hopeful as he smiled at her over breakfast.

She blinked and thrust from her mind the most recent news reports. "Yes?"

"Momma, on Saturday morning, the school is holding final tryouts for the soccer team. I was wondering…"

She smiled when he paused nervously. "Are you going to try out?"

"I'd like to. I met someone named Brad. He's been really friendly, and we've been practicing together after school. He thinks I'm good enough to make the team."

Lavishing attention on her children was her only relief from stress. "You seem hesitant."

He shook his head and grinned apprehensively. "I'm hoping you can come."

She winked at Lucia. "Sounds like your brother could use a cheerleader or two."

Lucia's eyes widened curiously. "What's a cheerleader, Momma?"

Sandra laughed. "Another one of those Earth oddities that your mother probably can't explain." Smiling at her son, she nodded. "What time? I'll be there and show you how Earth mothers make the best cheerleaders ever."

"Momma, only on Earth, I think. I'll look forward to your coming." Affectionately, he tousled his sister's hair. "You, too, Sparkles."

"Sparkles?" Sandra asked curiously as Morcai disappeared to leave for school. "That's a new name. Any special reason?"

Lucia's eyes held an oddly amused expression. "Brothers. Isn't that reason enough?"

Saturday morning started with rain, but bright sunshine quickly dispersed gray clouds. Forcing herself to ignore the influx of overnight bulletins, she left nashavris in her closet and dressed in a lightweight red sweater, black slacks, and sneakers. Morning prayers and breakfast were more lighthearted than any since their arrival. In a rush, they filed outside and climbed into their private transport piloted by a personal bodyguard doubling as chauffeur.

On the field, many young teenagers shouted welcome to the dark-haired Morcai. One in particular, with sandy hair and animated gestures, appeared especially excited. Quickly, coaches divided hopefuls into groups and called out instructions for initial warm-ups.

Glancing upward when a hand landed on her shoulder, she bounced to her feet. "Badrik! Farisa! I'm so glad you came! Where's Michahn?"

Both Badrik and Farisa hugged Lucia, then Sandra. Pointing toward the sidelines, Badrik laughed. "Close to the action."

While players were tested for speed and skill, parents cheered and shouted, groaned and encouraged. Tense and anxious, Sandra leaned far forward when Morcai stood in the center of the field to demonstrate ball handling techniques.

A mother beside her nudged her. "First tryout?"

Sandra's eyes darted toward the side. "That obvious, is it?"

Badrik excitedly interrupted. "Look! He has the same agility and accuracy as his badehr! That's exactly why Rodan and I hardly ever beat Warnach at pafla!"

Concentrating, Morcai flawlessly manipulated the ball until near the end of his demonstration when Sandra leapt to her feet and screamed out, "Way to go, Morcai!"

Dropping the ball, he stared in dismay at his suddenly chagrined mother. However, a smile quickly lit his face. Shrugging his shoulders in amused resignation, he waved at her. Despite the fumble, by the time tryouts ended, Morcai had earned a spot on the team. With a satisfied smile, he accepted hugs from his entire family and proceeded to introduce two of his teammates as friends from school.

The sandy-haired boy was named Brad Damron. Quickly, Sandra learned that her bench mate during tryouts had been Brad's mother. Both had glittering blue eyes and broad, friendly smiles. Laughing, Connie Damron suggested the families combine forces and attack a local pizza parlor to celebrate the boys' accomplishments.

Brad's friendly features and athletic appearance disguised his intense interest in current affairs. Excited to meet Sandra and Badrik, the teen launched a string of questions once a waitress left to place orders for beverages and food. Quickly, his mother called for a timeout. They were celebrating successful tryouts. Political queries could wait for another time.

The impromptu party proved a success. Brad and Morcai were obviously building a tight friendship. Badrik, Farisa, and Michahn were also integrating more comfortably into their alien environment. As usual, Lucia seemed content so long as her family was close. Connie and Sandra discovered the common bond of separation from the men in their lives.

When Badrik departed for Washington, Sandra invited Connie and Brad to spend the afternoon at her apartment. Lucia joined Nadana in the kitchen to prepare beverages and Chikondran-style desserts while Sandra and her guest chatted in the living room.

"Accepting this leave was a tough decision," Connie said, taking a glass of water from her young hostess. "Mark and I served together for years on board the Seeker. When hostilities broke out, families with children faced harsh decisions. We could have sent Brad to my brother, but Mark insisted one of us stay with him. With Mark's rank as commander, it seemed logical for me to take family leave."

Planting a quick kiss against Lucia's cerea-nervos, Sandra thanked her daughter and said to Connie, "Logic doesn't make it one bit easier."

Connie nodded sadly. "We both miss him. Brad practically grew up on board ship. I try to keep up appearances, but I'm really afraid."

Swallowing hard, Sandra watched condensation forming on her glass. "Every day is a trial. We've only heard twice from Warnach since we arrived. I can't stand listening to news reports.

I can't turn away from them, either. For me, it's torture not being there with him."

"I imagine the worst part is knowing that he's basically trapped."

Solemnly, Sandra tipped her face downward. Words clogged in a throat that swiftly thickened with emotion. Fortunately, Brad and Morcai made an energetic entrance, snatching dessert items from the platter Lucia had just placed on the coffee table.

Staring at gargantuan shadows looming against night-blue heavens, Warnach could hardly believe he was gazing at the darkened city of Kadranas. Moonlight eerily filtered through wispy cloud fingers. Grimly, he hoisted a wide strap over his shoulder and resolutely followed the leader of a security detachment assigned to protect him during the evacuation of Chikondra's beautiful capital.

On quiet, agile hovercraft, the security detail moved Chikondra's embattled leader and his advisors far from the city and into the concealing depths of Miferasud's densest forest. There, beneath the planet's surface, interlinking caves had long ago been transformed into naturally shielded bunkers and storehouses should the need ever arise. That afternoon, Zeterons had issued an ultimatum demanding unconditional surrender. If Chikondra refused, troops would descend the following day to take control of the planet by force.

Reports streamed into the underground command center the very next morning. Outnumbered, squadrons of fighters valiantly played games of seek, attack, and run. As the invasion continued, Chikondran pilots proved their cunning and their accuracy. From the outset, they had known they could only delay the inevitable. Recognizing the need to conserve lives and firepower, they retreated to soaring, craggy mountain ranges. From there, they would monitor Zeteron tactics and adapt with ever-changing strategies in hopes of preventing Chikondra's total collapse until sufficient Alliance forces could be rallied.

Siege. Warnach sat in morbid silence after the departure of aides who had just delivered fresh updates. Population centers were subjected to isolation, then attack. Children and the elderly filled evacuation centers. Men and women who had lived for peace learned firsthand the trials and tragedy of war. Not even four months had passed since the Zeterons had targeted Chikondra. How could he possibly hope his world would survive with what little Alliance assistance was able to break through the enemy armada surrounding his world?

Drawing in an angry, frustrated breath, he gazed upon a trio of photographs displayed in a folding frame. Lucia's gentle smile touched his heart. Vitality gleamed from the eyes of his son. Between his children, exotically fair features almost eased the remembered despair of their parting. Tips of long fingers touched images of beloved faces. His heart lurched. His solitary sense of peace came from the knowledge that they were safe.

Under constant guard inside converted caves, he soon felt days were indiscernible from nights. Beginning to suffer claustrophobia, Warnach finally decided to reject advice from his aides. He started joining guerilla-type raids against carefully selected Zeteron targets. Courageous, alert, and decisive, his leadership inspired those around him.

Midmorning. He had remained inside the previous night while one patrol coordinated a reconnaissance mission with soldiers from another camp. Zeteron attacks had suddenly lessened. Troops were converging on the site formerly occupied by the Kadranas Air Command Center. Warnach and his military strategists were convinced the reason held deadly threat.

Early indications from returning patrols proved ominous. Chikondran captives had been moved to the site. Forced into labor, they appeared to be building an extensive foundation on the northernmost corner of the base. Beneath spotlights positioned around the area, work continued underway even at night. A wide perimeter of troops and robots guarded the worksite while fighters continuously scoured surrounding airspace to prevent hostile incursion.

Observers couldn't be positive yet; however, trained eyes had studied the actions of ground supervisors, the layout, and construction materials transporting to the site. Early indications were that Zeterons were erecting some sort of tower.

Reviewing intelligence, Warnach recalled reading a rare report on Zeteron tactics from a planet virtually unknown to the Alliance. A scant handful of refugees had escaped and told stories of a tower that had cast a force field around their planet. The tower had prevented outside help and disabled worldwide power generation. Crippled, the planet had fallen, yet another conquered victim of the Zeteron Empire.

Warnach sat with elbows propped on his desk. His forehead rested against clenched fists. Straining to recall details of the account, he hadn't realized someone had entered his office until a hand came to rest on his shoulder. Blinking, he slowly lifted his head and twisted to look at his visitor. His eyes widened, and he jerked to his feet.

"What in the Great Spirit's name do you think you're doing here?"

Dark brown eyes regarded him with grave solemnity. "Warnach, they murdered Daltrehm. They killed my brother."

Warnach flinched. His stomach lurched. "His family?"

"I got them to the refugee center at Zahmichilá. When I heard about the resistance centered here, I came."

Warnach barely managed to hold skepticism at bay. "Lashira, I'm truly sorry about Daltrehm. He was a fine man. I fail to see why that brings you here."

Tears glazed her eyes. "Chikondra is my home, too. Zeterons murdered my brother. I'm here because I want to do whatever I can to help stop them."

Staring at her, he ground his back teeth together before exhaling a tense breath. "You know I can't afford to turn away a single set of willing hands. However, you must understand that this isn't some glamorous playground. This is war, Lashira. Ugly, bloody, and brutal. Just like Daltrehm, people are dying every day. If you're sure you can face that, you may stay. When you leave here, go to the right. Turn left at the end and go to the last chamber. Lieutenant Yihfrazh will find you an assignment."

For an extended moment, she gazed at him. Noting nothing more than cold regard, she shook her head and turned toward the door. Just before walking out, she stopped and looked around with sad eyes. "Warnach, this isn't the time to hate me."

Collapsing into his chair, he bent forward yet again. With his face buried in his hands, he ignored her as nervous fingers tracked tiny circles atop the golden ring of rafizhaq encircling his head.

Master Rodan Khalijar and Minister Sandra Sirinoya strode rapidly through brilliantly illuminated corridors until they reached the large conference room reserved for the Alliance's Security Committee. Followed by several aides, they wasted little time exchanging greetings.

Passionately, Rodan embarked on his newest plea to the committee. Alliance charters contained commitments from all allied worlds to defend the welfare of fellow members. Chikondra was in crisis. The Zeteron attack had escalated into a full-scale siege. Rehovotian journalists, including Sandra's friend, Deborah Levine, were risking their lives to breach the blockade in order to disseminate details of war being waged against a people whose history was devoid of such violence.

Committee representatives blanched, often averting their eyes from visual recordings. Still, while all agreed that help for Chikondra was necessary and would be forthcoming, they could not agree on how to expedite assistance. They argued that other planets could be in danger if left with too little military protection.

Rodan quickly realized that Alliance commitment to Chikondra was secondary to political images. Although committee members offered supportive rhetoric, they constantly retreated to topics that held no real substance, no viable solutions. Rising, he faced representatives with furious eyes. Enraged to the point he was unable to speak, he spun around and headed toward the door.

"Master Khalijar, wait. I'll join you in a moment."

He stopped at the sound of Sandra's voice. Her words had been spoken so calmly. Pausing, he turned around. The softness in her voice contrasted sharply with the fires blazing in her eyes.

Standing, she crossed the room and stood in front of a window. Sunshine enveloped her figure in a hazy cloud of light. "Ladies. Gentlemen. After attending these meetings all week, I'm frankly amazed and thoroughly disgusted by the lack of action from you who are charged with applying the most essential basics of the Alliance charter - that of defending each Alliance member in time of need."

A Garolian stood up. "Minister Sirinoya, if you intend to insult members of this committee, you may stop now. You have no right."

Sandra glared at him. "I am an Earth citizen and a member of this Alliance. My world's laws and our Alliance's principles give me distinct rights to speak frankly to every member of this committee. Each of you claims to uphold the Alliance, yet too many of you refuse to take any action while Chikondra suffers brutal attack.

"I do challenge this committee's irresponsible inaction while the Alliance member that welcomed each of you faces a horrible fate at the hands of vile invaders. You saw the reports just as I did. Cities bombarded without mercy. Mass graves. Stacks of bloody bodies. Those bodies were people who had been left dead or dying. What about the injured who didn't die? Can you imagine their pain and suffering? Of course not!

"I also question motives behind the inaction. For those of you who offer only excuses for your inaction, I wonder how loud your protests and demands would be if Zeteron had attacked your own worlds. This week's entire process has yielded no progress. None whatsoever. Today's meeting has shown me something I would never have believed had I not witnessed it myself. While we were discussing the extent of violence on Chikondra, I actually heard some of you whispering about lunch plans. The guilty know I do not lie. How shameful! How totally revolting!

"I leave you with this thought. Chikondra has inspired the Alliance since its inception. Its life and the blood of its people will ring the bell of death for many worlds because, if Chikondra falls, so falls this Alliance, one world at a time in a tragic game of dominoes. The defeat of Chikondra will give the Zeteron Empire a psychological victory unlike any other. And you, esteemed members of the so-called Alliance Security Committee, will have surrendered our Alliance with your inability to stand in courage to make a decision." Her eyes moved slowly from one stunned face to the next before she remarked sarcastically, "Enjoy your lunch."

"Sandra, you could have been somewhat more diplomatic...and perhaps less harsh."

Sitting in Master Devorius' office, she sat with eyes closed. "Explain gentle diplomacy to victims on Chikondra or any other world under Zeteron domination."

Nearly transparent irises widened, and he approached her. His hand grasped her shoulder. "My dear, your daring today has at least opened some eyes to inexplicable delay tactics. Debate already arises that could finally hasten approval of necessary military support. You must realize, though, that you set yourself up for personal attack."

Her features drew into a grave mask. "I need to go home, Master Devorius, but don't worry too much. I've already determined who will condemn me for saying what I did for personal reasons. Detailed reports are waiting in your message center. They contain verifiable data on what we might refer to as some fascinating conflicts of interest. Don't think for a second I won't fight tooth and nail against anyone who dares challenge me. The difference is that I won't hide the truth behind excuses, closed doors, and outright lies."

The venerable master smiled. "Perhaps Earth could finally fill a seat on the Security Committee. I know exactly the person I would recommend as the best representative."

Her eyes met his. "That is a thought if that candidate you're thinking of survives this disaster." Rising, she extended her arms and embraced one of her most dedicated supporters. "I really do need to go. Thank you."

Watching her leave, he shook his head. He should have expected her to arm herself before openly challenging powerful members of the Security Committee. The Zeteron Empire had decided the current upheaval created perfect opportunity to continue weakening the organization from within. Irony lay in her use of the word survival. He believed as did she. The fall of Chikondra would surely mark the beginning of the destruction of the Dil-Terra Interplanetary Alliance.

Chapter Sixteen

Huddled beneath thick bushes, Warnach held his breath as Zeteron troops pushed through the woods. His patrol had successfully destroyed a small camp of enemy soldiers with well-placed bombs. Replacements came quickly in search of guerilla fighters who were disrupting access to ground caches of weapons and supplies. After ten minutes of no sound and no life indications on scanners, Warnach signaled cautious resumption of their trip back to the caves.

As a result of the attack, the small band also rescued a young soldier being taken to Zeteron headquarters at the air command center. A sturdy volunteer carried the youth who had already been tortured and was unable to walk.

"Easy, Brehl. We're almost there." Warnach encouraged the wounded soldier whose face contorted in pain.

As they approached a hidden entrance to the caves, they again took cover. Zeteron air reconnaissance crisscrossed the area just above the trees. This time, they waited nearly an hour until Zeteron search efforts shifted south.

Leaving Brehl to undergo emergency treatment, Warnach headed dejectedly toward quarters that time and Chikondran hands had carved from solid stone. Inside, he glanced around. An office. If that's what it could be called. There was a desk near the far wall. A table, several chairs, and an upholstered settee. Geothermal power provided illumination and electricity for recharging power sources. To his right, a smaller chamber served as bedroom with an air-filled mattress on a carpet covering stone floors. Attached was a compact bathroom into which a shower and toilet had been fitted and plumbed for water sourced from natural springs.

Home. How he longed for open spaces. Green grasses. Colorful flowers. Fresh air. Singing birds. Spring rains. Home. How he had come to detest the always damp and stuffy confines of the web of tunnels carved so far beneath his world's surface. Sometimes, he felt almost as if life had regressed and that he had been drawn back into the womb, never again to be expelled to know the joys of living.

From a personal perspective, the afternoon had stirred bitter disappointment. Stalking and killing Zeterons, he had committed acts that appalled him. In doing so, he finally comprehended the pain Sandra had tried to express following Farsuk's assassination. Why? Why had it become so necessary for him to perform deeds he loathed?

Casting aside useless thoughts, he entered the tiny bathroom. Mechanically, he relieved himself, washed his hands. Staring into a narrow mirror, he winced at lines of worry now etched around the corners of his eyes. Stubble darkening his face showed hints of invading gray. He felt as if he'd aged twenty years since sending his family away.

Tossing his dirty shirt into a canvas hamper, he pulled on a lightweight sweater and headed toward the long chamber that served as a community dining area. A young woman showed him an unoccupied seat. Soon, she placed a bowl of thick vegetable soup and a plate of crispbread in front of him. Eating quietly, he let his mind wander.

"May I join you?"

He glanced upward with a blank expression. In resignation, he sighed and tilted his head toward the chair opposite him.

"The young man your patrol brought back will recover. I thought you might like to know."

He forced himself to respond. "Thank you."

"Warnach?"

A long pause. "Yes, Lashira?"

She appraised his somber mood. How she wished he would smile. "Do you still pray?"

"Every day." He answered truthfully, although he certainly had not prayed every morning and every evening as he had done before the Zeteron offensive.

"You should pray harder. I believe the Great Spirit will listen to you."

A piece of bread crackled as he bit off an edge. "Lashira, if the Great Spirit truly listened to me, not one of us would be hiding in these caves, nor would Zeteron ships be orbiting our world."

Her beautiful face softened. "You must not be praying hard enough, then. He will listen to you. I'm sure of it."

Growing impatient, he dropped a half-eaten slice of bread onto a plate and plunked his spoon into his bowl. "And you know this because?"

"I've been watching you. I've listened to what others say. You're facing here at home the same death and destruction you always worked so hard to prevent. You think the Great Spirit is ignoring you right now, and that makes you angry with Him. Still, you believe. Because you believe, when you finally decide to really pray, He'll listen." She stood up. "I have watch tonight. Try to get some rest."

That night, Warnach fell into exhausted sleep. After a few hours, he rolled from side to side on the mattress. Flinging covers off the bed, he quickly groped for their insulating warmth. Dreams tormented him. He traversed rivers of time as the past replayed itself. There she was. Glossy black hair falling to curve just above the upturned peaks of her breasts. Ebony eyes burning with promised passion. Cerea-nervos pulsating rhythmically. Smooth cinnamon skin gleaming. In his dream, his body prepared to take hers again.

Abruptly, he bolted upright. Stone walls coldly imprisoned him. Stinging tears scorched his eyelids. Sweat formed chilling beads on his forehead. Falling sideways, he fumbled in the darkness until trembling fingers curled around engraved metal. Drawing the ring to his chest, he curled into a fetal position. Squeezing his eyes shut, he choked on words he repeated over and over. "Ci'ittá mi'ittá, me'u Shi'níyah. Ci'ittá mi'ittá. Ci'ittá mi'ittá."

"We wanted you to be the first to know. With the Alliance Security Committee in a stalemate, we've assessed every other possibility. We've decided that we can't afford to wait any longer."

Her features might well have been carved from stone, considering the lack of emotion she showed. "What are your plans?"

"Admiral Mswati is already redirecting all Terran warships. He is also consulting with military advisors from all sympathetic worlds. Together, they are formulating a strategy to engage Zeterons."

"May I ask why now?" Her voice remained cool.

"Sandra," Eduardo replied, "we tried to act as cooperative members of the Alliance. You also know how hard we argued on behalf of Chikondra's defense. That tower the Zeterons are building - intelligence suggests it has uses beyond the planet's surface. If it can be tied into the abundant geothermal energy available on Chikondra, that tower can generate destructive force that can be aimed directly at any fleet within four adjacent sectors. I wish we could let Chikondran ground leaders know, but the net around Chikondra is tightening."

"Why do you believe when others don't?"

Eduardo sat down, his forward posture lending a sense of urgency. "I can't speak for the others. I don't understand them, nor do I think I want to. All I can tell you is that Earth's premiers and state leaders have unanimously decided to act as an independent Earth. Our decision is effective immediately."

Finally, she smiled her appreciation. "Eduardo, I do know you've tried to do this the right way. You have no idea how much I respect all of our premiers. I just hope that Mswati can pull plans together in time."

Arriving home that evening, she negligently tossed her things onto a table and headed directly to the kitchen. "Is Morcai in from practice yet?"

Nadana lifted a lid from a pan and stirred. "He's showering and changing for dinner."

"Lucia?"

"Reading."

Pensively, Sandra smiled and hugged Nadana. "Do you realize I'd be lost without you?"

Old features crinkled into a smile. "I'm glad you feel that way. Besides, spending time with Morcai and Lucia gives me much pleasure."

After dinner, the family gathered for evening prayers. When Morcai initiated opening chants, she noticed more passion in his voice than usual as her own silent prayers intensified. She prayed for her children, hoping they might never lose sight of their faith as they continued to adapt to a new culture. She prayed for the health of Nadana and Araman as constant worry hastened aging. Prayers offered for her beloved ki'medsah contained ever-increasing fervor.

"Momma?"

Lucia's hand against her cheek roused her. Blinking, she wondered when the others had finished their prayers. Sandra swallowed and forced a smile. "I'm sorry, sweetheart. I didn't mean to keep everyone."

Standing above her, Morcai grasped her hand and helped her up. "Momma, let's go upstairs. You need to go to bed."

Tossing and turning, Sandra rolled onto her side. Shoving her hand under the pillow next to her, she grasped her Kitak. Dragging it toward her face, she kissed cool metal. Her lips still lingered against the ring when a faint sound disturbed her. Sitting up, she was startled to see both Morcai and Lucia watching her from the foot of the bed.

Forcing herself awake, she frowned. "Why aren't you two in bed?"

"Momma, we want to talk to you." Morcai's voice held tones that reminded her of Warnach's.

"At two in the morning? You both have school tomorrow. I hope this is important."

Both of her children quietly moved and sat side by side at the end of her bed. Youthful faces were serious but tranquil. Morcai held his sister's hand while Lucia spoke first. "Momma, you know it's time to go home."

Shaking her head, Sandra wondered if she might be dreaming. "Home? This is home now."

"No, Momma. Chikondra is home. It always has been, even for you. It's time for you to go back."

"Lucia, what are you trying to say?"

"Momma," Morcai began, "you have to go back. Badehr needs you more than even he knows. You need him. Every day, we see your aura, and the light grows weaker. You need to be with him."

Sandra's jaw quivered. "I can't go back. I promised your badehr that I would bring both of you here to keep you safe."

"Momma, we are safe. Grandma and Grandpa check us every day. Nadana is here, and Maméi-mamehr, too. Badehr isn't safe and not just because of the Zeterons. He needs you to help him stay strong."

Her mind stalled. Gazing at her children, she said, "I can't leave you. Having children is a big responsibility. It isn't one I regret because I love you so much."

Lucia dropped her gaze to hands illuminated by moonlight filtering through window sheers. "We'll be safer if you go, Momma. You have to believe us. You have to find a way."

Leaning forward, Sandra stretched her arm out. Tucking her fingertips beneath Lucia's chin, she tilted the child's face upward. "It's late. Momma's tired, and you have school tomorrow. Let's make time to talk about this more on the weekend."

Saturday morning found them at her Uncle Rob's farm, bright and early. The Warner family had rallied to provide moral support for Sandra and her Chikondran family. Older women gathered over tea and coffee in the kitchen. Outside, other adults boosted children onto horses for rides along farm paths.

With more than enough guides to watch over young riders, Dave Warner took his daughter's hand and led her for a walk. Occasionally, they grinned at squeals of laughter carried on the breeze. Leaves fluttered and rustled above their heads. Nature wrapped them in a cocoon of calm.

Finally, he stopped. Lowering himself onto a fallen log, he propped one leg up and clasped his fingers together around his shin. "Mind a little fatherly advice?"

Wondering about the odd look on his face, she reluctantly plopped down onto a thick bed of brown pine needles. "What have I done this time?"

"It's not what you've done. It's what you need to do."

Her eyes narrowed, and her brow wrinkled. Puzzled, she asked, "What would that be?"

For nearly a minute, her father remained silent as he plainly wrestled with troubled thoughts. "Sandra, I've watched you closely ever since you moved here with the kids. At first, all I felt was relief that you were safe. Now, I'm scared to death for you."

"Scared? Why? You should be glad I'm not back home on Chikondra."

"You're right. I should be." His eyes closed. "The problem is that you're fading right before my eyes. I wish I could explain, but the life has all but disappeared from your eyes. The sparkle is gone. You can't begin to understand how hard this is for me to say, but you're barely half-alive without him. You need to find a way to go back."

Shocked, she stared at him. Stuttering, she replied, "Daddy, I… I can't go back. My children. They need me. Besides, I promised Warnach…"

"You promised him you'd get them to safety. You kept that promise. You know your mommy and I'll look after them. The whole family will. Now, it's time to keep the promises you made to him when the two of you married or unified or whatever the hell it was that you did."

Tears brimmed in eyes the color of the evergreens behind her back. "Daddy, I want to go to him, but I can't just leave and desert our children."

"Sandra, you have to go. Morcai and Lucia will be fine. You won't be if you stay. Even worse is that he won't survive. It took me years to figure him out. When I did, I still couldn't comprehend how much he loves you. Honey, that man needs you more than these trees around us need sun, soil, and water. Here, you've got your kids and his family. They've got all of us. There, he has no one. Without the three of you, he's totally lost and alone."

"Daddy…" Her children's words echoed through her mind. Suddenly, she could no longer withstand her swollen burden of pain and loneliness. Bitterly, she wept, grateful for her father's shoulder that she needed more than at any other time in her life.

The previous night had been disastrous. More than a dozen fighters had been killed with half that many seriously wounded. Attempting to learn more about the tower, a squad had been lured into a trap. Another unit had tried to help. Commanding a third patrol, Warnach had directed efforts to extricate injured soldiers. Without regard for his own life, he had engaged fire and drawn it away to create time for rescue and escape.

By the time they returned to base, morning had come and gone. Clever hiding places prepared in the event of emergencies had concealed them until Zeteron ground troops gave up. Thankfully, heavy storm clouds moved in, and torrential downpours discouraged further searches. Quickly, weary soldiers made their way into the tunnels from remote access points.

Although a godsend earlier, rainy weather outside created uncomfortable conditions inside. Humidity thickened the air. Dampness seeped through unsealed stone in some spots. Water formed puddles in several corridors and sloshed beneath their feet.

Returning to his quarters, Warnach breathed a prayer of relief that, although a faint musty smell hung in the air, everything was dry. Dragging off boots, soaked clothes, and sodden socks, he retrieved a towel to dry off. He had just pulled on dry trousers and socks when he heard tapping at the door.

The need for privacy prompted him to open the door and then quickly close it. Turning around, he gazed at Lashira. "You did well today."

She didn't smile. "I didn't come for your praise."

"Why did you come?"

Casting her eyes to the floor, she tried to dismiss the image of his half-nude body. "I…" Looking upward, she stepped closer and, with her right hand, grasped a muscular arm. "You were nearly killed out there today. Warnach, I don't know if I was ever that afraid in my life."

"Lashira," he answered tersely, "just like everyone else, I did what was necessary. Now, if that's all…"

Distressed eyes were pleading as both her hands took hold of him. "Today, more than ever, I understand the mistakes I made with you. Warnach, I love you. Almost losing you also made me realize that I never wanted you more than I do now. Don't send me away. Give me at least one chance to prove how much I care."

Caught off balance, he felt her arms slide around his back. Her breasts rose upward against his chest. Her mouth covered his as she sought the taste of him. For a moment, the dream he'd had weeks earlier flashed through his mind. Tired and lonely long years ago, he had taken her in hopes of winning her love. Tired and lonely now, he felt repulsed by her eager body, and he shoved her away.

"Stop it!" he growled furiously.

"Warnach," she murmured in a husky voice, "you need me, too. You wanted to respond. I felt it. We were lovers. We can be again."

Breathing heavily, he glared at her. "Why can't you leave the past where it belongs? Why?"

"Because I believe you still love me." When she reached out to touch him, he jerked away.

Searing bile rose and burned his throat. His lip curled in disgust. "Pity you, then, Lashira. I love only one woman."

"The Terran? The one who ran away to safety and left you behind?"

"You don't give up, even when you have no idea what you're talking about."

"Warnach, she's not here. She's not coming back, either. I won't ever leave you again. Together, we can comfort one another in the face of what's going on outside."

Staggering slightly, he sidestepped around her and flung the door open. "Get out."

Slamming the door closed, he stood motionless for only moments before he ran to the cramped bathroom. Falling onto the stone floor, he heaved until his guts emptied. Rising, he splashed icy cold water onto his face and rinsed bitter residue from his mouth.

With stumbling steps, he covered the short distance to the simple bed where he collapsed. With all his strength, he pressed his head between his hands. Praying with all his might, he begged the Great Spirit to let him live long enough to hold Sandra in his arms again and to watch his children grow up in peace.

Sandra offered her unexpected visitor a cup of tea. "I was quite astonished when I heard your name. How have you been?"

The ruggedly handsome man drank from his steaming cup before he said, "Quite well, actually. When my father died last year, he left me as the hereditary leader of our clan. Which reminds me. My mother really appreciated the personal message you sent her."

"I wish I could have delivered it in person."

Calvin Riley set his cup aside. There seemed little time for small talk. "Minister Sirinoya, Dargom owes you so much. Craig Brennan and I've met with other clan leaders. We've trained some of the finest pilots in the galaxy and expanded our space fleet."

Sandra's head tilted to one side. "I'm not sure I understand why you're telling me this."

"Minister Sirinoya, our leaders know Zeteron treachery on a personal basis. We're also convinced that if the Alliance continues to delay military intervention to help Chikondra, the results will be catastrophic for everyone, including Dargom. I'm here to inform you that Dargom's Parliament has voted to make its resources and military available for the benefit of Chikondra."

Her mind reeled. Dargom. Earth. Rehovot. All had pledged assistance. Slim hope it was, but it was a beginning. She smiled. "You do realize the potential for loss."

Beneath a shock of coppery hair, blue eyes gazed directly into hers. "I do recognize the potential. Unfortunately, no matter which path we choose, I'm convinced we all face enormous losses. However, if we don't resist, there's no hope at all, is there?"

A week later, she forced smiles and embraced her children. "Listen to your grandparents. And to Nadana and your uncles. And don't forget. Your Badehr loves you." Her voice cracked. "I'm sure he loves you as much as I do."

Lucia and Morcai hugged their mother tightly. "Tell Badehr we love him. Tell him to be strong until we come home."

Clinging to their youthful optimism, Sandra hugged them once again and followed with a final round of kisses. Grateful eyes met those of Mamehr, Nadana, and her parents. Turning, she linked her arm with Badrik's and headed toward his waiting transport. Flattening her nose against the window, she waved farewells until the transport ascended into cloud-dotted skies.

Staring at the back of their military chauffeur's head, Badrik sat with his arms crossed tightly over his chest. His profile revealed clenched jaw and tightly drawn lips. His demeanor was stiff, cold, and distant.

Settling back for the flight to Earth's Space Control Center, she closed her eyes. "To answer your questions, yes, I know exactly what I'm doing, and yes, I do intend to go through with this."

His head tilted sharply backward. "This is madness, Sandra. Sheer madness."

She stared at his obstinate profile. "You're right, Badrik. It is insanity, but there's no other choice for me. We need to alert Chikondrans on the ground about the tower. They also need to know that help is coming. After all our camping and hiking excursions, I know Miferasud almost as well as you and Warnach. I'm sure I'll get there."

His jaw shifted from side to side. "Have you considered the fact he might not be there? That he might be dead already?"

She didn't flinch. "He isn't dead. I would know. However, he does need me."

"And if you're killed trying to run the Zeteron blockade?"

"If that happens, then we must accept it as the will of God." Finally, she stretched out her hand and rested it on his tense thigh. "Badrik, I'm sorry to worry you this way, but you know that I'm the best-trained person available. Just as when Earth forces rendezvous with the Dargomans and Rehovotians, you'll be the best person to command them. Each of us must do what we both wish weren't necessary."

Twisting on the seat, he gripped her shoulders and stared into her eyes. "Swear to me you'll be careful, sister. If you die, I'll never forgive myself."

Her smile was tenderly sympathetic. "Big brother, no matter what happens, there'll be no need for you to forgive anyone, especially yourself. You'll have done no wrong. The decision is mine and mine alone. I must go to him."

Badrik breathed in and out. "Do you know how angry he'll be?"

"Don't fret so much. He'll understand. Besides, it won't make any difference once I get there."

"I want you to change your mind."

For a moment, her thoughts drifted back to the hours before dawn. In bed, nestled between her children, she had lain awake. Even with them so close, much of her soul had felt disconnected. Her father had said she and Warnach needed one another to survive. He was right. She smiled reassuringly. "It must be this way, Badrik. Without him, I'll die anyway."

"Emilio?" Sandra's eyes widened in stunned wonder. "What in the world?"

"Chica! It's been far too long!" The tall, handsome Latino greeted her with a huge hug and kisses for both cheeks.

"An odd time to say hello when I'm about to leave!" she exclaimed.

"So I know. I have little time. I just arrived for a short visit home. I wanted to wish you well and tell you that many of us will be lighting candles and praying for you."

Shaking her head, she grinned. "And?"

Taking her hand, they walked inside behind Badrik. "Your Chikondran brother is none too happy about this."

"No, he isn't. Tell me now. Why have you really come?"

He stopped and turned to face her. "Chica, the truth is that I only arrived back on Earth this morning to deliver crucial reports regarding the crisis. Our premiers have had me shuttling from planet to planet. There are many worlds now willing and ready to turn sympathy into action. Behind the scenes, I've been working on what might be considered a new alliance, one based on the true principles for which Chikondra stands. When you go, take with you the knowledge that you'll not be long alone in the struggle."

"Emilio, I…"

"I know, Chica. It's neither an easy concept nor an easy direction. However, it's an unfortunate path that those who truly seek peace must follow." He leaned forward and embraced her. Looking at her once again, he smiled. "I've always been proud to call you my friend but never more than today. *Dios te bendiga.*"

Within half an hour, she stood at the base of the shuttle ramp. Badrik hugged her tightly. "I promise, little sister. We'll take good care of Morcai and Lucia. Go with our prayers."

Despite miles of tunnels winding underground, the cave base had grown more confining than ever since his latest encounter with Lashira. Occasionally, he found himself forced to endure her presence during briefings and training. He also found it necessary to tolerate her during strategy sessions because she had quickly proven herself valuable as both guide and soldier. Avoiding her as much as possible, Warnach concentrated on his own growing capabilities as a military strategist.

Two weeks after her visit to his quarters, he lay beneath overhanging stones on a steep hillside. Tall grasses and leafy bushes blocked him from view. Peering toward the construction site, he filed extensive mental notes about size, supports, and internal workings rapidly progressing in precisely planned stages. Upon a broad base the height of a two-story building, a narrow structure had quickly risen. He prayed his presence would remain undiscovered so he could deliver rough sketches and notes back to base for further analysis.

Stiff limbs complained when he finally edged out of his niche. Concealed by the blackness of night, he began the painfully slow process of returning to the caves. Halfway there, he dropped to the ground and rolled toward a copse of low brambles. However, evasive action hadn't been swift enough. Lazon rays speared through the darkness.

Minutes later, he groaned as a heavy boot kicked him in the hip, rolling him onto his stomach. Another boot landed heavily on his back, shoving downward and pinning his upper body against hard ground. Harsh voices growled orders for him not to move. Finally, rough hands dragged him up by his jacket. Clutching his right arm, Warnach stared at captors in Zeteron uniforms. Although his arm burned as if on fire, his expression revealed nothing.

The officer in charge sneered menacingly. "Such a prize we've found. You're Sirinoya, aren't you?"

Remaining silent, Warnach's only reaction was a slight tilt of his head. The Zeteron officer slammed a powerful fist into Warnach's midsection, causing him to double over. "Let that be a lesson. When I ask a question, I expect a clear answer."

Catching his breath and straightening slightly, Warnach faced the sallow-faced attacker. "My apologies," he choked out breathlessly. "I am Warnach Sirinoya."

Swaggering as he turned to his men, the officer chuckled. "When we return to base, I think the captain will be quite pleased with this prisoner. Secure him, and let's get back."

Leaden steps slowed his progress despite impatient shoves from Zeteron troops. Limping grew more pronounced as pain in his bruised hip radiated into his leg. The lazon burn to his arm and shoulder sent searing sensation crawling through his flesh, making him feel shaky and nauseous. Weak and dizzy, he stumbled and pitched forward to the ground.

Voices suddenly cried out. High-pitched pings pierced the air. He tried to move, but his body refused to respond. Something hard banged against the side of his head. Loud, noisy commotion faded into a muted cloud. Consciousness sank into sucking black mire. Following a faint moan, his body grew totally still.

CHAPTER SEVENTEEN

"Staring toward home won't get us there any faster."

As if in slow motion, she glanced around in response to the comforting sound of a familiar voice. Sad and forlorn, she forced a ghost of a smile. "I wish your ship could travel as fast as my thoughts."

Forsij Tibrab placed a reassuring hand against her shoulder. Gazing through the observation window, he said, "You should rest while you can. Once we reach Chikondra, you will need all your strength."

Wearily, her head fell sideways to rest against her friend's arm. "Something's wrong, Forsij. I feel it."

Finding no surprise in her comment, he sighed. "How serious?"

She answered very quietly, "I'm not quite sure. I sensed pain, then struggle. Now, all I feel is strange darkness."

He hesitated before placing his arm around her and guiding her to an upholstered bench. "Do you think he's dead?"

For several moments, her eyes held indescribable blankness. Fingertips of both hands moved in slow circles atop her Kitak. When he began to wonder if she had even heard his question, she shook her head. "No. He's still alive."

Forsij sighed heavily. "Sandra, if he's still alive, he needs you. Once you reach the planet's surface, you're going to have to make your way to Miferasud to find him. There's no way we can know how difficult that path will be or how long it will take. Trust me, dear one. You must rest while you can."

Pursing her lips together, she raised her face. Stretching slightly, she kissed his cheek. "You're right. Forsij, would you do me a big favor before I return to my quarters?"

He smiled. "If I can."

"Will you go with me to the ship's Brisajai and pray with me?"

By the following day, prayer and meditation had restored her resolve as well as her ability to concentrate. After breakfast, she met with Forsij to prepare briefings for the trio of commandos due to transfer within hours from Earth's starship Comanche. Then, she met with the Dargoman pilots already on board.

Calvin Riley had decided to personally pilot the arrow-shaped Rapier assault fighter, renowned for speed and versatility both in space and underwater. His ship had been stripped of all unnecessary equipment to make room for three passengers. The plan was for Alliance vessels to perform a variety of maneuvers within Zeteron scanning range but just beyond Zeteron firepower. Riley's ship and a second Rapier carrying the remaining commando and essential supplies would race between the two Chikondran moons and slice through Chikondra's stratosphere for a dangerously steep descent into the ocean. If they succeeded in running the blockade, they would submerge and head for shore. The mechanics of the flight had been successfully tested both on Dargom and on Earth. The current challenge lay in avoiding Zeteron lazon cannons.

Sandra followed Forsij through the Curasalah's corridors as they headed toward the hangar deck to meet commandos who had volunteered to accompany her to the hidden base at Miferasud. After the incoming transport navigated the pressurization chamber and came to rest on deck, she waited to welcome hardy souls willing to join her on what many considered a suicide mission.

The first two commandos exited the transport. Introducing themselves as Lieutenants Sally Baines and Diego Mesa, each exuded confidence. They showed no personal reservations about guiding a civilian diplomat on such a rugged, perilous mission. Dedicated to their cause, they assured the notable Minister Sirinoya that she could look forward to delivering essential information to Chikondra's embattled resistance. The Terran commandos were then escorted to their quarters.

Sandra glanced around. Her eyes suddenly widened, and her mouth dropped open. Automatically, her arms flew out, and she rushed forward. "Mac! What are you doing here?"

Blue eyes lit up as he returned her embrace. "Temporary transfer. I find life quite an irresistible adventure when it coincides with your travels."

Stepping back, she grinned. "Are you telling me you're the third commando?"

"That I am." He then acknowledged Forsij's greeting before the three headed toward an officer's lounge for tea.

Setting her cup on a saucer, she shook her head in disbelief. "I still can't believe Admiral Mswati would dare endanger one of his finest starship captains on a mission like this. You must admit. It doesn't make sense."

"Mswati and I have been friends for a long time. He considers this little excursion critical if he's going to succeed in launching offensive action against the Zeterons. He trusts my observational skills and my judgment."

Knowing the Terran officer more by reputation than personal experience, Forsij studied Captain McAllen. Listening to the conversation freed him for closer scrutiny. The Chikondran captain sensed emotions deeper than McAllen would ever admit. One glance toward Sandra reinforced a feeling of empathy. Without her conscious awareness, fingertips of one hand lightly tapped against her Kitak.

The journey toward Chikondra kept busy with continual briefings and preparations for the blockade run. Dargoman pilots repeatedly inspected their ships and continually performed minor adjustments to compensate for differences in weight distribution. In the meantime, when Sandra wasn't deep in meditation or in conditioning exercises, she reviewed detailed maps of the planned route from the seashore to Miferasud over rugged terrain and through thick forests. Mac and the commandos checked equipment and discussed basic plans and options in the event of emergency.

Following dinner the evening before the mission, Sandra headed toward the observation deck. Forsij had outdone himself as host. Food had been excellent, and the company amiable and optimistic. Although she had been present in body, her mind had drifted constantly. One minute, she thought of Morcai and Lucia. The next, her thoughts shifted direction, seeking even the slightest connection to her ki'medsah.

Distant stars trailed streams of light as the Curasalah continued its flight. Black heavens were otherwise devoid of color or life. The faint, steady hum of efficient engines created subdued, monotonous background noise. Sensitive feet detected slight vibrations. Air around her felt cool. Detached aloneness ended when an arm extended around her shoulders.

"You look so isolated," Mac said softly. "Why is it I always seem to find you shouldering such heavy burdens?"

A slight waving of silken hair was the only indication she had moved. "I can't tell you how many times I've wondered about that same thing. All I ever really wanted was to help the peace process and dedicate myself to family and friends."

"Instead, you've become Earth's galactic heroine."

She breathed out a shaky sigh. "Being a heroine is far from anything I ever had in mind. Fighting a war was never part of the picture."

"You're not a soldier. You're a diplomat, and you're right. War shouldn't be part of your picture. Sandra, you have two children to think of, not to mention your own safety."

"I left my children safe with people who love them."

Gently, he spun her around. His gaze locked on serious features. "We can find our way to the Miferasud base. You don't have to do this."

Her expression grew distant, soaring ahead to Chikondra. Her eyes misted and closed. "I wish that were true. He needs me, Mac. Almost as much as I need him."

Mac's open hand rested against her cheek. Her expression broke his heart. "You realize that I'm damned jealous of him, don't you?"

Her eyebrows knit together, and she looked up. Comprehension escaped her. "Jealous? I'm not sure I understand."

"Why do you think I really came?"

"I…" Her voice trailed off. With a blank look, she shrugged her shoulders.

"Sandra, I love you. I have for years. When Mswati informed me of your plans, I threatened to resign my commission if he didn't authorize me to go with you. There was no way I could let you face that kind of danger alone."

Widening eyes regarded him with incredulity. "Mac," she murmured brokenly, "I didn't realize. I…"

Handsomely mobile features assumed a wry look that transformed into regret. Still, he couldn't tear his eyes away from her shocked face. "Forgive me. I never meant to say that, but it's all true."

Her chin quivered. "I wish I knew what to say, Mac. You know I absolutely adore you."

He nodded. "My bad luck that I found you years too late." Firmly, he grasped her shoulders. "Forget everything I just said. You should be trying to sleep. Tomorrow promises to be the start of what I expect to be a formidable ordeal."

Shaking her head, she started past him and then stopped. She reached upward and caressed his cheek. "Goodnight, Mac."

She had been gone barely five minutes when Forsij Tibrab appeared. "Good evening, Captain McAllen. I thought you would be asleep by now."

Mac glanced around at the Chikondran officer and turned back to stare into empty space. "I needed to clear my head before retiring to my quarters for the night."

Forsij again studied the Terran before turning to gaze out the same window. "I expect yours to be an especially hard task when you reach Chikondra."

A slight twitch pulled at the corner of Mac's mouth. "Ground warfare is never easy. Commando warfare is always worse, especially when one's real passion embraces the freedom of commanding a ship."

"Or when one's deepest passion in life belongs to another."

Mac's eyes narrowed as he twisted around. "Excuse me?"

Forsij smiled sympathetically. "I do not judge. I first met her nearly twenty years ago and realized immediately how unique she is. In my opinion, Warnach Sirinoya is the most fortunate man alive to have found a woman like her to love, especially when one considers how much she loves him in return. Wouldn't you agree?"

Mac gazed into the impenetrable darkness of Captain Tibrab's eyes. He wondered if he only imagined unspoken significance in the officer's words. However, before he could comment, Tibrab smiled, wished him goodnight, and left.

Arriving at the far edge of the Chikondran solar system, Forsij Tibrab constantly monitored activities of escort battleships. His crew had performed duties with unparalleled precision as cargo was stowed, braced, and secured on the Dargoman assault craft. Calvin Riley repeated procedures to be followed once the Rapiers reached open water. Commandos rechecked personal gear. Mac performed final inspections.

Escorted on the arm of Forsij Tibrab, Sandra was the last of the mission team to appear on deck. Drawn into a concentrated mask, her face reflected calm determination. Squared shoulders and straight back created an air of authoritative command. Garbed in fatigues and boots, she looked every bit the part of a soldier except for the gleaming band of golden rafizhaq circling her head.

"Captain McAllen, I deliver your guide for this mission." Forsij looked straight into the Terran captain's eyes. "My advice is to trust her instincts. My most fervent request is that you deliver her safely to my friend."

Mac's head dipped respectfully. "Your advice is well received, Captain Tibrab. I promise to do all possible to fulfill your request."

Forsij turned from Mac. He gave Sandra a gentle smile. "Dear one, your ki'medsah needs you. May the Great Spirit bless your heart with courage and your path with holy light."

Ignoring the presence of Chikondran military personnel, Sandra lifted her arms and encircled Forsij's neck. "Dear friend, I carry your prayers in my heart. Thank you for all you've done. May God keep you safe." Lightly kissing his cheek, she then smiled and turned, placing her hand in Mac's so he could boost her into the Rapier.

His head turned on the low, hard pillow. Light and shadow leapt and danced through his brain. Muffled sounds trapped him in a fluttering cloud. Arms and legs, leaden and numb, failed to respond. His own heartbeat, impelling life-giving blood through his veins, was the only thing of which he was certain. The total void of unconsciousness reclaimed its hold on him.

Time passed. Sunshine filled his vision. Summer foliage adorned lush woods surrounding his ancestral home. Children's laughter drifted on lazy breezes. Morcai and Lucia sounded so happy and carefree.

Peaceful satisfaction seeped into weary limbs. Deep beds of evergreen needles cushioned his back from hard ground. Her fingertips grazed the length of his neck with erotic invitation. The palm of her hand, firm and insistent, flattened over the expanse of his chest. His nostrils flared, filling with the sweetness of her scent. His lips parted, hungering for the passion imparted by her mouth.

A husky moan escaped his throat. His body had endured its separation from hers for too long. His arms responded, needing to hold her close again. Deep and passionate, he felt the gently probing kiss.

Abruptly, he jerked his head to the side. Groggy but instantly awake, he rolled onto his side, pushing himself onto the support of one elbow. "Damn you! Damn you, Lashira!"

Lashira's stricken face swam into focus. "Warnach. Praise the Great Spirit. You're finally awake."

He heaved in several breaths between gritted teeth. Angry words slurred thickly. "What do you think you're doing?"

Hesitating, she leaned forward and pushed him back onto the pillow. Her voice was remarkably steady. "I couldn't help myself. You looked so peaceful, so happy. Wherever you were, I wanted to be there with you."

Clamping his eyes shut, he consciously fought to clear his mind. Slowly, he again pushed himself into a sitting position.

Glancing around quickly, he realized he was in a partitioned section of the infirmary. Pressing the heel of his left hand against his temple, he questioned her. "What happened?"

"I convinced Captain Jizmatlah that you were too late returning. We went searching and saw that a Zeteron patrol had taken you prisoner. We rescued you."

He remembered sudden confusion but nothing more. "Then what?"

"Here," she said, pulling his arm down. "Drink some water. You need to hydrate yourself."

Shaky hands lifted the cup, and he took several sips of the refreshing liquid. When she took back the glass, he finally gazed into her face. "Did we lose anyone else?"

"No. One wounded. Minor. You've already had two HAU treatments." Seated on the edge of the narrow cot, she covered his hand with hers. "Warnach," she began, her voice softening, "I haven't left you. Not for a minute. I couldn't. Don't let the past continue to separate us."

Weakly swallowing, Warnach's head shook slightly. "Any distance between us, Lashira, is your own creation."

Sorrowful eyes watched as he slid his hand from beneath hers. "Have you no mercy for me? Do you honestly hate me that much?"

Staring at her, Warnach couldn't repress a certain pity. "My heart holds no space for hatred."

Hopefulness sparked in her eyes. "Does that mean you really still care about me?"

A masculine voice interrupted them. "Master Sirinoya, I'm glad to see you're awake." The physician cast disapproving eyes toward Lashira. "Miryah Ehmedrad, will you excuse me?"

Minutes later, the doctor studied scan results. "You've recovered quite well. The lazon wound will likely cause weakness in your shoulder and arm for perhaps a week. Other than that, a day or two of rest should restore you."

Warnach nodded appreciatively. "Thank you, doctor. Could you ask one of my aides to bring clean clothing?" Suddenly, he stopped, his eyes wildly darting around. "My Kitak! What happened to my Kitak? Where is it?"

"Calm yourself, Master Sirinoya. Simlani Niflatish removed it with a ceremonial cloth before we placed you inside the HAU."

A wave of nausea subsided, and Warnach sucked in a breath of relief. "Eyach'hamá eu Yahvanta. For a moment, I was afraid…"

Mentally noting his patient's spontaneous reaction, the doctor remarked, "I am relieved that, despite trying circumstances, you do not forget the most important facets of our lives."

Sensing veiled reference to Lashira, Warnach's eyes met those of the doctor. "I would prefer death rather than dishonor sacred vows made in love and faith."

Approval reflected in the doctor's smile. "I shall summon your aides. I shall also ask the Simlani to bring your Kitak."

Streaking between Chikondra's two moons, Dargoman pilots steered sleek vessels in sharply twisting maneuvers to avoid lazon fire from swiftly approaching Zeteron fighters. Terran and Dargoman starfighters swarmed in and fired against the enemy while Calvin Riley adjusted his ship's trajectory for entry into Chikondra's upper atmosphere.

Despite internal cabin pressurization, Sandra grimaced against the compression flattening her body against her seat inside the Rapier. With eyes squeezed tightly shut, her heart pounded as blood throbbed through her veins. Never had she encountered such physical force as the Rapier's screaming dive that seemed to go on forever.

She was startled by the abrupt, jarring shock when the ship pierced the surface of Chikondra's ocean. Then, she felt an almost immediate sense of leveling. Her head swam dizzily, and she forced herself to draw in slow, deep, regular breaths. No wonder they had been warned against eating or drinking anything until after reaching the planet. Despite an empty stomach, she felt a powerful urge to regurgitate.

"Everyone all right?" Calvin Riley's voice couldn't quite restrain a teasing note.

White-faced, Baines nodded. Mac grinned. "Quite a ride, Mr. Riley. My compliments."

"And you, Minister Sirinoya?"

Sandra sought relief through humor. "I'm not quite sure. Maybe if we could recover all my lost parts you left up in orbit..."

Chuckling, Mac released his harnesses and turned around to face her. Grasping trembling hands, he noted ashen features and glazed eyes. "Not a fan of roller coasters, I take it?"

"Roller coasters? No."

"All right, my friends. Heads up. We have complications."

Crisp command instantly saturated Mac's voice. "What sort of complication?"

"O'Rourke made it with Mesa, but he's advising we have a flock of nasty birds up top. Our signal blockers must be working, or they'd be firing into the water by now. We're not going to be able to surface for a while."

"Suggest you hold steady position. They'll expect us to head toward shore."

"Agreed," Calvin responded. Communicating with O'Rourke, they all unfastened harnesses and stretched as much as possible within the confining space of the Rapier.

Hours later, the ships broke the surface. Sheathed in darkness, the arrow-shaped vessels bobbed in ocean waters. Riley looked worried. "Under power, we're maybe an hour from land. However, I'm concerned that Zeterons might be waiting. Any new suggestions?"

Mac looked at Baines. "Lieutenant, any ideas?"

"We have rafts."

Calvin shook his head. "An hour under power in these ships. In motorized rafts, you look at reaching the shore beneath midmorning sun. You'll make perfect targets."

Mac felt Sandra's hand curve around his. As he watched her face, haunting memories crept into his awareness. "Sandra?"

Heavy eyelids fluttered and opened. "Please. I need quiet."

Baines and Riley exchanged odd glances. Mac held an index finger to his lips, signaling silence. Minutes passed. They watched curiously. Her head moved from side to side, and her lips formed silent sentences. Finally, she stilled. Moments later, she asked, "Calvin, can we safely get the rafts into the water with our gear?"

"Aye, Minister Sirinoya, but it's a long journey. You must realize that you'll be exposed once the sun rises."

She smiled. "Get us a little closer. I'll take care of the rest."

Not quite half an hour had passed before the Rapiers stopped. From hatches opened just above the waterline, two rafts were deployed and floated on the rippling ocean. Trailing behind the boats, buoyant, waterproof packs were filled with supplies and equipment. Baines and Mesa entered one raft. Mac maneuvered into the second raft and extended his hands to Sandra, who perched on the hatch's threshold. Firmly in his grasp when a swell raised both Rapier and raft, she tumbled on top of him.

Peering from inside, Calvin laughed. "Sorry for the unfortunate exit, Minister Sirinoya. I wish you a more solid landing onshore."

Pushing off Mac's chest, she shook her head. "I'm certain Captain McAllen appreciates that wish more than I."

Mac whispered wickedly, "I think not. A desperate man appreciates any opportunity he can get to hold the woman of his dreams."

No matter what, she couldn't find it within herself to be angry. "Sit up. We've got work to do." She shifted her gaze out to sea and then to Riley. "Help is coming. Whatever you do, swear that you and O'Rourke will say nothing to anyone other than Captain Tibrab."

Riley's rakish expression grew serious. "Help? What kind of help?"

"Swear it, my friend." Serious eyes met those of her companions. "The same goes for all of you. I need your oaths of secrecy if we're to reach shore safely."

Mac's eyes narrowed for a moment. "Baines? Mesa? Are you willing to swear such an oath?"

Curious, each vowed to keep whatever secret the minister required. Mac met Sandra's waiting gaze. "You know I'll keep any secret you ask of me."

"Thanks, Mac." Smiling, she told Riley, "As soon as we clear your ships, back off slowly and return at will. Oh, and don't be surprised by anything you see."

Rolling swells raised and lowered the dark-colored rafts. Moonlight reflected sparkling glints of light off the water. Fascinated, Mac watched Sandra's expressions change. Slowly, she raised her hands. "No one move."

Unexpectedly erupting through the water's shimmering surface, silver projectiles hurtled skyward, carving tall, sweeping arches through the air before splashing back into the sea. Within minutes, one of the creatures lunged forward, sliding its upper body across the raft's side.

"Hello, my friend!" Sandra cried out as her arms wrapped around the sleek body. "How glad I am to see you again!"

Clicks and whistles sounded from behind the one she hugged. With Mac clutching her belt to keep her from falling overboard, she leaned forward to caress each of five Quazon. "A new friend, I see! I'm so glad to meet you."

For a matter of seconds, Mac twisted his head enough to look toward the other boat. Perplexed commandos stared in utter confusion. When the large male slid back into the water, five tapered snouts protruded from the sea. Glittering eyes fixed on Sandra, who talked to them as though carrying on a normal conversation.

At long last, she settled back into the boat. "A change of plans. Zeterons are patrolling the waters and the beach where we intended to land. My friends will guide us to a safe spot to go ashore. They also have a better route for us to travel to Miferasud. It's further in terms of distance but won't take as long because of less rugged terrain and fewer enemy patrols."

"Your friends." Mac sat back and stared at her. "Sandra! They're fish!"

Her face screwed up disapprovingly. "They're mammals, not fish. They're called Quazon, and they're more intelligent than all of us combined."

"Excuse me?"

She gave a curt shake of her head. "Mac, these creatures are sacred angel spirits on Chikondra. That's why you can't say anything about meeting them."

Almost wondering if stress had caused her to lose her mind, he recalled her actions on Dargom. "Do you mind me asking how you know about this safer route?"

"The Quazon told me." She tried to avoid sounding impatient. "Mac, if you must know the truth, they communicate with me telepathically. I know it sounds unbelievable, but..."

"Unbelievable? More like preposterous!"

"Have it your way," she responded impatiently. "You can just get back inside the Rapier and leave me with the Quazon. They'll take me to shore. Then, I'll make my own way to Miferasud."

"Think again, sweetheart. Where you go, I go." Mac cast skeptical eyes toward Quazon faces. "You honestly mean these creatures communicate with you? Intelligently?"

Exasperation draped over her features. Glancing toward the Quazon, she shook her head. "Some people need hard lessons, my friends."

Rising from the water in an amazing demonstration of synchronized balance, all five Quazon filled Mac's face with streams of salty seawater. Then, in a synchronized wave, they lunged forward into the water and swam ahead.

Wiping his face with his arm, Mac glared at her in mock anger. "Not fair."

"Just start the motors and follow them. Otherwise, I'm jumping overboard and hitching a ride."

While the Terrans followed torpedo-shaped bodies leading the way through open waters, Mac observed in amazement when the apparent leader fell back numerous times as if to check on Sandra. Lying on her stomach, she dangled her arm overboard, fingers outstretched to touch the Quazon. Having traveled to many worlds, he had often heard about legends and read of spiritual and psychic encounters. Never had he expected to be caught up in one of them.

Just as hints of pinkish-gold edged above the horizon, they caught sight of shore. High cliffs plunged into shallow waters guarded by enormous, craggy rocks. Sandra glanced around. "Stop the motors. We need to paddle our way closer before higher tides move in."

Silver guides proceeded with ultimate confidence. Sandra and Mac rhythmically dipped oars into the ocean. Mesa and Baines followed. As they headed toward one particularly large stone formation, Sandra called out, "They say our heads are too high. Toss the tethers into the water and lie low in the rafts."

Following her commands, they felt themselves being pulled and pushed. Slimy, dripping rock faces were barely a foot above sidewalls of their rafts. They soon discovered themselves inside a large cave. Small openings permitted the entry of morning sunlight. Quickly, Mesa climbed onto a broad sandbar and helped Baines out. While she secured the raft and started dragging up equipment, Mesa pulled Mac and Sandra onto dry sand.

Kneeling close to the water's edge, Sandra gratefully acknowledged her friends. "I know. That's why we came. We'll do everything possible to stop the invaders." Her voice broke. "I won't forget. I love you, too."

Leaning forward, Mac's hands spanned her waist and helped her stand. "If I hadn't seen it with my own eyes," he whispered, "I wouldn't have believed it."

"That's how I felt the first time I met them," she said while watching Quazon bodies glide beneath the water's surface and disappear.

With equipment secured and personal hover transports ready, Mac turned to her. "What now?"

"There's a short tunnel off to the left. We follow it until we reach stone stairs. Step carefully because they're slick. When we reach the top, two Luradrani are already waiting. We'll eat with them and rest before we head for Miferasud."

"Luradrani?"

Sandra nodded. "Chikondran priests, if you will. The Quazon told me they're gatekeepers here for Chikondra's sacred Efi'yimasé Meichasa."

Rodan sat beside Eduardo de Castillo and John Edwards. Leaders from Earth, Rehovot, and Dargom had attracted many sympathetic Alliance members. Public outcry had arisen on those worlds in support of the original, embattled seat of the Alliance government. Forging a new coalition, their worlds broke ranks from those who advocated abandoning Chikondra.

They also hoped to assemble a larger force for the protection of planets in their own solar systems.

Rodan's eyes shone with gratitude. "I cannot express how much I appreciate your courage and your loyalty. I assure each of you that, if my world survives, my people will never forget your actions."

President Capret, head of state from Koozikra, dipped her face respectfully. The slightly indented channel that divided her skull into halves revealed rhythmically vibrating blood vessels. "Master Khalijar, your world never should have been subjected to this attack without military support. Had my planet not been so far away, we surely would have delivered help sooner."

Rodan swallowed against the knot in his throat. "My people resist with courage. They knew our truest friends would come as quickly as they could. Now, for the good of all, it is our task to ensure that the Zeteron tower is disabled before it becomes fully functional. I cannot ask any of you to send ships into battle to face certain death."

Nolj Kirimaris, now senior ambassador from Simartis Major, asked the question troubling all present. "Master Khalijar, if that tower really has the capabilities we begin to see, we have little hope of saving Chikondra. The Zeterons will then surely expand their aggression into the heart of the Alliance. Are you certain the message will arrive about the necessity to disable the tower?"

Rodan met her gaze. Images of Sandra and Quazon teased his mind. "As we speak, that message is en route, and yes, I am confident the dispatch will be delivered. With all my heart, I believe our messenger will not fail."

"Thank you, Kaliyah," Rodan said later as his daughter cleared plates from the table. Lifting a glass of dessert wine, he tasted amber liquid and sighed. "Dargom's pilots certainly accomplished a miracle."

Badrik nodded. "How strange it feels knowing that the fate of our world now lies in Terran hands."

Farisa rested her elbows on the table and, holding her glass between her hands, voiced disagreement. "Only the escort is Terran. I've come to believe Sandra is as much Chikondran as any one of us sitting here."

A glint of light sparked in Mirah's eyes. "You make a valid point."

Badrik's expression remained serious. "I cannot deny that her connection exceeds my comprehension."

Rodan set down his empty glass. "Reinforcements will soon arrive from Medron. In the meantime, let us pray her connection is not severed by Zeteron lazons."

Chapter Eighteen

Sandra secured straps on her knapsack. Stopping at the tunnel opening to the outside, Mac waited as she paused and said, "Esteemed Luradrani, we thank you for your kindness. Please, keep us in your prayers."

The elderly priest bowed his head. "Minister Sirinoya, it has been our honor to serve you and your comrades. Our prayers go with you in the hope you bring fulfillment to ancient prophecy."

Later, Mac helped her descend the ledge where, years earlier, Badrik and Warnach had sat when they had made their pilgrimage to Efi'yimasé Meichasa. Once on solid ground, Mac's firm grasp prevented her from moving. Blue irises fixed on her face. "I'm not sure English was the best means of communication back there. What did he mean by fulfilling ancient prophecy?"

Her shoulders rose. "In all honesty, I don't have a clue. All I know is that Chikondran religious often speak in poetic riddles that usually confuse me. Whatever he meant doesn't really matter right now. We need to reach Miferasud."

Sheltered by velvety night, Warnach sat beneath a tree near a remote entrance to the cave base. Holding his left arm across his chest, he massaged tender muscles. Leaning back against the tree's smooth trunk, he closed his eyes and enjoyed the simple pleasure of breathing fresh air.

The music of night birds ushered him into a dreamlike state. Memories of life with his ki'mirsah invaded. To his deathbed, he would carry images of the night they had celebrated Shi'firah. In many ways, that night had been the true beginning of the life she had taught him to cherish. Her promises of loyalty and devotion had remained constant. Her love had introduced him to wonders and awed him with miracles.

For just a moment, his hand drifted upward and touched his Kitak. No matter how great any distance that had ever separated them, he always sensed when her thoughts were of him. At that moment, he felt distinct vibrations. As his hand dropped, he smiled. Knowledge that she was directing loving thoughts toward him provided balm for his weariness.

"Warnach?"

Reluctantly, he relinquished private retreat and opened his eyes. "What now, Lashira?"

Sitting in front of him, she gazed longingly. "Why do you always speak so harshly to me?"

His eyes lifted impatiently. "Lashira, you do little to inspire me otherwise."

"They told you I saved your life."

He expelled a sharp breath. "Yes, they did, and I have thanked you. What more do you want?"

Her chin quivered, and she looked away. "Not so much. A little kindness. More than anything, a little of the love we once shared."

"I credit you with one thing," he grumbled. He then stood and brushed clinging dust from his pants. "You do persevere."

Rising, she turned as he edged past her. Watching him disappear into the entrance, she felt her heart sank. Lowering herself, she sat on ground that she imagined still held the warmth of his body. Tears eased down her cheeks. Her mind and body ached with need for him. Somehow, there must be a way to reach him, even if only for a little while.

With her back to the curving wall of a narrow crevasse, Sandra felt Mac's body press her more tightly against rough, unyielding rock. Zeteron troops had decided to take a break no more than ten meters from their hiding place. Sally Baines' boots were inches above her head. The four Terrans huddled in tense silence for more than an hour until enemy soldiers headed along a path opposite their intended route.

Climbing out, they hastily gathered equipment shoved into the fissure. Mounting quiet hover transports, they resumed their trek along wooded paths. Occasionally, Mac glanced in awe at Sandra. She insisted that Quazon had warned her about the approaching enemy and guided her to safe hiding. Quazon or no, they were rapidly nearing Miferasud. By the time they reached their destination, the journey would likely be shortened by three or four days.

On the sixth night, they made camp just within the easternmost boundaries of the Miferasud preserve. Surrounded by trees with trunks five meters in diameter, they kept close together. While Mesa stood watch, the others prepared light, high-energy meals over small, disposable, radiant heat-cubes. With temperatures dropping, hot food was a welcome treat after a day that had frequently required them to hike on foot rather than use their hover platforms.

Cool breezes swept down from nearby mountains. Sandra shivered. Mac sat down and wrapped them both in his jacket. "Is it always this chilly?"

"It's not unusual around here. The mountains here are famous for currents that sweep down from their ice caps."

"Any new warnings popping into that head of yours?"

She snickered. "Ah, ever the disbeliever."

"Wrong, my dear. I'm convinced. You gave me no choice. What's next?"

Grateful for their shared warmth, she snuggled closer. "Logically, we should expect more Zeteron patrols. Ideally, we should be able to reach the cave entrances after another short hike of, say, six or seven hours on foot."

"On foot? Why can't we use the hovercrafts?"

"From here on, the forest is far too dense. Personally, I don't fancy smashing into one of these choktilal trees."

"Good point. Why don't you try to sleep some? Maybe your fishy friends can find a nice clear path to help me deliver you to this hidden base."

Dawn kissed quiet forest with soft light. Rising and stretching, Sandra could hardly believe that, within a short journey, Zeterons tormented Chikondra's people and waged war against the most populous region of the planet. Glancing at sleeping comrades, she slipped into the woods for a few moments of privacy. Returning, she knelt and urgently grasped Mac's shoulder.

"Shsh," she whispered. "I heard voices in the distance. We need to break camp and get moving."

Rapidly, they assembled equipment and brushed away signs of their presence. In semi-darkness, they sought cover. Crouching behind a tall, dense patch of thorny mirmaja, they held their breaths and listened to boots crunching through the undergrowth. Sandra's eyes closed, and she almost felt like crying. Shocked by the sudden sound of her voice, Mac pitched forward to his knees.

"Greetings on this morning granted by the Great Spirit," she called out in Chikondran. As footsteps halted, she cautiously crawled out from beneath clinging, scratching bushes.

A young commander hauled her to her feet. "Minister Sirinoya?" The officer's face showed even more shock than Mac had felt. Returning early from three days of reconnaissance, he had never dreamed of encountering the renowned Terran diplomat. "How did you get here? What are you doing?"

Her relieved smile quickly faded. "We've brought critical information. I must reach your commanders urgently." Ray weapons suddenly pointed toward the bushes. "Stop! I travel with three Terran officers. My people would not allow me to come alone."

With a sharp tilt of his head, the squad commander signaled his patrol to lower their weapons and help the others escape prickly brambles. Once everyone had gathered together, the commander ordered his squad to help the Terrans with their packs and then took the lead. Along the way, in excellent English, he updated them on recent developments. He expressed his most significant worries about the strange tower near the former air command. Although still incomplete, trial rays were often aimed at nearby cities or into space. With Zeterons heavily guarding the perimeter, Chikondran freedom fighters had found no way to reach the tower. Neither did they know how to neutralize it.

Following hours of traipsing through thick forest, they stopped. Voice signals mimicked native birds and alerted guards to their approach. Quickly, they hurried ahead and entered a tunnel opening that, from above, looked like nothing more than a gigantic downed choktilal.

Curious eyes stared at the dirty, disheveled Terrans descending further and further into the depths of the cavern base. The commander instructed his troops to take Mac and the others to quarters where they could shower and change. Etched by war into a youthful face, deep lines eased into a courteous smile. "May I assume you wish me to take you to Master Sirinoya?"

Sandra's mouth spread into a nervous smile. "Your assumption is a good one."

Minutes later, one of Warnach's aides glanced upward as he strode swiftly through a corridor. "Eyach'hamá eu Yahvanta! Minister Sirinoya! Such a surprise!"

Glad upon learning that Warnach was alone inside his office, she peeked around a half-opened door. Her heart skipped a beat. How tired and dejected he looked as he gazed into a familiar triple frame. Pensively, she allowed her fingers to rub back and forth along her Kitak. As if in direct response, he touched his Kitak. Then, setting the frame back on the desk, he stood. Turning around, he leaned over a monitor displaying strategic information.

With tentative hesitancy, she entered the dreary office. Swallowing nervously, she hoped her voice didn't falter. "Me'u ki'medsah, you mustn't be angry with me."

Sharply pivoting, Warnach froze and stared. "Sandra?"

She dared a smile. "Warnach, I had to come. I couldn't bear the separation another day. Please, don't be angry."

Within seconds, his arms imprisoned her. "Me'u Shi'níyah," he whispered brokenly as he frenziedly kissed every part of her face. "Sandra? Is this possible? Am I dreaming?"

Frantic lips met. Desperately, they clung to each other as their kiss deepened. Resisting when he would have broken their bond, she tangled her fingers into his hair. Finally, barely able to breathe, they parted. Long fingers laced into her hair as his thumbs caressed circles where Kitak rounded her temples. Glazed eyes joyfully drank in her image.

"Me'u Sandra," he murmured as his lips feverishly brushed her forehead, "I am completely furious with you." He kissed her eyelids. "That can wait." He kissed her nose. "Shi'níyah, how I've missed you."

The sound of his voice was like healing tonic seeping into the far reaches of her soul. Heated lips injected fresh, vital warmth. "Me'u Warnach," she whispered when he clutched her tightly, "I love you. I love you so much."

Standing in the center of his office, they relished the incoming tide of relief. Currents, much like those that had once swept them into Ku'saá, now revitalized their bonded spirits. Momentarily freed from fear of violence and war, their hearts and thoughts focused on their precious union.

Swaying, Warnach finally led her to the loveseat where they sat down. Eyes of darkest brown studied her countenance. Tenderly, he smiled. "You look so tired, me'u Shi'níyah."

Closing her eyes, she nodded. Her stomach growled loudly. "Tired, smelly, and hungry, I'm afraid."

He chuckled lightly. "My quarters are cramped, but I do have rudimentary bathroom facilities. You could take a shower. Afterward, we can get something to eat while we talk."

"I'd love a shower. It's been days. I left a knapsack outside the door with clean clothes. Would you mind?"

"Go through that door, and you'll find the bath."

While she showered, he sat on the end of the bed and pulled items from the large backpack. Shaking his head, he couldn't help grinning. Compact, lightweight, battery-powered hairdryer and curling wand. Hairbrush and leak-proof cylinders of personal toiletries. Just beneath those lay the pouch of vacuum-packed garments. Extracting the bag, he opened it and removed essential, functional clothing—three pairs of slacks, long-sleeved pullovers, a sleep shirt, socks, and underwear. Holding a shirt to his cheek, he savored the smoothness of the fabric and the faint scent belonging to her.

"I'm much softer than that shirt. Less wrinkled, too."

He laughed and got up. Reaching her, he kissed first her lips, then damp, towel-dried hair. "I don't dare remove that towel you're wearing, or you'll never get to eat."

Giggling and stepping away from him, she picked up grooming items and undergarments. "I won't take long."

True to her word, she soon emerged with long hair smoothly curving around her shoulders and a gleam in her eyes. Again, he went to her. His fingertips traced the edge of the lacy bra covering full breasts. "I believe this may be worse torture than the towel."

Seeing smoldering desire in his eyes, she smiled. "Feed me, and let me rest a little. After that, I promise to make up for any unintentional torture."

"I love your promises," he whispered huskily as his face nuzzled against her sensitive neck. "Finish dressing so I can help you keep this newest one."

She pulled on shirt, slacks, and socks. Flipping open a flap on the side of her pack, she removed a pair of lightweight slip-on shoes. Straightening, she shook her head in dismay. "I must be tired!" Disappearing into the bathroom, she came back, Kitak in hands held out to him. "It's been so long. Will you put it on?"

His grin faded as he took the golden ring from her. As he'd done so often throughout the years, he kissed the diamond. Adjusting the ring around her head, he kissed the stone again after tilting her face upward. "Me'u Shi'níyah, it has been much too long. Ci'ittá mi'ittá."

With her arm tucked beneath his and their fingers laced together, he guided her through busy tunnels. Frequently, he lifted their hands and kissed her fingers. Reaching the dining area, he stopped long enough to order dinner trays. Then, without once releasing her, he headed toward a table in a deserted corner.

After they were seated, he leaned forward and again grasped her hands. His expression was intense. "You must forgive me. I can hardly bear to let you go."

Her face dropped as she stared at elegantly sculpted fingers wrapped tightly around hers. "Your touch feels so good."

Quiet moments were interrupted when their trays arrived. Praying first, he sat back in his chair and affectionately gazed at her. "Tell me. How are my children?"

Nibbling a buttered roll, she smiled. "Morcai is spirited and fun-loving. He's made many friends. He also earned a spot on his school's soccer team. Badrik says he plays soccer the way you play pafla. Hard, fast, and accurate."

Pleasure and pride gleamed in Warnach's eyes. "He must be a terror, then."

"A gifted player, so his coaches say. On the other hand, he's serious about his studies and never fails to pray or read from your Book of Faith."

Warnach's features softened. "And my Lucia? How is she?"

Sandra set aside her fork and dabbed her mouth with a napkin. Evergreen irises misted. "Lucia perplexes me. She does well in school and has a couple of friends, but I've never known anyone, child or adult, as serene as she is. Everyone comments on what a blessing she's been since we left Chikondra. I sometimes think Nadana only survives because of Lucia."

"Lucia has always been especially sensitive and nurturing."

"Strong, too. They both told me to tell you how much they love you and miss you. Lucia was very insistent that I tell you to stay strong until they return home."

Sadness crossed his face. "I miss them so much it hurts. How I hope the day will come when I can hold them again."

Leaning forward, she stroked his hand. "It will, Warnach. We're stronger together. Our children understood that and, despite my resistance, pushed me to come back. I can't explain exactly why, but I trusted in their wisdom."

He couldn't quite meet her gaze. "The wisdom of children. So simple and untainted."

"Your children are especially wise. I credit Quazon."

As they finished eating, their conversation drifted. Leaving war-related discussion for briefings the next day, he inquired about friends and family on Earth. Tensely, he questioned her about the harrowing trip through the Zeteron blockade and the resulting cross-country hike to Miferasud. Glancing around, he stopped in the middle of a question about the headlong dive from orbit. Excusing himself, he stood and crossed the dining room.

He greeted the Terran with a quickly executed bow. "Captain McAllen, welcome."

McAllen's blue eyes briefly darted toward the corner table where Sandra waited. "Master Sirinoya, it's an honor to see you again."

Noting the captain's furtive glance without comment, Warnach smiled. "It seems I owe you a great debt for my ki'mirsah's safe arrival. Would you care to join us at our table?"

Mac smiled and followed him to the table where Sandra sat. "For a few minutes. I'm supposed to meet the others who came with us."

"I'm surprised you haven't eaten yet," Warnach remarked.

"I have to admit. After I got a shower and sat down, the next thing I knew, I was waking up."

Sandra chuckled and looked at Warnach. "I'm afraid I gave him an unexpected wake-up call this morning. I heard voices in the distance. We scrambled into hiding. Fortunately, those voices belonged to a Chikondran patrol."

Warnach smiled and then addressed Mac. "I understand your arrival on Chikondra was somewhat unusual."

Mac laughed aloud. "Unusual. An understatement if ever there was one. Dargoman Rapiers diving headfirst from orbit into the ocean. Some of us tumbling face-first into rafts in the middle of the night." He paused before continuing. "A complete change of plans and the strangest guides I've ever met."

"Strange?" Warnach asked, his forehead creasing in puzzlement. "How so?"

Before Sandra could utter a word, Mac replied, "Would you believe sea creatures? Sandra, what was it you called them? Quazon?"

Warnach's head jerked around as he faced his ki'mirsah in disbelief. "Quazon? Quazon revealed themselves to him?"

Shrugging, she nodded. "Zeterons were waiting where we planned to go ashore. The Quazon led us to another place. They called it Efi'yimasé Meichasa."

Hardly knowing what to say, Warnach's mouth dropped. "Efi'yimasé Meichasa?"

"Rocks like none I've ever seen with an entrance so low we had to lie down while Sandra's ocean friends pushed and pulled us into a cave where we could get onto solid ground."

Warnach gazed at Mac with new esteem. "Has Sandra mentioned that you mustn't say anything to anyone about meeting Quazon?"

The low, secretive tone of the question reminded Mac of the oath he'd given Sandra. Sheepishly, he apologized. "I'm sorry. I didn't mean to…"

She smiled in response. "With Warnach, it's all right. He knows already."

Mac's eyes questioned them both. "She did. Is it really so important?"

With a nod, Warnach reached for Sandra's hand and replied, "Most certainly. Quazon are angels sent to watch over our people. I cannot emphasize how rarely Quazon reveal themselves. They allow no one to see them except those whose intentions are important for my world. Their affection for Sandra exceeds unique. Chikondrans believe those who encounter them are blessed."

Something about Warnach's explanation baffled Mac. Perhaps it was because the Chikondran leader was so well educated and sophisticated but still believed in what many would consider nothing more than superstition or mythology. Whatever the case, the creatures had certainly delivered his party safely ashore.

"Master Sirinoya, if that's the case, then I shall consider myself a blessed man and keep the secret. Now, if you'll kindly excuse me, I'm quite sure you'd appreciate some private time with this remarkable lady." They all stood. Mac gave Sandra a loose hug, shook hands with Warnach, and headed toward the table where Baines and Mesa had just sat down with a group of Chikondran officers.

Dark eyes thoughtfully fixed on his lifemate's face. "Shi'níyah, what other surprises do you have for me?"

"Surprises?" she asked.

Speculatively, he eyed her. "Do you not remember Efi'yimasé Meichasa?"

Hesitating, she said, "Yes. The pilgrimage. The one you made with Badrik before Morcai was born."

"Exactly. Efi'yimasé Meichasa is the most sacred place on all of Chikondra. I find it fascinating that Quazon took you there."

After a prolonged silence, she dismissed the matter as one with significance she might never understand. Her fingers withdrew from his grasp only to form delicate circles on top of his hand. Smiling seductively, she said quietly, "I feel much better now. I'm also thinking of my latest promise to my ki'medsah."

Sensual lips spread into a smile. "Shall we go?"

Reaching his quarters, Warnach pulled candles from a storage cabinet and lit them. When he turned around, she had already pulled back blankets on the low mattress. When she came closer, he noted shimmering light in her eyes. Slowly, he removed her Kitak and, with eyes closed, savored her touch as she took his. Reverently, he brought together the two rings and watched as they reunited. Placing their rejoined Kitak aside on a storage cube, he straightened and allowed her to undo the buttons of his military jacket. Letting it slide from his arms to the floor, he shivered as she pulled his high-necked sweater above his head. Cool hands pressed against his bared chest, and she leaned forward to place trembling kisses against his shoulder.

Pausing, her hand suddenly went to his arm. Her index finger traced along the fading red mark left by the lazon hit he'd sustained. Troubled eyes rose. "I was right. You were hurt."

"You knew?"

"I felt it. When I was on the Curasalah, I told Forsij. I was so afraid."

Gently, he kissed her forehead. "Let's not think about it. Right now, all that matters is that we're together."

Dismissing remembered fear was impossible. Instead, that fear heightened her need for him. "Warnach," she gasped softly as her mouth opened, begging his kiss.

Responding instantaneously, he indulged in the taste of her while his hands feverishly sought direct contact with the smooth skin of her back. Breaking their kiss only long enough to remove her shirt, they quickly found themselves touching one another while shedding remaining clothing. Her full breasts pressed against his chest. His hands cupped her hips. Her fingers laced into his hair.

Within moments, he guided her toward the bed and carefully lowered her. Kneeling, he leaned over her, drawing long, languorous caresses across her shoulders, downward over the curve of her breasts, and along her velvety smooth abdomen. Loving her with hands and eyes, he marveled at the courage that had brought her to him.

"Warnach," she whispered, "come. Lie down beside me. Let me touch you."

Thick, ebony lashes fell. His head tilted back into the pillow as her lips trailed moist kisses along the strong column of his neck. Feathery touches along his arms, chest, and stomach set afire every nerve in his body. Exploding desire sent his body into writhing, twisting spirals as, unable to withstand the onslaught of her erotic caresses, he dragged her to him.

Rising above her, he gazed down into eyes begging for the union that created such indescribable pleasures. She whimpered and, raising her head, kissed the slight hollow at the base of his throat. "I need you, Warnach. Please. Don't make me wait."

With a low, muted groan, he granted her wish. Reconnected to her in such totality, he escaped into the refuge of her being.

Feverish touches banished fear from their minds. Throbbing nerves responded to frenetic strokes and caresses, whispers and kisses. She matched his movements with wild abandon. Searing passion drove them as they sought ever-deepening connection. Abruptly, they reached climactic heights of staggering dimension.

For the first time in months, sleep came to him sweetly. She murmured words of love, praising him for his skill in pleasing her. Her fingers soothingly stroked tired muscles. Her lips gently pressed calming kisses above his beating heart. Snuggling close to him, she pulled covers around them and whispered, "Ci'ittá mi'ittá, me'u Warnach. Ci'ittá mi'ittá."

Eyelids blinked before opening. He stared into darkness. Shifting slightly, he smiled at the way her body matched the curve of his. Tapping at the door. That must have been the sound that had wakened him from passion-induced sleep. Gently lifting her arm away and tucking blankets over her nude body, he slid off the mattress and stood up. Taking his robe from a stool and shrugging into it, he crossed hard, cold floors to respond to his midnight visitor.

From the open door of the attached office, yellow light streamed in as Lashira hurried inside. Tears filled her eyes, and her hands shook. "I'm so sorry to disturb you, but I needed to talk to someone. Oh, Warnach, it was so awful."

Shaking off the effects of deep slumber, he mumbled, "Awful? What was awful?"

"Our patrol should have returned this morning, but we came across a stack of bodies. Warnach, they even killed the babies. I'd never seen anything like that. We dug trenches and buried them."

With drowsiness ebbing, his eyes closed. "The extent of Zeteron brutality no longer surprises me." He sighed. "Go. Get some rest."

Swiftly, she pushed herself into his arms. "Warnach, I can't bear being alone. Not after what I saw today. I can't."

"Lashira..."

Frantically, one hand clenched the lapel of his robe while the other gripped his sleeve. "No, don't send me away. Not again. I need you more than I've ever needed anyone in my whole life!"

He heaved in a deep breath. "I told you already..."

"Me'u Warnach, I know what you said, but she's gone. Don't be so cruel as to keep sending me away. You know we're going to die anyway. Just once. Love me just tonight. I don't even care if you pretend she's the one you're making love to..."

"Warnach?"

Both Warnach and Lashira jerked their heads toward the bedroom entrance. Standing there, Sandra clutched a blanket half-concealing bare breasts. Stunned, Lashira dug her fingers into thick fabric. "What? What is she doing here?"

Grasping slender wrists tightly, Warnach wrenched Lashira's hands free of his robe. When it fell open, he angrily tugged it closed. Pleading eyes shifted to Sandra. "Shi'níyah..."

So furious that she forgot her nakedness, Sandra dropped the blanket and went to Warnach's side. Glaring at Lashira, she shook her head in disdain. "I'm here because my place is with my ki'medsah. How dare you intrude like this?"

Too shocked to move, Lashira trembled visibly. "Warnach? I beg you. You said your heart had no room to hate me. You must still love me."

Swiftly crossing the short distance to the bedroom door, Warnach picked up the discarded blanket and returned to wrap it around his lifemate. "Lashira, I don't hate you. After all these years, I also seriously doubt I ever really loved you, but I am sure of my love for my ki'mirsah."

Ignoring Sandra's presence, Lashira insisted. "But she left you!"

"You did ask why she's here, didn't you? Lashira, you insinuated once before that Sandra deserted me. The truth is that she had to be tranquilized before I could send her to safety. Against my wishes, she came back after risking her life running the Zeteron blockade. That is love you can't possibly comprehend. For you, Lashira, love is whatever satisfies your selfish whims at any given moment."

"That's not tr…"

"Lashira," Sandra interrupted coldly, "perhaps you have convinced yourself that you really love Warnach. I don't know. I also don't give a damn. I just want you out of our lives. Permanently."

Piteously, Lashira sobbed Warnach's name as he grasped her shoulders, spun her around, and pushed her into the corridor. When she turned back, his eyes blazed. "Lashira, one last thing. I will never betray Sandra the way you betrayed me."

With Lashira gone, he wearily leaned his forehead against the closed door. He expelled a harsh sigh of exasperation. Feeling the gentle weight of Sandra's hand against his back, he sighed again. "I'm sorry. I was so overjoyed seeing you that I totally forgot about her."

Slipping her hand beneath his arm, she led him into the bedroom. Spreading the blanket over the mattress, she waited while he went to wash his face. Sad-faced, he returned. Hesitating almost fearfully, he rubbed a wide tress of her hair between his fingers. "Sandra, I swear..."

"Warnach, I heard every word she said. Even if I hadn't, I would have trusted you without needing to ask." Her face turned just enough for her to lightly kiss his fingers. "Let's go back to bed."

Propping himself on his elbow, he leaned over her as she lay beside him. His free hand tenderly stroked her hair. "Shi'níyah, I..."

Breathing in deeply, she snaked her hand between them. Curving fingers grasped him firmly. "Warnach, don't tell me. Show me how much you love me."

Chapter Nineteen

Fingers, aged and thin, affectionately stroked the thick, even braid adorned with a pink ribbon. "You're up early, child."

On her knees in a cozy den substituting as Brisajai, Lucia did not look around. "I needed to pray, Nadana. To thank the Great Spirit."

Despite advanced years, the old Simlani remained spry as she joined her nephew's daughter on handmade kneeling pads. "Why do you thank the Great Spirit so early in the morning?"

Lucia's attention remained fixed on a yellow flame dancing atop a scented candle. "Badehr's heart is filled with relief," she replied softly. "Momma is with him again."

"How can you be sure?"

Lucia twisted her head at last. "Quazon told me last night when they visited my dreams."

Nadana dropped her face. Silent for several moments, she still wondered. Could it be? "Do they visit often?"

"More often now than before we left home."

Nadana kept her voice steady. "The spirits of Meichasa rarely visit one's dreams. Do you know why they visit yours?"

Lucia's mouth, shaped much like Warnach's, curved into a delicate smile. "Of course, I do. We both do."

Focusing meditative techniques, Nadana stilled her old heart that wanted to leap and race like that of a high-spirited youth. "Child, I only read and imagine."

"No, my Respected Simlani, you read. Then, you see truth through eyes of faith."

How anciently wise the young girl sounded. How suddenly formal, too. "I wished always to serve the Great Spirit with my faith."

"He knows, and He sees, Respected Simlani. According to Quazon, you're blessed by the Great Spirit. He understands your difficulty living far from Chikondra. He is pleased that you believed enough to understand my need."

Tears pricked Nadana's eyelids. Frail looking hands trembled. "The times ahead may be even more difficult for all of us."

Lucia's almond-shaped eyes continued to stare at the flame on the burning candle. "The darkness on Chikondra is terrible, Respected Simlani. Our people are suffering."

"Your badehr is very strong and very brave, Lucia. He will help them as much as he can."

"He is helping them. Momma will help him. It still won't be enough. The darkness is too strong."

"What more can we do, child? We pray every day."

Lucia smiled again. This time, her small hand slid across the short distance and touched her aunt. "You must never stop praying. You cannot let the others stop praying, either."

"And you?"

"Respected Simlani, only light can defeat darkness."

Sweeping into the briefing room with an air of unmistakable authority, Badrik cast his eyes around the gathering of high-ranking officers. Black beard and piercing eyes created a daunting image that commanded undivided attention. Reaching the curved chair reserved for him, he paused and bowed according to Chikondran custom.

"I apologize for my delay. I was reviewing new bulletins just reaching CCEC. Is everyone here so we can begin?"

Disciplined military minds then analyzed every shred of information available regarding Zeteron ships, armament, positions, and tactics. Detailed star maps were projected onto a domed, room-sized screen that provided visual dimension of the occupation pattern maintaining the blockade against Chikondra. Employing impressive knowledge and strategic expertise, admirals and generals discussed data and developed plans for launching the formidable armada preparing to go to Chikondra's defense.

Admiral Mswati's ebony face reflected apprehension. "General Sirinoya, this plan addresses the number of Zeteron vessels and their capabilities. Our forces are not yet an exact match for the enemy, but I have absolute confidence in the skills of our commanders and assault forces. We also have sufficient troops to land on Chikondra to confront Zeteron land forces. That leaves one major issue unresolved."

Badrik nodded. “The tower. According to reports just received, the rays Zeterons are firing into space grow more threatening.”

“Troop transports cannot land if it isn’t disabled.”

Badrik met the respected admiral’s questioning gaze. “Admiral Mswati, you’re right. Even with the armada we’ve amassed, it would be foolhardy to send forces too near the planet. The tower’s firepower is too dangerous. We can only hope the Chikondran resistance can find a way to cripple the tower.”

Concern sparked in the admiral’s eyes. Leaning forward with an intense expression, Mswati met Badrik’s direct gaze. “There are few officers in our fleet who can equal McAllen’s command capabilities. Everyone here knows Minister Sirinoya’s reputation. Whether we like it or not, we must give them sufficient time to disable that tower.”

Badrik tersely agreed. “In the meantime, we must forge ahead with strategies for the defense of all our worlds.” Verbalizing indescribable dread, he paused. “We must also develop alternative plans in the event we must abandon Chikondra.”

Inside a small cave obscured from view by wildly spreading bushes, Warnach crouched near the opening and peered along the dusk-blanketed path they had taken. All was quiet with no sign of armed pursuers. “We’ll rest here for the night.”

Wearily, he dragged the small pack off his back and deposited it on the cave’s floor alongside his weapon. With an ironic smile, he glanced over at Mac. “The diplomat who truly believed war could always be averted through negotiation.”

Dropping onto hard ground, Mac released a sharp sigh as he recalled something he had read years ago. "Diplomacy requires discussion. War requires no discussion and is nothing more than negotiation by force. The problem with war is that people die."

Sitting down and drawing his knees toward his chest, Warnach gazed at the man who busied himself by adjusting a dim lantern. "Captain McAllen, I wasn't aware you could be so cynical."

Settling in for a less than comfortable night after a long day of climbing, hiking, and hiding to observe the Zeteron tower, Mac shrugged. "Cynical? Maybe. More like my perception of reality."

Occasionally glancing at handheld scanners and communications scramblers, the two men ate unappetizing nutrition bars. Squeaks and chirps of nocturnal insects drifted from outside. Occasionally, the sounds stopped as Zeteron transports passed low over the forest canopy. As soon as the moan of engines disappeared, the insects resumed their night symphonies.

"You're certain no vicious animals inhabit this cave?" Mac inquired.

Black brows lifted. "Fortunately, not in this region. Only the odd serpent or spider."

Mac cast a furtive glance around shadowy stone walls. "Great. I'd rather face the big ones."

Warnach chuckled grimly. "None are quite so dangerous as our Zeteron visitors." Settling back against smooth rock, he closed his eyes and let his mind drift.

"Seeing a world as beautiful Chikondra in the throes of invasion and occupation must be painful."

Breathing out a sigh, Warnach nodded almost imperceptibly. "It is. Separation from my children is a thousand times worse."

"I can imagine," Mac replied quietly as his thoughts turned toward his estranged son.

Peering at Mac through half-closed eyes, Warnach realized how little he knew about the Terran officer. "Do you have children, Captain?"

"A son," was the matter-of-fact response. "He lives with my ex-wife. She makes certain I rarely see him."

"I'm sorry," Warnach replied. "I didn't know."

"Don't worry. I've spent years getting used to it."

"I don't understand how you ever could. My son is fifteen, and my daughter is nearly twelve. Having them in my life has been an incomparable experience."

"I've attempted a closer relationship with Gil. His mother always interferes."

Warnach reached for a tube of water. Taking a drink, he set it aside and studied his companion. "I'm curious. How is it that your superiors ordered a highly-skilled starship captain to undertake a ground assignment in the hostile environment here?"

Blue eyes narrowed. Unable to discern ulterior motives from Sirinoya's expression, Mac's shoulders lifted in a non-committal shrug. "They didn't. I volunteered when I heard about the mission."

"Volunteered?"

"Yes, volunteered. In fact, I insisted. After Dargom and the Ashapat incident, Sandra and I became good friends. I wanted to help."

Black brows arched slightly. Otherwise, Warnach's face remained unemotional. "I didn't realize you were so close."

For several long moments, Mac avoided looking at his companion. Low light from the lantern did little to dispel night's shadows. Mac found that a relief in the face of Sirinoya's tactfully probing comments. "She's an intriguing woman. I've never met a woman so much in love. She's so devoted to you. You're definitely a lucky man." Despite the darkness, Mac could sense the Chikondran's smile.

"I've never thought in terms of luck. When it comes to my lifemate, I consider myself a man blessed." Warnach pulled a thin thermal sheet from his pack and, lying on his back, covered himself. "Still, I find it odd that you'd leave a command post for a mission like this."

"I tend to be protective where my best friends are concerned. I figured no military escort would look out for her the way I would." Settling in for the night, Mac turned onto his side.

Warnach yawned. "Whatever the reason, I very much appreciate your willingness to protect her."

"The actions of a complete fool," Mac muttered sarcastically under his breath.

✧✧✧

"Everything is ready. I don't think Derma'ad Badrik or his chauffeur will notice."

Lucia smiled thoughtfully. "That leaves the hard part. Getting from the transport onto the shuttle."

Morcai plopped down onto his sister's bed and fell back on the pillows. "Yes, getting off the transport and onto the shuttle, then off the shuttle once it reaches the starship, and staying hidden onboard the starship without starving until we reach Chikondra. Oh, don't forget the part about starving on the way to Chikondra."

Grinning, she gently smacked him on top of his head. "Big brothers. Always worried about food."

Morcai's face turned serious. "Food? What else is there to worry about?"

Lucia's smile faded. "You're right. It won't be easy. I think we need help."

"Or a better plan. My suggestion is we pray about it tonight. With Nadana. She should know what we're planning."

Lucia stared into her lap, and her hair formed a waving cascade that concealed her expression. Whispering, she said, "You don't have to do this, Morcai."

Sitting up, Morcai placed a protective arm around his sister's slim shoulders. "We're both Sirinoya. I also have a name to live up to. Your faithful guide I'll be as long as the Great Spirit lets me."

That evening, silence marked most of dinnertime. Nadana's wise, old eyes constantly shifted from one face to the other. Her charges were far too serious. Finally, placing her fork on her plate, Nadana rested her elbows on the table and gazed at Morcai and Lucia. "You both look too solemn. Do I get an explanation?"

Morcai faced her directly. "We've been thinking of night prayers."

A curt shake of her head revealed Nadana's surprise. "Night prayers? Isn't it a bit early?"

"Not really," he responded. "So much is happening, Nadana, including what we need to share with you."

"So serious, is it?"

Lucia rose and sweetly smiled. "Morcai and I can clear the table, Respected Simlani. Would you prepare for early prayers?"

Noting Lucia's odd change to formal address, Nadana inclined her head. "I shall wait for you."

Lifting her face when the children entered the den, Nadana observed their somber demeanor. Her heartbeat quickened, but she remained calm. "Candles are lit. Are we ready to start the incense?"

"Not yet," Morcai answered in a subdued voice. "Lucia wants to tell you something first."

Reaching out, Nadana grasped the young girl's hands. "Come, child. What is it you wish to say?"

Childlike innocence assumed new dimension as Lucia faced her great-aunt. "Respected Simlani, you've understood since the beginning. Tomorrow marks my twelfth birthday. The time has come for me to undertake the Great Spirit's intentions for my life. Your help is needed."

Nadana bowed her head reverently. "May the Great Spirit's blessings be upon us, Guardian of Light. How may I help?"

"Morcai and I must find a way to return to Chikondra. We thought about sneaking into Derma'ad Badrik's transport and then getting to one of the starships. I'm hoping for a better way. We need your advice as much as we need your prayers."

The lurch in the old Simlani's stomach left her slightly dizzy. "Lucia, this is a terrible time to return to Chikondra. If you're discovered onboard a starship, you and your brother could face great trouble."

"Getting to the starship will be the hardest part. After that, I'll become stronger as we get closer to Chikondra. Nadana, you must help us find a way. Then, after we're gone, you have to keep Grandma and Grandpa from finding out too soon - so no one starts searching for us."

"I know little of how things work here on Earth. There's also little time. Badrik plans to leave Earth within days."

Morcai slid across the floor. His hands reached for his aunt's. "Then, we must pray hard and ask for guidance, Nadana. Will you lead us in prayer?"

Nadana's eyes shifted and rested upon Lucia's serene features. "Child, would the Great Spirit not listen better to you?"

"Respected Simlani, I'm still a child preparing to prove my devotion. Morcai is my protector, but you are a holy woman, serving faith with faith. Prayers of the faithful, combined as one, carry the greatest power of all."

Sitting on Lucia's bedside, Nadana gazed affectionately into young features. Dark hair waved, reflecting lustrous highlights. Bone structure shaped a face mostly like her badehr's but with slight roundness reminiscent of her mamehr's features. Full lips were definitely inherited from Warnach just as wide, expressive eyes had come from Sandra. Cerea-nervos were slender and delicately shaped. All in all, Nadana thought her the most beautiful little girl she had ever seen.

Smiling encouragingly, Nadana stroked long hair. "I'm quite sure they'll both think of you on your birthday."

"I know they won't forget." Sensitive lips quivered. "Nadana, I miss them very much."

"We all do, child, but not nearly as much as your brother and you. Now, try to sleep. Remember. I'll pick you up early at school. Then, we'll go to Badrik's house to celebrate with your mamèi-mamehr. Your Uncle Roy also called today. When I told him we're going to Washington tomorrow, he asked if he could stop by to see you and Morcai. That will be especially nice for your birthday." Touching cerea-nervos lightly, Nadana marveled at the sense of light filling her being as she wished Lucia goodnight.

"There you are. You shouldn't be outside."

With a desolate expression, she glanced over her shoulder. "Today is our baby's birthday."

Warnach wound his arms around his lifemate and rested his chin on her shoulder. "Perhaps, if we stare hard enough into the heavens, she'll feel our thoughts."

Chilly night air made his nearness all the more comforting as she snuggled backward against his body. "She's so beautiful, Warnach. And Morcai. He's strong, like you."

His sigh ruffled strands of her hair. "They're both wonderful. We were exceptionally blessed to have them."

"I love them, Warnach. I'd do anything to keep them safe."

"That's why I sent them to Earth." Painful memory prompted a pause. "That's also why I sent you away."

Turning slowly, she gazed into features lit only by moonlight. "Are you still mad at me for coming back?"

"Furious," he murmured, gently resting his forehead against hers. "At the same time, your presence revives me. I needed you more than I realized."

Placing her palm against his face, she concentrated on the subtle vibrations of his cerea-nervos. "Me'u ki'medsah, I never wanted to worry or upset you."

"I know." His embrace tightened. "Ku'saá demands our unity, me'u Shi'níyah."

A sudden disturbance roused them as several men raced toward them. "Inside! Zeterons are coming!"

With frenetic urgency, Warnach dragged Sandra from the edge of the tiny clearing. Rounding an enormous pile of boulders, he shoved her through the tunnel opening and hurried the others in after her. Furtively glancing around, he then plunged through the entrance while guards inside secured the camouflaged doorway.

Dragging himself off the dirt floor, he listened carefully for sounds of weapons. Turning to one of the soldiers who had been on watch, he hissed a low whisper. "Did they see you?"

"I don't believe so. We were on duty when we saw them coming this way. There must have been at least twenty."

"Did your entire watch make it inside?"

"Two were still in the trees, sir. I'm more worried about a scout patrol that was on its way in."

Anxious minutes later, Warnach led the way to a different exit. Despite his protests, Sandra refused to remain behind and grabbed a rifle on her way out. Joined by the other Terrans and several Chikondrans, the group carefully threaded its way through thick woods. Shrieking sounds of ray weapons pierced the night. Shouts and cries saturated the forest.

Crouching or crawling on their bellies, Warnach's squad spread out as they neared the far side of the skirmish. Through thick cover, they sighted Zeterons boldly approaching the small band of Chikondrans who had placed themselves between the invaders and a nearby entrance to the tunnel refuge. They could not wait for better position. With time seemingly trapped within a sordid warp, shouted commands and fresh fire exploded in a confused frenzy. The ensuing battle lasted several minutes that assumed the dimension of eternity.

When weapons silenced, eerie darkness descended. Thick clouds blocked out earlier moonlight. Tense quiet was broken by haunting coughs, moans, and wheezes. Bodies lay scattered across weedy paths and at the bases of trees. Cautiously, heads peeked out from cover.

Low to the ground, Sandra edged along the trunk of a rotting tree and found herself barely two meters from where Lashira huddled for cover amid a tangle of dry, straggly branches. Swiftly, with Lieutenant Baines close to his side, Warnach moved into the open and advanced toward a wounded soldier. Two enemy soldiers leapt from behind a tree and aimed.

"Warnach!" Sandra cried out and fired her weapon, striking one of the Zeterons.

A second weapon fired, missing Warnach but striking Baines.

"Lashira! No!"

Ignoring the warning and evading Sandra's futile attempt to grab her, Lashira sprang from her hiding place and fired her weapon. The Zeteron pitched backward just as Lashira's scream echoed through the forest. Instantaneously, Sandra jumped forward, catching Lashira in time to prevent a hard fall to the ground.

As more Chikondran soldiers closed in and captured enemy stragglers, Sandra called out for help. Racing toward them, Warnach hurtled over the tree trunk. Falling to his knees, he breathed raggedly with fear. "Sandra!" he gasped. "Are you hurt?"

"No, but Lashira..." Her gaze instantly fell to the other woman's head cradled in her lap.

Looking down, Warnach was sickened by the sight of scorched clothing and charred flesh oozing steamy blood. Scrambling closer, he grasped the hand reaching for him. "Lashira, don't be afraid. We'll get you inside."

Tears streaked along dusty cheeks. Hesitant words rasped. "No, Warnach. It's too late. I… I won't make it."

"You can make it. The HAU's will help." His head shot up. "We need help over here!" Seeing Mac hurrying toward them with a handheld HAU, Warnach returned his attention to Lashira.

"No. Just listen to me."

Leaning closer to hear her, he nodded. "What is it?"

"Warnach, I'm so sorry I hurt you. I…" Weakly, she coughed as blood began to trickle from the corner of her mouth. "I do love you. Do you believe me?"

Swallowing hard, he solemnly answered, "I believe you, Lashira. Now, be quiet while Captain McAllen uses the HAU."

"No use. I'm dying." A gurgling sound distorted her voice. Her eyes begged him. "Say you still love me. Please?"

Warnach's eyes swiftly rose to Sandra's face. Glancing downward, he gently stroked Lashira's face. "I don't want to see you die, Lashira. Truly I don't." His voice broke. "I just can't say I love you because I don't."

Her eyes closed. "I'm so sorry," she murmured. Suddenly, she shuddered violently, and her eyes wildly sought his before rolling upward into a motionless, sightless gaze.

Stunned and horrified, Warnach stared. His whispered prayers then joined others in a strangely rhythmic round rising above the forest canopy. He gathered Lashira's petite body into his arms and, staggering to his feet, led the macabre parade of dead and wounded to safety.

While volunteers helped Simlani Niflatish cleanse and anoint the dead for burial, medical staff efficiently tended the wounded. The Terrans had delivered six newly developed, compact HAU's that proved a blessing inside the infirmary where Sandra comforted and encouraged injured patients. Mac stayed with her when Warnach left for his quarters to change clothes.

"Sandra," Mac said softly as he took her arm, "come. You're ready to drop. We both need a break."

Without protest, she went with him to the nearly empty cafeteria. A cook brought a pot of fresh tea while other hands set mugs and sweetener on the table. Focusing on her troubled face, Mac poured tea for them both. When she only stared into the steaming liquid, he quietly commanded her to drink. Mechanically, she lifted the cup to her lips and set it back on the table.

"If you want to talk about it, I'll listen. If you'd rather cry, I've got broad shoulders." Receiving a wobbly grin for his efforts, he asked, "What was that all about back there?"

She swallowed hard. "Lashira and Warnach once lived together."

"You're kidding. I didn't think that was the Chikondran way."

Nervous hands curled around the mug for something to do. "It isn't, and it ended years before I ever met him. She disappeared for ages only to suddenly show up when I was pregnant with Morcai. When she found out that Warnach and I had unified, she went crazy. She even assaulted Warnach's mother and me. After that, she disappeared again for years before showing up here."

"How do you expect him to react to her death?"

Eyelids blinked back hot tears. "I don't know. He looked so devastated." She choked back a sob. "Lashira's been like a specter haunting him for years, but I know he must have really cared about her. I despised her, Mac, but I did try to save her tonight."

"Come with me." Taking her hand, he led her to a long tunnel where they walked back and forth several times before entering a small chamber. Inside, gentle fingers lifted her face. "Sandra, listen. I know how much you love him, and I'm pretty sure he loves you every bit as much. I seriously doubt he blames you for her death."

Turning, she paced erratically. "Mac, what if he does? What if he suddenly decides that he made a mistake with me? What if, deep down, he thinks I wanted her dead?"

"Sweetheart, you're making no sense at all. I'm sure he heard you warn her, and I know I'm not the only one who saw you try to stop her. You were courageous and effective out there tonight, and I'm certain you did everything in your power to save her."

"I've just never seen him the way he was tonight. That look on his face! He didn't say a word. He just picked her up and walked away. Mac, what do I do? What do I say to him?"

"Shi'níyah?" Warnach stood in the dimly lit doorway, his countenance darkly somber. Noting her abrupt start and stricken expression, he ached over the fear he had overheard in her voice. Forcing a grim smile, he said quietly, "Captain McAllen, would you kindly excuse us?"

With a nod, Mac paused long enough to give Sandra a reassuring smile before he disappeared.

Seeing his lifemate seemingly frozen in place, Warnach slowly approached her. Tender fingers rubbed a dirty smudge from her cheekbone. "You owe me an explanation."

"Ex...expla..." Tears finally spilled from her eyes. "Warnach, I swear to you. I tried to stop her. You have to believe me."

"Shi'níyah, I saw what happened tonight. What I want to know is how you could doubt my faith in you. How could you possibly think I would ever blame you?"

Distancing herself from his disturbing gaze, she stared at shadows on uneven stone walls. "You didn't believe she'd die. The look on your face...you were so angry. Then, you just got up and carried her away. I couldn't move. I was so numb I didn't know what to do."

"It's always painful to watch someone die, especially a violent, useless death. No matter what she ever did, Lashira didn't deserve to die that way."

"It was my fault! I should have tried harder. That's what you were thinking, wasn't it?" Pivoting sharply, she bolted past him and fled.

Chasing after her, he caught her just as she reached a remote exit from the tunnels. Roughly grabbing her, he hauled her backward. "No, Sandra! It's too dangerous out there!"

"Leave me alone!" she cried. "Go away and leave me alone!"

"Shi'níyah!" His arms tightened as she tried to push him away. "Stop it! You've got to listen to me! Sandra, please!" Efforts to escape him failed. Fearful she might flee again, he locked his hands behind her. "Me'u Shi'níyah, it wasn't your fault! I know that! The only one blaming you for what happened tonight is you."

Trembling, she buried her face against his shoulder and wept. "Warnach, I…"

"Shi'níyah, everything will be all right," he cooed soothingly. "We're still together, and nothing matters more than that. I'm beginning to think you're in shock yourself. Come." Clinging to her tightly, he turned and led her through a side tunnel toward the privacy of his quarters.

Emerging from the tiny bathroom and changed for the night, she crawled into bed. Lying beside him, she listened to his prayers for the peaceful repose of those who had lost their lives that evening. His final entreaties were for the family he loved so dearly.

When she would have rolled onto her side away from him, he stopped her. "Shi'níyah," he whispered, cuddling her close, "I want you to think about something. Even though I knew Lashira was dying tonight, I couldn't lie to her. I couldn't say I loved her when the lie would have hurt you. You're my life, Sandra. You must never forget that. Ci'ittá mi'ittá, me'u Shi'níyah."

Her open palm pressed firmly above his beating heart. "Ci'ittá mi'ittá, Warnach. Ci'ittá mi'ittá." Tremors shook her hushed voice. "I love you so much."

Threading their way through thick forest, Warnach and Mac again headed for the tower, hoping to spot some weakness in Zeteron defenses. After a frustrating day revealing no new possibilities, they started back toward base. When steady rain moved in, they took refuge for the night inside yet another small cave.

Mac laid out light, communications devices, and weapons in precise order. Beneath a thermal blanket, he pulled his coat around him and shivered. "This rain is cooling things down."

"Not unusual this time of year," Warnach replied distractedly.

"Are you still worried about her?"

"I always worry about her. No one fully comprehends all she's endured through the years."

"She's entitled to some weakness every now and then. She seemed much better when I talked to her last night."

Warnach's brows lifted. "You spoke with her? When?"

"While you were visiting infirmary patients. She apologized for getting so emotional."

"I hated leaving her this morning. She had a restless night. Several times, she called out our children's names in her sleep. If there weren't so few of us familiar with this region, I never would have left her."

"Get some sleep. The more rested we are, the sooner we get back tomorrow."

The next afternoon, the sun shone brightly over the forest as both men carefully checked for unwanted observers and then disappeared below ground. Heading directly to his quarters, Warnach entered. Softly, he called out, "Shi'níyah?"

Receiving no response, he checked inside the bedroom. Everything was neat and orderly. Frowning, he left to look for her. Twenty minutes later, he still hadn't located her, and no one with whom he spoke could recall seeing her since the previous day. Deciding she must have found a private corner to read or think, he returned to his rooms to take a quick shower and change into clean fatigues.

Back inside the bedroom, something struck him as odd. What was it? Scanning the room, he noted storage cubes and personal effects. Plagued by uneasiness, he again looked from corner to corner. Everything was in its proper place. A final inspection prompted the rise of nausea. Not everything. The backpack she had brought was missing. So were her boots. "Damn it!" The expletive exploded from him as he turned and ran from the room.

Racing through the tunnel, Warnach collided with Mac, who was on his way to the dining area. "Whoa! What's wrong?"

"McAllen! It's Sandra! She's gone!"

Tightly gripping Warnach's shoulders, Mac nearly shouted, "Gone? Gone where? What are you talking about?"

Twisting his head to the side, Warnach responded through gritted teeth, "No one I spoke to has seen her today. I went to our quarters to look for her. Her backpack and her boots are gone."

Mac's heart thudded leadenly within his chest. Calm derived from years of military discipline allowed him to marshal self-control. "Come on. Let's get something to drink. You need to calm down, and we both need to think."

Warnach stared at lazy swirls of steam rising from amber liquid. "I can't believe she just left. I know how despondent she felt - and preoccupied, but I honestly thought we'd settled what happened the night Lashira died."

Mac's jaw twitched from side to side. "About Lashira, I think you did. What bothered her most was the fact she was forced to kill again."

Warnach's voice shook slightly. "I told her to stay behind that night."

"And let you face the danger alone? Even I know her better than that. The question now is where she's gone and why. Do you have no idea at all?"

"All sorts of ideas, just none specific enough to launch a search." Warnach downed his tea. "I've got to find her."

"What you need to do is to think. You know her better than anyone else. I don't believe for a minute she would leave without a word. Where would she go? With whom might she have been willing to talk?"

Dropping his face, Warnach unconsciously began to rub fingers along his Kitak. An odd awareness seeped into his thoughts. She was alive. She was wearing Kitak. That much alone imparted a sense of relief. He met Mac's waiting gaze. "She would have prayed." Rising quickly, he ran from the dining area with Mac close behind.

Entering the Brisajai, Warnach went to the stone altar and lit a candle. Falling onto his knees, he chanted a brief prayer. He looked up when Simlani Niflatish approached from the opposite side of the chamber. "Respected Simlani," he greeted with a respectful bow of his head.

"Master Sirinoya, I heard you had returned. I've been looking for you."

Warnach stood, hope sparking in his eyes as he exchanged a glance with Mac. "You needed to speak with me?"

Niflatish nodded. "More to the point, I have a message for you."

The weight of the world descended on Warnach's chest. "From my ki'mirsah?"

The young Simlani bowed his head, but a strange expression crossed his features. "Your ki'mirsah asked me to tell you not to worry. She said she had a critical matter to attend."

"Did Minister Sirinoya say where she was going?" Mac inquired when Warnach seemed unable to speak.

Simlani Niflatish's face reflected concern. "No, but she asked that no one try to follow her." He reached into a pocket and, producing a folded note, handed it to Warnach. "She gave me this and said to tell you she'll be safer alone."

Trembling hands opened the page.

"Me'u Warnach, I ask you to trust me and pray for me. I promise I will return as soon as I possibly can. You must not forget. I always keep my promises. Ci'ittá mi'ittá, Warnach. Sandra"

"What does it say?" Mac demanded.

Tensely, Warnach shook his head. "That she'll be back." He looked at the Simlani. "She said nothing else?"

The young priest shook his head. "There was something else. Something I'm afraid I didn't quite understand. She said to tell you to have faith. She needed to answer the voices of those who had summoned her and who would guide her."

Meeting Warnach's expression with shock, Mac blurted out, "Quazon?"

Warnach reread Sandra's note. "Quazon. That's the only possible explanation."

Simlani Niflatish stared. "Quazon? The angels of Meichasa?"

Meeting the holy man's questioning gaze, Warnach forced a brief, tense smile. "Respected Simlani. Meichasa's angels speak to my ki'mirsah. Through her, both Captain McAllen and I have met them."

"She speaks with Quazon?" Passages from the Book of Faith swept through the young man's mind as he recalled hushed whispers from his last night in Tichtika. Trembling, he asked, "Can we now hope that prophecy comes to deliver us?"

Mac groaned in frustration. "Not again. That word is starting to scare me."

Warnach jerked around. "What word?"

"Prophecy." Mac shuddered involuntarily. "That's almost exactly what the Luradrani told us when we left the caves where the Quazon took us. He said something about her bringing fulfillment of ancient prophecy."

Warnach's expression reflected the startled bewilderment on Niflatish's face. Unlike the Simlani, he failed to grasp clear significance. "Prophecy? What prophecy? What did Sandra say?"

Baffled and worried, Mac shook his head. "She said she didn't know what he meant."

Warnach looked to Niflatish for answers. "Respected Simlani, please, help me understand. I fear for my ki'mirsah's life."

Simlani Niflatish inclined his head. "Master Sirinoya, we must say nothing more of this until the time is right. The Great Spirit alone will determine when He will reveal His prophecy. In the meantime, we must do as your ki'mirsah requested. We must pray."

Still perplexed, Warnach looked to the spirit guide for an explanation. "Respected Simlani, I don't understand. What does prophecy have to do with my ki'mirsah?"

Niflatish reverently lit cones of Efobé. Tendrils of smoke swirled intoxicating fragrance throughout the Brisajai. The holy man then knelt and smiled reassuringly. "Master Sirinoya, do you recall the legend of Mi'yafá Si'imlayaná?"

Love. Life. Legend. Prophecy. With overwhelming force, the powerful tides of each converged and flooded his very soul.

Alertly, Mac caught Warnach, who swayed dizzily. The captain staggered and lost his balance when the Chikondran leader stumbled. Both men fell to their knees. Not knowing what to say or do, Mac watched and waited.

Covering his face with his hands did nothing to erase mental images sweeping through his mind. Vibrations circled his head, penetrating his heart and soul with her love. Could all the little pieces of their life possibly fit together as foretold? Could he really look forward to salvation for his people? Could he somehow find sufficient courage to cling to faith without doubting? Whatever the case, he understood with staggering, absolute clarity why she had gone.

Terrified realization plunged like daggers into his heart. His hands fell limply to his sides. Tears coursed down along his cheeks. "Respected Simlani, I beg you to pray for my family. My ki'mirsah has gone to bring my children."

Chapter Twenty

Deborah Levine's hazel eyes scanned the short corridor. Waiting until several crewmen disappeared, she rushed her two veiled companions toward a TC. Inside the transit compartment, she announced the single-use code that signaled the polymer-enclosed platform to move to the launch deck. Reaching the restricted area, the three were met by a waiting officer.

"The ship is ready. Hurry before anyone questions why there are four instead of two."

Cropped brown curls bounced as she acknowledged the instructions. "Let's go."

As planned, the foursome quickly strode toward the silver-skinned ship that was constructed utilizing Rapier design augmented by Rehovotian technology. Calm and purposeful, they mounted the ramp and disappeared inside. As soon as the hatch was shut and secured, Deborah sighed in relief. "I hope you all realize this was the easy part. Zeterons will do everything in their power to stop us from reaching the planet's surface."

Dragging the veil off her head, Lucia smiled confidently. "They can't stop us now."

Discarding his veil, Morcai looked at his sister with a mock grimace. "Lucia, I may be older, but remember one thing. No matter what, you get to explain all of this to Badehr and Momma."

From the front, a voice said, "I hope that explanation will also save me from your badehr's wrath. And that of your derma'ad."

While Deborah fastened the children's harnesses, Lucia only shook her head. "There's no need to worry. Trust me."

Swiveling around in the pilot's seat, the pilot gazed with stern eyes at his young passengers' faces. "You realize that your derma'ad could end my career over this."

Mysterious lights shone from dark eyes that locked onto his. Shivers raced along his spine as he felt the penetration of her mind. Strange thoughts, alien to his being, reinforced understanding of the critical nature of completing the mission he had undertaken. Within the depths of his soul, he comprehended that his choice had been a dictate of faith superseding any military obligation or duty.

Observing the silent exchange, the Rehovotian journalist secured her own safety restraints. Wondering if she would ever comprehend the source of voices that had prodded her into undertaking this bizarre venture, she sat back and closed her eyes. "We're ready to verify for properly secured personnel restraints."

Alert eyes scanned security readouts. All restraints and locks were functional for pilot and crew. Complex displays skimmed across lighted screens. Life-support systems operating ideally. Engines powering to impressive, optimum efficiency. Drawing in a deep breath, Forsij Tibrab entered codes to engage flight systems for their exit from the Curasalah into free space.

Gripping sensitive controls, he maneuvered the ship through heavy traffic comprised of starships, battle cruisers, and military transports converging under the joint command of Earth's Admiral Mswati and Chikondra's General Sirinoya. Smoothly piloting his ship, Tibrab reached the nearest end of the Alliance armada more than an hour later.

Aligning his position with other ships, he rechecked instrument readouts and scanned decoded messages for any sign of problems or discovery. He verified functionality readings of the ship one final time. Everything appeared in perfect order. Silently, he prayed that his skills would match the extreme test at hand.

In a calm voice, he addressed his unusual crew. "We're ready to break away. I will guide the ship out of formation and then accelerate engines quickly. We have forty minutes before our course places us in position for the descent from the far side of Kayah'mayah. I request prayers for the pilot and our safe escape from Zeteron detection."

Deborah Levine cast her glance toward Lucia. The girl stared straight ahead without blinking. Worried eyes met those of Morcai. Serious but calm, the teen nodded reassuringly. "I trust my sister. So should you."

Aboard the Curasalah, Badrik whisked onto the command deck. "Commander Drehmijian, have you seen Captain Tibrab?"

Lifting eyes from a continual feed of data, the commander shook his head. "No, sir, not since he left for his quarters."

Disconcerted, Badrik requested a general page to the captain. No response. Looking puzzled, Drehmijian paged again. When there was still no response, Badrik issued orders to search the ship for the missing captain. The general's growing annoyance was interrupted when an urgent message arrived from Admiral Mswati.

Frustrated and worried, Badrik issued commands to continue the search for Tibrab. He then turned and left for the arrival deck. Reaching the command console, he watched an incoming transport slowly settle onto the landing pad. Before a computer voice completed the all-clear announcement, he was already heading straight for the Terran personnel shuttle.

Taken aback as the single passenger disembarked, Badrik shook his head. "I never expected to see you onboard military spacecraft."

Hazel eyes assessed Badrik's strained expression. "I apologize for letting you find out this way about my work as an intelligence officer."

"I had no idea. Since this can't possibly be a social visit, shall we go to my quarters for private discussion?"

Striding quickly through busy corridors, they remained silent during a TC ride that swiftly delivered them to the officers' deck. Entering the private lounge, Badrik turned to his guest. "I must apologize if I've been brusque. I can't locate the ship's captain, so your arrival comes at a rather awkward time."

"Quite the contrary, Badrik. My timing was precisely planned."

"Excuse me?"

With a sweeping wave, Roy Warner suggested they sit down. "We have to talk, Badrik. Urgently."

"Druska! What a delight to see you. Please, come in."

"Mirsah Sirinoya, I do hope I'm not disturbing you."

"Of course not. My sister is upstairs reading, and I was just..."

Beautiful blue eyes noted lines creasing Araman Sirinoya's forehead. "Worrying, perhaps?"

Araman laughed self-consciously. "I seem to do little else nowadays. Please, come and sit down."

Casting her gaze around the living room, Druska smiled at the many family portraits grouped on occasional tables. Declining an offer of refreshments, she forced herself to keep to her purpose for the visit. "Mirsah Sirinoya, I must ask you to forgive me, but I came to discuss an important matter with you."

Strain immediately tightened Araman's mouth. "Please, Druska. Don't tell me you've come to inform me that one of my children has..."

Immediately, Druska leaned forward and grasped Araman's hands. Golden hair fell forward, concealing regret. "No, Mirsah Sirinoya. I've heard nothing like that. I..." She paused, nervously wetting delicately shaped lips. "I came to ask about Morcai and Lucia."

Lack of comprehension reflected in Araman's eyes. "Morcai and Lucia?"

"Yes. Actually, I was wondering if I could talk to them."

Breathing a sigh, Araman smiled. "I'm sorry. After Lucia's birthday party last week, Sandra's brother, Roy, left with them. He offered to take them back to their grandparents' house."

Consternation quickly clouded Druska's features. "They left with Roy?"

"Yes. He said they needed to go back to avoid missing school."

Shaking her head, Druska stared at hands clenched together in her lap. That made no sense at all. After several seconds, she again grasped Araman's slender hands. "Mirsah Sirinoya, I came after talking with the Warners. They're worried."

"Worried? Why?"

"Worried that Morcai and Lucia shouldn't be away from classes so long."

Araman immediately stiffened. "Are you saying they're not with Mr. and Mrs. Warner?"

"Sandra's parents think the children are still here."

Rising on trembling legs, Araman turned to call Nadana. To her surprise, her sister already stood at the bottom of the stairs. "Sister! Morcai and Lucia! Something has happened to them! They're not with Sandra's parents!"

Calmly, Nadana crossed the room and wrapped a comforting arm around her younger sister's shoulders. "Araman, sit down. Please."

"Sit down! My grandchildren are missing! How can I just sit down?"

Nadana's eyes closed tightly. She had expected more time to prepare an explanation for Araman when the right moment came. Expelling her breath in a rush, she met her sister's panicked gaze. "Araman, the children aren't missing."

Druska's curved eyebrows lifted. "You know where they are?"

"Not at this precise moment."

Angrily, Araman cried out, "What kind of answer is that? Do you know where they are or don't you?"

"Sister, calm yourself. You must let me explain."

"Explain what? I just want to know where my grandchildren are!"

Thin, ancient shoulders rose and fell. Rising, Nadana went to a bookcase and removed a familiar book she had brought with her from Sandra's apartment. Clutching the large volume to her chest, she sat down and ran wrinkled hands over the richly embossed surface. Opening the cover, she read aloud the title, translating to English for Druska's benefit. "The Coming of Mi'yafá Si'imlayaná."

Growing irritated, Druska leapt to her feet. "I don't know what some old book has to do with this, but two children are missing, and I'm calling authorities in to deal with the matter."

Nadana glanced up. "Minister Collins, you're Sandra's closest friend. You know very well that she completely trusts her Chikondran family. You also know her strong stance that her children should be taught to honor the faith of our people. Is that not true?"

"Of course, I know all that. Tell me what that has to do with the disappearance of Lucia and Morcai!"

Although her stomach churned and her head suddenly throbbed, Araman forced a calmer voice. "Druska, please, let my sister explain."

Focusing on Araman's pale face, Nadana forced a smile. "Search your heart, dear sister. I believe you've suspected the truth nearly as long as I."

Tears began to draw crooked tracks along softly withered cheeks. "Are you sure, Nadana? Are you sure this is truth and not wishful thinking?"

"My sister, read again the prophecy. The pieces of the puzzle fit together too well. Even the Camudahmni have recognized this. That is why I was asked to come to Earth instead of remaining behind with our people. I never expected such happenings in my lifetime. I find it nearly inconceivable."

Araman dragged the book from her sister's lap onto her own and turned several pages. Distraught eyes fell upon an elegantly drawn illustration. Lifted from the sea on a platform supported by Quazon, the child of prophecy was surrounded by shimmering clouds of light. Elaborate script formed the simple caption that she read aloud. "Child called Light."

"Excuse me," Druska interrupted impatiently. "This isn't making any sense."

Araman's chocolate-colored eyes held more astonishment than fear. "Druska, ancient prophecy tells of dark times bringing war, death, and destruction to Chikondra. A guardian warrior would remain to defend his world only after sending away his beloved lifemate, who had come from a faraway star. She would take their children to safety but, unable to face life without him, would return to his aid. The prophecy goes on to say that, at the Great Spirit's appointed time, their children would also return. A faithful first child would escort the chosen Guardian of Light, the one the prophecy calls Mi'yafá Si'imlayaná. Sent by the Great Spirit, she will spark defeat of the dark forces."

Fresh aggravation sparked in Druska's eyes. "What does ancient prophecy have to do with Morcai and Lucia? They're children, for God's sake!"

Rising from the sofa, Araman walked to a table. Picking up a picture frame, she gazed into the once happy faces of her son and his family. Returning to sit on the arm of the sofa, she replied to Druska's question. "There are too many details to explain completely. However, Warnach's life perfectly fits the legend's description of a guardian warrior. In our language, Warnach means fierce warrior, and Sirinoya means guardian of peace. For us, Sandra comes from the faraway star. Morcai's name means faithful guide. The legend speaks of the portal closing with the coming of the second child to this union. Remember what happened to Sandra when Lucia was born."

Shaking her head in growing consternation, Druska glared at them both. "You're saying you both believe this?"

Nadana faced Druska with unflinching directness. "You may have lived on my world, Minister Collins, but there is much you could never know. As my sister said, there are far too many details to dismiss as mere coincidence."

"Do you really expect me to believe that Lucia is some holy child prophesied Lord knows when? You think she's this so-called Child of Light?"

"Do you forget?"

Uncertain about the question, Druska stared impatiently. "Forget what?"

"Dargom. Sandra's obsession with light. Her vague references to light that led to the rescue of trapped ministry personnel, including you and your husband. Do you remember how she often called Lucia her sweet light?"

"I remember, but I still don't..." Halting abruptly, Druska caught her breath. Layers of logic peeled away, revealing insight that surprised her. "Child of Light. Lucia. The name means..."

Araman's mouth spread into a solemn smile that quickly faded. "Now that you understand, say that you'll also pray. My grandchildren have gone home to Chikondra."

Despite a constant, throbbing headache, Warnach concentrated on evacuation plans. Although discovery of this side of the modified caves was unlikely, southernmost tunnels were under direct attack. Escape routes were jammed with personnel fleeing with all the equipment and supplies they could carry.

Apprehension marked expressions on his aides' faces. "Master Sirinoya, you cannot risk capture. If our people continue to resist, it's because your example inspires them to courage. We can always return once we're certain this section of tunnels remains undetected."

Mac backed the aides. "We all want to help the others, but we stand to lose everything if we try. It's practically nightfall. With Zeterons concentrated in the south, we can avail ourselves of darkness to move up the mountain to the reserve caves."

His advisors and Mac were right. Decisively, Warnach issued orders to begin immediate evacuation. His aides swiftly filed out of the room, leaving their leader behind with only the Terran officer.

"You know you can't stay."

Warnach returned Mac's burning gaze. "She won't know where to go."

"Are you and that Simlani so certain she went to get your children? The very idea sounds preposterous to me."

Closing his slim, powerful computer and shoving it into a padded case, Warnach shook his head in frustration. "I pray that I'm wrong. Whatever the case, I don't want her returning to find this base deserted."

Mac rubbed taut tendons pulling from his neck to his shoulder. "Maybe my opinion doesn't count since I'm only an ungodly Terran, but my money's on Sandra. Those sea friends of hers got us here safely the first time. Add their help to Sandra's spunk and stubbornness… I almost pity the poor Zeteron who would dare threaten her, especially if she's protecting her children."

Pausing, Warnach thoughtfully assessed the officer from Earth. "You do know her well."

Sapphire eyes met the Chikondran leader's penetrating look. "On Dargom, she amazed me. While we were with the Yezabrá, there was plenty of time to talk. Then, I brought her here. Yes, I think I do know her well. Well enough to believe in her."

Warnach's jaw clenched, but his voice remained steady. "You're in love with her, aren't you?"

Without even flinching, Mac's blond head tilted only slightly. "My feelings are irrelevant. If she did go for the children, she went because Quazon told her to do so. If that's the case, they'll get her where she needs to be. That means you need to get out of here."

Breathing in deeply, Warnach glanced around. "I'll meet you at the rear exit in ten minutes." Once Mac left, he hurriedly gathered essential items and stuffed them into a large duffle with a shoulder strap.

On his way out, he paused at his desk. Picking up the folding frame, he stared longingly at faces smiling back at him. Pressing beloved images over his heart, he prayed out loud. "Loving Great Spirit, I beg your sweet care for my children and my ki'mirsah."

Sandra reclined against a weatherworn boulder. With fully charged rifle by her side, she drifted into a light sleep. Waking to loud, cheerful calls from a curiculitl bird, she shook morning chill from her limbs. Dawn's earliest rays began to filter through the tight thatch of tree branches above. Quietly, she got up and prepared for yet another solitary day of travel.

Mounting the hover transport, she rose above ground and agilely leaned first one way and then another while avoiding trees in rapidly thinning forest. Soon. Soon, she would return to the caves where she had come ashore with the other Terrans. Soon, she would learn why Quazon voices had been so urgent.

By midmorning, she stopped near a stream to rest. Leaning forward, she cupped her hands to scoop sparkling, fresh water to drink. Sitting back on a patch of thick grass, she munched a dry protein bar without tasting it. Her mind wandered back to Miferasud.

Pensively, her head moved from side to side. Lashira's death had shocked her more than Warnach. Analyzing her reactions that night, she sighed in regret. Guilt. An attack of conscience had turned her upside down. She had been so furious when she had heard Lashira begging Warnach to make love. What had she said? Ah, yes. She had told Lashira she wanted her permanently out of her life.

Time alone provided the chance to reason through complicated feelings. In reality, events that night had moved too quickly for her to react from resentment or anger. In retrospect, she knew her warning to Lashira had been shouted simultaneously with the shots that had killed her rival. The resulting outburst had been a reflection of self-doubts fueled by Warnach's odd, silent retreat from the battle site. Guilt had collided with irrational fear, creating an emotional overload.

Rising, she smiled to herself. Now, she thought, she knew what to tell him when she returned. That is, after she tried to explain the promise made long ago to the Quazon that she would come to them whenever they asked. Hopefully, he wouldn't be too angry to listen. Trudging up the bank toward the HT, a broader smile lit her features. She would find a way to make him listen.

Just before noon, light breezes carried the salty scent of the ocean to tease her nostrils. Bringing the HT to a soft landing, she gazed skyward. Reaching into her backpack, she pulled out another nutrition bar to ward off hunger pangs. Resolutely, she climbed back onto the HT for the final leg of her hasty trip.

Reaching the sea, she marveled at the shimmering beauty of rippled ocean revealed by golden sunlight. Magenta-hued clouds drifted across the faces of moons already visible in afternoon skies. How strange the connections her mind made. The sight reminded her of the scarf that had been attached to her Kitaska to conceal her face the day of her unification to Warnach. How blissfully happy she had been that day.

Stopping the transport and stepping off onto sea-kissed sands, she entertained fleeting wishes to return to that time in her life. Again, looking inward, she accepted that revisiting precious memories was quite sufficient. Although it would have been difficult to believe then, her love for Warnach had grown exponentially since their unification.

Staring upward toward the cave's high ledge, she heaved a sigh, feeling extremely glad her ascent was far less steep coming from this side. Quazon voices were clear. Her presence was urgently needed. Beneath brilliant light reflected by a slowly retreating sun and Chikondra's moons, she began the climb up the cliff's rocky face.

By the time she reached the ledge, her fingers ached from tightly grasping stone holds and from nails broken into the quick. Her throat scratched with dryness. Ankles protested the pressured stretches she had performed while pushing herself ever closer to the entrance of the main cave. Sore and hurting, she finally pulled herself safely onto the ledge.

Looking down, she could hardly believe how far she had come without mishap. The thought crossed her mind that she had needed the physical triumph to help her set straight the perspective that had begun to falter the day of Baadihm Farsuk's assassination. Facing separation from Warnach and now their children, she had steadily slid into a dismal pit of depression. This unplanned trek had provided an unusual opportunity to delve into her deepest emotions and reconcile issues tormenting her, thereby achieving a kind of personal cleansing.

A fleeting prayer of gratitude crossed her lips in the hope that Warnach would understand and forgive her for leaving the way she had. Then, drawing her feet firmly onto the ledge, she stood and turned toward the enormous, yawning mouth of the main cave of Efi'yimasé Meichasa.

No more than a few feet inside the huge cavern, she stopped and bowed. "Esteemed Luradrani, good afternoon."

The elderly Luradrani returned her salutation. "Minister Sirinoya, we have awaited your return. Welcome."

Sandra's eyes narrowed in surprise. "Awaited...? You expected me?"

"Of course. Meichasa's angels advised us you would come."

Her eyebrows shot up. "Quazon? They speak to you?"

"Do not be surprised. Luradrani Hadrezh and I are caretakers of this holy site. The angel spirits communicate with us whenever necessary."

"I see," she replied softly. "I came as fast as I could."

"This pleases them, especially considering the very real dangers you might have encountered."

Solemnity transformed her expression. "Quazon brought precious blessings to my life. I could never turn my back on them."

The Luradrani smiled approvingly. "They have much to ask of you, Minister Sirinoya. You must recall those blessings and never once doubt Meichasa's angels."

After letting him place her weapon and the HT beneath a rock-covered hollow in the cave's floor, she followed in silence as he led her further inside the caves. Reaching the central chamber via a different route than Badrik and Warnach had used years earlier, she saw the table was set for six. Puzzled eyes met his. "More will come?"

Merely nodding, he poured a cup of water from a handmade pottery pitcher. "You must be thirsty. Drink."

Obediently, she downed the cool liquid and handed the cup back. She then removed her pack and placed it near one of the cots lining a far wall. Although not nervous, she waited with some anxiety for him to speak.

"You have journeyed far. To your left, that tunnel slopes downward to a pool of naturally heated spring water where you may bathe. We left towels, gown, robe, and sandals for you. Just remember. The waters rise from a sacred source."

Memories again. "Like the pool at the Brisa'machtai in Tichtika?"

Graying features brightened. "Exactly. Others summoned by Quazon will soon arrive. Go so that you may welcome them."

Disrobing in the candlelit cave, Sandra arched her foot so her toes could test bubbling waters. Immersing herself up to her neck, she relished the flow of tension from her body while her arms and hair floated upon the pool's frothy surface. Wishing fervently that Warnach could be with her was useless, she decided, and instead, dunked her head underwater before rising from the water and stepping out onto etched stones.

Remembering that other guests were arriving, she wrapped her hair in a towel before buffing her skin dry. She noted grooming items and clothing as a curious, transient thought entered her mind. The Luradrani had worn gray ceremonial robes. As she stepped into golden sandals, white gown, and robe, a surreal moment akin to déjà vu struck her. Shi'firah. Wistfully sighing, she thoroughly missed her ki'medsah.

Chapter Twenty-One

"General?"

Badrik's fierce expression unnerved the deck commander. "I said notify all Chikondran ships to prepare to arm and launch attack drones. Stagger launch sequences three minutes apart. Launch only upon my order. When the drones are within forty seconds of the tower's last known firing range, aim all weapons at the tower. Fire in alternating sequence until ordered to halt."

Commander Drehmijian hailed other vessels to transmit General Sirinoya's orders. "Sir, what about vessels under Admiral Mswati's command?"

Stiffly erect, Badrik stared at magnified images on the observation monitor. "Mswati's ships will temporarily fall back."

Confidently trusting his instincts, Drehmijian approached Chikondra's top military leader. "Sir, may I respectfully request to speak with you privately?" Moments later, the officer studied the general's countenance. "Sir, I do not presume to question your tactics or your strategies. However, I believe it is my responsibility to express concern about the potential loss of so many drones."

"Commander," Badrik responded, "your concern is valid and noted with appreciation. Mswati and I are in agreement at this moment. Chikondrans must assume the lead to assure the safe arrival of our world's salvation. Our best hope is to divert Zeteron attention."

"Sir, I apologize if I don't understand."

Glancing at the time, Badrik started toward the door of the enclosed consultation room. Pausing before pressing the control pad, he suppressed anger and fear as well as hope. Turning halfway around, he saw lingering questions on the younger man's face. "Commander, are you a man of faith?"

Disconcerted, Drehmijian returned Badrik's speculative gaze. "Sir, despite all that Chikondra suffers, I remain a faithful man."

"Good. The time is now when Chikondrans must combine faith with strength to liberate our world. Notify the captains commanding our other ships that Captain Tibrab is on his way to the planet's surface."

Incredulously, the young officer stared. "Captain Tibrab? On his way to Chikondra? Why, sir?"

"Because he is obviously a man of great faith. He risks his commission, his career, and his life to undertake a most perilous mission." Badrik's heart pounded. "Commander, onboard the ship your captain pilots is the Great Spirit's promised salvation for our people."

"Sir?"

Badrik's voice lowered. "With nothing more than hope and sheer faith, Commander, today, we become participants in prophecy. Today, if men and women of faith succeed, Chikondra receives Mi'yafá Si'imlayaná."

Tibrab monitored the steady influx of data displayed on the Chamalyeh's command console. The ship was perfectly aligned with the trajectory calculated to sweep them from space into Chikondra's atmosphere. If he could accurately maintain the vessel's angle, the orbiting Kayah'mayah would shield them from the tower's rays except for about ten seconds before entry. After that, they would remain vulnerable to Zeteron fighters during their dive toward the ocean.

A green light flashed. Resolutely, the captain pressed the command pad. "Chamalyeh responding to hail. This is Captain Tibrab."

A pause. "Forsij, old friend, I expect a very detailed explanation from you."

"General, let us pray that I live long enough to offer that explanation."

"Should you see my niece and nephew, tell them their derma'ad is furious, but he does understand. Tell them they have his love and his blessings."

"Message understood and complete." Forsij paused. "Badrik, my friend, don't forget to pray."

Badrik's voice was quietly firm. "My prayers have already begun."

Divorcing himself from all emotion, Forsij concentrated on instrumentation readouts. Engines rapidly reached maximum power. Without hesitation, he engaged propulsion units that instantly propelled the ship toward the gigantic planet below. Exterior peripheral lenses captured brilliant flashes of light above the curvature of Kayah'mayah. However, the Chamalyeh's pilot barely noticed signs of efforts to draw Zeteron fire from the lone ship racing into Chikondra's upper stratosphere.

During rapid adjustments of speed and angle for the plummet into the ocean, an alarm sounded. Watching monitors, Levine cried out, "Zeteron fighters approaching!"

Forsij's heart pounded as, taking manual control, he deftly maneuvered the responsive ship to evade starfighters undertaking pursuit. Rolls, banks, and turns put Rehovot's Chamalyeh through angry, screaming tests of stability and flight agility. Still, Zeteron pilots pushed their ships through the skies in deadly chase. Fiery lazon blasts sliced through the heavens. Skillfully, Tibrab continued evasive maneuvers. He couldn't afford the scant few seconds necessary to readjust the Chamalyeh's dive angle so the ship would pierce the ocean's surface without breaking apart.

Suddenly, two starfighters multiplied to four. Only years of training prevented panic. Thoughts raced through his head. Options? Did any exist? Had he brought two innocent children to face naught but doom?

Unexpectedly, he heard Lucia's voice call out in words he didn't quite comprehend. Almost simultaneously, the skies over Chikondra erupted into blinding bursts of sheer light. Shipboard monitors showed nothing but undulating waves of white. Instruments flashed erratic, meaningless signals. Trusting nothing more than feel and instinct, Forsij Tibrab forcefully gripped manual controls.

Thirty seconds passed before instrumentation resumed normal function. Monitors revealed no further sign of Zeteron attackers. Forsij Tibrab instantly lowered the ship's nose for its death-defying plunge into the sea.

White knuckles gripped the captain's chair on the Curasalah's bridge as Badrik stared at observation monitors. The indescribable burst had filled the entire deck with white, painfully blinding light. Officers who had risen from their seats slowly dared to reopen astonished eyes that turned unspoken questions to their general.

Spinning to face the captain's chair, Commander Drehmijian broke through shocked silence in a smooth voice. "General Sirinoya, communications are jammed with inquiries. Respectfully, sir, may I suggest you communicate to our fleet what just occurred?"

Numbness eased from Badrik's body. Mere faith had exploded into faith-filled certainty. Nodding, he asked Drehmijian to open secure frequencies to all Chikondran vessels holding battle-ready positions. Sitting and tightly gripping the arm of the captain's chair, he breathed in deeply and leaned forward.

"Fellow Chikondrans, you have delivered excellent performance, and my pride in each of you is boundless. Answering anxious inquiries, there is no need to fear. Our drones drew the tower's fire as planned. To the faithful, I invite each of you to join me in the ancient Eyach'hamá prayer of gratitude. Although work and sacrifice remain, the light we just witnessed heralded deliverance of ancient prophecy. That light belonged to our promised Mi'yafá Si'imlayaná."

Onboard dozens of star cruisers, officers and crewmembers alike stopped ordinary tasks. Many fell to their knees as Badrik's words carried through sound systems into engine rooms, across flight decks, and into every operational area. Most could hardly believe the general's declaration. Not one resisted the fount of rising hope. The Great Spirit had not forsaken them. His Guardian of Light had been sent to rescue His people of faith.

Simlani Niflatish's awed expression held the same shock as on faces of fellow Chikondrans peering toward the heavens as light brighter than any had ever seen gradually dissipated into multitudes of fading sparkles against darkening evening skies. Murmured questions arose in a soft rush. Nearly paralyzed by the sight, Warnach could not tear his eyes away from the shimmering aftermath of the dazzling display.

"Master Sirinoya?" Niflatish grasped Warnach's upper arm. "Now, you see for yourself. The miracle we just saw has the power to deliver renewed hope and inspiration in the quest to liberate our world. Our people are weary and afraid. You already know the source of that light. You must help them understand."

Following a prolonged pause, Warnach faced the young spirit guide. "Do I dare? What if we're wrong?"

The spirit guide's expression conveyed reassurance. "In your heart, you know we aren't mistaken. Even if we are, our people need hope again. After the miraculous sign we just witnessed, no one will doubt. If they must face more death, let them do so inspired and consoled that the Great Spirit has not abandoned them. Look within, Master Sirinoya, for answers that lie inside your soul."

Pensively, Warnach dropped his eyes to the ground. Images coursed through his mind in a blur. Morcai's ability to see auras. His son's infantile description of light that hurt his eyes even before Lucia's birth. From the very beginning, light associated with Sandra's second pregnancy. Since, oddities. One after the other. He suddenly recalled the healing of the Yezabrá children and the mysterious flashes of light several claimed to have seen. Rarities, he thought, beginning years earlier when he had taken Sandra to the beach and first encountered Quazon.

"Niflatish, gather everyone inside the caves. Allow me a few moments for private prayer."

Approval shone from the spirit guide's eyes. "Be joyful, Master Sirinoya. By entrusting his precious Guardian of Light into your care, the Great Spirit not only acknowledges you. He honors you."

Adjusting her Kitak as she entered the primary chamber at Efi'yimasé Meichasa, Sandra looked up at the sound of a familiar voice. Stopping abruptly, a surprised smile spread across her face. Her arms instantly stretched out as she hurried forward. "Forsij! What in the world? I never expected to see you here!"

Forsij Tibrab's eyes closed as he received her greeting. Releasing her, he breathed out a worried sigh. "Sandra, how glad I am to see you safe and looking so well."

Sensing his anxiety, she frowned questioningly. "Is something wrong?"

"Let's just say I dread the risk I've taken with our friendship. I pray you will come to understand and forgive me."

"Forgive you? For what?" Noting the forward tilt of his head, she turned around. Evergreen irises widened with shock. "Morcai? Dear God!" Rushing to her son, she wrapped him in a powerful embrace. Tearfully kissing his face, she scolded him. "Oh, Morcai! You know you shouldn't be here! It's too dangerous! How could you?"

Pushing her away, Morcai smiled nervously. "For the same reason you're here, Momma. I had to come."

"The same reason? I came back to Chikondra because of your Badehr."

Reaching out, he stroked his fingers through her damp hair. "Momma, I meant being here tonight. We had to come."

Without conscious thought, she took a single step backward. "We? We had to come? You mean you and Captain Tibrab?"

He faced her squarely. "No, Momma. Not just the captain and me."

Rising nausea threatened to overcome her. "Morcai, tell me you haven't brought your sister with you."

"In truth, Momma, she brought us."

Incredulous, Sandra stared at her son. Her jaw trembled so hard that forming speech hurt. "Y…your sister. Where is she? Is she all right?"

Morcai grasped her hands. "Lucia is fine. Momma, she's with Quazon."

"Quazon?"

Luradrani Tlimaln placed a comforting arm around Sandra's shaking shoulders. "I know this must be difficult for you to comprehend, Minister Sirinoya. You will understand later. For now, you must go to your daughter. We will guide you."

The Luradrani caretakers lifted heavy antique lanterns and led the way. With Sandra in the middle, Morcai and Forsij followed the holy men through shadowed caves. Reaching the spot where the cave system opened to the sea, they gazed out over rolling waves kissed by eerily beautiful moonbeams. Everyone gasped simultaneously in wonder.

Luradrani Tlimaln's voice created mysteriously muted echoes inside the stone cave. "Centuries ago, Chikondra met its destiny at this very spot when the Great Spirit delivered our world's beloved Mehrashahm. Tonight, with love and mercy, the Great Spirit fulfills promises spoken by holy prophets." The priest reached for Sandra's hand. "Minister Sirinoya, please, come forward."

Her glance darted to her son's face. Noting an unreadable expression, she then faced Tlimaln. Letting the elderly Luradrani take her hand, she tentatively moved toward the circular portal. Looking outward, she saw that water, swelling with inbound tides, steadily rose. Fearful jitters and rattled nerves caused her teeth to chatter and her skin to crawl with gooseflesh.

With welcome relief, familiar voices penetrated her mind. Not the humorous chirps and comical whistles that had prompted laughter so often throughout the years. Instead, she heard settled sounds. Purposeful hums and vibrations growing into distinctive whispers. In the distance, beams of light struck the uneven surface of the ocean where two sleek Quazon leapt from the sea, performing ballet-like acrobatics above the water.

As their voices sounded closer, clouds of brilliant light forced those inside the cave to squint. From within billowing, shimmering mist, a more defined shape moved closer and closer. Balanced atop some invisible platform of energy created by sacred Quazon, the lighted image clarified into a well-defined figure extending a foot to step onto the stone ledge.

Instinctively, Sandra reached out. Protectively grasping delicately boned hands sliding into hers, she gazed into beloved features belonging to her daughter. So focused was she on Lucia that she failed to realize that Forsij, Morcai, and the two Luradrani were all on their knees with heads bowed.

Drawing Lucia tightly to her breast, Sandra caressed her daughter's long black hair. "My baby," she whispered brokenly. "My sweet baby, how your Momma loves you."

The Luradrani rose, chanting in unison a formal greeting in the old language of their world. "Qu'vimasa'i bri'insha'á eu Chikondra, Mi'yafá Si'imlayaná."

Only the last words registered clearly in Sandra's consciousness. Lifting her head, she swiftly looked from one side to the other and then back outside. Astonished, she saw multi-colored sparkles crackling in the air and Quazon suspended in utter defiance of scientific laws of gravity. Their voices filtered into her nearly numb brain.

"Child from the Distant Star, into your care we again deliver the Great Spirit's promise. Trust in The One who blessed your life with love, then deliver this sacred Child called Light to her people. They will know that within her veins flows the blood of Mehrashahm and Perazhan, spiritual mamehr and badehr to all Chikondra's people. Just as Mehrashahm and Perazhan led Chikondra's people from spiritual darkness into the light of faith, this Child called Light will guide them out of the darkness of unprovoked war. Heed our bidding. Lose not your courage, Child from the Distant Star, neither your faith. Believe as you have always believed, and all will come right."

Light and Quazon gradually faded into night. Rippling waters lapped gently against outer walls as swollen ocean receded. Fresh air drifted through the window hewn by nature from solid rock. Moonbeams invaded with misty illumination. Unique quiet enfolded those who had witnessed the advent of Chikondra's awaited prophecy.

While still holding Lucia tightly with her left arm, Sandra turned and reached for Morcai. Embracing both her children, she kissed each one. Unwilling to release them quickly, she rested her chin atop Lucia's head and, with eyes closed, silently prayed. Her promises had been given years ago to Meichasa's angels. Her supplications for strength she sent to God whom she loved.

Finally, she allowed Morcai and Lucia to leave her protective embrace. The serenity that softened her features seemed almost contradictory considering the path lying before her. To her daughter, she said, "My heart breaks to think of you following this course. It will be so hard and even painful."

Lucia's eyes clung to her mother's face. "I already know it won't be easy, Momma, but Chikondra's people need my help."

"Tell me truly, sweetheart. Are you certain you want to go through with this?"

"Momma, don't worry." An enigmatic smile transformed tender features with confidence. "I will do this because this is who I am."

Wetting her lips with the tip of her tongue, Sandra nodded and drew her son closer. "You then have my total support added to that of your brother here."

Morcai looked from his mother's face to his sister's. Their auras glistened, expanded, and touched. Solemnly, his young man's voice penetrated the silence. "Momma, thank you for understanding."

Sandra's expression softened. She met her son's gaze and delicately traced fingertips along his maturing cerea-nervos. "I'm not sure I'll ever fully understand. This whole thing scares me to death. However, your badehr and I taught you always to live your faith. I can only admire you for your courage, your devotion - and for your loyalty in not deserting your sister."

"Thank you, Momma. I see myself as rather fortunate to have such an exciting baby sister." Morcai then grinned. "Now, if you don't mind, the Luradrani have already disappeared to set the table for dinner. I'm starving."

"And I have the typical big brother. Always thinking of food." Adoring brown eyes glittered in flickering candlelight as she snaked a slender arm around Morcai's waist. "This time, he's right. I'm hungry, too."

Laughing softly, she turned to see Forsij waiting patiently. "Children. My challenge and my blessing. Will you join us?"

Still awed at being included in such a momentous event, Forsij barely managed a smile and bowed slightly. "I shall be most honored to accompany you."

Damp, chilly air drifted into the section of the caves where cots were kept for sojourning pilgrims. Drawing a thick, rough blanket around her shoulders, Sandra rose from her bed. After sliding sock-covered feet into sandals, she quietly moved to the two small beds where her children slept. Bending forward, she lovingly pushed strands of hair from Lucia's eyes and tucked a blanket snugly around her shoulders. Peaceful features belonged to the child Sandra almost wished her daughter could always remain.

Turning, she smiled at the sight of her son's long leg sprawled over the edge of his cot. Lifting it back onto the bed and tugging the cover across him, she marveled at slumber so deep that he continued to sleep as though nothing had happened.

Entering the chamber used by the resident Luradrani as primary living quarters, she was pleasantly surprised. Silent and smiling, Luradrani Tlimaln offered her a mug of steaming Tzitua. With a tilt of his head, he suggested she might wish to join Captain Tibrab in front of a low, sculpted fire-bowl. With a slight nod, she approached and, dropping her hand lightly onto Forsij's shoulder, spoke her first words of the morning. "May I join you?"

Quickly rising, Forsij held her mug while she settled onto a thick mat woven of native grasses. Handing her the cup and lowering himself beside her, he did as she and stared into yellow and blue flames dancing merrily above their firewood stage.

His voice softly broke contemplative quiet. "Sitting here, I've wondered how I could possibly face you and Warnach. How do I ask forgiveness for bringing them back here?"

Sipping strong tea, Sandra stared at the fire. "Forsij, as angry as I know I could be, I'm not. I don't begin to comprehend all of this, but I know we're all supposed to be here. Forgiveness just isn't part of the equation. Reliance on faith and friendships seems most important."

Strain eased from Forsij's cinnamon features. "Your understanding helps. I dreaded facing you even more than Warnach or Badrik."

She gave him a sideways glance. "Am I so fearsome?"

"Not really," he mumbled, mentally placing safe distance between them. "Are you aware I wasn't alone in bringing them?"

Her forehead creased. "No. Who else came?"

"Deborah Levine. She escorted the children onto the Curasalah. She disguised them and claimed they were members of some secret religious sect from Rehovot. Admiral Mswati granted them special permission to board. Your brother, Roy, arranged it."

"Roy?" Curiosity swelled. "Roy's involved in this?"

"He was the one who convinced Deborah and me to bring the children. I refused until he explained to me that he was acting on the request of Quazon. He promised their message would reach me even though I had never seen them."

Stupefied, her gaze fixed on his face. "Roy hears them, too?"

"Apparently. I wouldn't have believed him except that Warnach told me years ago about your relationship with them. After we met with your brother, Deborah and I also started hearing the voices."

Musing over yet another perplexing revelation, she shook her head sharply. "This gets more unbelievable by the minute. Where's Deborah now?"

Forsij's sighed heavily. "I'm not sure what happened. Despite a ship's controlled environment, you know firsthand the forces exerted by such a steep dive. After gradually rising to the ocean's surface, she complained of a headache but managed to help us get equipment out for the final approach to shore. Quazon were already waiting. For a few minutes, she looked ecstatic as they interacted with her. Suddenly, she tumbled into the ocean. I tried to pull her into the raft, but a large Quazon simply bore her away."

Tears blurred Sandra's vision. "Dear God. I don't know what to say. Because our lives were too often at opposite ends of the Alliance, Deborah and I never had time to be close. I always knew she wasn't especially happy except with what she believed she could accomplish through her work. That she would sacrifice herself this way..."

Forsij reached out and took Sandra's hand. "She was a courageous woman with a noble purpose. My people believe that dying in the company of Quazon leads to eternal freedom and peace for the spirit. You mustn't forget. They are personal servants of the Great Spirit."

Leaning to the side, she rested her head against his arm. Quietly, she murmured, "Forsij, how can I ever hope to deal with all this? How?"

"As I now try to cope. Rely on faith. In your case, focus on your children. Cling to the love you share with Warnach. Strength will rise from that love."

Nightfall. Blackened skies sharpened the contrast of the light beam spearing out from the Zeteron tower into the depths of space. Reports continued to filter back to the makeshift command post. Technicians worked at a furious pace. Occasional escapees from the labor camp delivered terrible snatches of conversations about deadly capabilities expected on the tower's completion.

The day's final briefing felt more like handfuls of dirt thrown onto a coffin holding a person not yet dead. Warnach felt trapped with no possibility of escape. The idea of his people enslaved by brutal Zeteron taskmasters tormented him. Day and night, his thoughts retraced every reconnaissance mission and reviewed details of every report. There must be a way to reach that tower and disable it. Only then could Alliance ships and troops offer any significant assistance.

"You know, you might be able to think this through if you'd take a break."

Warnach breathed in deeply. "That tower symbolizes the destruction of my world and doom for my people. I can hardly take time for myself when they look to me for leadership from this disaster."

Mac huffed a heavy sigh. "No matter what happens, they respect the fact that you've stayed."

"Cities are overrun. Families are torn apart. They're lucky if they're only separated. My people do not possess the mentality to wage war."

"And still they fight as bravely as any I've ever known. Part of that is because they have a leader who stands with them. They've resisted despite unfathomable odds."

Warnach fell silent. Watching peoples from other worlds suffer the horrors of war had driven his struggle to promote peace. Secretly, he had always harbored fears about war coming to Chikondra. With that fear now reality, he waged personal battles to sustain both faith and strength. Encouraging tired soldiers, cheering the wounded, and comforting the dying was exacting a terrible personal price. For a while, after Sandra had joined him, his outlook had improved. With her gone...

Observing his tense lapse, Mac studied the darkened landscape, seeking any sign that might warn of encroaching Zeteron troops. "I'm scared, too. I expected her back days ago."

Warnach's jaw tightened. "Except that we're here now. If only I could sense her so I'd know she's safe. I'm ready to damn my people and go search for her."

"You could do that. Not a soul here would blame you. The problem is that you know that's not what she'd want you to do. Besides, that priest of yours is dead certain she'll come back."

"She nearly died once because I stayed somewhere when I should have gone to her. Right now, that memory haunts every waking moment."

Mac studied his grim profile. "Where would you go? Where would you begin to look? You have no better idea about that than I. Face it. We have no choice but to wait and hope."

Warnach watched a shooting star cross the sky. Sighing, he turned to reenter the cave. "There is one thing we can do. We can pray."

While Morcai and Lucia huddled beneath a rocky overhang, Sandra shielded them with her own body. Forsij crouched close by, hiding behind a thorny copse of mirmaja. Approaching voices definitely belonged to a Zeteron night patrol.

Morcai whispered. "Lucia, did you hear what Momma's friend, Calvin, said?"

"About what?"

"Shsh," Sandra hissed softly.

"Spiders," Morcai answered, ignoring his mother. "He said the Zeterons captured on Dargom panicked over spiders."

Rolling over, Sandra placed her hand across Morcai's mouth. "Shsh. They're getting closer."

Lucia responded to her brother. "Want to find out?"

"About now would be good, Sparkles. I can smell them."

Straightening and readying herself to defend the children, Sandra sucked in a startled gasp. Never had she dreamed so many spiders inhabited Chikondra. Little ones. Big ones. Skinny ones with long legs. Fat hairy ones. Giant ones big enough to swallow a Terran tarantula. Spiders and more spiders, all marching toward gruff Zeteron voices. Suddenly, chaos. Yelps. Shouts. Howls. Terrified squeals.

"Momma, we can get out now. It's safe."

"Safe? The forest is overrun by spiders! Don't you dare move!"

Lucia giggled. "Momma, I asked them to help. They won't hurt any of us. Just the Zeterons."

"What?" Sandra exclaimed in dismay.

Morcai grasped his mother's shoulder. "Zeterons. They're scared to death of spiders. Calvin Riley told us. Sparkles here can communicate with every animal alive on Chikondra. Now that we know Calvin wasn't joking, we don't have to worry so much."

"It's true, Momma. If you let us out of here, we can prove it."

Nerve-wracking minutes later, stealthily working their way through heavy woods, Sandra and Forsij stared in disbelief. Half a dozen heavily armed Zeterons lay sprawled on the ground. Surrounding them and crawling on top of them, spidery sentinels seemed to proudly stand guard.

Confidently, Lucia stepped from behind her mother and walked fearlessly into the midst of paralyzed Zeterons. Legions of spiders parted to allow her unimpeded progress. Turning in a circle, she looked from one soldier to the next. Her young face held sadness. "My friends," she addressed the arachnid army, "thank you for your help tonight. I know you don't kill for pleasure, but these men intended to murder us all. I may yet again have to ask for your help."

An hour later, they reached a sheltered spot where they felt safe spending the night. Rationing what little food was left, Sandra shook her head. "I saw it, and I still don't think I believe it."

"Momma, the forest creatures love Chikondra, too," Lucia explained thoughtfully as she bit into a tasteless nutrition bar. "This is their home as much as it is ours. With only a little guidance, they'll help us."

Hardly able to believe the sight of fallen Zeteron soldiers, Forsij said, "If only they could guide us to your badehr's camp."

Morcai grinned at his sister. "Sparkles has already been talking with the birds. They told her earlier that we're close. We should get there tomorrow."

"Sparkles?"

Sandra barely stifled laughter at the look on Forsij's face. "He started calling her Sparkles back on Earth. I finally realized it has to do with the way he perceives her aura. My child of light and my child who sees the light."

Morcai nodded with satisfaction. "And my Momma, who lights the way with her smile."

Sandra froze for a moment. The tone in his voice had held both humor and affection. Swallowing final crumbs of food, she smiled at him. "That was a beautiful thing to say, Morcai."

Unembarrassed, her son said, "Badehr always told us you're the most beautiful woman he ever knew. I think he was right."

Standing outside his command shuttle, Badrik bowed to Admiral Mswati. "My people appreciate your patience. I am confident Captain Tibrab will find a way to get the children to Warnach. After that, I can only hope that we will soon see positive headway against Zeteron ground capabilities."

The deep tone of Mswati's voice conveyed both wisdom and commitment. "General, we share a driving need to do something more than wait. Unfortunately, we must remind ourselves that patience is essential more during war than at any other time in men's lives. The tragic irony is that war is also when we can least afford time for patience."

Stiffly nodding agreement, Badrik shook hands according to Terran custom and then departed for the Curasalah. During the short trip, his mind covered the detailed strategy discussed with Admiral Mswati. Carefully planned forays with drones had provided opportunities to assess steady increases in enemy firepower. The already formidable power of the tower's rays, augmented by the fleet of Zeteron warships, was sufficient to deter any major offensive because losses would be staggering to the point of crippling Alliance forces. Starfighters and troop ships would remain at the ready. The Terran admiral had been right. There was nothing more to do except wait and hope for the tower to be neutralized on the ground.

Back on board his ship, General Sirinoya reviewed key status reports. Masking troubled thoughts, he left the bridge under Drehmijian's capable command. Brisk strides carried him through busy corridors. Reaching the Brisajai on the officer's deck, he entered quietly to avoid disturbing others in meditation. Discreetly approaching the low altar, he lit a candle and a single cone of Efobé before kneeling to pray.

Badrik's mind directed troubled questions to the Great Spirit. How was it that a people who had always lived for peace had been forced into ruthless, bloody war? Why had he been called upon to leave his beloved ki'mirsah and son on an alien world in order to command men and women in battle where many would surely die? How had he not known that his niece and nephew had stowed aboard Chikondra's command ship and then sneaked away with his own best friend to return to their beleaguered world? Why must he worry every moment for the lives of his brother and sister? Why? Why? Why were there so many questions with no real answers?

His lips moved in prayer. Faith. His badehr had always taught him that faith was the single most important key to facing even the worst calamity. For a moment, Badrik wondered if his faith had collapsed beneath the weight of command. Unwilling to accept the concept, he continued to pray until a gently rolling wave suffused his body. He felt the warm ocean waters of Chikondra bathing him in comfort. Quazon voices responded to his supplications.

When Badrik finally opened his eyes, the candle he had lit flickered with dying flame. He smiled. Perhaps that flame had helped rekindle his spirit. Returned was his sense of being a blessed man. With perspective restored, he rose and retired to his quarters. For the first time since his departure from Earth, he slept a restful slumber.

Chapter Twenty-Two

"Are you sure they're up there?" Forsij asked doubtfully. Receiving a curt nod from Lucia, he gritted his teeth while assessing the steep, obstacle-strewn path ahead. The thought crossed his mind that years of service onboard a starship had softened his athletic prowess.

Reaching into her backpack, Sandra withdrew her carefully wrapped Kitak and placed it on her head. Since departing the caves at Efi'yimasé Meichasa, she had carried it to avoid any chance of light refracting from the ring's diamond. Settling it into place brought instant relief. Allowing her fingertips to rest against cool metal, she grimaced at her perception of deepening gloom in Warnach's mood. Bleakly, she met Forsij's questioning glance. "They're up there."

Just inside one of the caves, Mac noticed the fleeting, shadowed expression that crossed Sirinoya's face during a briefing with soldiers who had just returned from reconnaissance. Simultaneously, the fingertips of his right hand briefly stroked the band around his head. Memories flitted through Mac's mind.

He had watched Sandra do the same thing numerous times. She had once explained that she often sensed her ki'medsah's feelings vibrating through Kitak.

Saying nothing, Mac eased out of the cave. Having thoroughly explored rugged surroundings, he scanned frontal approaches from right to left. He then checked sentries posted in trees near the mountain summit. Everything was quiet. Trusting instinct, he headed left to make his way around to the eastern side of the wind-carved, time-worn mount.

Carefully sidestepping along an extremely narrow stretch an hour later, Mac stopped abruptly and held his breath. Closing his eyes, he listened intently. His heart swelled with relief. Carried by the breeze, her voice reached his ears. He soon peeked around a tall boulder. In a cheery voice, he called out, "Nothing quite like uninvited guests."

Sandra's head instantly tilted backward. "Mac! What are you doing?"

"Obviously looking for you," he laughed while reaching for Lucia's hands. Strong arms pulled her up. "Here you go, little lady."

Soon, Mac successfully guided them safely to where the path widened enough to walk normally. Armed soldiers cast surprised glances at the unexpected party nearing the cluster of camouflaged cave openings.

"Momma," Lucia said, grasping Sandra's jacket sleeve, "may I see Badehr now?"

Mac dropped onto one knee and brushed aside curls straggling down onto the girl's smudged forehead. "I'll take you straight to him."

Sandra glanced at Morcai. "Follow your sister." Without entering the cave where Mac disappeared with Lucia, she leaned around and peered into the artificially lit chamber. With his back to the entrance, Warnach sat on a makeshift bench while listening to two officers. Noting movement in one of the officers' eyes, he started to pivot on his hip. Before he could, Lucia embraced him from behind with slender arms encircling his neck.

Sheer relief replaced sudden shock. "Lucia!" he exclaimed as he clutched her tightly to his chest. "Me'u Lucia!"

"Badehr," she whispered tearfully into his ear, "I've missed you so much, Badehr. Oh, Badehr, I love you."

Sensitive lips pressed kisses against dusty braids and sweaty cheeks. "I love you, too, dear one. Oh! How I love you!"

Clutching her tightly, he looked up and saw the waiting face of his son. Gently releasing his daughter, Warnach stood and reached out to Morcai, dragging him into his arms. "My son! I love you, too." His voice caught in his throat. "I so feared I'd never see you again."

Stepping backward, one hand reached for Lucia while the other gripped his son's upper arm. "You've grown so tall." Proud tears stung his eyes as he captured them both in a shaking embrace.

Moments later, Morcai protectively held his sister by the shoulders. Bravely, he faced Warnach. "Badehr, I know you wanted us to stay on Earth with Maméi-mamehr, but you must let us explain."

Swallowing painfully, Warnach acknowledged Morcai's direct approach with respect. "My son, we will make time to talk. I know you both well enough to know you would not have come back here without very good reasons."

Relief sounded in Morcai's heavy sigh. "Thank you, Badehr. First, you should talk to Momma. She's waiting outside."

Lucia clung to Warnach's hand. "Momma was really worried. She carried her Kitak to keep Zeterons from seeing any light shine off it."

Pausing, he knelt and lightly kissed the tip of his daughter's nose. "Thank you for telling me that. Now, Jaizia here will show you two where to clean up before we get something to eat. In the meantime, I'll go take care of your momma." Standing, he squeezed Morcai's shoulder before silently heading outside.

Silvery gray twilight cast shadows over dense forest stretching across Miferasud Park. Glancing to his right, he saw soldiers moving into caves for shelter. Far to his left, he saw his ki'mirsah. Alone and leaning with her back against uneven rock walls, hers was a desolate image.

Slowly approaching her, he shook his head admonishingly. "You brought Morcai and Lucia, but you didn't even come inside with them. Why?"

Recalling her emotional outbursts just before leaving, she was certain she detected disapproval in his voice. Without opening her eyes, she turned her face away from him. Renewed dread filled her at trying to explain everything. "Warnach," she murmured, "considering how upset I was before I left, I wasn't sure how to face you. When I went to answer the summons from the Quazon, I had no idea it was because of Morcai and Lucia. I really didn't know. Then... There was no way for me to leave them behind."

"Sandra," he said in a quiet, firm voice, "look at me." When she resisted, he reached out and turned her face toward him. "I said, look at me."

Reluctantly, her eyelids fluttered and opened. In all the years they'd been together, she had never seen such an expression on his face. Her chin quivered, but she didn't flinch. Neither did she surrender to an urge to cry. "Warnach, I know you deserve a better explanation. I have no idea what to say."

Tenderly, he placed his index finger against trembling lips. "I promised my children we'd all talk soon. Right now, I think their mother owes their badehr some restitution for all the terrible worry she caused."

Bringing his forehead to bear against hers, he initiated the energy exchange that now readily flowed between them. Receiving as much as he gave, he leaned heavily against her body before forcing himself to withdraw. His breath came in short gasps as his face nuzzled against her neck. Huskily, he whispered, "You shouldn't be able to do that."

Her arms snaked around his waist. Resting her cheek against his shoulder, she closed her eyes. "How many things in our lives shouldn't be but are?"

His bearded chin rested on her head. Thick lashes drifted downward. "Me'u Sandra, you've filled my life with miracle after miracle. I want you not to worry. I already know about Lucia."

Narrowing eyes questioned him as she pushed him away. "You do? How? When? Why didn't you tell me?"

Soothingly, he caressed her face. "I do. I didn't tell you because you were already gone. I was sick with worry. When Niflatish gave me your note, years of memories exploded into the reality I still wonder if I can accept."

"Oh, Warnach, how I wish you could have been there. When Quazon lifted her from the ocean, they were all suspended in mid-air. Lucia was surrounded by light, and she looked so angelic and so beautiful - like an impossible dream."

"I can only imagine. Later, I want to hear every single detail, but you look exhausted. We can eat together as a family and talk awhile. How does that sound?"

Almost too tired to move, her head dipped in a nearly imperceptible nod.

"One last thing. Please, Shi'níyah, stop doubting me the way you did tonight. No matter what we face here, you are the one miracle that sustains me. I may not always understand everything, but my trust in you is complete."

"Me'u Warnach, I'm so sorry," she whispered, lightly touching her lips to his. "You know how much I love you."

Midnight. From outside, sounds of the tower firing deadly rays at regular intervals seemed incredibly far away. Warnach tightened his arm around Sandra's waist. Crackling beneath a waterproof pad, dried grasses formed their newest bed. For several moments, he listened to the even breathing of his children, who were sleeping close by. He needed them even more than he hated having them in that cave. In the morning, they would talk further with Lucia. For the moment, he felt even more tired than his family. Closing his eyes, he surrendered to much-needed sleep.

Rolling onto his back, he stared at the rocky ceiling. Noises drifting into the cave indicated the war-weary camp was beginning to stir. Raising his head and seeing Morcai and Lucia still asleep prompted complex, bittersweet feelings that their arrival had been no dream. His heart ached as he thought of exposing them to the ugly realities of war.

Reluctantly drawing himself upward, his gaze fell upon his ki'mirsah. As he carefully leaned over her, his lips lightly grazed her temple. Reacting with a gentle sigh, she tucked her chin beneath the edge of their blanket. Glad to see her resting, he dragged himself to his feet and stretched. Then, going to his children, he knelt and tucked blankets around their shoulders to ward off morning chill.

"Forsij, you're up early," Warnach greeted the captain outside as both men accepted cups of steaming Tzitua from an aide.

"I was debating the value of a hasty escape."

Puzzled, Warnach stared at him. "Escape? From what?"

"From whom. You and I had no time to talk last night."

"Ah, I see." Warnach breathed slowly in and out. "If anything, I regret that you were drawn into this."

Forsij's eyebrows lifted as he sipped his tea. "The choice was mine to make. After what I was blessed to witness, I have no regrets."

Warnach's line of vision drifted across forest canopy just beginning to lose its luxurious cloak of autumnal yellows and reds. "Simlani Niflatish counseled me to expect this. Despite everything I know to be true, my mind resists accepting Sandra's description of what happened at the ocean."

Forsij nodded. "Although I personally witnessed the miracle, I still find comprehension overwhelming." Following a thoughtful pause, he continued, "I've watched your daughter grow stronger and more confident with each passing day. You and I may find our most difficult challenge will be following one so young."

Warnach's face fell. Waving curtains of hair concealed his expression. "Forsij, I held her in my arms moments after her birth. Since then, Sandra and I have protected her and cared for every aspect of her life. How do we face exposing such a sweet, loving child to this hideous war?"

Hands came to rest on his shoulders. "As much as it breaks both our hearts, we must learn to acknowledge the destiny she freely accepts."

Warnach's eyelids closed over teary eyes. Tilting his head backward, he rested it against Sandra's midriff. "Shi'níyah, why aren't you still asleep?"

Her fingers affectionately combed through waves now sparsely threaded with silver strands. "The sun is up. Your ki'mirsah is a morning person. Remember?"

Wrapping his fingers around her right hand, he pulled her closer to sit with them. "Are Morcai and Lucia still sleeping?"

She nodded and paused to thank an aide who quickly offered her a cup of freshly brewed Tzitua. "I heard you and Forsij talking. You were both right, you know. It hurts to think of them exposed to this war. On the other hand, we've been given no choice but to follow the course. Lucia may be a child, but I can tell you. She knows exactly what she's doing and why."

Forsij noted shadows lurking in his old friend's eyes. "Sandra is right. Even when we were on board the Chamalyeh, Lucia's presence dominated the flight. When Zeteron fighters pursued us, she called out something, and suddenly, it was as if the entire universe had been enveloped in blinding light. The next thing I knew, Zeteron ships had vanished, and I was diving into the ocean."

Warnach's wide, sweeping eyebrows lifted high. "So that explains the light we all saw."

"You saw it even here?" Forsij's brown features wrinkled in disbelief.

"It was as if a tidal wave of light washed across the entire sky. For a while, it was so bright we could barely look. Then, the light dissipated into millions of sparkles that gradually faded."

"May I join you?" Mac inquired hesitantly.

The two Chikondrans smiled, and Forsij shifted positions to make room for Mac on a narrow, crude bench. "We were just discussing the lights you saw in the skies here."

Questions shone from blue eyes. "That was days ago. You must have still been near the ocean."

A short laugh escaped from Forsij. "Actually, on the verge of diving into the ocean. Lucia was the source of the light. That's what eliminated the threat of Zeteron fighters."

"Your daughter?" Mac asked, directing an incredulous gaze toward Warnach.

"My daughter," Warnach replied, almost mechanically. Turning toward Sandra, he noted her silent, downward stare at solid, packed ground. "Shi'níyah, you're so quiet. What are you thinking?"

Seconds passed. Shrugging and then shaking her head, she sighed. "I keep trying to sort this all out in my head. No matter what, I find myself asking if any of us ever had any choice in this."

Forsij's voice held gentle warmth. "We always have choices, Sandra."

"Do we?" she asked, finally facing them with evergreen eyes that moved from face to face.

Sensing disturbance within her thoughts, Warnach set his mug on the ground and took her hand. "Tell us what you mean, Shi'níyah."

"Destiny. Predetermination. It's something I never really believed in. Now, I can't decide whether to feel angry, betrayed, or both. When I think of the life I've lived, I wonder if the decisions I made were really mine. If I had known, I might have done something differently to prevent my children from facing this turmoil that confronts us." She paused, nervously biting at the inside of her cheek. "Because this was all laid out in prophecies, there were never any options. I despise the thought that I've been nothing more than a puppet in a play written centuries ago."

Her words struck with profound impact. Warnach and Forsij exchanged perplexed looks as they considered a concept challenging their faith. Warnach's thoughts stalled. Forsij breathed shallowly.

Standing, Mac was the one who broke tentative silence. "In my personal opinion, destiny doesn't necessarily equate to predetermination."

Meeting his gaze directly, Sandra questioned him. "I heard that Niflatish told you about the legend of Mi'yafá Si'imlayaná. Given what's happening, how can you possibly justify that statement?"

Abruptly, with a sharp flick of his wrist, Mac sloshed cold tea across the ground. "As I see it, predetermination means that everything is dictated beforehand. Every word. Every thought. Every action. I don't believe for a single minute that some omnipotent deity would bother with something so trivial. On the other hand, destiny is more like a destination we can reach in an infinite number of ways. There may be people and situations intended to cross the paths we travel, but our decisions and reactions are ultimately a matter of choice given to us by Divine Will."

"That may be true, but I still don't see where I ever had any choice in the matter. This was all going to happen no matter what I did," Sandra countered.

"We all had options and possibilities, Sandra. No one forced us to go in any specific direction."

"I can't accept that. When I remember the story of the Guardian of Light, it's all outlined in such specific detail. Just thinking about it scares me."

"Momma, there's no need to be afraid. You only have to see it differently."

Sharply twisting, Sandra looked up at Lucia's sleep-softened features. "Lucia…"

"Come, dear one," Warnach beckoned. "Forsij said earlier we need to learn how to listen to you. You seem to have specific ideas about Momma's concerns."

Letting her badehr pull her onto his lap, Lucia regarded her mother's troubled expression with wide eyes. "Your friend is right, Momma," she began seriously. "Yesterday, when Morcai started to tell Badehr why we came, Badehr told us that he knew we wouldn't have disobeyed his wishes without good cause."

"How does that relate to our discussion, Lucia?"

"Momma, Morcai is sensible and faithful. So am I. Badehr trusted us and our reasons for coming because he knows what we've been taught and how we think. It's just like when you always seem to know in advance what we'll do before we do something. You know because you understand us so well.

"It's the same with the Great Spirit. He sees into our souls. Like you and Badehr, He knows us so well that He expects what kinds of decisions we'll make. The big difference is that the Great Spirit is so wise and powerful that He sees far into the future, so He knows what will happen before it ever does."

Curious, Warnach questioned his daughter. "Dear one, is that how you explain the legend?"

Lucia breathed in deeply. "Even Momma's religion from Earth has prophecies. Prophets there predicted lots of things, like details about the life of Jesus before he was even born. The Great Spirit, or God, like on Earth, knows that there's an evil force in the universe. Because He sees what will happen, He talks to especially faithful people so they can write about warnings and blessings, and remind everyone to pray for help. That way, people can be ready for the important times."

Smiling tenderly, Forsij leaned forward. "What about you, Lucia? Your momma is upset thinking that you were born only because of the legend."

"Sir, the Great Spirit plans all His children, but He does let them decide what to do with the lives He gives them. For me, it might be different. Maybe He did send me with a special purpose, just like He sent Mehrashahm to Chikondra and Jesus to Earth. I don't know." She shrugged. "All I know is who I am and what I have to do. I don't worry because I do what Momma and Badehr always told me. I pray and trust the Great Spirit."

Breaking thoughtful silence, Sandra reached for her daughter. "I don't think I'll ever understand all this, but having you and your brother does make everything worthwhile."

Slender fingers twisted into golden brown hair. Expressive eyes fixed on fair features. "Momma, maybe I don't explain things very well, but I do know what is right, like being happy because our family is together again."

Mac and Forsij silently rose and left as Warnach and Sandra together embraced the daughter whose wisdom far exceeded her tender years.

John Edwards stared at field reports. Ships from the Medron System were only days from Chikondra. The extra firepower would be essential to defeating the Zeteron war machine orbiting the heavens around Chikondra.

"You're far away."

A slightly crooked smile lifted one corner of John's mouth. "I can't stop wondering what's happening there."

"Give her time, John. You remember how far the ocean is from that tower. You know she'll make it."

"Angela, it scares me to death when I think about her and the children being there now. If I had only known they were masquerading as Rehovotians… I wish I'd never given Roy permission to travel to the war zone. I still wonder how in God's name he convinced Badrik to let them go to the surface."

Angela sat down in an easy chair inside John's study. "You forget something. Morcai and Lucia are her children and every bit as creative and stubborn. Times two. No matter what, they would have found a way to get there, and you know that, too. They're even more different from normal kids than Diana and Sandra were. You can't take the blame for something beyond your control."

"I suppose not," he breathed out in frustration. "Mswati's communiqué still has me in shock. Beyond the fact that Morcai and Lucia are back on Chikondra, the admiral's confidence that they'll turn the tide against this invasion is next to impossible for me to understand."

Rising, Angela crossed the study and sat on the edge of her husband's desk. "Second-guessing and worrying yourself into a frazzle will get you nowhere. You have important work to do organizing the new alliance. My advice is to believe in Sandra the way you always have. You can't deny her knack for turning desperate situations around."

"Is it a knack or dumb luck?" John eyed his wife gravely. "If it's luck, what happens if her luck runs out?"

"There you are."

Turning her head, Sandra smiled over her shoulder. "I needed some time to think."

Gingerly stepping over loose stones connected to a steep incline, Warnach joined her on a narrow ledge. "You certainly picked a place hard enough to find."

Pensively, she smiled. "You're wearing Kitak. You could find me anywhere if you tried."

Taking hold of her hand, he looked out across darkening heavens. "To my detriment, I fear I'm not nearly as perceptive as you." Long moments passed in silence before he spoke again. "Are you still angry?"

Her eyes stared at distant storm clouds. "Not really. Lucia's explanation made me think."

"And?"

A muffled laugh escaped. "I remember something I said a long time ago about being born to love you. I've decided it doesn't matter much anymore whether this is all through choice or intent. Loving you and our children counts more than anything else."

Quietly, Warnach breathed out a sigh. "What I remember is something you've told me more than once. You said that we need to treasure and be grateful for the seconds and minutes of our lives. I've been blessed with more than my fair share of those treasures since I met you."

Finally, she gave him a wide smile. When it faded, her gaze was direct. "The assault on that tower will be more dangerous than anything we've ever done. I want you to know that I'm very greedy when it comes to sharing those treasured times with you. Don't you dare take them away from me."

Darkening brown eyes appraised the demand in her expression. "I have every intention of growing old with you, me'u ki'mirsah."

Chapter Twenty-Three

"This rain is a blessing in disguise," Mac stated as he shrugged out of dripping raingear. "Mesa got the transmitter installed, and it's ready to alert the fleet. If something goes wrong after the signal is triggered and the attack is delayed or fails, the transmitter is far enough away to keep Zeterons from detecting our camp."

Warnach smiled tersely at the Terran and then looked around at men and women who had served long months under deplorable conditions and against impossible odds. Ignoring concerns about how many would die over the next few days, he spoke in a firm voice. "The plan delivered by Captain Tibrab will alert the Alliance fleet, thereby giving them the advantage of surprise. Our task is to escort Mi'yafá Si'imlayaná to the tower. She promises divine assistance in neutralizing Zeterons on guard there. You know what to expect. You understand the danger. If anyone feels they cannot carry through, feel free to withdraw now with my gratitude for all you've endured to this point. Beyond that, it's time for us all to get some rest before tomorrow night's assault."

A stone-faced female officer stood. "Master Sirinoya, you will not face this fight alone. I am confident that I speak for all my comrades when I say we will never abandon you, nor will we desert Chikondra." Nervously, she forced a smile. "May the Great Spirit deliver us from Zeterons." The voices of her fellow officers, affirming her stand, drowned out her muttered last words, "And spiders."

Commander Drehmijian interrupted Badrik's concentration on the most recent update of the fleet's deployment. Sternly, but without sounding harsh, Badrik responded, "Yes, Commander?"

"Three ships of alien origin are rapidly approaching the fleet. We just received a hail directed to you personally."

"To me?" Badrik frowned. "From whom?"

"You're being hailed by a Captain Kimasou."

"Kima...? Sidrihn!" Abruptly rising to his feet, Badrik leaned forward. "I'll respond to the hail here. Make certain the exchange is scrambled. Take a seat."

"Greetings, General Sirinoya, on this day created by the Great Spirit."

"And to you, cousin! Your voice comes as a most welcome interruption."

"I told you we would return. The transmission devices you installed on our ships have proven quite useful in monitoring conditions confronting you."

"Then you know you haven't chosen an ideal time for a family reunion."

"Perhaps not happy times for a reunion, but families share the bad as well as the good. We bring help that I'm certain will prove useful."

Badrik closed his eyes and breathed deeply. The Yezabrá had kept their word. "Cousin, it is good your arrival is near. Stay alert and keep frequencies open. By the way, did your people manage to preserve the legend of Mi'yafá Si'imlayaná?"

After a prolonged pause, Sidrihn said, "We did. It's an intriguing story to tell our children."

"My cousin, a story it is no longer. I'll explain more soon, but we await the actions of the real Mi'yafá Si'imlayaná."

Again, a pause. "Lucia?"

Badrik's eyebrows dipped low. "How did you know?"

"My son, Ehmrihm, insisted he was saved when the Great Spirit's Light visited him. Lucia was the only one with him when he was cured. The conclusion comes easily."

Terminating communications with the Yezabrá ships, Badrik stared at Commander Drehmijian. "Alert our captains and Admiral Mswati regarding Captain Kimasou's ships."

The Curasalah's second-in-command arose but stopped at the door. "General Sirinoya, may I be so bold as to ask who is Lucia?"

The military aspect of Badrik's character subsided briefly, revealing to the younger Drehmijian a different side of the man leading Chikondran space forces. Anxiety replaced strident notes in the general's voice as Badrik quietly answered the question. "Lucia is a twelve-year-old girl. She is also my brother's daughter."

Efobé essences perfumed chilly air. A motley assortment of containers held candles and prevented drafts from extinguishing their yellow flames. Chambers inside the caves were filled with men and women on their knees. All prayed in advance of the afternoon and night ahead. Before a makeshift altar, Lucia knelt between her parents. Morcai prayed beside his mother. Simlani Niflatish chanted cherished prayers composed generations earlier.

Solemnly, Lucia bent forward, touched her forehead to the makeshift altar, and then pulled herself to her feet. Slender and tall for her age, she projected an ethereal image as she slowly strode past physicians, nurses, technicians, and freedom fighters who dared to reach out for a furtive touch of her hand or clothing in passing. The Respected Simlani had revealed the child's identity. No one doubted. All fervently believed that, within the presence of a twelve-year-old girl, they would find deliverance from the Zeteron curse.

Sandra scrutinized her children's faces with features drawn into a concentrated mask. Silently, she dipped her fingers into a pot and smeared oily black smudge on cheeks and foreheads as camouflage. Pulling a knit cap firmly over her own head, she concealed her Kitak that she feared to leave behind. Grim-faced, Warnach swiped blackened grease across his lifemate's cheeks. Joining hands, the Sirinoya family offered one last hasty prayer for the success of their critical mission.

Every resistance fighter who could be summoned converged near the cave outpost to join the death-defying mission to the occupied Kadranas Air Command Center. Agile soldiers climbed up sturdy tree trunks and securely perched high above the ground to deploy signal blocking devices that would disrupt electronic scans for humanoid life forms. Once the signal disruptors were activated, others stealthily spread around the targeted area, concealed themselves, and waited.

Suspended in chilly autumn air, twilight mist eerily blew in sweeping billows across broad meadows. Under heavy guard, captive Chikondrans pressed into slave labor were being herded from the tower's massive base. The looming threat of heavy rain had ended the workday early. With moons and stars obliterated by thick clouds, nightfall blanketed the forest in thick, unnatural quiet.

In severely hushed whispers, Mac and Warnach noted the positions of sentries and robotic weaponry surrounding the tower's perimeter. Even if Zeteron guards were disabled, armed robots would require tactical teams to advance with extreme caution. Orders were relayed to squad commanders. Meeting Sandra's gaze, Warnach swallowed uncomfortably and then authorized transmission to the space fleet he hoped still awaited their initial signal.

Fifteen minutes later, the strangest army he had ever seen advanced across the damp forest floor. Spiders. Thousands of the creatures swarmed toward the tower. Illuminated by floodlights sweeping the pavement skirt of the deadly edifice, waves of arachnids swept toward soldiers who immediately panicked. Howls and terrified screams filled the night as some ran while most fell.

Arriving at the edge of the clearing, Lucia held up her hand, signaling those with her to stop. Pointing at the robotic sentries still in position, she whispered, "They're armed and activated. Stay here."

Before anyone could stop her, she stepped forward. Motion sensors on top of the devices reacted to her movement and spun, firing beams in her direction. Deadly rays met a shell of dazzling light that instantly shielded her body. White light repulsed fiery beams, reflecting them straight back to their sources. Zeteron robots immediately collapsed into smoking, molten piles of useless rubble

Swift feet carried the primary assault team toward the tower's main entrance. While Warnach and Sandra bodily protected their children, Mac and two others attempted to force open the main entry door.

"Damn it!" Mac cursed explosively. "The damned thing is sealed tight!" Swinging around and flattening his back against the wall, he hissed, "What now?"

Lucia wriggled free from behind her mother and slid toward the door. Her hands moved in a circular motion over thick metal. Again, light surrounded her and flowed from her hands. Suddenly, crackling static electricity engulfed the door. Within seconds, it gave a creaking groan and crashed inward.

From the far side of the base, ominous sounds rapidly approached. Alerted to the offensive, Zeteron soldiers were quickly advancing to reinforce the base's falling defenses. Joined by Mesa and three Chikondran freedom fighters, Mac launched himself inside the enemy facility. Spiders dangled from silken threads and crawled along walls. Petrified Zeterons cowered in corners or lay lifeless on hard floors.

"Lucia! Baby, what now?" Sandra gasped as she covered the entrance.

"We have to find the control room, Momma!" For several nerve-wracking seconds, the girl closed her eyes. Jerking her head to the left, she pointed. "That way!"

"Morcai! Go with your momma!" Warnach cried out. "I'll stay here with the others to hold off any Zeterons!"

Dashing through a circular corridor, they reached a glassed room filled with lighted control consoles. Two Zeteron soldiers huddled in a corner, fearfully eyeing an advancing stream of spiders. A third had climbed onto a chair and boldly aimed a lazon pistol at the floor. Bursting through the doorway, Sandra fired. The soldier tumbled to the floor just as the others collapsed from assault by arachnid attackers.

"Sister! Hurry! We don't have much time!"

"Watch out for me! I have to do this carefully to control the direction of the explosion!"

"Morcai! Guard your sister! I'll cover the door!"

Tightly squeezing her eyes shut, Lucia floated her hands across controls and lighted displays. Agonizingly long moments passed as the sounds of battle outside grew in volume and intensity.

"Lucia! There's not much time!"

Sounding from the opposite side of the main entrance, Zeteron voices shouted furiously. Pivoting, Sandra raised her rifle.

Suddenly, Lucia's eyes flew open. "Here's what I wanted!"

Momentarily transfixed, Morcai stared as his sister's entire body transformed into pure energy that flooded the tower's control system. Snapping and crackling expanded into fiery, miniature explosions. Abruptly materializing and spinning on her heel, Lucia shouted, "Momma! We have to get out! Fast!"

Heavy footsteps rapidly pounded closer. Grabbing the door and pulling her children into the hall, Sandra shouted at Morcai. "Get your sister out of here! Get to Badehr!"

"Momma!"

"Go!" she commanded as she dropped to the floor and sprayed the corridor with an arc of scorching rays.

Lazon blasts crisscrossed the curving hallway. Confusion erupted into sheer bedlam when enemy troops encountered a retreating swarm of spiders that turned in a fresh assault. Inside the control room, sizzling flames from the control console spewed acrid smoke into the hallways. Low to the floor, Sandra heard the screech of a lazon ray just above her head. Watching a Zeteron soldier in front of her pitch forward, she shot a backward glance over her shoulder.

A loud voice shouted out as a hand shot through the smoke, grabbing her and dragging her to her feet. "Let's go!" Racing through the corridor, they reached the main entry, dropped to the ground, and rolled outside.

High-pitched ray weapons fired blistering bursts that turned the night into massive pandemonium. Officers roared commands in Chikondran and Zeteron. Fighters screamed high above them and chased through the heavens, flashing blazing spears of light that pierced clearing mountains of clouds.

Freed, Chikondran laborers snatched up weapons and joined trained soldiers and resistance fighters in the battle against Zeteron invaders. Desperately scanning the chaos, Mac clutched Sandra's hand and, bolting across the tower's foundation, lunged toward the protection of nearby trees. Tumbling and then staggering to their feet, they raced further into the woods as Chikondrans shouted to vacate the tower's perimeter. Suddenly, Sandra felt a shove against her back and plunged forward into a mad roll down a steep hill. Landing with a thud against a tree, she cleared her head with a hard shake and gasped to catch her breath.

Seconds later, a rumble shook the ground seconds before a thunderous roar reverberated through the night. Trees swayed. Branches cracked and fell to the ground. Birds squawked and screeched. Chunks of rock and debris crashed and rolled down the hill. Smoke, dust, and steam filled the air. Bits of stone and metal rained down from the skies. Shocked eyes stared at the blast of crimson fire that abruptly shafted straight up into the heavens.

Her dazed mind reeled. Frantically, she forced herself to focus. Casting her eyes around, she saw others who had joined her wild descent. "Mac!" she cried out. "Mac!"

"Sandra! Here!"

On hands and knees, she scrambled over rough ground toward the familiar voice. "Mac! I'm coming!" Sliding a little further down the embankment, she reached an enormous boulder sheltered by thick shrubs where Mac had landed. "Mac!" she exclaimed. "You're bleeding!"

With a groan, he pushed himself up with his left arm. "I caught my right arm on a tree branch or something. Damn! It hurts like hell!"

Wrapping her arms around his shoulders, she maneuvered him around the rock for more cover. "Here, let me check. Hold this so I can see," she whispered, reaching into a pocket and producing a tiny flashlight. Dragging his jacket off his shoulder, she examined the bloody gash. "Good news is that you haven't damaged an artery, but I've got to stop the bleeding and close this wound."

Through gritted teeth, he hissed, "Do whatever you have to."

Reaching into another pocket, she pulled out several rolls of bandages. Efficient fingers swiftly created pads that she pressed over the gaping cut. Rapidly, she wrapped long strips around the pads and tied them in place. Fumbling with a snap on an inside breast pocket, she took out a handheld HAU and passed it several times above the hastily dressed wound. "We don't have time for more, but this should close it enough to reduce the bleeding until you get proper medical care."

Admiring eyes had studied her concentrated expression throughout the process. "Are you always so prepared?"

She shrugged. "I try. Now, you've got to get out of here, and I have to find my family."

"Sandra, you can't go traipsing alone out there. It's too dangerous. There were others with him. They'll get him and the kids to safety."

"They're my family, Mac. I'll get you some help. Then, I've got to go."

Reaching out, his left hand clutched her arm and dragged her toward him. Searing pain in his right arm receded from consciousness as he pulled her face to his and kissed her. Releasing her, he stared into eyes he adored. His voice faltered. "Sandra, I know you belong to him. That doesn't make me love you less. I'm terrified you'll get hurt. Don't go out there by yourself. Please. I'm begging you. Don't go."

Breathing raggedly, she stared into his handsome face while searching for words. Nearby voices thankfully diverted her attention, and she crawled around the protective cover of bushes. "Mesa! What a godsend! Captain McAllen's hurt. He needs help back to camp."

"Thank heavens! We were searching for you!" Lieutenant Mesa said as he and four other Chikondrans rounded the boulder. "What about you, Minister Sirinoya? Are you all right?"

"Bruised and had the wind knocked out of me, but okay otherwise." She inhaled deeply. "He's got a huge cut on his right arm. He's lost a lot of blood. I bandaged it and used an HAU, but he needs real medical attention."

When Mac was dragged to his feet, he swayed dizzily. "Easy there," Mesa instructed as the Chikondrans steadied him. "Let's get out of here."

Gently, Sandra placed her palm against Mac's dirty cheek. "They'll take you to safety."

"Sandra." Frustration permeated the sound of her name. "Don't."

"I have to, Mac. They're still out there in the middle of all this. I feel it."

Anger gushed through his body at the weakness preventing him from going with her. "Mesa," he ground out, "these gentlemen will take care of me. You go with Minister Sirinoya. If she gets hurt, you answer to me. Understood?"

Sounds of battle echoed all around. Threading their way around toppled trees, fallen branches, and other obstacles strewn by the explosion proved painfully slow and tedious. They were constantly forced to stop and hide from Zeteron patrols. Prowling the woods, the enemy was intent on finding any stragglers from the assault force. As soon as voices faded, the two Terrans grimly resumed their advance with Sandra leading the way.

Dawn's skies brightened above them. They abruptly stopped. Bursts of lazon fire zinged through the air ahead of them. Rolling beneath prickly undergrowth, Sandra closed her eyes and shoved her fingers underneath her knit cap. Vibrations within Kitak confirmed her instincts. Not far ahead, Warnach lay trapped, defending their children.

"How good are you with that rifle?" Mesa inquired as his face tautened into fierce lines while he checked his weapon.

"As good as I have to be."

Mesa's head cocked in acknowledgment. "Let's get closer. You go left. No reason not to use the wrist communicators now. I'll signal you."

Quickly, they split and hurried through thick forest. Crouching behind a tree, Sandra peered ahead. Zeteron soldiers were beginning to press forward, heading toward a rock formation jutting out of the ground. "Mesa! How many?" she hissed into the black band circling her wrist.

"I count about fifteen," came the terse response. "Are you clear to fire?"

"Ready!"

"Now!" Rising and aiming his laser rifle, Mesa fired. Caught by surprise in crossfire, Zeterons instantly dropped to the ground. Those not hit stubbornly advanced on their original quarry. Their commander knew he had a prize ahead, ready for the taking. That prize would also provide excellent hostage protection.

Emboldened by the sound of reinforcements, the soldiers with Warnach increased their efforts to repel heavily armed attackers. When one of his guards fell, Warnach grabbed his legs and dragged him behind the rocks. "Morcai!" he growled and shoved the extra rifle toward his son. "Stay with your sister!"

Snatching up his own weapon, Warnach launched himself through stiff grasses and joined fire. Explosive tension mingled with the shrill, deadly shrieks of ray weapons. Hearts throbbed. Lungs heaved. Heads pounded. Sandra leapt out from behind the tree and raced forward. Her rifle spat scorching rays ahead of her. Mesa followed suit.

Return fire from Zeterons halted. Bodies lay sprawled across the tiny clearing. Sudden quiet jarred nerves. Mere moments burgeoned into seconds lasting an eternity. Chikondran soldiers cautiously lifted heads above concealing grasses. With guns at the ready, they began to rise to their feet. When Warnach finally stood, his eyes instinctively sought those of his ki'mirsah.

"Badehr!" The warning shout, bursting into what had been eerie quiet, was accompanied by the instantaneous zing of rifle fire.

As if in slow motion, she watched a wounded Zeteron officer groan and fall sideways onto the ground. Her eyes swept toward the resolute expression on her son's face as he held his rifle, ready to fire a second time. Swiftly lunging forward, she then collapsed to her knees. Terror and despair showed in every motion as she gathered Warnach's body close to hers. "Warnach! Warnach!"

Chapter Twenty-Four

Admiral James Mswati's ebony features pulled into a fierce mask. With quiet patience that rivaled the stealth of his hunter ancestors, he made a final assessment of his prey's strength and position. Intellect collided with strange irony. His forebears had hunted food for survival. He, too, was turning to the hunt, not for food, but for survival nonetheless.

Implicitly trusting his instincts, he had waited without ever doubting the signal would come. He had already ordered his fleet of warships to raise shields and assume offensive positions. When the spectacular ball of flame spewed from the planet's surface, he smiled his grim satisfaction. In a cool, firm voice, he issued a string of new commands, including the launch of squadrons of starfighters to join Chikondran fighters deployed after reception of the ground transmission.

The tower's explosion had ignited a torch-like shaft of fire spiraling into the heavens. Urgent strategic exchanges and status reports saturated communication frequencies. Battlecruisers initiated fire as they engaged a surprised Zeteron fleet whose commander had arrogantly believed Alliance forces would posture and then retreat in the face of superior numbers. Alliance starfighters streaked through the void of space, aggressively engaging Zeteron squads.

Badrik Sirinoya monitored carefully choreographed chaos. Chikondran assault vessels pursued the primary goal of disabling the largest Zeteron vessels. Terran pilots demonstrated clever prowess against enemy fighters. Dargoman Rapiers sliced through Zeteron ranks while spilling destructive firepower onto battleships hastily trying to maneuver into defensive positions. Chamalyeh ships courageously streaked perilously close to pummel enemy transports with disruptor rays. Two of the Yezabrá ships headed directly toward the Zeteron command ship. Meanwhile, Sidrihn Kimasou's sleek, more compact starship angled its trajectory to enter Chikondran air space with an escort of Alliance fighters.

"General Sirinoya!" Mswati's commanding voice hailed the Chikondran leader.

"Sirinoya here, Admiral. Advise."

"Scouts report two enemy assault ships approaching from the far moon. Intercept and engage."

"With pleasure, Admiral!" Scowling, Badrik shouted orders. "Drehmijian! Order the Mipari and the Netlalka to set course for Neralahm and intercept enemy vessels inbound from its far side!"

The remaining Yezabrá ships released a rapid volley of disruptor cannons. A Zeteron starship suddenly exploded. The Curasalah shuddered from resulting shock waves. Crew members throughout the ship scanned for signs of damage to the Chikondran flagship. All attention focused on maintaining the vessel's formidable presence in a battle for the very survival of their world.

To the utter surprise of the Alliance military command, Zeteron formations began breaking up, and enemy warships began to scatter. The destroyed starship had carried their command team. Zeteron strategists had not anticipated the concentrated onslaught of an unexpectedly aggressive Alliance fleet. Defeat was a concept they would resist by retreating to regroup, assess, and revise tactics.

Badrik consulted with his brilliant Terran counterpart. Despite reservations, Mswati understood. Had his family been on the embattled planet below, he, too, would have wanted to be there. Accepting full command of the Alliance armada, Mswati wished General Sirinoya good luck.

Leaving the Curasalah under Drehmijian's command, Badrik ordered a Cuseht to be readied. Speeding through the flagship's bowels, he mentally prepared himself for whatever lay ahead. Emerging on the launch deck, he donned flight suit on the run and climbed into the waiting ship. Briskly barking orders, he secured harnesses and raced through launch protocol. Within minutes, he cleared the Curasalah and, accompanied by a dozen starfighters, hurtled through space toward his beloved Chikondra.

Rodan Khalijar tightly gripped the glass in his hand. His chest had tightened, making it difficult to breathe as he tensely viewed startling images inbound from home. Chaotic battle scenes unfolded with the sickening knowledge that men and women were facing death rather than meekly submit to Zeteron subjugation renowned for its cruelty.

Eduardo de Castillo nervously leaned forward in his chair. The wide screen brought the war for Chikondra painfully close to home. "Mswati is a brilliant strategist. Rehovotians descend from some of the most effective and tenacious fighters in Earth's history. Every Alliance ship out there is staffed by people fighting to protect their worlds as much as yours."

Unable to tear his eyes from the secure broadcast, Rodan nodded slightly. "Badrik and Warnach are descendants of an ancient tribe on Chikondra that has always inspired my world. Even though war was never part of our history, I'm confident that the Sirinoya won't easily surrender."

Rodan swallowed forcefully against the knot in his throat. "Combat has already begun. Why has the tower not already fired?"

"Initial reports are inconclusive," John Edwards stated matter-of-factly. "We're not sure why Chikondran starfighters deployed." Tightly gripping the arms of his chair, John then abruptly bolted to his feet. A flash of light suddenly dominated the screen. "What the hell?"

Rodan gasped. "The tower! It must be the tower! Ground forces destroyed it!" Shocked eyes met those of his Terran friends. "They did it! They destroyed the tower! Now we can afford to hope!"

Tension did nothing to diminish the still handsome face of Peter Collins. Exchanging worried glances with Druska, each tenderly grasped one of Araman Sirinoya's hands. Receiving advice that the Alliance battle for Chikondra had begun, they had come personally to inform her to prevent her hearing news from unofficial sources that might distort information that was sketchy at best.

Araman's features stiffened with fear. "My sons are not men of war. Morcai and Lucia are just children. They shouldn't be there."

Druska said sympathetically, "We know, Mirsah Sirinoya. On the other hand, Badrik and Warnach are both strong and resourceful. They also know that Zeteron conquest will be catastrophic for the entire Alliance if not stopped. You have to believe in them."

Nadana leaned forward in a chair opposite her sister. "Druska is right. We must believe in them. Don't relinquish your faith in the promises of prophecy."

Araman's chin quivered. "My faith falters when I think of the very real possibilities that they might be killed. All of them… the children, my sons, and Sandra. What happens if I lose them? What am I to do then?"

Peter's optimistic tone of voice held reassurance. "I prefer to think of how soon we'll see them again. I refuse to believe they'll all die there. It just won't happen."

Druska stroked Araman's trembling hand. "Mirsah Sirinoya, I agree with my husband. I believe in all of them. Besides, we all know my best friend and her talent for succeeding against staggering odds."

Too frightened even to cry, Araman stared blankly in her sister's direction. Woodenly, she responded, "I want to hold my sons and my grandchildren again. As much as I believe in Sandra, even she's just one person against the Zeteron fleet."

"Yes, that's true," Peter agreed. "She isn't alone, though. She fights this battle with courageous Chikondrans and an armada comprised mostly of Terrans and Terran descendants. There is one thing certain. The ingrained psychology of my people will not endure the loss of our freedom. That mentality will fuel Sandra's fight and everyone else under Admiral Mswati's command."

Extracting her hands, Araman arose on shaky legs. She needed something to do to ease the sharp edges of fear. "I think some hot tea might do us all well."

"McAllen!" Forsij ran to help soldiers bringing the injured captain to safety. Supporting Mac around the waist, they headed into a reclaimed tunnel complex. Within minutes, the Terran was taken into the bustling infirmary, where medical personnel rushed to treat rapidly swelling numbers of wounded resistance fighters.

Limited bed space was reserved for critical cases. Carefully, Forsij lowered McAllen to the cavern floor and placed a mat between the officer's back and rough, cold walls of stone. The Chikondran captain knelt, his eyes searching Mac's ashen face. "Master Sirinoya?"

Mac weakly muttered a response. "A group of soldiers got him and the children away from the tower. I don't know which direction they went."

Forsij's heart crashed heavily into the pit of his stomach. Nearly choking, he had to ask. "And Minister Sirinoya?"

Eyelids lifted, revealing pain-glazed eyes. "Mesa. She went with Mesa to look for them." Mac clutched Forsij's wrist. "I begged her not to go. It's bedlam out there."

Forsij's eyes burned. "I'll lead a team out now. We'll do everything possible to find her."

Blue Terran eyes met black Chikondran eyes. "Captain Tibrab, look for her children and Master Sirinoya. If she's still alive, she'll find them."

A medic appeared and knelt beside McAllen. Forsij straightened above them and stared downward. "Nothing will stop me. I will find her."

"Momma?" Morcai's hushed voice shook with terror as his mother frantically tugged scorched fabric away from Warnach's body.

When other hands joined her efforts, she glanced upward. "Morcai. Your sister. Where is she?"

"By the rock. She collapsed after we got out." Seeing panic cross his mother's face, Morcai forced a reassuring smile. "She'll be all right, Momma. Really. Destroying the tower took a lot of energy. She warned me ahead of time and said not to worry."

"Morcai, are you sure?" Sandra demanded.

Her son's frightened eyes strayed toward his badehr's face. "I'm sure, Momma. I wouldn't lie. I'll take care of Lucia. You take care of Badehr. He needs you the most."

A hand firmly grasped Sandra's shoulder. Mesa's voice was coolly composed. "Minister Sirinoya, base landing pads are just past that line of trees. Alliance ships are coming in and landing. I've alerted them to the emergency. Let's move your husband closer, so we can get help."

Rapid breathing literally hurt as she covered the hideous lazon burns on her lifemate's body. Her jaw locked as she concentrated on the task at hand and then watched several soldiers slide a makeshift stretcher under his motionless form and hurriedly make their way through trees standing between them and ships they could hear but not see. Several times, she cast backward glances to make sure that Mesa, who carried Lucia, followed. Never leaving his sister's side and keeping a rifle at the ready, Morcai matched the Terran's fast pace.

Breaking through brush and using ray guns to cut a wide swath through protective fencing, they were met by an awe-inspiring sight. A silver-skinned Cuseht had just landed with an escort of four Dargoman Rapiers and one of the Yezabrá ships.

"Quickly!" Sandra shouted. "Someone get over there to get help! Mesa, help me with this HAU!" Tossing a second handheld HAU she had carried, she heard a faint moan. She instantly dropped to her knees. "Warnach? I'm here, Warnach. I won't leave you."

Weakly, the tip of his tongue passed over parched lips. "Lucia. Morcai," he whispered.

"They're safe." For a matter of moments, she closed her eyes and forced herself to sound calm. "Help is here."

"Shi'níyah," he murmured. "Never forget. Ci'ittá mi'ittá."

"No, Warnach," she returned sternly. "You're going to live! I refuse to let you die! You listen to me now! You are not going to die!"

"Sandra!"

Never releasing the hand she clutched so desperately, Sandra looked up. "Badrik! Thank God! Help me!"

Rushing to her side, Badrik crouched low and gently placed his hand on Warnach's shoulder. "Brother! Don't leave us now. You must live to see peace return to Chikondra." His eyes rose to meet Sandra's. "Come. The Yezabrá ship is the fastest. We'll take him to a critical care HAU."

Rising as soldiers again lifted Warnach's body, she shook her head. "No, Badrik. He won't make it. The ocean! We have to go to the beach house! Now!"

"Sandra..." Years swiftly peeled away in his mind. Memories flooded his brain. His initial protest evaporated. "Hurry, then!"

Inside the Yezabrá vessel, Warnach was strapped to a reclining seat for the short journey to the sea. While Badrik directed Sidrihn, Sandra stayed with her ki'medsah. The hum of engines filled her ears as she leaned over Warnach's body. Touching his face, she felt his changing temperature. Panic filled her as she literally sensed his life ebbing. Planting her feet firmly, she positioned her hip securely on the edge of the fully reclined chair.

Suddenly, Sandra cried out, "Warnach! I won't let you die!" Badrik spun around in reaction to the utter terror in her voice. Badrik's eyes widened, and his jaw trembled. She had leapt onto the seat and straddled Warnach's waist. Bracing herself with her arms, she pressed her forehead firmly against her ki'medsah's cerea-nervos. In constant repetition, she chanted, "You will live. You will live. You will live."

The Yezabrá ship reached the ocean in less than fifteen minutes. Instruments indicated that the beach was deserted.

Rehovotian Chamalyeh fighters joined Rapiers in crisscrossing the skies to protect the landing ship.

Firmly, Badrik grasped Sandra at the waist and helped her down from her precarious perch. Frightened eyes noted his brother's pallor and shallow breathing. Badrik's stomach pitched when he glanced upward at a medic who, scanner in hand, sadly shook his head. The unspoken message was clear. Warnach was dying.

The seat holding Warnach's body was removed from its base for use as a stretcher. Anxious footsteps then carried him out of the ship and across wind-carved sands.

Running ahead, Sandra hastily loosened her boots before kicking them off. She then raced in a headlong dash to ocean waters just beginning to reflect dawn's rose-colored skies. "Please," she begged piteously toward the horizon. "Please, help him!"

On the shore, Yezabrá Chikondrans aimed confused looks at her before turning questioning eyes to Badrik. His jaw set firmly. She was his sister. He would trust her. Besides, he thought, there was nothing he or anyone else could do for Warnach.

Suddenly, she froze. Turning, she called out, "Badrik! They're here! Hurry! Bring him in!"

Within moments, the padded seat served as a raft and bobbed on low tides rolling toward shore. Strong arms carefully guided the dying Chikondran master further out until they reached the Terran who watched every movement. As the others respectfully backed away, Badrik held onto the seat and watched Sandra lean over and kiss Warnach's silent lips.

Sleek, smooth bodies emerged from beneath the surface. Their somber mood severely contrasted with the cheerful whistles and excited chatter of previous encounters. Circling, their telepathic conversation with Sandra was more apparent than ever before.

"They say I was right to bring him here. Let go of your side."

Aching fingers released the long safety strap still attached to the seat. An adult Quazon glided through the water and grasped the floating band between strong jaws. Badrik then watched as Sandra stroked Warnach's hand and bent forward. He heard the break in her voice as she murmured against his brother's ear, "I love you. Ci'ittá mi'ittá, me'u Warnach."

Moments later, Badrik stared toward the horizon as Quazon bore away the body of his beloved brother. Bitterly hot tears stung his eyes and burned scorching tracks along his cheeks. His heart felt ready to burst, its swelling sorrow too great to contain. Powerful hands shook as he whispered toward dawning skies, "I send you in peace to the Great Spirit, my beloved brother. In peace and love do I send you."

Turning, he realized he stood alone in morning's quietly sighing tides. Slowly wading toward shore, he saw that Sandra had lowered herself onto the beach. With legs bent and arms wrapped around them, she rested her chin on her knees. Evergreen eyes gazed blankly toward the watery horizon.

Directing a grateful glance toward respectfully waiting Yezabrá, Badrik knelt in front of the Terran he called sister. "We must go now." Emotionally shattered, he dragged in a sustaining breath. "Warnach now sleeps peacefully with Meichasa's angels."

Shock was swiftly replacing earlier sheer determination, and her head moved shakily from side to side. "I can't go. Not yet. You don't understand."

Tenderly, Badrik stroked her cheek. "Sister, Morcai and Lucia need you now more than ever."

Her voice quivered. "They also need their badehr. I have to keep the faith. I have to believe."

Overwhelming sadness filled his soul. He wondered how long he could withstand the onslaught of grief tearing at his insides. "Sandra, the house is here. You can rest inside a while if you want."

"No," she replied firmly. "You go rest with the others. I'll stay here. I need to be alone."

Lacking will to argue with her, he nodded. "Very well. I'll leave guards outside the house. Just in case. You come in when you're ready." He had walked about two meters away when the sound of his name stopped him. "Yes?"

"A long time ago, they told me to stay strong and never lose my faith. They promised me all would come right. I have to believe. I can't fail. *I… I have…to believe.*"

Sorrowfully, Badrik resumed his solemn walk to the house where his family had once shared so much happiness and so many blessings.

With elbows propped on the conference room table, Rodan covered his face with his hands. He could still hear the quake in Badrik's voice in the VM that had delivered dreaded news. So absorbed in shock, he never even heard the door when John and Eduardo returned from briefing journalists anxiously seeking updates.

"Rodan? Are you all right?"

Brown eyes held profound sorrow. Rodan shook his head, hardly knowing what to say.

Fear sparked in John's eyes. "Tell me. What's wrong?"

Forcefully swallowing against his constricting throat, Rodan looked away. "I heard from Badrik. Our fleet has destroyed a number of Zeteron vessels, including five battleships and their command ship. It seems the Zeterons were relying on the tower and were unprepared for an all-out assault. Their blockade is falling apart." His voice cracked. "Sandra and the children are safe, but..." He paused again. "Badrik's message said we've lost Warnach."

Shock robbed John of breath, and he fell heavily into a chair. "Oh, my God. No."

Eduardo firmly grasped John's shoulder. "I'm so sorry. I know how close you were."

John gazed at Rodan's stricken face. "What happened?"

"Badrik didn't go into details. I think he was too shaken." Rodan pushed his chair back and stood. "I hope you gentlemen will excuse me. I have personal obligations to Warnach's family."

Eduardo responded when John remained mute. "We'll contact you immediately in the event of any changes. Rodan, please, convey my condolences to the family."

After shamelessly bullying those treating him, Timothy McAllen contacted Terran officers in charge of troops landing on Chikondra. Despite doctors' protests that he needed additional treatment, the captain ordered a military transport to pick him up. After receiving an update from Captain Tibrab, Mac decided it was impossible to remain in the infirmary when he could never rest without seeing for himself that she was getting the comfort and support she must surely need.

The expansive shoreline stretched out beneath afternoon sun. The small ship had barely settled when Mac was impatiently waiting to disembark. Ignoring throbbing pain in his arm, he swiftly strode toward the house surrounded by military personnel. A guard opened a door, and Mac hurried inside.

"General Sirinoya," he greeted somberly. "I came as soon as I heard. I can't tell you how sorry I am about your brother."

Badrik inclined his head. "Thank you, Captain McAllen." With a wave of his arm, he invited his unexpected visitor to sit. "Warnach's death is a tragedy not only for my family but for my entire world."

"He was a courageous man who commanded the greatest respect." Mac gravely regarded the Chikondran general. "I checked on Morcai and Lucia before I came. They're both well. When I left, they were inside the tunnels with the Simlani - praying." Exchanging a glance with Forsij, who stood across the room, Mac tentatively continued, "Sandra? How is she?"

Badrik's eyes revealed the grief-stricken battle he waged. "I'm not sure what to tell you. She has spent nearly the entire day on the beach. She refuses to come in to eat or rest. The best we've been able to do is to coax her to drink some water. She just sits and stares out to sea."

Mac's shoulders lifted with the deep breath he inhaled. "She must be on the verge of collapse. We headed for the tower early yesterday afternoon. Then…"

"I've tried, but I can't reason with her, nor can I force her to go. Neither can I bring myself to leave her. I'm doing the best I can to provide tactical advice from here until she…"

Badrik's voice wavered before he managed a weak smile. "I know the two of you are close friends. Perhaps you could try to reason with her. She needs to rest. Her children... They'll need her."

A Chikondran officer silently led McAllen outside and pointed toward the beach. Leaden steps carried Mac across brown, brittle grasses. Looking toward the skies, trained eyes spotted ships streaking through the upper atmosphere. En route, he had heard reports that Zeteron forces had incurred heavy losses after the arrival of the Yezabrá vessels armed with firepower far more destructive than anything known to the Alliance. Enemy ships not damaged were quickly dispersing, attempting to escape into deep space. Ground troops were finding themselves stranded and facing legions of Alliance soldiers landing all around Chikondra.

Abruptly, Mac stopped. His chest contracted. Still and quiet, she sat alone with someone's coat wrapped around her shoulders. Wearily, she hunched over legs bent to support her head. For a moment, as tears stung his eyes, he asked himself how many years it had been since he had really cried. At that moment, feeling her hurt, he wanted to hold her - to cry with her for her pain and his own years of lonely sadness. Knowing that was impossible, he sucked in a deep breath and went to her.

Lowering himself onto white sand, he reached out with his uninjured arm. His large hand rubbed comforting circles across her back. "Sandra?"

He could never have prepared himself for the face that turned to him. Her features were tightly drawn. Streaks of oily smudge stained her face. Rose-colored lips pressed into a thin line. Eyelids were heavy with deepening fatigue. Evergreen eyes showed resistance against exhaustion while refusing to give way to tears.

"Sandra," he began softly, "you know you can't stay out here like this."

Her whispered response sounded like dry leaves swept from their trees by winds heralding the onrush of winter. "I have to wait, Mac. I have to believe."

Regretfully shaking his head, he stroked her cheek. "I know how much you loved him, but he's gone now. You have two children waiting for you. They don't need to see you this way."

"You don't understand, Mac. Quazon. They promised all would be right. I have to stay strong. I just have to keep faith."

"Sweetheart, listen to me. Keeping faith sometimes means giving up what you can't have any more without surrendering your love. His entire family needs you. More than anything, his children need their mother. Loving him means staying strong enough to protect and care for everyone you both loved most without sacrificing his memory." Mac paused. "You also owe it to him to take care of the woman he loved more than anything else in his life."

Her voice quivered. "I can't leave. Not yet. I just can't."

Patiently, he negotiated with her as one might deal with a frightened child. "All right. You don't have to go. Not until you're ready. However, you could show some compassion to his brother. General Sirinoya is inside, trying to direct the offensive from here while coping with his own grief. He won't leave you because he's also sick with worry. You could go inside, eat a little, and get some sleep. That would at least give him some relief."

Bleakly, she again stared out to sea. Her mind struggled. Their voices were strangely silent. Where were they? Where had they taken her beloved ki'medsah? Swallowing several times, she turned back, locking her eyes on Mac's face. "I'm so tired, Mac. In my whole life, I don't think I've ever felt this tired."

"Let me take you inside. Please?" With one arm in a sling, he clumsily stood up. He watched as she tentatively grasped the good hand he offered. After she stiffly unfolded herself and rose, he led her to the house.

Inside, Mac watched as Badrik Sirinoya stood up in surprise. Arms immediately stretched out and wrapped around the woman who slowly went to him. For the longest time, they held one another. Images from Dargom flitted into his mind. Years ago, Mac had first witnessed the bond the two shared. He could hardly avoid thinking that he had never been that close to anyone at any time in his life.

Almost an hour later, she sat at the kitchen table. Grateful for clothes still on hand for the impromptu trips the family made to the beachfront, she had showered and donned pajamas and robe. Staring at a half-eaten bowl of stew, she hardly had enough energy to lift a spoon, let alone chew and swallow.

"Sister," Badrik pleaded tenderly, "just one more bite. Please? For your big brother's sake?"

Her mouth widened but failed to form a smile. Swallowing a last bite, she met the approving expression on Badrik's face. Moments later, she leaned against him as they headed toward a bedroom. Sliding beneath blankets, she looked at him with eyes barely able to resist sleep. "Thank you for letting me stay."

Badrik nodded as he pulled the covers up around her. "Are you going to try to sleep with Kitak on?"

She nodded once. Fluttering eyelids were surrendering to total exhaustion. "Badrik?"

"What, little sister?"

Words slurred thickly. "You are the very best big brother." As her eyes closed, she murmured, "You'll always be my hero."

Mirah and Farisa held Araman between them. Violent sobs had shaken her petite body for nearly half an hour. Tears coursed down soft, wrinkled cheeks. Rodan knelt in front of her.

"Mirsah Sirinoya, we all share your grief. We loved him, too. All of Chikondra will mourn his loss for years to come, but his example is one that will surely inspire our world's recovery. In that sense, the legacy he leaves will keep him alive forever."

"I don't care about legacy," Araman choked out. "My son! My son is dead!"

"Araman," Mirah cooed gently, "not one of us can imagine the depth of your sorrow, but you can't make yourself sick. You must remember. Warnach leaves behind his son and daughter. They will need the family they love. In a way, he still lives through them. You must think about his children."

"Badrik is still there. You know him. He still faces the same risks. I…"

Farisa swallowed her own fear on a barely restrained sob. "Mamehr, Rodan is going to help me take you up to bed. Then, I'm going to give you a neuro-sedative. You can't keep this up. We've lost Warnach. We can't bear losing you, too."

Once Araman had drifted into deep, tranquilized sleep, Farisa turned frightened eyes to question Rodan. "Badrik. Did he say how things were?"

Rodan faced her question directly. "When he sent the VM, he was at the house in front of the beach. Sandra refused to leave, and he refused to leave her."

"He wouldn't leave her. He knows this could easily destroy her."

Rodan's chest expanded with the huge, tremulous breath he forced into the bottom of his lungs. "She'll make it, Farisa. I have to believe that she won't fail Warnach's children."

"Lucia," Morcai softly addressed his sister. "What are you doing now? Your aura keeps changing color."

Without moving or even opening her eyes, she answered quietly, "Focusing, Morcai. Feeding energy to our people. It isn't easy. Please, pray with me."

Nervously, Morcai sat beside his sister. "Lucia, you didn't see Badehr. Momma was so afraid. I'm afraid, too."

"I know, Morcai. There's nothing we can do. For now, our people need my help. You pray for Momma to stay strong and for the fighting to end soon. Only then will things come right."

Watching his sister, Morcai wished for some of the tranquility that swept her deeper into trance. He wondered how he would ever shut out the memory of ending a man's life. He questioned how he could ever forget the sight of his badehr's scorched body or the expression on his mother's face. With dogged determination, he turned his heart, his thoughts, and his fears to the Great Spirit. Clinging to faith, he prayed for his mother and his badehr.

Sandra's head rolled to one side on the pillow. Her troubled heart surged and then quieted. Eyelids remained closed. She feared waking. Even in the exhausted, sleep-drugged recesses of her mind, the knowledge that he would not be there terrified her.

A fluttering touch. Dreaming. She had to be dreaming. She turned away. Again, the tender touch gently drawing through sleep-tumbled hair. Maybe the battle at the tower had been nothing more than a terrifying nightmare. How often had Warnach caressed her hair that way when he thought she was asleep? Rolling over again, she slowly lifted her eyelids.

Nighttime darkness engulfed her. She heard no sounds outside the bedroom. Awareness stealthily crept into her waking brain. Light. Faint, shimmering light. An oval of glistening light, hovering above her.

"Sandra?"

The voice sounded vaguely familiar. Or did it? Pulling her weary, aching body upright, she blinked several times. As her vision cleared, she began to discern a figure enveloped within the misty cloud. Nauseating waves rolled through her stomach. Her hands began to tremble as she stared hard at the figure now leaning above her.

"Do not be afraid. I could never hurt you." The figure straightened and beckoned to her. "Will you come with me?"

Instinctively, she knew she was safe. Ignoring her weariness, she rose from the bed, pulled on her robe, and slid feet into slippers. Then, she stared at the iridescent figure, not quite knowing what it expected of her. Unsure whether she saw or felt the reassuring smile, she nodded. In silence, she followed the cloud of light into the hallway.

"We must be very quiet. I will take you out through the side door."

As they passed through the lounge, the figure paused and gazed down at Badrik, who had fallen asleep on the sofa. The cloud of light momentarily brightened before its edges expanded to touch Badrik and then softened into a glistening glow. "Come," sounded the muted, barely audible whisper.

Outside, the figure escorted her slowly toward the sandy shoreline. Tides spread frothy waters onto the beach and then receded. The two stopped and gazed at Chikondra's shining moons suspended above the vast ocean. Gradually, the figure stopped and turned to look at her as she lingered in questioning hesitation.

"Who…?" As she started to ask the question, the cloud seemed to dissipate, allowing her to distinguish features of the person who had awakened her.

"Do you now recognize me?"

Her breath caught in her throat. How was this possible? She studied the distinctive, carved features of the masculine face that gazed upon her so affectionately. Soft breezes brushed waves of long, silvery-white hair around his face and shoulders. That smile was unforgettable. Those eyes held so much gentle wisdom. She nodded in awed recognition.

He stretched out his hand. "Will you walk with me?"

Tentatively, Sandra extended her hand. When his long fingers curled around hers, confusion filled her eyes. Although his hand felt warm and real, it did not feel like human touch.

His smile again reassured her. "Come, dear one."

Silently, they strolled along the same stretch of beach she had walked years ago on her honeymoon. The cherished memory brought a faint smile to her face. She felt her companion's eyes upon her, and she met his gaze.

"Dearest Sandra, you have shown so much courage and devotion to this world that is not your own. You also proved that prayer is a mighty force when offered with unquestioning, undoubting, unconditional love."

"I don't know what you mean," she replied quietly.

He laughed softly. "Of course, you don't. Many, many years ago, I saw him nearly destroyed by anger, grief, and shame. I counseled him to faith. At the same time, I questioned if my own faith was strong enough to help him. I recall a night much like this one. With every bit of strength I possessed, I prayed and prayed for hours until I collapsed. Do you know what I prayed for?"

Her footsteps slowed, and she turned inquisitive eyes to his. "That he would be healed?"

"No, my child. I boldly prayed for a miracle. I prayed for someone who would love him completely and teach him to be happy." He reached up and tenderly stroked her cheek. "No one in the universe could have loved him more than you have. Not even me."

Her jaw quivered, and her chest tightened. "He gave me every reason to love him."

"Child, you grace the Sirinoya tradition with honor. You are a loving daughter to Araman, who possesses a soul filled with unparalleled kindness and beauty. Chikondra now rises from darkness because of Mi'yafá Si'imlayaná, the daughter you bore Warnach. You gave him a son whose future will be a beacon to this world and others seeking true peace. You also made Warnach happy. Such miracles exceed any humble hopes I ever conceived."

"I…" Words caught in her throat. Her heart beat erratically. "Is it possible…?" She stuttered to a stop and started again. "My heart is breaking without him. Badehr, is it possible for you to hold me?"

The ethereally handsome face glowed. His arms extended, enfolding her within his protective spirit. More reluctant than she, he stepped away from their embrace. Again, so sweetly reminiscent of Warnach's endearing habit, he caressed her hair.

Glimmering tears shone in her eyes. "Why did you come tonight?"

"I wanted to know you in this time. I must also ask for your help."

"I don't know how I can."

His eyes studied features so different, yet so like those of his own people. "Sandra, Araman needs to come home. Your world has welcomed her and given her refuge, but she belongs here. My grandchildren, Michahn included, need your example. Only you will be able to tell Badrik and Araman that I always watch over them. You must tell my family how proud they have made me and how much I love them. I came also to deliver a message." He noted her involuntary grimace of pain.

"Yes?" she asked in a strangled whisper.

"Child, close your eyes, and listen carefully." Watching her, he observed uncertain hesitation before she obediently squeezed her eyelids shut. "The Great Spirit now summons me home. However, He also commends the way you have followed the counsel of Meichasa's faithful angels. He wants you to know. They have never broken a promise. They never will."

For the briefest of moments, she felt his lips against her cheek. Even with her eyes closed, she sensed when Morcai Sirinoya's presence began to fade. A faint whisper tickled her ear. "Daughter, they told you many years ago. This place would always await you whenever you needed to be healed and restored. Your soul never forgot."

Finding herself in complete solitude on the beach, she no longer possessed sufficient will to resist the onslaught of total desolation. Rivers of tears cascaded down her face. Her knees weakened, and she sank into deep, soft sand. Chilly breezes chafed damp cheeks. Hands trembled with the cold of night. Within her breast, her heart throbbed. Months of fear and worry and death swelled inside her. Her consciousness registered a nearly overpowering desire to scream out her pain, but some unknown power stifled her cries before they were born.

Warm hands firmly grasped her upper arms. Someone had missed her and had come to look for her. Ashamed for causing more unnecessary worry, she reluctantly opened her eyes. Black eyes intensely searched her face.

"You just couldn't leave, could you?"

Evergreen eyes widened. Her mouth fell open as a powerful quake shuddered throughout her body. Dumbfounded, she could utter not a single sound.

Drawing her into his arms, he held her more tightly than ever before. "Me'u Shi'níyah, I heard when you said you wouldn't let me die. You were right. You didn't. Your faith and your love saved my life."

In their age-old ritual, ocean waters swished onto shore and danced back into the sea. Moonlight bathed the night with beams of silver. Secure again within his embrace, she discovered yet another miracle as she reclaimed her perfect place to be. With her arms encircling his neck and her face against his shoulder, her voice broke with sobs of joy. "Ci'ittá mi'ittá, me'u Warnach. Ci'ittá mi'ittá."

About the Author

Despite living all her life in Columbus, Ohio, Sandra Valencia was always captivated by international themes. Having studied several languages, she adds zest to her life by traveling abroad to experience the wealth of different cultures personally. Since childhood, she has had many experiences commonly categorized as paranormal activity. Those experiences have been a treasure chest of ideas and concepts often woven into her writing.

Ms. Valencia's writing career began when she consolidated two decades of dreams into the series Legends from Turand. In Song of Turand and Return to Turand, haunting poetry enhanced vivid prose in the romantic, thought-provoking tale of a nation and its leaders in the dramatic struggle to overcome a brutal occupation army. Both men and women embraced the characters and story in ways that amazed and humbled the author.

After another series of dreams prompted more than four years of daily writing, she released Guardian Redeemed. This first book in The Chikondra Trilogy introduced a romantic saga fraught with personal, social, and political challenges in an intergalactic setting. Whispers from Prophecy continued the often mysterious epic as a distant empire threatened a peaceful alliance of worlds and those who labored to eliminate the grave threat of war. Ms. Valencia has been deeply gratified with messages from American readers as well as readers from Australia, Brazil, Colombia, England, Italy, Mexico, The Netherlands, Portugal, and Sweden. She sincerely hopes that the trilogy's climactic finale, Lest Darkness Prevail, will continue to satisfy her readers' desire for more of what one reader called a "uniquely elegant" writing style.

Married and the mother of two sons who challenge her intellectually and spiritually, she enjoys nature, gardening, classical and Latin music, and the company of treasured friends.

CPSIA information can be obtained
at www.ICGtesting.com
Printed in the USA
LVHW111632100920
664499LV00013B/58/J

9 781633 373945